SYCAMORE PUBLIC LIBRARY

W9-AAC-826

7/03

The Business of Dying

The Business of Dying
SIMON KERNICK

 St. Martin's Minotaur ✎ New York

SYCAMORE PUBLIC LIBRARY
103 E. STATE ST.
SYCAMORE, IL 60178
815 895-2500

THE BUSINESS OF DYING. Copyright © 2002 by Simon Kernick. All rights reserved. Printed in the United States of America. No part of this book may be used or reproduced in any manner whatsoever without written permission except in the case of brief quotations embodied in critical articles or reviews. For information, address St. Martin's Press, 175 Fifth Avenue, New York, N.Y. 10010.

All the characters in this book are fictitious, and any resemblance to actual persons, living or dead, is purely coincidental.

www.minotaurbooks.com

Library of Congress Cataloging-in-Publication Data

Kernick, Simon.
    The business of dying / Simon Kernick.—1st St. Martin's Minotaur ed.
        p. cm.
    ISBN 0-312-31401-9
    1. Police—England—Fiction. 2. Police corruption—Fiction. 3. England—Fiction
I. Title.

PR611.E76B87 2003
823'.92—dc21   2003040640

First published in Great Britain by Bantam Press
A division of Transworld Publishers

First St. Martin's Minotaur Edition: June 2003

10 9 8 7 6 5 4 3 2 1

For Sally

Thanks to all those who helped in both the writing and the publication of this book.

You know who you are.

Part One

INTRODUCING THE DEAD

1

There's a true story that goes like this. A few years back a thirty-two-year-old man abducts a ten-year-old girl from the street near her house. He takes her back to his dingy bedsit, ties her to a bed, and subjects her to a brutal hour-long sex ordeal. It might have been a lot worse had the walls not been paper thin. One of the neighbours hears the screams, phones the police, and they come and knock the door down. The girl is rescued, although apparently she still bears the scars, and the perpetrator is arrested. Seven months later he goes on trial and his lawyer gets him off on a technicality. Apparently she takes the legal view that it's better that ten guilty men go free than one innocent one's imprisoned. He returns to the area where he committed the crime and lives the life of a free man. The lawyer gets her money, courtesy of the tax-payer, as well as the congratulations of her partners on a worthy performance. They probably even take her out for a celebration drink. Meanwhile, every parent in a two-mile radius of this guy is living in fear. The police try to defuse the situation by saying they'll keep a good watch on him, but admit there's nothing else they can do. As always, they appeal for calm.

Three months later, the girl's dad gets caught pouring petrol through the guy's letterbox. The police, for once, have been true to their word and are actually watching the place. He's arrested, charged with arson and attempted murder, and remanded in custody. The local newspaper sets up a campaign to free him and starts a petition that gets something like twenty thousand signatures. Predictably the powers-that-be ignore it, interest fades, and then, before his case comes to trial, the dad hangs himself in his cell. Is this the tale of a progressive, forward-looking society, or one that's about to go down the pan? You tell me.

But the moral of the story, that's easier. If you're going to kill someone, plan it.

9.01 p.m. We were sitting in the rear car park of the Traveller's Rest Hotel. It was a typical English November night: dark, cold and wet. Not the best time to be out working, but who can choose their hours these days? The Traveller's Rest didn't look very restful at all. It was one of those modern redbrick structures with loud lighting, revolving doors, and that curse of modern times, a weekly karaoke night. The one thing going for it was the fact that the front car park had been shut for resurfacing. This meant our quarry would have to come round the back, away from the main entrance, and hopefully away from any stray civilians. Would they smell a rat? I doubted it. Not until it was too late anyway.

I hate the waiting. It's the worst part. It gives you too much time to think. So I lit a cigarette and took a long but guilty drag. Danny wrinkled his nose but he didn't say anything. He doesn't like smoking but he's not the kind to make a big deal about it. He's a tolerant sort. We'd been talking earlier about this case of the 'alleged' paedophile and Danny had been the one supporting the lawyer's ten guilty-men argument, which was typical of him. And bullshit too. Why the suffering of many is seen as being preferable to the suffering of one is beyond me. It's like running a TV station where twenty million viewers want to see gameshows and two million want to see operas, and only showing operas. If the people who believed it ever ran a business, it'd go bust in a day.

But I like Danny. And I trust him. We've worked together a long time and we know each other's capabilities. And that, in our line of business, is the key.

He opened the driver's side window to let some air in and I shivered against the cold. It really was a shitty night.

'Personally, I'd have gone after the lawyer,' I said.

'What?'

'If I was that girl's dad, I would have gone for the lawyer rather than the rapist.'

'Why? What good would that have done?'

'Because there's an argument that the rapist couldn't help what he did, that his urges were just too much to handle. I'd still cut his balls off, but that's not the point. The point is, the lawyer had the choice not to defend him. She was an intelligent, rational woman. She knew what he'd done and still she did all in her power to put him back on the streets. Hers was therefore the greatest crime.'

'I don't understand that argument at all.'

'The greatest evil in the world comes not from those who perpetrate it, but from those who excuse it.'

Danny shook his head like he couldn't believe what he was hearing. 'Jesus, Dennis, you're beginning to sound like some sort of Angel of Death. You want to calm down a little. It's not as if you're whiter than white yourself.'

Which was true. I wasn't. But I consider myself to have principles – codes of conduct to which I strictly adhere –

and that, I felt, gave me the justification to say my piece.

I was about to tell Danny this when the radio crackled into life.

'All right, they're here,' hissed the disembodied voice. 'Black Cherokee, three occupants. It's them.'

Danny started the engine while I slid silently out of the car, flicked the cigarette away, and walked towards the spot where the Cherokee would appear, knowing that this was going to be the one and only chance I was going to get.

There was a clank as it hit the speed ramp, then it came round the side of the main building and drove slowly into the car park, looking for a place to stop. I broke into a jog, waving my hands to get the driver's attention. In my Barbour jacket and shirt and tie, I looked every inch the harassed businessman.

The Cherokee continued moving but came to a halt as I reached the driver's side window and banged on it. 'Excuse me, excuse me.' My voice was different now. Higher pitched, less confident.

The window came down and a hard-looking sod with a square jaw that looked like it was made of cast iron glared out at me. I put him at about thirty-five. My face dissolved into nerves. Both the driver and his front- seat passenger, a smaller, older guy with Brylcreemed hair and a greasy face, were already relaxing. They saw me as no threat. Just a man who pays his taxes and does what he's told for a living. I heard the one in the back mumble something but I didn't even look at him.

'What do you want?' demanded the driver impatiently.

'Er, I was wondering . . .'

I brought the gun up from my pocket, had this momentary paranoia that I might not have released the safety, and shot him twice in the right eye. He made no sound, simply fell back into his seat, head tilted to one side, and shivered out the final ounces of his life.

The front passenger swore loudly and immediately flung up his arms in a futile effort to protect himself. I leaned down slightly to get a better view of him and pumped out a further two rounds. One hit him in the elbow, the other in the jaw. I heard it crack. He shrieked in pain and then coughed violently as his mouth filled with blood. He tried to retreat in his seat, scrabbling about like a madman, unable to accept the fact that it was all over. I steadied myself and fired again, hitting him square in the forehead. The window behind him bloomed with red and his greasy features immediately relaxed. So far the whole thing had taken about three seconds.

But the one in the back was quick. He was already swinging open the door and coming out with what looked like a gun in his hand. I didn't have time to take a closer look. Instead I retreated three steps and squeezed the trigger as he came into view. I got him somewhere in the upper body but still he kept coming, and fast. I continued firing, holding the gun two-handed, teeth clenched against the noise that was exploding in my ears. The momentum of the bullets forced him backwards, driving him into the door. He did a manic, confused dance to the tune of the gunfire, his arms and legs flailing, and angry red spots appeared like pox on his crisp, white shirt.

And then the magazine was empty and everything stopped as suddenly and dramatically as it had begun.

For a second he remained upright, holding onto the door for support, the energy almost visibly leaking out of him. Then he sort of half fell, half sat down, losing his grip on it in the process. He looked down at the blood on his shirt, and then at me, and I got a good look at his face, which I didn't want at all, because it was young, maybe late twenties, and his expression was all wrong. What I mean is, it wasn't the expression of a sinner. There was no defiance there, no rage. Just shock. Shock that his life was being stolen from him. He looked like a man who didn't think he deserved it, and that was the moment when I should have known I'd made a terrible mistake.

Instead, I turned away from his stare and reloaded. Then I stepped forward and shot him three times in the top of the head. The mobile phone he was carrying clattered noisily to the ground.

I dropped the gun into my jacket pocket and turned towards Danny, who was now bringing the car round.

Which was when I saw her, maybe fifteen yards away, standing in the light of the rear firedoor, a bag of rubbish in each hand. No more than eighteen and looking right at me, still too shocked to realize that what she was witnessing was real. What do you do? A movie pro would have taken her out with a single shot to the head, although there was no guarantee I'd even have hit her from where I was standing. And anyway, I'm not interested in hurting civilians.

Her hand went to her mouth as she saw I'd seen her, and I knew that any moment she was going to let out a scream that would probably wake the dead, which, with the dead only just being dead, I didn't want at all. So I lowered my gaze and hurried round to the passenger door, hoping that the gloom and wet had obscured my features enough to make any description she gave worthless.

I jumped in and kept my head down. Danny didn't say a word. He just hit the pedal and we were out of there.

It was 9.04.

The journey to our first change of transport took exactly four minutes and covered a distance of approximately two and a half miles. We'd parked a Mondeo in a quiet piece of Forestry Commission land earlier that day. Danny now pulled up behind it, cut the engine, and got out. I leaned under the passenger seat and removed a full five-litre can of petrol which I liberally sprinkled over the car's interior. When it was empty, I got out, lit a book of matches, stepped back so I was well out of the way, and flung them in, followed by the murder weapon and the two-way radio I'd been using. There was a satisfying whoosh as the petrol ignited, followed by a wave of heat.

When they came across the mangled wreckage it wouldn't tell them anything. We hadn't left any fingerprints and the car itself would be almost impossible to trace. It had been stolen in Birmingham six months ago, given new plates and a respray, and stored in a lock-up in Cardiff ever since. In this line of business, you can never be too careful. Contrary to popular belief, most detectives couldn't detect a heartbeat on a speed addict, but you never know when you might be up against the next Ellery Queen.

We now followed a pre-arranged route for four miles through a mixture of B and single-track roads and it was 9.16 when we pulled into the car park of Ye Olde Bell, a busy country pub on the edge of an affluent looking commuter village. Danny drove up to the far end and stopped behind a burgundy Rover 600.

This was where we parted.

'Did that girl get a good look at you?' he asked as I opened the door. They were the first words he'd spoken since the shootings.

'No, we'll be all right. It was too dark.'

He sighed. 'I don't like it, you know. Three murders, and now we've got a witness.'

Admittedly it didn't sound too good when he put it like that, but at the time there was no reason to think that we weren't in the clear.

'Don't worry. We've covered our tracks well enough.'

'There's going to be a lot of heat over this one, Dennis.'

'We both knew that when we took the job. As long as we keep calm, and keep our mouths shut, we won't feel any of it.'

I gave him a friendly pat on the shoulder, and told him I'd call him the next day.

The Rover's keys were behind the front driver's side wheel. I got in, started the engine and followed Danny out of the car park. He turned south and I turned north.

And that should have been that, but tonight was not my lucky night. I'd barely gone three miles and was just short of the turning that would take me back to London when I hit an improvised road-block. There were two Pandas with flashing lights at the side of the road: officers in fluorescent safety jackets were milling about a BMW they'd already stopped. My heart gave an initial jump but I quickly recovered myself. No reason to worry. I was a man on my own, unarmed, driving a car that had never been within five miles of the Traveller's Rest, and they wouldn't even have the vaguest description of me yet. The clock on the dashboard said 9.22.

One of them saw my approach and stepped out into the road, flashing his torch and motioning for me to pull up behind the other car. I did as I was told and wound down the window as he approached the driver's side. He was young, no more than twenty-three, and very fresh-faced. They say you can tell you're getting old when the coppers look young. I could just about have been this kid's dad. He looked really enthusiastic as well. That wouldn't last. A second officer stood a few feet behind him, watching, but the other two were preoccupied with the driver of the other car. None of them appeared to be armed, which I thought was a bit foolish under the circumstances. I could have run this roadblock and they wouldn't have had a chance.

'Good evening, sir.' He leaned down into the window and gave me and the car a gentle once-over.

It always pays to be polite. 'Evening, officer. How can I help?'

'There's been an incident at a hotel called the Traveller's Rest on the A10. About fifteen minutes ago. You haven't come that way, have you?'

'No, I haven't,' I told him. 'I've come from Clavering. I'm on my way to London.'

He nodded understandingly, and then looked at me again. You could tell that for some reason he wasn't entirely convinced, although I don't know why. I'm not the type who arouses suspicions. I genuinely look like a nice guy. There shouldn't have been any alarm bells.

But there were. Maybe I'd just met the new Ellery Queen.

'Have you got any identification, sir? Just for the record.'

I sighed. I didn't want to have to do this because it could well cause me a lot of long-term problems, but I didn't see that I had much choice.

For a split second I baulked.

Then I reached into my pocket and removed the warrant card.

He took it, inspected it carefully, looked back at me, then back at the warrant card, just to double check, probably wondering why his instincts were so wrong. When he looked back again, he had an embarrassed expression on his face.

'Detective Sergeant Milne. I'm sorry, sir. I didn't realize.'

I shrugged my shoulders. 'Course you didn't. You're just doing your job. But if you don't mind, I'm in a bit of a hurry.'

'Of course, sir, no problem.' He stepped back from the car. 'Have a nice evening.'

I said goodnight, and put the car in reverse. Poor sod. I remembered only too well what it was like to be out on nights like these, being paid a pittance to stand around for hours on end with the rain pissing down on your head. Knowing that the people you were meant to be looking for were probably miles away. Oh, the joys of being a uniformed copper.

I waved as I drove past, and he waved back. I wondered how long it would take him to lose the enthusiasm; how long before he, too, realized that by playing by the rules he was just banging his head against a brick wall.

I gave him two years.

2

I used to know a guy called Tom Darke. Tomboy, as he was known, was a buyer and seller of stolen goods. If you'd nicked something – whatever it was – Tomboy would give you a price for it, and you could be sure that somewhere down the line he'd have a customer who'd take it off him. He was also an informant, and a good one too if you measure such things by how many people his information convicted. The secret of his success lay in the fact that he was a likeable character who was good company. He used to say that he listened well rather than listened hard, and he never asked too many questions. Consequently, there wasn't a lot that went on among the North London criminal fraternity that he didn't know about, and such was his affability that even as the local lowlifes were going down like overweight skydivers no-one ever suspected old Tomboy of being involved.

I once asked him why he did it. Why, as the Aussies would say, did he dob in blokes who were meant to be his mates? Because the thing was he didn't really strike me as the grassing sort. He came across as being a decent bloke who was above such petty deceptions. Tomboy had two answers to this question.

The first answer was the obvious one. Money. There were good rewards on offer for information on criminals and Tomboy needed the cash. He wanted to retire from the game with his freedom intact because he believed that with the onset of technology, and its availability to the police for fighting crime, the writing was on the wall for middle-ranking career criminals such as himself. So it was a case of making hay while the sun shone, building up a nice little nest egg (he'd set a target limit of £50,000), and then getting the fuck out.

The second answer was that if he didn't dob them in, someone else would do it anyway. Criminals are usually notorious braggarts. Since they can't tell the whole world what they've done for fear of retribution, they like to boast about their exploits to one another. And since by definition they're a dishonest lot – as Tomboy once said, 'Whoever heard of such a thing as honour among thieves?' – sooner or later someone's going to inform on them if the money's right. All he did, if you believed his rationale, was get in there first.

So that was Tomboy's philosophy. There's no point in not doing the deed because one way or another it's going to get done, and if you're going to get paid to do it, all the better. I thought about that as I drove home through the rain that night. If I hadn't killed those men, someone else would have shot them. Either way they ended up dead. If you're in the line of business where you make enemies of people who'll pay to have you killed, you've got to be prepared to accept the consequences. That was how I justified it to myself, and that was how Tomboy had always justified it to me, and it had never done him any harm. In fact, it appeared to have done him a lot of good. The last I'd heard he was living out in the Philippines. He'd made his fifty grand, probably a lot more knowing him, and had invested it in a beach bar and guesthouse on one of the more far-flung islands.

He'd sent me a postcard from there a couple of years back in which he'd extolled the virtues of the laid-back tropical lifestyle. It had ended with him saying that if ever I fancied a job working at his place, I should let him know.

More than once I'd felt like taking him up on the offer.

It was getting close to eleven o'clock when I got home that night, home being a rented one bedroom flat at the southern end of Islington, not too far from City Road. The first thing I did was take a long hot shower to wash the cold out of my bones, before pouring myself a decent-sized glass of red wine and settling down on the lounge sofa.

I turned on the TV and lit a cigarette relaxing properly for the first time that day. I took a long slow drag, enjoying the fact that a potentially hazardous job had been completed successfully, and flicked through the channels until I found a report on the killings. It didn't take long. Murder's a numbers game. Kill one person and you barely make the inside pages. Kill three, especially in a public place, and it's big news. It adds a bit of excitement to the mundane grind of people's lives, even more so when it bears all the hallmarks of a so-called gangland shooting. Shootings are entertaining because they're not too personal. They make good conversation points.

Understandably, details were still very sketchy. The programme I was watching had a young female reporter on the scene. She looked cold but excited to be involved in what was potentially a meaty, career-enhancing story. It was still raining, only now it had turned into that light stuff that always seems to soak you more. She'd positioned herself in the rear car park and you could make out the Cherokee in the background about twenty yards away, behind reams of brightly coloured scene-of-crime tape. There were a lot of police and forensic staff in lab coats swarming all over it.

The report didn't last long. The girl confirmed that three people had been murdered – no idea as to identities – and speculated that they'd been shot. She then wheeled over the hotel's deputy manager, a tall, spotty young man who looked like he'd just got out of school, for his comments. They weren't, it has to be said, very enlightening. Squinting through his spectacles, he explained that he'd been working in the reception area when he'd heard a number of faint popping sounds (they all say that) coming from the rear car park. He'd thought nothing more of it but then one of the kitchen workers had come running in screaming and shouting that there'd been a murder. He, the deputy manager, had bravely gone out to investigate and had immediately discovered my handiwork, which was when he'd called the police. 'It was very shocking for all of us,' he told the reporter. 'You don't expect this sort of thing in a quiet area like this.' They all seem to say that as well.

The reporter thanked him before turning back to the camera and breathlessly promising further information as and when she received it. She then signed off, and it was back to the studio. It seemed I'd made her night anyway.

I took a drink of wine, taking my time swallowing it, and switched over. There was a programme about great white sharks on the Discovery Channel, and I sat watching that for a while, not really paying too much attention. Although I tried to empty my mind of the day's events, it was difficult not to think about the murders. I suppose it was only now that the full enormity of what I'd done was beginning to sink in. Three lives snuffed out, just like that. It felt like I'd crossed a threshold. I've killed before, I suppose that's obvious by now, but only twice, and in vastly different circumstances.

The first time was twelve years ago. I'd been one of a number of armed officers who'd turned up to a domestic incident at a house in Haringey. A man was threatening his common-law wife and their two young children with a gun and a carving knife. They'd got people trying to negotiate with him over the phone but the guy was drugged up to the eyeballs, shouting incoherently, and they weren't really getting anywhere.

Siege situations are the most frustrating a police officer can get involved in. You've got very little control over events so you can never really relax an inch, just in case something happens. But more often than not, nothing does. The suspect mulls over his actions, finally works out that he's trapped and that he's not going to get out of there except in handcuffs or a box, and eventually releases his hostages and simply walks out the door. It's frustrating because you want to be doing something to help end the situation, yet in most ways you're pretty much irrelevant to it.

On the day of the Haringey siege I remember it was hot. Stiflingly hot. We'd been on the scene about an hour and had the place completely surrounded when, without warning, our hostage taker had suddenly appeared in the front window, naked from the waist up, holding his gun. He was a big guy with the beginnings of a pot belly and a tattoo of an eagle straddling his chest. He'd shouted something from behind the glass, then opened the top part of the window and stuck his head out, shouting something else unintelligible. I was ten yards away behind a car on the street. Another officer was crouched down beside me. He was about fifteen years older than me and his name was Renfrew. I remember he got pensioned off a couple of years later after he got a glass in the face trying to break up a pub fight. Renfrew cursed the guy under his breath. You could tell he wanted to shoot him. Why not? The guy was just a waste-of-space dopehead who caused a lot more harm to the world than good. But Renfrew was a pro and, like a lot of coppers, he had one eye on the pension, so he was never going to do anything that might jeopardize his career. I was still a bit idealistic in those days. I didn't think about the pension. I thought about the wife and kids stuck in there with an unpredictable maniac.

I'd had an earpiece on. The chief superintendent spoke into it. Don't fire, he said. We're still negotiating. Keep him in your sights, but don't fire.

Then, just like that, our target had brought the gun up and pointed it wildly towards us. The chief superintendeant hissed something else into my earpiece, but I didn't hear it. It looked like the suspect was going to pull the trigger. I knew he wouldn't hit me from where he was standing. I had good cover, and he looked too stoned to aim straight, but I was still nervous. And angry. This bastard was just showing off his power, knowing we'd have to stand there like lemons, hamstrung by our limited rules of engagement. That got me, it really did.

So I'd fired. Two shots from the Browning. Straight through the window and into his upper body. One of them got him in the heart, but the autopsy confirmed that either of the bullets would have been fatal on its own. He died instantly, I think. Certainly before anyone could administer first aid.

I was offered psychological counselling and I took it because I was told that if I didn't, it would look like I didn't care that I'd killed a man. It didn't do me much good, mainly because I genuinely didn't care that I'd killed him. In fact, I was quite pleased. He'd wanted to kill me and I'd got in there first. But of course I didn't tell the counsellor that. I told him I deeply regretted having to take a life, even if it was in the line of duty. I guessed that was what he wanted to hear.

There was an inquest, and I was forced to give evidence. There was even talk about a criminal trial, especially when it was discovered that the gun he'd been holding was a replica, and I was suspended for close to two months, although that at least was on full pay. On the second day of the inquest, I was leaving the building by a side door when I ran into the common-law wife and her brother. She spat in my face and called me a murderer while the brother punched me in the side of the head. A uniformed officer intervened before things went any further, but the incident taught me two things. One, never rely on the support of people you're trying to help. As politicians have often found out to their cost over the years, the hand that pats you on the back one day can just as easily grab you by the balls the next. And two, never rely on anyone else for support either. In this world, you've got to get used to the fact that, in the end, you're always on your own.

No blame was ever officially attached to me over the killing of thirty-three-year-old Darren John Reid (who, it turned out, had a grand total of twenty-nine convictions, including eleven for violence, four of which related to his missus), but it might as well have been. I was taken off any further firearms duties (and have been to this day); banned from keeping guns privately; and my path up the career ladder slowed down one hell of a lot over the next few years. Crime, it seems, only pays when you're a criminal.

I'm not a bad man, whatever those who like to sit in judgement may think. When I started out I really did believe I could make a difference. My sole motivation was to take the bad guys off the street and bring them to account for the crimes they'd committed. After the Reid shooting, I slowly stopped caring. I suppose I finally realized what all defence lawyers know: however well intentioned its designers may have been, the law in practice only serves to help the criminal, hinder the police, and ignore the victim.

Having got to a point when I was as cynical as that it was only a matter of time before I fell in with the wrong company. The wrong company being, in my case, about as wrong as you can get, although when I first started doing business with Raymond Keen, one of North London's more colourful entrepreneurs, I wasn't to know quite how far it would go.

I've had a business relationship with Raymond for about seven years now. At first it wasn't too serious; nothing like that ever is. Just a few tips here and there, a helpful advance warning of impending police action, a sale of the odd bit of dope that went missing from police custody. Small things, but like cancerous lumps, small things that inevitably grow bigger. I wasn't even that surprised when two years ago he asked me to kill a bent businessman who was refusing point blank to pay him the twenty-two grand he owed him. The businessman was a nasty piece of work. One of his sidelines was importing kiddie porn. Raymond offered me ten grand to get rid of him. 'It'll strike a blow for creditors everywhere,' he'd said, although I wasn't quite sure how many creditors would follow his example and write off their debts with that degree of permanence. But ten grand's a lot of money, especially when you're on a copper's wage and, once again, he wasn't the sort of bloke anyone was going to miss. So one night I waited for him outside the lock-up he used. When he came out and walked over to his car, I emerged from the shadows and followed. As he opened the door, I pushed the silencer against the back of his hairless head and pulled the trigger. One shot was all it needed, but I added a second for good measure. Pop pop. All over. And I was ten grand richer. It was very easy.

But three men dead in one go? Danny was right, there was going to be a lot of heat over this one, although Raymond, who was the instigator of the whole thing, didn't appear too worried that any of it would get back to him. But then Raymond wasn't really the worrying type – which, I suppose, in his line of business, is something of a plus.

It was getting late. I drained my wine, drank a glass of water from the tap so that I didn't dehydrate myself, and made my way to bed. Looking back now, I already had a bad feeling about the whole thing but I was trying hard not to admit it to myself. Raymond Keen had paid me forty grand for killing those men. It was a lot of money, even after Danny had got his 20 per cent cut. Enough to justify a lot of things.

But nothing like enough to justify what was to follow.

3

Things started going downhill at exactly ten past eight the next morning. I'd been up for about twenty minutes and was in the kitchen making myself some toast for breakfast when the land-line rang. It was Danny, which was a bit of a surprise. I hadn't expected to hear from him today. He sounded agitated.

'Dennis, what the fuck's going on?'

'What the fuck's going on what?'

'Have you not seen the news this morning?'

I experienced the first stirrings of fear in my gut. 'No. No, I haven't. What's the problem?'

'The targets, that's the problem.'

'What do you mean?'

'They weren't who you said they were, Dennis. Just switch the TV on and you'll find out.'

I paused for a moment, trying to collect my thoughts. This wasn't what I wanted to hear. The most important thing, though, was not to say too much over the phone. 'All right, listen. Sit tight, don't worry about anything. I'll check things out and call you back later.'

'This is bad, Dennis. Very bad.'

'I'll call you back later, OK? Just stay calm and carry on as normal.'

I rang off and immediately looked around for my cigarettes. I needed to think things through, to try to locate what the fuck had gone wrong.

When I'd found them, I lit one, went through to the sitting room and flicked on the TV. I didn't hang about, I went straight to the news channel, but they were already on to something else. So I flicked on Ceefax, unable to suppress the feeling of dread at what I was going to see. I knew it was going to be bad, it was just a case of how bad.

It was the top story. Unlike the other stories, the headline was in bold block capitals, telling even the most shortsighted viewer that this was big news.

I had committed these three murders for Raymond Keen. Raymond had told me that the men were drug dealers, violent drug dealers, who were causing some associates of his serious trouble. But the headline staring back at me wasn't saying that at all. It was saying, TWO CUSTOMS OFFICERS AND ONE CIVILIAN GUNNED DOWN OUTSIDE HOTEL.

For a couple of seconds, I had this irrational idea that I'd opened fire on the occupants of the wrong Cherokee, but a couple of seconds was all I needed to scupper that particular one. I'd shot the people I was meant to shoot all right. Raymond Keen had set me up. For whatever reason, he'd wanted these men out of the way and had duped me into killing them. He knew that if he told me they were violent criminals whose business was supplying the masses with hard drugs, I'd have no problem pulling the trigger.

29

I sighed loudly and sat back on the sofa, willing myself to calm down. A serious mistake had been made, there was no denying that. But it had been Raymond who had orchestrated it. What mattered now was that I kept my nerve. There'd be a far bigger police operation to find the killers of two hard-working customs officers than there would have been to find the people who'd put away three low-level gangsters, which meant I was going to have to be extremely careful. I needed to know what it was these customs officers were doing, and who the hell the civilian was who was with them. Armed with that knowledge I could at least work out how how likely it was that the police could get on to Raymond. The whole thing was odd because I didn't think Raymond would ever get himself involved in the type of situation that put him and his business empire at risk. You don't get to his position and stay there by executing representatives of the forces of law and order.

I possess a mobile phone that's registered in the name of a man I've never met before, and that man always pays the bills. Whenever I need to make contact with Raymond I use that phone, and I used it now.

Unfortunately, it was Luke who answered. Luke is Raymond's personal assistant and bodyguard. He's the strong, silent type who tends to look at you as if you've just patted his bottom and blown him a kiss; all simmering rage and barely suppressed violence. Legend has it he once broke a love rival's legs with his bare hands, and he's supposedly an expert at some highfalutin martial art whose name I forget. Useful to have around in bar-room brawls, but that's about it.

'Yeah,' he grunted, by way of a greeting.

'It's Dennis, I need to speak to Raymond.'

'Mr Keen's not available.'

'When's he going to be available?'

'I can't tell you that.'

Conversations with Luke can be frustrating. He always acts like he's the heavy in a very cheap gangster flick.

'Give him a message. Tell him I need to speak to him urgently. Very urgently. He'll know what it's about.'

'I'll let him know you called.'

'Do that. And if I don't hear from him by the end of the morning, then I'll come looking for him.'

'Mr Keen doesn't like threats.'

'I'm not threatening him. I'm just telling you what'll happen if I don't hear from him.'

He started to say something else but I didn't bother waiting around to find out what it was. I rang off and put the phone in the pocket of my dressing gown. What a start to the fucking day.

I'm not a panicker by nature. I can sometimes be thrown off course by a shock, especially a big one, but I can generally pull myself together without too much difficulty. This, though, was different. Not only had I jeopardized my livelihood and freedom, I'd broken every moral rule I've ever made. I'd killed men who, on the surface of it at least, didn't deserve it.

I went back into the sitting room, located another cigarette and lit it, coughing violently as the smoke charged down my throat. I switched off the Ceefax and aimlessly flicked through the channels.

The phone rang again. The landline, not the mobile. I let it ring. It wouldn't be Raymond, and if it was Danny, I didn't want to talk to him for a while. Not until I had a better idea of what I was going to do. After five rings the answerphone kicked in. My bored voice told the caller I wasn't in but if he left a message with a number and the reason why he was calling me, I'd get back to him. Or her, I suppose. If my luck was in.

The beep went, then my immediate boss's voice came on the

line. I nearly jumped out of the seat. What the fuck did he want? Surely the trap hadn't closed that quickly?

'Dennis, it's Karl.' His voice sounded weary. 'I need you in now.' There was a short pause before he continued. 'I'm down at the canal just behind All Saints Street. It's eight twenty-five a.m. and we've got a body down here. If you get this message within the next two hours, make your way over. Otherwise just get down to the station. Cheers.'

He hung up.

As if I didn't have enough work on my plate without a murder to add to it. I was already investigating two rapes, an armed robbery, a missing housewife, a motiveless stabbing, and Christ knows how many muggings. All of which had occurred in the last month. In the last seven days I'd put in a grand total of fifty-nine hours' work on the job, as well as organizing last night's little foray, and I was exhausted. The problem these days was twofold: one, we didn't have anything like the manpower we used to have, or that our colleagues have abroad, because no-one wants to be a copper any more; and two, we have far more crime, especially crimes of violence. I suppose the one is caused by the other, at least in part. There's something about criminals these days too – and I'm not counting myself here – they tend to use violence a lot more casually. They take more pleasure in it too. Hurting or killing someone is no longer simply a by-product of committing a crime. To a lot of people it's part and parcel of the buzz they get out of it. At least when I'd put people down, I thought I was doing the world a favour. I might have made mistakes, but they were mistakes made in good faith.

I continued smoking the cigarette until it was down to the butt, then I used it to light another one. When that one was halfway down, I knew I could hold back no longer. The thing is, I can never sit still when there's a new investigation starting, particularly a murder. I get a kick out of catching killers – maybe for the wrong reasons, I don't know, but it makes me feel good letting them know it's me who put them down, and fucked up their whole lives.

And, if nothing else, getting involved in this one would at least stop me mulling over matters I could do nothing about.

So I stubbed out the cigarette in the already overflowing ashtray and headed down to Regent's Canal, the grimy scene of many a heinous crime.

4

It was twenty to ten and raining when I arrived at the murder site. A uniformed officer stood at the entrance to the towpath talking to a guy in a trenchcoat who looked like a journalist. It's amazing how quick these people sniff out a story; it's like they've got an extra sense that can detect a fresh kill from miles away. I pushed my way past the journo, who gave me a dirty look but thought better of saying anything, and nodded to the uniform. I recognized him from the station, although I couldn't put a name to him, and he evidently recognized me because he stepped aside and let me through.

This part of the canal was fairly well looked after. The old warehouses had been knocked down to be replaced by office blocks that were built a few yards further back from the waters edge. A well-trimmed lawn had been laid down in the extra space with a couple of benches to add to the park-like feel.

The painstaking, monotonous hunt for clues was already in

full flow. There were about two dozen people widely scattered across the scene as they picked, probed and photographed every patch of earth. At the canal's edge stood four police divers, fully kitted up, ready to enter the treacle-like water. One of them was talking to DCI Knox, my boss's boss. He would be the senior investigating officer on a case like this, responsible for making sure that the investigation ran smoothly and nothing was missed. Almost certainly the key to a conviction lay in these few square yards.

A tent had been erected at the entrance to a narrow gap between two of the buildings. This was where the body would be and where it would remain until it had been examined and photographed in minute detail. I could see my boss standing next to the tent, talking to one of the forensic team. I made my way over, nodding to two CID men I recognized: Hunsdon and Smith. They were standing by one of the benches taking a statement from an old guy who had a Jack Russell on a lead. I guessed the old guy had discovered the body. His face was pale and troubled, and he kept shaking his head, as if he couldn't believe what he'd seen, which he probably couldn't. It's always difficult for people when they come into contact with the handiwork of murderers for the first time.

My boss turned round and nodded a curt greeting as I approached. It was a cold day, but DI Karl Welland was sweating. I thought he didn't look well. This was nothing new. He was overweight, red in the face, highly stressed, and, if my memory served me right, the wrong side of fifty. Hardly a candidate for a ripe old age. He looked worse today than usual, though, and his pale skin was covered in vivid red blotches. I felt like telling him he needed a holiday, but I didn't. It's not my business to offer lifestyle advice to my superiors.

He excused himself from the conversation he was having and

led me into the tent. 'It never gets easier, you know,' he said.

'The dead'll always keep dying, sir,' I told him.

'Perhaps, but do they have to die like this?'

I stopped and looked where he was facing. The girl couldn't have been more than eighteen. She was lying on her back in the paved alleyway between the two buildings, legs and arms splayed open in a rough star shape. Her throat had been cut so deeply that the wound had come close to severing her head, which was tilted at an odd angle to the rest of her; thick dried blood had splattered across her face and formed in irregular pools on either side of the body. Her black cocktail dress had been ripped badly around the chest area, exposing a small pointed breast. It had also been pulled up round her waist. She hadn't been wearing any underwear, or, if she had, she wasn't any longer. There was also a lot of congealed blood around the vaginal area, suggesting that her killer had stabbed her there as well, although I thought immediately that this would have been done after death as there didn't appear to be any defensive wounds on her hands or lower arms. She had died quite quickly, I was sure of that. Her face was screwed up in pain and her dark eyes bulged out, but there was no fear in them. Surprise maybe, shock even, but no fear. She was still wearing one of her shoes, a black stiletto. The other lay on its side a few feet away.

'She must have been freezing dressed like that,' I said, noting that she wasn't wearing any stockings or tights, nor were there any in the vicinity of the body.

'Looks that way,' said Welland. 'She was partially covered with an old rug when we found her. It's already gone off to the lab.'

'What do we know so far?' I asked, still looking down at the corpse.

'Not a lot. She was found just before eight o'clock this

morning by a bloke walking his dog. There hasn't been a great deal of effort to conceal her, and it doesn't look like she's been here that long.'

'I'd say by the way she was dressed, she was a Tom.'

'I think that's probably a fair assumption.'

'Goes off with a punter to a nice secluded spot, he pulls the knife out, puts a hand over her mouth, and the rest is history.'

'Looks that way, but we can't tell for sure. A lot of girls go out scantily clad these days. Even in weather like this. The first thing we need to do is identify her. You're on the squad for this one, Dennis. DC Malik'll be working alongside you, and you'll be reporting to me. DCI Knox is the SIO.'

'I've got a lot on at the moment, sir.'

'You're going to have a busy week, then. I'm sorry, Dennis, but we're short on bodies, if you'll excuse the pun. Very short. And it seems the world's lowlifes are all busy at the moment. What can I do?'

What could he do? He was right, of course. We were snowed under, and in those circumstances it's a case of all hands to the pumps. I was already losing my initial enthusiasm, though. It just didn't look at first glance like it was going to be an easy case. If this girl was a prostitute, it was highly likely we had a sex killer on our hands. If he'd been a clever boy and had worn gloves and avoided leaving any liquid evidence at the scene of the crime, then finding him was going to be an uphill battle. Whichever way you looked at it there was going to be a lot of legwork.

I looked back at the pathetic corpse of the girl. Some mother's daughter. It was a lonely way to say your goodbyes to the world.

'I want to get this one solved, Dennis. Whoever did this . . .' He paused momentarily, choosing his words. 'Whoever did this is a fucking animal, and I want him in a cage where he belongs.'

'I'll get on to it,' I told Welland.

He nodded, wiping his brow again. 'You do that.'

5

At 1.05 that afternoon, I was sitting on a bench in Regent's Park smoking yet another cigarette and waiting for my rendezvous. The rain had long since cleared and it was even threatening to be quite a nice day. I'd already attended the briefing session back at the station where Knox had worked hard to instil some enthusiasm and grit into the inquiry, not an easy task as no-one felt there was much hope of intercepting the perpetrator quickly. I'd now got Malik on to the task of identifying her, which, if she was a Tom, wouldn't take too long.

I liked Malik. He wasn't a bad copper and he was efficient. If you asked him to do something, he did it properly, which doesn't seem to be a common trait with a lot of people these days. And he wasn't idealistic either, even though he'd only been in the Force for five years and was university educated, which is usually a pretty dire combination. So many of the fast-track graduates who go shooting up through the ranks have all these big ideas about trying to understand the psychology and economics of crime. They want to find out what motivates and drives criminals rather than simply doing what they're paid to do, which is catch them.

I looked at my watch again, which is something I do constantly when I'm early for a meeting or the other person's late. In this case, the other person was late, but then Raymond was never the most punctual of people. I was hungry. Apart from the toast I'd forced down myself earlier that morning, I hadn't eaten in close to twenty-four hours and my stomach was beginning to make strange growling noises. I was, I decided, going to have to improve my diet and start eating more regularly. One of the DCs had told me that sushi was very good for you. The Japanese eat it all the time and, according to him, they have the lowest incidence of lung cancer in the industrialized world, even though they're the heaviest smokers. Raw fish, though. It was a high price to pay for a life of rude health.

'Care to join me for a walk, Dennis?' said Raymond, interrupting my thoughts. 'Or would you prefer to continue your meditation?'

There he was, bright as a bell, a wide smile on his big round face, as if the whole world were his playground and all was fair within it. That was Raymond Keen for you. He was one of those big, bouncy guys who simply oozed *joie de vivre*. Even his haircut, a magnificent silver bouffant of the kind so beloved of middle-aged men who want to put one over on their balding contemporaries, and which sat on the top of his head like a curled up Cheshire cat, seemed designed to tell the world what a jolly character he was, which was a little odd when you considered that one of his more active and lucrative sidelines was running a funeral parlour. But Raymond, as became clear when you got to know him, was a man with a deeply ironic sense of humour.

'I'll join you, I think,' I told him.

I got up and we started to walk across the grass in the direction of the boating lake. Some kids who should have been in school were playing football and a few mothers were out strolling with prams, but other than that the park was quiet.

I didn't beat about the bush. 'What the fuck happened, Raymond? You told me I was shooting drug dealers.'

Raymond attempted a rueful smile but he didn't look overly guilty. 'Give me a break, Dennis. I could hardly have told you the real targets, could I? You wouldn't have shot them.'

'I know I wouldn't have shot them! That's the point. You got me involved in something that's against everything I stand for.'

Raymond stopped and looked at me, a smile playing on his lips. Angry or not, it was obvious he knew there was nothing I could do about the situation. He had me pinned, and he knew I knew it.

'No, Dennis. That's where you're wrong. You got yourself involved. Admittedly, I embellished the truth a little bit—'

'You mean you lied.'

'But I needed them out of the way, and knowing – and all credit to you for this, Dennis – knowing your moral standpoint on this sort of thing, I thought I'd withhold some of the details. But I don't want you to lose sleep over it. These blokes were pondscum. They were blackmailing some associates of mine and the associates wanted them out of the way.' He sighed meaningfully. 'They were corrupt men, Dennis.'

'And that's meant to make me feel better, is it?'

'If it's any consolation to you, it makes me feel bad as well. I don't like the idea of men dying. Human life is a very precious thing, not to be taken away lightly. If there was any other way, any other way at all, you can claim a bet that I would have tried it.'

The phrase 'claim a bet' was one of Raymond's favourites, even though it meant absolutely nothing, and I'd never in my life heard a single other person utter it. Hearing it now annoyed me.

'Raymond, you have fucked me up. Do you have any idea the sort of pressure the murder of customs officers is going to generate? It's not like shooting three dealers who no-one's going to miss. These were family men who died doing the job they loved.'

'They were blackmailers who died because they were trying to blackmail the wrong sort of people. That's what they were.'

'But that's not what the media are going to say, is it? To them, these guys are the thin blue line, brutally murdered in the line of duty. They're going to be clamouring for a result on this. And you can claim a fucking bet on that.'

'Don't be facetious, Dennis.'

'I'm being serious. Deadly serious. The pressure to get a result on this one is going to be massive.'

'But they're not going to get a result, are they? We've done everything needed to cover our tracks. It was a well-planned operation. All credit to you for that, Dennis. It was a professional job.'

He started to walk again, and I followed. To him, the conversation was effectively over. He'd said his piece, tried to smooth the ruffled feathers of his part-time employee, and now it was time to move on.

I then did a stupid thing, a very stupid thing, that was to cause me and plenty of other people a lot of grief. I told him I'd been seen.

That stopped him dead. Which, of course, I knew it would.

'What do you mean?' There was an edge to his voice now and I wasn't sure if it was anger or nervousness. Probably both. Immediately I regretted opening my mouth. I'd just wanted to punch a hole in the smug air of confidence he was exuding, and it looked like I'd been only too successful.

'I mean, I was seen. One of the staff, a kitchen girl or something.'

'Did she get a good look?'

'No. It was dark and raining, and she was a fair way away.'

'How far?'

'Fifteen, maybe twenty yards. And I had my head down.

I doubt if she could give much of a description.'

'Good.' He seemed mollified. 'Why didn't they say anything about that on the news?'

'On something like this, where there's evidence that it was a planned killing, they won't want to risk putting the witness in any danger. Also, they'll still be questioning her.'

'How come you didn't shoot her?'

'Would you have wanted me to?'

'Well, it mightn't have been a bad idea.'

'What? Four killings? Come on, Raymond, this is England, not Cambodia.'

'Well, if you didn't think she saw anything, then I suppose there'd have been no point.'

'I *don't* think she saw anything.'

'Maybe not, then. There's no point killing anyone unnecessarily.'

'Especially when human life's such a precious thing.'

Raymond glared at me. He wasn't the sort of man who liked having the piss taken out of him. 'I don't really think you're in a position to get on your high horse, Dennis, do you?'

'So what were these customs men doing, Raymond, that was so bad they had to die?'

'As I said, they were blackmailing some associates of mine. Associates who are very important to the smooth running of my business.'

'That doesn't really answer my question.'

'Well, my apologies, Dennis, but that's all the details available at present.'

'It said only two of them were customs. Who was the other one?'

'Why so interested? You can't bring them back.'

'I want to know who I killed, and why.'

Raymond sighed theatrically. 'He was another piece of pond-scum. He thought he was setting the other two up. In that, he was wrong. Now that's all I'm going to say on the matter.'

I took a last drag on my cigarette and stubbed it underfoot, still feeling pissed off.

'Look, think of it from my perspective,' he continued. 'Just for a moment. I needed the job done and you're the best man I've got for that sort of work. It's unfortunate that your main talent lies in that direction; it's a particularly barbaric skill to possess, but there you go.'

'You didn't have to use me. A man like you's got other contacts.'

'What did you expect me to do? Ring round and get quotes in? I had no choice, Dennis. That's the long and the short of it. I had no choice.'

'Don't ever ask me to do anything like that again.'

Raymond shrugged, seemingly none too concerned. 'Last night was a one-off. It won't happen again.' He looked at his watch, then back at me. 'I'm going to have to go. I've got a punter at two o'clock.'

'A dead one or a live one?'

'She's deceased,' he said sternly. 'A car accident. Beautiful-looking girl, and only twenty-three . . . her whole life in front of her.' He crossed his hands in front of him and was silent for a moment, I assumed out of respect for the dead. Then it was back to business. 'Anyway, I've got to prepare and time's getting on. I don't want the poor thing to be late for her own funeral.'

'That's very thoughtful of you.'

'Thoughtfulness costs nothing, Dennis.'

'Which reminds me. There's the small matter of my remuneration.'

'As if I'd forget.' He fished a key out of the breast pocket of his expensive-looking suit and chucked it over to me. 'The money's in a locker at King's Cross. The same place as last time.'

I put the key in the inside pocket of my suit, resisting the urge to thank him. There wasn't, I concluded, a great deal to thank him for.

Sensing my continued annoyance, he flashed me a salesman's smile. 'You did a good job, Dennis. It won't be forgotten.'

'No,' I said. 'Somehow, I don't think it will.'

After we'd parted company I grabbed a sandwich at a café just off the Marylebone Road. They didn't do anything with sushi in it so I ordered smoked salmon, thinking it was probably the next best thing. The sandwich tasted like cardboard, but I wasn't sure whether that was as a result of the poor-quality bread or my own numbed tastebuds. I ate about three quarters of it, washing it down with a bottle of overpriced mineral water, then smoked two cigarettes in quick succession.

On my way back to the station I called in on Len Runnion at his pawn shop just off the Gray's Inn Road. In some ways, Runnion was one of Tomboy's successors. He dealt in stolen goods of pretty much every description, using the pawn shop as a cover. He had none of the class of Tomboy, though. A very short man with a leering smile that made Raymond's look genuine, Runnion had cunning, ratlike eyes that darted about when he talked. And he never looked anyone in the eyes, which is something I can't stand. To me, it means they've got skeletons in the closet. From what I knew of Runnion and from what I could guess from his general demeanour, I expect he had a whole graveyard in his.

In the armed robbery I was still effectively investigating, the two robbers had held up a post office and, after stabbing the postmaster's wife and one of the customers, had got away with several hundred vehicle tax discs as well as a small sum of cash. I strongly suspected that they were amateurs who wouldn't really know what to do with the discs other than sell them on to other criminals. Professionals don't knife two people for that sort of return. It was a fair assumption then that they'd try someone like Runnion as a possible conduit for the goods, and if they had I wanted to know about it.

Runnion claimed ignorance of any tax discs. 'What would I do with them?' he asked me as he polished some garish-looking costume jewellery. I stated the obvious and he told me that he wouldn't have a clue where to sell such things. I didn't believe him, of course. Men in his line of business always know where to unload contraband. I told him that the perpetrators had stabbed the postmaster's wife and one of the customers during the course of the robbery, and that the customer had been lucky not to bleed to death. 'He was sixty-one years old, trying to protect the members of staff.'

Runnion shook his head in mock disbelief. 'There's no need for that,' he said. 'Never any need for violence. It's all about forward planning, isn't it? If you use forward planning, no-one gets hurt. The kids these days, they just don't have any. It's the education system, you know. They don't teach them anything any more.'

This was probably true, but you don't need to hear it from a toe-rag like Len Runnion. I told him firmly that if he was approached by anyone offering stolen tax discs he should play them along a bit, get them to come back again, and inform me straight away.

He nodded. 'Yeah, yeah, no problem. Goes without saying. I don't have no truck with bastards like that.' Which, of course, he did. Among other things, Runnion was well known for supplying firearms, usually on a rental basis, to whoever needed them. We

might never have caught him for it, but that didn't mean anything. We knew he did it. 'If I hear anything, I'll make sure
you're the first to know, Sargeant.'

'You'd better do, Leonard. You'd better do.'

'And will there, shall we say, be a little drink in it for me if I
come good?' The eyes darted about like flies in a field of shit.

'I'm sure we'll be able to come up with something,' I told him,
knowing that bribery was usually more effective than threats.
After all, as a police officer, what could I threaten him with?
That we'd look into his business affairs more closely when we
had the time? It would hardly have got him quaking in his boots.

It was five to two by the time I got out of Runnion's shop.
Rather than continue my journey to the station, I thought I'd
phone Malik to see how everything was going.

He picked up after one ring. 'Miriam Fox.'

'Miriam?'

'That's our victim,' he said. 'Eighteen years old, just turned.
Ran away from home three years ago. She's been on the streets
ever since.'

'Miriam. It seems a funny name for a Tom. I assume she was
a Tom.'

'She was. Six convictions for soliciting. The last was two
months ago. Apparently she came from a good home. Parents
live out in Oxfordshire, father's something big in computers.
Plenty of money.'

'The sort of people who call their kid Miriam.'

'It's a rich girl's name,' Malik agreed.

'A runaway, then.'

'That's what I can't understand. All over the world you've got
people struggling to get out of poverty and make a better life for
themselves, and this girl was trying to do exactly the opposite.'

'Don't ever try to understand people,' I told him. 'You'll just be disappointed. Have the family been informed?'

'The local boys are round there now.'

'Good.'

'I've got her last known address here. A flat in Somerstown, not far from the station.'

I had to hand it to Malik, he didn't hang about. 'Has it been sealed yet?' I asked him.

'Yeah. According to the DI, they've got a uniform down there at the moment.'

'Keys?' It was always worth asking this sort of thing. You'd be amazed how many times simple things like means of entrance to an abode got overlooked.

'I had to pick them up myself. The landlord was one cheap bastard. It turned out she was late with the rent. He asked me what he could do to get hold of the money she owed him.'

'I hope you told him where to get off.'

'I told him he'd have to talk to her pimp. I said as soon as I got his address, I'd give it to him.'

I managed my first smile of the day. 'I bet that pleased him.'

'I don't think there was much that was going to please him today.' Anyway, the DI wants us to check out the address. See what we can find.'

I told Malik where I was and he said he'd come by and pick me up en route. He rang off and I lit a cigarette, sheltering the lighter from the cold November wind.

As I stood there breathing in the polluted city air, it struck me that maybe Malik was right. What the fuck had Miriam Fox been thinking about, coming here?

6

For me, one of the worst jobs in policing is looking through the possessions of a murder victim. A lot of the time when a murder's an open-and-shut case, which mostly they are, it's not necessary to have to do it, but sometimes there's no choice, and it's a painful process, the reason being that it puts flesh and bones on people, gives you insights into what made them tick, and this only serves to make them more human. When you're trying to be rational and objective, this is something you could really do without.

Miriam Fox's flat was on the third floor of a tatty-looking townhouse that could have been improved dramatically by a simple lick of paint. The front door was on the latch so we walked right in. Bags of festering rubbish sat just inside the entrance and the interior hallway was cold and smelled of damp. Thumping techno music blared from behind one of the doors. It annoyed me that people lived like this. I was all for minimalism, but this was just letting things go. It had nothing to do with poverty. It was all about self-respect. You didn't need money to clear away rubbish, and a can of paint didn't cost much. You could get a lot of paint, plus brushes for everyone, for the price of a few extra-strength lagers or a gram of smack. It's all about priorities.

A uniformed officer stood outside the door of flat number 5. Someone in flat number 4, which was just down the hall, was also playing music but thankfully not as loud as the guy downstairs. It also sounded quite a lot better – hippy stuff, with a woman singing earnestly about something or other that was obviously important to her. The uniform looked pleased to be relieved of his guard duty and made a rapid exit.

I checked the lock quickly for signs of tampering and, seeing none, opened the door.

The interior was a mess, which I suppose I expected. At least it was in keeping with the rest of the building. But it wasn't the mess of someone who'd gone completely to pot and no longer cared about her surroundings, which is a lot of people's image of the desperate prostitute. It was a teenage girl's mess. An unmade sofa bed took up close to half the floor space of the none too spacious living room. It was liberally sprinkled with clothes, not the sexy ones a Tom wears to attract her customers, but leggings and sweaters, stuff like that. Normal stuff. There were two threadbare chairs on either side of the bed and all three items of furniture faced an old portable TV that sat on a chest of drawers. There were pictures on the wall: a couple of impressionist prints; a colourful fantasy poster of a female warrior on a black stallion, sword in hand, blonde hair waving in the imaginary wind; a moody-looking band I didn't recognize; and a few photographs.

I stopped where I was and gave the place a quick once-over. A door on the left led to a bathroom while one on the right led into a kitchen that didn't look to be much bigger than a standard-sized wardrobe. There was only one window in the whole flat as far as I could see, though thankfully it was large enough to throw a bit of light into the place. The view it offered was of a brick wall.

On the floor in front of me, amid the teen magazines, empty KFC boxes, Rizla packets and other odds and ends, was a huge round ashtray the size of a serving plate. There were maybe ten or fifteen cigarette butts in it, plus the remains of a few joints, but what caught my eye were the pieces of screwed-up tin foil, the small brown pipe, and the dark patches of crystallized liquid, splattered like paint drops inside.

It didn't surprise me that she was a crack addict. Most of the girls are, especially the young ones. It's either that or heroin. It's what keeps them tied to their pimps, and it's why the money they earn is never quite enough.

I lit a cigarette, figuring it wasn't going to make any difference. Malik gave me the briefest of disapproving glances as he put on his gloves but, like Danny the previous night, he didn't say anything.

We got to work without speaking. Malik started on the chest of drawers on which the TV sat. We both knew what we were looking for: little clues, things that in themselves might seem irrelevant to the untrained eye but which, taken together with what else the investigation threw up, could be used to build up a basic picture of the life and ultimately the death of Ms Miriam Fox.

She must have been quite a pretty girl once. There was a photograph of her pinned to the wall at a slightly uneven angle. In the picture, she was standing in the room we were in now, dressed in a pair of jeans and a sky-blue halter top that exposed a pale midriff. She didn't have any shoes on and her bare feet were long and thin. One hand was on her hip while she ran the other through her thick black hair. She was pouting mockingly at the cameraman. I think the pose was supposed to be sexy, but the overall impression was that of a young girl trying hard to be a woman. I didn't know her, and would never know her, but at that moment I felt sorry for her.

The drugs had taken their toll. Her face was gaunt and bony, the eyes sunken and tired. It looked like it had been months since a decent meal passed her lips, which was probably true. But there was hope in the photograph too, or should have been. The damage didn't look permanent. Given time, some sleep and a healthy diet, she could have turned things around and become pretty again. Youth, if not luck, had been on her side.

There was a mirror shaped like a smiling moon next to the photograph. I saw my reflection in it and I couldn't help feeling that I was also beginning to look ravaged by the wrong sort of living. My cheekbones were protruding too much. So pronounced were they that it looked as if they were trying to escape from the rest of my face. To add to my misery, tiny webs of burst blood vessels I hadn't noticed before had popped up on either side of my nose. They were still pretty small, three of them altogether the size and shape of money spiders, but they worried me because now they were there, they were going to be there for ever. Youth, unfortunately, was not on my side.

There's nothing worse for a vain man than seeing reality catch up and hit him. I've always thought of myself as quite a good-looking guy and, to be honest, that's what more than a few women have told me over the years. No-one looking at the face I was looking at would have said that now.

There were two passport-type photos, still attached to each other, tucked into the mirror between the plastic coating and the glass. I removed them as carefully as I could and took a closer look. They'd obviously been taken one after another in one of those photo-me booths you get in railway stations and the occasional department store, because they were essentially the same picture. Two laughing girls, arms round each other, faces pressed together. One of the girls was Miriam Fox, the other was younger and prettier. The younger girl had blonde curly hair cut into a bob and, in contrast to Miriam, a round cherubic face with a cute smattering of freckles. Only the eyes, nothing like as bright as the rest of her, trying to look happy but not quite making it, told you that maybe she too was a street girl. I put her at about fourteen, but she could have been as young as twelve. They were both dressed in thick coats and the girl had a winter scarf round her neck, so I guessed the photo was fairly recent.

They looked like good friends. Maybe this girl, whoever she was, could fill in some of the gaps in Miriam Fox's life. We'd have to try to locate her, if she was still around. I put the photos in my notebook and moved over to a battered-looking wardrobe next to the bathroom door.

We went over everything bit by bit. Malik discovered a wad of notes: eight twenties, a fifty (how often do you see one of those?) and a ten. He appeared quite pleased with the find, although I wasn't sure why. A prostitute keeping cash in her flat was hardly a revelation.

'It means she definitely planned on coming back here,' he told me.

I told him that that's what I would have assumed anyway. 'If she picked up a punter and he just turned out to be the wrong sort of guy, then there's no question that she went out intending to come back here. Why wouldn't she?'

Malik nodded in agreement. 'But we're still trying to discover a motive, aren't we?' he said evenly. 'And at least this provides evidence that she wasn't running away from something and got caught before she could escape. It gives more credence to our theory of a dodgy punter.'

Credence. That was an interesting word. Malik was right of course. It did help to close off alternative theories, leaving us scope to focus our enquiries on certain areas, but I thought that maybe he was unnecessarily complicating matters. Malik was trying to look at it from the angle of Sherlock Holmes, and you didn't need to do that. If a prostitute gets her throat slashed and her genitalia mutilated, and her body's discovered on the edge of a notorious red light district with the clothing interfered with, it's fairly obvious what's happened.

Or so I thought.

There was nothing in the wardrobe that told us anything. There were a couple of drawers in there containing various knick-knacks; some books, including two by Jane Austen, which caused me to raise my eyebrows (how many whores read Jane Austen?); a bag of dope; an unopened carton of Marlboro Lights; a jewellery box filled with costume jewellery. Nothing unusual, but no address book or anything like that, which might have thrown up a few clues. The man who'd killed her may well have been one of her regulars, someone who could have been in love with her but whose love was not being reciprocated. Out of frustration, he kills her. Out of rage, he mutilates the corpse. An address book might have contained the details of this man, if he existed. But of course, these days things are a bit different. She might have kept details of her clients in a palmtop PC or on a mobile, rather than writing it down on paper. Obviously, in a block of flats like this you weren't going to keep readily saleable items such as electronic goods on display for your neighbours to pinch, so I presumed if she owned anything like that, and it seemed highly likely that she had, she would have hidden it somewhere in the flat.

'Did she have a mobile on her when they found her body?' I asked Malik.

'I don't think so,' he said, shrugging. 'But I'm not sure.'

I thought about phoning and asking Welland, then decided it would probably be easier just to look for it. I couldn't recall him saying anything about a mobile in the briefing. 'Give me a hand lifting up this bed, will you?'

Malik lifted it up while I peered underneath. Apart from a lot of dust, another book (which turned out to be another Jane Austen), and a pair of knickers, there was nothing there. I stood back up and Malik put the bed down again.

I was wondering where to look next when there was a loud knock on the door. We both stopped and looked at each other. The knocking came again. Whoever was on the other side wasn't particularly patient. I was keen to find out who it was, so I stepped over and opened it before he could knock again.

A stocky black guy, late twenties, was glaring at me. He didn't hang around. 'Who the fuck are you?' he demanded, pushing past me into the flat. He stopped when he saw Malik in his rubber gloves standing by the bed, and immediately twigged. I closed the door to prevent any quick escape. 'You're Old Bill, aren't you?' he added, somewhat unnecessarily.

'While you're here, sir,' I said, walking up behind him, ' we'd just like to ask you a few questions.'

'What's going on?' he asked, whirling round to face me.

I could see him calculating the possible reasons why we were there and whether it was worth him hanging about. It didn't take him long to decide that it wasn't. He shoved me once, very hard, in the chest and made for the door. I stumbled but somehow managed to stay upright. He grabbed the handle, pulled the door open and tried to slam it in my face. He almost got me as well but my reflexes didn't let me down and I managed to dodge it and run out after him, Malik hot on my heels.

I used to be a sprinter when I was at school, and at the age of thirteen I did the hundred metres in 12.8 seconds, but thirteen was a long time and a lot of cigarettes ago.

But I was still quick over short distances and as he rounded the corner and charged down the stairs, two at a time, I was only a few feet behind him. The door was slightly ajar and he pulled it open and kept running pretty much in one movement. But I was closing. As I reached the top of the steps I dived onto his back and grabbed him in a desperate bearhug. 'All right, come on!' I panted in as authoritative a voice as I could muster. But it didn't seem to work. He kept running, at the same time shaking himself out of my grip, and managed to plant an elbow in my face. I yelped but continued chasing, one hand stretched out try-ing to grab him by the collar, wondering amid the pain in my lungs exactly how I was going to bring this guy to heel.

Suddenly he slowed abruptly, half turned so he was sideways on to me, and brought back his fist ready to throw an almighty punch. Momentum kept me going and, even though I knew exactly what was going to happen, I had no way of stopping it. His fist connected perfectly with my right cheek, sending me completely off balance. My head pounded with the shock of the blow and I bit my tongue as I fell against a wall. My legs wobbled precariously and then went from under me, and I fell backwards onto the pavement, hitting it arse first.

Malik immediately screeched to a halt beside me. 'Are you all right, Sarge?' he yelled with more concern than I would have expected from him.

'Get after him!' I panted, waving him away. 'Go on, I'm fine.'

Which was bullshit, of course. I felt like death. My lungs were bursting and the whole right side of my face throbbed. I opened my eyes and my vision was partly blurred. Still sitting where I'd fallen, I watched as Malik disappeared up the street, all five feet eight of him, armed with nothing more than harsh words. Somehow I didn't think an arrest was imminent.

I was going to have to give up smoking. I couldn't have run much over thirty yards all told and it felt like I'd done a mile at a sprint. The problem with not taking regular exercise, especially when you combine it with a shit lifestyle, is you don't realize quite how unfit you really are. I was going to have start going back to the gym, even though my membership had lapsed close to two years ago. I couldn't embarrass myself like that again. That cheap piece of dirt, who from the way he acted was no doubt Miriam Fox's pimp, could have kicked the shit out of me if he'd wanted to, the contest was that one-sided.

Across the street I could see a middle-aged woman staring out of her window in my direction. She looked like she felt sorry for me. When I caught her eye, though, she turned away and was gone.

As I gingerly got to my feet, I found myself experiencing an impotent rage. He'd made me look a fool. I wished I'd had the gun I'd been using the previous night on me. I could have blown that fuck apart. I wouldn't even have needed to tire myself out. I could have just strolled down the steps, taken aim at the middle of his back, and fired at leisure. He might have been a solid boy, but I'd yet to come across anyone whose skin deflected lead.

Malik came back into view, walking without urgency, and the rage passed. We'd get him. It was just a matter of being patient. Maybe, just maybe, once he'd been released again, I'd track him down one evening and put him to sleep. The thought made me feel better.

Malik looked pissed off. 'I lost him,' he said, stopping in front of me. 'He was too fast.'

'I know I shouldn't say this, but I'm sort of glad you didn't corner him.'

'I can handle myself, Sergeant. Anyway, you're the one who took the pasting. Are you all right?'

I rubbed my cheek and blinked a few times. My vision was still a little blurred but it seemed to be moving back towards normal. 'Yeah, I think so. That bastard had a good punch on him, though.'

'I saw. So who do you think he was?'

I told him, and he nodded in agreement. 'Yeah, I'd have thought so too. So what do we do about him?'

'It won't take long to find out his name. There'll be plenty of uniforms on the streets tonight, talking to the other Toms. They'll find out who he is. Then we'll just reel him in.'

It dawned on me that he might also be the pimp for the blonde girl in the photo with Miriam, and I suddenly felt protective towards her. She was too young to be selling herself on the street and too vulnerable to be under the thumb of someone like him. The sooner we picked him up the better.

We went back to searching the flat but, though we spent close to another half an hour in there, we didn't find anything else of note. I checked in with Welland and he told us to speak to the other occupants of the block, which turned out to be something of a fruitless exercise. Number 1, the one playing the techno music, steadfastly refused to answer the door, which was probably because he couldn't hear us. A few more hours of that and he wouldn't be able to hear anything. Number 2 wasn't in. Number 3, a colourfully dressed Somalian lady with a young baby in her arms, couldn't speak English. She recognized Miriam's picture but I think she thought we were looking for her because she kept pointing upstairs. Without a Somali translator, there wasn't a lot more we could do, so we thanked her and left.

Number 4 eventually answered the door after we'd knocked at least three times. He was a tall, gangly bloke with John Lennon glasses and a badly trimmed goatee. He took one look at us and immediately clicked that we were police. In our trenchcoats and inexpensive suits, we were never going to be anything else. He didn't look too pleased to see us, which was no great surprise since the unmistakable aroma of freshly exhaled dope smoke was easing out of the gap in the door.

I did the introductions and asked if we could come in. He started to say that it wasn't a good time right now, which is what they all say when they've got something to hide, but I wasn't going to let this one go, not after drawing blanks everywhere else in the place. I told him that it was a murder inquiry, and that we weren't interested if he'd been smoking blow in the privacy of his own home. Malik, who came more from the zero-tolerance school of policing (where it suited him, of course) gave me the standard disapproving look I was beginning to get used to from my subordinates, but I ignored him.

The guy really didn't have much choice so he let us in and turned the music down. He sat down on a large beanbag and, waving in the general direction of the other beanbags assembled around the cluttered room, let us know that we too could sit down.

I told him we'd remain standing. He looked a mixture of nervous and confused, which was fine by me. I wanted to make him take this discussion seriously, to get him to rack his brains for information that could be of help.

As it happens, I didn't get a lot. His name was Drayer. He added that his first name was Zeke, but I told him I didn't believe anyone would have called their kid Zeke, not at the time he was born, which had to have been at least forty years earlier. He insisted that it was. I asked him if that was the name on his birth certificate. He admitted it wasn't. 'And have you changed it by deed poll?' He reluctantly conceded that he hadn't.

Eventually, I got it out of him that his real first name was Norman. 'Norman's an all right name,' I told him. 'It's no worse than Dennis, which is mine.'

'I know it's no worse,' he said, and left it at that. Cheeky bastard.

It turned out that Norman was a poet by trade. He performed his poetry in some of the local pubs and clubs and had also had a few bits and pieces published in various anthologies. 'It doesn't pay much,' he confided, 'but it's a clean life.' Looking round his worn-out living room, I wasn't sure I'd have used that description for it, but there you go. Everyone's entitled to their own illusions.

Norman appeared genuinely upset when he found out it was Miriam who'd been murdered. He hadn't really known her, he said, as she'd tended to keep herself to herself, but whenever he'd run into her in the hallway she had always smiled and said hello. 'She was a nice girl, you know. Made the effort. There aren't many like that in this city.'

We both nodded in agreement. 'It can be an unfriendly place,' I said, stating the obvious. 'Did Miss Fox have many visitors? Particularly male ones?'

'Er no, I don't think so,' he said, thinking about it. 'I saw one man go up there a couple of times.'

'What did he look like?' Malik asked.

'He was muscular, well formed. Attractive, I would think, to women. And there was a fire about him, a passion. An anger almost. As if somewhere inside him was a volcano waiting to erupt.'

'That's a truly terrible description,' I told him. 'Try again. Was he tall, short? Black, white?'

'He was black.'

I described the guy who'd just clouted me and it quickly

transpired that they were one and the same. Well, at least he'd been right about one thing. There'd certainly been an anger there.

'How often did he come and go?'

'I saw him maybe two or three times in the hall or on the stairs. He never spoke to me.'

'Over how long a period?'

He shrugged. I think he was pissed off that I'd mocked his descriptive skills. 'I don't know, maybe three months.'

'And when was the last time you saw him?'

'A couple of weeks ago. Something like that.'

'Not within the last two or three days?'

'No.'

'How long have you been here?' Malik asked.

'About a year now.'

'And was Miss Fox already here when you moved in?'

'No, she wasn't. She came . . . I don't know, about six months ago.'

'And you can't remember any other male visitors?'

He shook his head. 'No, I don't think so. Should I have done?'

'I thought poets were meant to be observant,' I told him. 'You know, viewing their surroundings and commenting on what they see.'

'What do you mean? What are you talking about?'

'She was a prostitute, Mr Drayer. Didn't you know that?'

It turned out he didn't, which was probably because there hadn't been any other male visitors that he recalled. She'd clearly kept her business and personal life separate. I showed him the photo-me images and asked him if he recognized the blonde girl. He said he did. He'd seen her a number of times coming and going with Miriam. 'They seemed like good friends. They used to laugh together a lot. Like schoolgirls.'

'That's what they should have been,' I said.

We asked him a few more questions about his own back-ground and what he knew about the other people in the flats, but didn't get any information of significance. If anything, Norman knew even less about his other neighbours than he'd known about Miriam.

It was just after a quarter to six when we finally got back to the station and reported to Welland, who'd taken up residence in a small office next to the incident room, from where he could control his end of the inquiry. He was pissed off because one of his witnesses in another case, a girl testifying against her ex-boyfriend who'd knifed someone in a pub fight, had decided to pull the plug and keep her mouth shut. Apparently someone had persuaded her to change her mind with a small threat of violence, leaving Welland's case in tatters.

'I've had the CPS on the phone all afternoon,' he moaned between vacuum-cleaner-like drags on his cigarette. 'Making a fucking fuss like they're fucking whiter than white.'

Malik made the mistake of asking if she'd had protection.

Welland glared at him. 'That fucking knifing happened three months ago and the trial doesn't start until February. I can't have a man with her all that time. Where the fuck am I going to get him from? Magic him up out of thin air?'

Malik backed off, knowing better than to get involved in one of Welland's rants. Welland finished his cigarette in three angry drags and used the butt to light another one. 'Anyway, what happened to your face?' he asked me eventually. I told him, and he shook his head angrily. 'We'll put a warrant out on him as soon as we've got his name. He might be able to throw some light on this. Did you find anything of interest there?'

I shook my head. 'Not a lot. There was no address book or mobile phone or anything, nothing that would give us any idea of her client list.'

'We're just going to have to ask around among the King's Cross girls tonight. See if they can throw up any names.'

'She's bound to have had a mobile,' I said. 'Have we got anyone checking whether there was one registered in her name?'

'Yeah, I've got Hunsdon on it at the moment, but it'll take time.'

I told him about the girl in the photographs and suggested it would be a good idea to try to trace her.

'Yeah, you're right. She might be able to help. There's a meeting tomorrow at eight thirty sharp. We'll be getting the preliminary autopsy findings, so make sure you're there. No fucking oversleeping. It's important we get momentum on this one,' he said by way of conclusion. 'You know what they say about the first forty-eight hours.'

I did indeed, but my momentum had gone for the day. The right side of my face still ached, and since I was going to have to be in early again, I decided it was time to knock off. I asked Malik if he fancied joining me for a drink, more out of politeness than anything else, since I didn't think he'd say yes. He looked at his watch for at least two seconds too long, then smiled and said why not, which was unusual for him. He generally liked to get away at the end of the shift back to his family, which was fair enough, although he wasn't averse to socializing with the bosses if he thought it would do him some good.

We adjourned to a pub called the Roving Wolf, which was a haunt for CID and some of the uniforms. It was busy with the after-work office crowd, a few of whom I knew by sight, and I said hello to a couple of people as I pushed my way to the bar and ordered the drinks – a pint of Pride for me, a large orange juice for Malik. We found a table in the corner away from the scrum, and I lit a cigarette.

'So, who killed Miriam Fox, then?' he asked, sipping his drink.

'Good question.'

'What do you think?'

'Well, it's early days yet, and a lot depends on the result of the autopsy, but I suppose my first thought's the obvious one, and that's because the obvious one's usually the right one.'

'A pervert?'

'I think so. You've got to say, it points that way. She died at the scene, there's no doubt about that. The area round the body was too bloodstained for her to have been taken there after death. And the location suggests she wasn't killed by someone who knew her. It's the sort of place she might well have gone for privacy with a punter, and the sort of place a killer might have gone for privacy with his victim.'

'So what do you reckon our chances of a result are, then?'

'Too early to say. If the killer's been careless like a lot of these guys can be, then we're sorted. Forensics'll have him in no time.'

'Unless, of course, he's not known to us.'

I didn't like to think of that scenario. 'True. But someone who can do that . . . you know, grab a young girl from behind and cut her throat from ear to ear. Even in this day and age, I don't think there are many who could. Someone like that is likely to have done something that's brought him to the attention of the police before. But if he's planned it, and he's been careful, and he's picked someone who doesn't know him from Adam—'

'Like a prostitute.'

'Like a prostitute, then he could be miles away by now.'

'And what do you think? Do you think he's a planner or someone who just can't control his urges?'

'Well, my gut feeling is that he's a planner. But I haven't really got anything to back that up with, except for the fact that he picked a good spot to take her out, and he obviously knew what he was doing. What about you? What's your take on it?'

Malik smiled wearily. 'I think it's depressing that we learn all these investigative skills, yet how much do we actually ever need them?'

'What do you mean?'

'Well, unless the guy's an idiot or we get a lucky break, then we're not going to catch him, are we? No matter how clever we are.'

'Policework's all about lucky breaks, but you know what they say: in the end, you make your own luck.'

'Well, I hope we get lucky, then, because otherwise it's just a matter of waiting, isn't it?'

'He may not kill again,' I said. 'Sometimes they don't.'

'And if he doesn't, then he may never be brought to justice.'

'That's the trade-off. Let's just hope it doesn't come to that. To successful forensics,' I said, raising my glass.

'To successful forensics,' Malik intoned, not looking completely convinced.

For a few moments we both sat in silence, mulling things over. I took a long sip of my drink, thinking that I was glad the day was over.

'Did you hear about that shooting in Hertfordshire last night?'

My mind immediately snapped to attention. To be honest, I hadn't thought about last night's activity since my meet with Raymond. It might sound callous, but I'd been too busy. I felt a short rush of regret when Malik mentioned it, but it was a lot weaker than it had been earlier. I felt bad at what had happened, but what was done was done. Time can sometimes be a rapid as well as a great healer.

'Yeah, I did. I reckon there's more to that one than meets the eye.'

'So do I. I've got a friend, a guy I used to go to college with. He's a DC up in Hertford. They're handling the case. For the moment anyway.'

'Yeah, I heard. What's he got to say about it so far?'

'I haven't spoken to him yet. I expect he's under the cosh a bit. Same as us. I thought I might try him this evening, that's if they're letting him home for the night.'

I took an easy gulp of my pint, knowing that I was going to have to approach this carefully. 'When you do speak to your mate, find out a bit more about this case. It intrigues me.'

'And me. It's an interesting one. Looks like a gangland hit. It makes you wonder what those customs men were investigating.'

It did that, all right. 'Whatever it was, it must have been pretty big.'

'Well, you'd think so, wouldn't you? I think the key lies in finding out whoever the guy with them was. The civilian. When you know what his involvement was, I think you'll have the motive, and with something like this, once you've got the motive, you're two thirds of the way there.'

'It's proving it, though, isn't it? This was obviously well planned so you'd assume whoever was behind it has covered their tracks pretty well. You might find out who they are, but it's building a case against them that matters.'

Malik nodded. 'You've got to get someone to talk, that's always the key. Something like this, there's got to be a fair few people involved, and one or two of them are bound to get cold feet.'

I thought of Danny. Would he break? I doubted it. He'd known what we were going to do and had been happy enough to get involved. But Malik was right. There were a fair few people involved, some of whom I didn't know from Adam. Any one of them could end up talking, although it was a bit late to worry about that now. I was glad that, through Malik, I at least had a means of finding out how well the investigation was going.

'One way or another, it's going to be a difficult one to crack,' I added. 'Time consuming.'

'Perhaps. But definitely interesting. I'd love to talk to the man who did it. You know, the one who actually pulled the trigger.'

'Why? What'll he tell you? I expect he did it for money; something nice and mundane like that.'

Malik smiled. 'I'm sure he did – it's almost certainly a professional hit – but it takes a special kind of man to shoot dead three people without a second's thought. Just like that.' He clicked his fingers to signify his point. 'People he's almost certainly never met before. People who've never done him any harm.'

'You'd probably find that whoever did it was pretty normal underneath it all.'

'Normal people don't murder each other.'

This time it was my turn to smile. 'Normal people murder each other all the time.'

'I don't agree with that. Most murderers might look normal, but there's always something rotten inside that makes them do what they do.'

'I don't know. It's not always as cut and dried as that.'

Malik stared at me intensely. 'It *is* always that cut and dried. Murder's murder, and the people who commit it are bad people. There's no two ways about it. It's a black-and-white issue. Some murders aren't quite as horrific as others, but none of them are justifiable. Under any circumstances. They're just different shades of black.'

I could tell he felt passionately about what he was saying and thought it best not to say too much more on the matter. You never know when such conversations can be regurgitated and used against you somewhere down the line. So I conceded the point and the conversation drifted on through the awkward avenues of small talk before inevitably coming back to the case. After all, what else was there to talk about?

We both concluded that Welland was right about momentum. If we didn't turn up clues in the next few days, and it really did turn out to be someone unknown to the victim – which I have to say is what everything seemed to point to – then the bottom would fall out of this case very quickly and we'd be left with nothing. Either waiting for our mystery perpetrator to strike again (a worrying enough scenario in itself) or losing him for ever amid the vast ranks of the unsolveds, which somehow I felt would be even worse.

Malik stayed for two drinks to give him the opportunity to buy me a brew back, then it was time for him to return to the family seat in Highgate where his pretty wife and two young children awaited him. He offered to share a taxi with me but I decided to stay put for a while. I was hungry, but I fancied one more drink before I headed back to the flat. I'd got the taste of beer now.

One of the regulars, an old guy with a raspy voice whom I knew vaguely, came and joined me and we chatted about this and that for a while. Normal shit: football results, the price of beer, what a fuck-up the government was making of everything. Sometimes it's nice to talk to civilians. It doesn't require you to rack your brains in case you missed something. Things just flow along nice and easy. But when the guy started going on about his wife's pickled-onion-sized bunions, and I started thinking that I hoped I'd be dead by the time I got to his age, I knew it was time to go.

It was eight o'clock when the cab dropped me off outside my front door. The iron-grey cloud cover that had sat above the city most of the morning had now broken up completely, you could even make out the odd star. The temperature had dropped accordingly and the night had a pleasant wintery feel about it.

The first thing I did when I got inside was phone Danny, but he wasn't at home. I tried him on his mobile but got diverted to the message service, so I left one telling him to be in at five p.m. the next day so that I could drop the money round to him. Then I showered, washing off the dirt of the day, and thought about food.

I found a carton of something called creamy prawn risotto in the freezer. It said 'ready in twenty minutes' on the sleeve and the photo didn't look too unappetizing so I defrosted it in the microwave. While it was cooking, I took my usual seat on the sofa and switched on the TV, turning straight to the news channel.

Two passport-type photographs dominated the screen. They were of the Cherokee driver and his front-seat passenger. The driver looked different from the previous night. In the photo he was smiling broadly and there were laughter lines around his eyes. It gave you the impression that he'd probably been quite a nice bloke when he was alive. Old greasy face next to him looked better as well. He was still staring moodily at the camera, like he'd just been told off by someone twenty years his junior, but he'd lost the shiftiness he'd been exuding the previous night, and it looked like he'd washed his hair and given it a decent comb, which had improved his appearance no end.

The report named the driver as Paul Furlong, a thirty-six-year-old father of two young children, and his passenger as forty-nine-year-old Terry Bayden-Smith, who'd been with customs since leaving school. Bayden-Smith was divorced and presumably had no kids because none were mentioned.

Their faces disappeared from the screen to be replaced by a male reporter in a fleece coat standing outside the Traveller's Rest. There was still police tape everywhere and the Cherokee remained where it had stopped beside me, but activity had dwindled. A uniformed officer stood in the background guarding the scene, but he was the only person I could see. The reporter said that there'd been more than sixty detectives assigned to this case and that the police were confident of finding the killer. There were apparently a number of ongoing lines of inquiry but the reporter quoted a senior police source as saying that a quick result was unlikely.

I wondered if Raymond had been telling the truth when he'd said they'd been corrupt. Would it make what I'd done any better? Probably not. Once again I found myself wishing I hadn't got involved. Corrupt or not, there was going to be a huge amount of pressure on the investigating officers. Unlike us, they'd get all the resources they needed as well, always the way in high-profile cases where the public are clamouring for arrests. Again, very little mention was made of the third victim of the shooting, and they still weren't naming him, which surprised me. I was going to have to press Raymond to find out who he was. By now I was fairly certain he was more than just another piece of pondscum.

The murder of Miriam Fox didn't get a look-in, not even on Ceefax. I suppose a dead prostitute just doesn't carry the same kind of glamour, although that would certainly change if another Tom went the same way. There's nothing the public likes more than a serial killer, especially when he's not targeting them.

I ate my food while watching *Family Fortunes*. As always, Les Dennis did his best with only limited resources, kind of like the Metropolitan Police. Neither family was over-bright and the Dobbles from Glasgow had accents so thick that you had to wonder how they'd made it through the auditions. Les made a few jokes about needing a translator and laughed heartily as he tried to keep things going, but you could tell he was getting a bit tired of it. In the end they lost to the English family whose name I forget, and who went on to win the car.

After that I watched a film. It was a romantic comedy and it would have been quite entertaining but I had difficulty concentrating. I kept imagining the family of Paul Furlong huddled together in their living room, their faces red and tearstained. In my mind, the kids were a boy and a girl and they had blond hair. The boy was the older, maybe five, and the girl was a pretty little thing, about three. The boy kept turning to his mother who had her arms round both of them and asking why their dad was gone and where he had gone to. The mother, her voice breaking with emotion, said that he'd gone to heaven because sometimes that's where you have to go if God wants you for a particular reason. I thought of myself as a young kid and wondered how I would have felt if someone had snatched away my dad. My dad was dead now. He'd died five years ago, and it had been a blow even then, because I'd always held him in high esteem. When I was five, he'd been king of the world because he'd known everything there was to know about anything. It would have torn me apart if someone had taken him away then.

In the end, I could torture myself no more. Sitting alone in a poky flat, wallowing in the guilt of depriving kids of their father, was always going to be a recipe for disaster. So when the film finished, and the couple who hadn't been able to stand the sight of each other at first predictably got together and disappeared off into the sunset, I went to bed.

It was a measure of my exhaustion that I was asleep almost before my head hit the pillow.

7

Most nights my sleep is a blank space where nothing happens but that night was different. I dreamed of many vague things and woke up time and time again. Everything was a jumble, a messy kaleidoscope of images and thoughts and memories that for split seconds were ice cold in their clarity, but just as quickly faded like dying film heroes as I moved on to the next one.

Only one dream stayed in the mind. It came in the grey time just before dawn. In this dream, I was in a television studio watching an edition of *Family Fortunes*. I was up in the audience, but the audience was just a blur. The studio was very dark but there was a light that shone on Les Dennis, so you could see him well enough, and I remember that he was wearing a pink suit with a lime green shirt. Les was introducing one of the families but I couldn't make out their name because everything was too dark. He spoke to each of them in turn, and as he stopped in front of an individual player a light shone down on that person so you could see who was who.

First there was the driver of the Cherokee, Paul Furlong. He only had one eye, the other was just a bloody mess where I'd shot him, but he looked happy enough, and he laughed when Les told a joke. Then there was the front-seat passenger, Bayden-Smith. He still looked morose and most of the top of his head was missing. When he spoke, his voice sounded slow and drawling like a record on the wrong speed, and it took me a couple of seconds to work out that this was because his jaw was hanging off his face at an odd angle. I remember thinking that I was glad he didn't have kids. Then there was the back-seat passenger, but I couldn't really see his face very well and he kept looking away. Les tried to put him at ease by saying that he'd heard he was a very good skateboarder and inviting him to elaborate. But still he wouldn't look at us. Miriam Fox, who was standing next to him in a slinky black dress, her throat sliced from ear to ear, put a protective arm around his shoulders.

'You're Miriam,' said Les.

'That's right,' said Miriam in a pleasant voice.

'And what brings you here, Miriam?'

'I'm here with the dead.'

'Here with the dead!' laughed Les. 'That sounds good!' And he looked at the audience, and they all laughed too. 'And who's this?' he added, looking towards the person on the other side of Miriam. I couldn't see who it was because the light wouldn't shine on her and she was silhouetted in the darkness, but I had a dread feeling of familiarity. She was small, smaller than Miriam, and I thought I could make out curly hair.

'Is it your sister?' asked Les, still smiling, and Miriam suddenly looked very sad, as if Les had touched upon some secret tragedy. She started to say something but the words didn't come out or, if they did, I didn't hear them.

There was a long pause, and the audience fell silent.

Then Les turned back towards us, and he too looked troubled.

'These are the dead,' he said.

And then I woke up, sweating and frightened.

Part Two

HUNTING THE LIVING

8

'Miriam Ann Fox, aged eighteen, died from a single stab wound
to the neck delivered from behind. The wound was almost two
inches deep, suggesting that it was a) a very sharp bladed knife,
and b) a very strong person delivering the fatal blow. From the
angle of the wound we can surmise that the perpetrator was considerably taller than her. She was five feet three; he, and I think
we can safely assume it was a he in this case, is almost certainly
between five feet ten inches and six feet two. The victim either
bled or choked to death as a result of this one wound. The
pathologist thinks that the perpetrator held her up while she
choked and died, then laid her out on the ground on her back,
before stabbing her four times in the vaginal area.'

'So he didn't have sex with her then?' asked one of the
assembled group.

It was 8.35 the following morning and Malik, me, and the
fourteen other detectives assigned to the Miriam Fox murder
hunt were sitting in the incident room while DCI Knox, the
official head of the investigation, stood next to a whiteboard
giving his summary of what we knew so far. Welland sat next to

him, but was once again not looking himself. If someone had asked me for a diagnosis of his condition I would have said his batteries had gone flat, which seems to happen more and more to coppers of a certain age, and I wondered briefly how much longer he was going to last on the Force.

No such concerns about Knox, who was a big charismatic guy with a deep, resonant voice that swept across the room. 'There's no evidence that she had sex either immediately prior to or immediately after her death,' he continued. 'According to the pathologist she died at some point between eight and ten on Sunday night. Now we've spoken to a number of the girls who work the area and she was seen by at least two of them at about eight p.m., which was when she generally started her shift. She spoke briefly to one of the girls, and the girl said that there was nothing untoward about her. She then moved down the street to her usual spot, which is the corner of Northdown and Collier Street, and from there she was picked up by a car – a dark blue saloon, we haven't got the make yet – and driven away. Usually the girls try to get the number of the cars but, sod's law, no-one did this time.'

There was a resigned murmur from the assembled men, including me. You don't expect to get too many lucky breaks in the course of your work, but on a case like this you need a few.

Knox paused to take a sip from his tea. 'They didn't drive very far though, as we know. The victim was killed at the spot where she was found. As the crow flies that's no more than a few hundred yards from where she was picked up. It's important we trace this car. We've got a dozen uniforms who are going to be doing house-to-house in the vicinity to see if anyone can remember seeing a vehicle fitting the description near the scene. If we're lucky' – more groans –'somebody might even have got a look at him. He would have been heavily bloodstained after the killing.

We're checking CCTV on every possible site from where she was picked up to where she was discovered, but so far nothing's turned up.'

'None of the Toms recognized the car, then?' asked Capper, who was a DS, the same as me. I didn't like Capper; never had. He had an unpleasant haircut and constant bad breath, but I wouldn't have held those things against him particularly, not on their own. It was the way he sucked up to senior management I didn't like.

Knox shrugged. 'They see a lot of dark-coloured saloons in their line of business so no-one remembers this one.'

'You said that the Toms tended to make notes of punters' registration plates.' It was me speaking this time.

'That's right.'

'Do they ever keep records of them?'

He shook his head. 'No, it doesn't appear so, not according to any of the girls who were spoken to last night. We still might get the number, though. We'll be appealing for information on *Crimestoppers* and in the area itself. Boards'll be going up round there this morning, so someone's memory might get jogged. We need to find out if she had any punters who she went with on a regular basis. Most of them usually do. We've got two statements from girls testifying that she was picked up on more than one occasion by someone in a red TVR, although no-one ever saw his face. Apparently she had a friend, a girl by the name of Molly Hagger, who used to work the streets with her, I believe you've got a photo of her, Dennis, but she hasn't been seen for several weeks.'

I felt a brief stab of fear. So that was her name. Molly. And now she was missing. 'There was a photograph of her with the victim at the victim's flat,' I said. 'It looked recent, so I think it would be useful to talk to this Molly.'

'If we can find her.'

'Have we got an address for her?' I asked.

Knox nodded. 'We think so. One of the girls said she thought she was staying at Coleman House. It's a council-run children's home over towards Camden. We haven't contacted anyone down there yet so I want you and Malik to pay the place a visit and see if you can find out where she is, and if any of the other people there have any information on the victim.'

I nodded. 'Sure.'

'We've also got to bring in the victim's pimp, who we've now identified as Mark Wells. Dennis met him briefly yesterday.' He looked across at me and winked, much to the amusement of everyone else. 'Wells has a long record of violence, including attacks on women, and at the very least we can bring him in for taking out DS Milne.'

Again there was more laughter. I managed a strained smile to show that I could take a joke, just like the next man, not that I felt much like laughing. My face still hurt and a darkening bruise had appeared under my right cheekbone overnight.

'We're applying for a search warrant for his house and a warrant for his arrest, both of which should be with us by mid-morning. We're going to lean on him hard. He's a cocky bastard by all accounts, but he's going to have useful information about the victim, and it's essential we extract it from him. He's also a suspect. So far, our only evidence of sexual assault is the stab wounds around the vagina, so it's quite possible that the killer's attempting to make it look like a sexual assault when, in reality, it wasn't his prime motivation. Now I don't want to put too much stock on that theory, because at the moment it is just a theory, but we've got to bear it in mind. And that means taking a close look at Mark Wells.'

He paused again, took another sip of his tea. 'We also need

the names of everyone in a three-mile radius of here who's been picked up for soliciting at any time in the last two years, giving particular preference to anyone with convictions for violence or sex offences. And we're going to need to interview them all.' Several people groaned, and Knox managed an understanding smile. 'Look, it's not going to be easy – it never is – but we've got to explore every possible avenue, and that means talking to the sort of people who could have done this, i.e. men who are known to be violent to women. This murder hunt is twenty-four hours old, ladies and gentlemen. At the moment the body's still warm but it's going to cool down fast, so we've got a lot of work to do. One hell of a lot. I want this killer brought to justice and I know you're the people to do it.' He accompanied this last sentence by enthusiastically whacking one of the desks with the palm of his hand, which was a very Knox-like gesture. I'm sure sometimes he thought he was working on Wall Street.

Brave words, too. Whether they'd be matched by deeds or not, though, remained to be seen.

The remainder of the meeting was spent organizing who was going to be doing what, and took about ten minutes, including questions. Welland was going to be leading the raid on Mark Wells's place as soon as the paperwork came through, which annoyed me a little bit. Since it had been me the bastard had hit, I wanted to be on the team which brought him in, but I suppose at the same time I also wanted to find out more about Molly, and it was going to be difficult to do both.

It was 9.20 when Malik and I left to go round to the Coleman House care home. Times were hard in our division of the Metropolitan Police and budgets tight, so we decided to save the taxpayers some money by taking the bus. In the end, though, it would probably have been quicker to walk. An accident on the Holloway Road had snarled up the traffic and we were stuck in it, stopping and starting, for what seemed like hours.

I told Malik about my dream as we sat there watching the world go by, or not as the case might be. It had genuinely rattled me. 'You know, I know it sounds stupid, but it was almost like some sort of premonition.'

He couldn't resist a grin. 'What? You think Les Dennis might be in danger?'

'I'm serious, Asif. This wasn't like any dream I've ever had. You know me. I'm not superstitious, and I'm not spiritual or anything like that. I'm not even a Christian. So it's nothing to do with my state of mind. It was just it was so vivid that when I woke up I was absolutely positive this Molly girl was dead.'

'Explain the dream to me again.'

I went through it all with him, missing out the details of the dead customs men, and whispering so that none of the other passengers, a mixture of old grannies and foreign students, could hear what I was saying. I didn't want them thinking I was some sort of nutter.

By the time I'd finished, we'd travelled the sum total of about thirty yards.

Malik shook his head and gave me the sort of look that suggested he thought it was grossly unfair that he should be taking orders from someone with such a tenuous grip on reality. 'Look, Sarge, I wouldn't worry about it. You know, a dream's just a dream. The chances are this girl's all right.'

'I hope so. I didn't like the sound of the fact that she hasn't been seen for a couple of weeks.'

'Only by the local streetwalkers. Maybe she's changed. Maybe she's realized that prostitution and drug addiction is no way to lead a life.'

I laughed. 'Do you really believe that?'

'Well, it's unlikely . . .'

'Dead right it is.'

'But it's possible. And anyway, maybe she's just plying her trade somewhere else. There's got to be more chance of that than of her being dead in a ditch somewhere.'

Malik said these last few words a bit too loudly and a couple of people turned round and gave us funny looks.

'Yeah, you're right,' I said. 'You've convinced me.'

But he hadn't.

We exited the bus on Junction Road when it became obvious that we weren't getting anywhere and took the tube, which thankfully was still running pretty much as normal. It was 10.20 when we got out of Camden station. It was slowly turning into a sunny winter's day, so we walked the rest of the way.

Coleman House was a large redbrick Victorian building on a road just off the high street. One of the third-floor windows was boarded up, but other than that it looked quite well kept. A couple of kids, a boy and a girl, sat on the wall in front of the entrance, smoking and looking shifty. The girl was wearing a very short skirt and a huge pair of black platform-soled trainers that, set against her spindly legs, made her look mutated. They both looked at us as we approached and the boy sneered. 'Are you coppers?' he said.

'That's right,' I told him, stopping in front of them. 'We're investigating a murder.'

'Oh yeah? Whose, then?' he asked, looking interested. Morbid little bastard.

'Well, why don't we start with you telling me your name?'

'What's it got to do with me? I haven't done nothing.'

'You can't make him give you his name,' said the girl confidently, looking me in the eye. I put her at about thirteen, and she would have been quite pretty except for the angry cluster of whiteheads around her mouth and the excessive use of cheap make-up. Thirteen, and she was already a barrack-room lawyer. I had a feeling they were all going to be like that in a place like this.

'I'm not trying to,' I told her. 'I'm just interested in knowing who I'm talking to.'

'If you want to talk to him, you need an appropriate adult present.'

'So, when did you graduate from law school then, young lady?'

She was about to come up with some other smart-alec answer but we were interrupted before she could get it out.

'Can I help you, gentlemen?'

The speaker was an attractive white female, early forties. Quite tall – about five feet nine – and, from the sound of her voice, someone in authority.

I turned in her direction and smiled, opening fire with the charm. 'I hope so. My name's DS Milne and this is my colleague, DC Malik. We're here as part of an ongoing inquiry.'

She managed a weak smile. 'Really, what now?'

'It's a murder investigation.'

'Oh.' She looked taken aback. 'Was there any reason why you were talking to the children?'

'I was just introducing myself.'

'No you weren't,' said the girl. 'He was trying to find out who we were.'

'Well, I'll take over from here, Anne. Aren't you and John meant to be with Amelia?'

'We're just having a quick smoke,' said the girl, not bothering to look up.

'Perhaps you'd better come inside, gentlemen, and we'll talk in there.'

I nodded. 'Of course. And you are?'

'Carla Graham. I manage Coleman House.'

'Well, then, please lead the way,' I said, and we followed her through the double doors and into the building.

The place had the unwelcoming feel of a hospital: high ceilings; linoleum floors; health-related posters on the walls warning against shared needles, unwanted pregnancy, and a whole host of other obstacles to a happy and fulfilling life. And there was a nasty reek of disinfectant in the air. Dr Barnardo's this wasn't.

Carla Graham had a spacious office at the other end of the building. She ushered us in and we took seats facing her across her sizeable desk. There were more doom-mongering posters in here as well. One showed a huge photograph of a young child, no more than five, covered in bruises. The caption above it read: Stamp on Child Abuse. Below the photograph it added: Not on Children.

'So, what's happened?' Carla asked. 'I hope none of our clients are involved.'

'Clients, meaning children?' It was Malik asking the question.

'That's right.'

'We don't really know, which is why we're here.' I then told her about the discovery of the body the previous day.

'I didn't hear anything about that,' she said. 'Who was the poor girl?'

'Her name was Miriam Fox.' Carla's expression didn't hint at recognition, so I continued. 'She was an eighteen-year-old prostitute, a runaway.'

She shook her head and sighed. 'What a waste. Not a shock, because the potential for this sort of thing to happen's there all the time. But a terrible waste, all the same.'

Malik leaned forward in his seat and I immediately got the feeling that he didn't much like Carla Graham. 'I assume you didn't know her?'

'I don't know the name, no.'

I took the photo of Miriam posing for the camera out of my suit pocket and passed it over to her. 'This is her. We think it's a recent picture.'

She studied it for a long moment before handing it back to me. As I took it back I noticed she had graceful hands with well-kept, unvarnished nails.

'She looks vaguely familiar. I may have seen her before with one of the clients, but I couldn't say for sure.'

'We've been talking to some of the other girls who work the same area as Miriam did and they say she was particularly friendly with a girl called Molly Hagger. They said that Molly lived here at Coleman House.'

'Lived is the right word. Molly was a client of ours for some months but she walked out about three weeks ago now and we haven't seen her since.'

'You don't seem too worried about that, Ms Graham,' Malik said, only just about concealing his dismay that she should take the loss of one of her 'clients' so lightly.

'Mr Malik,' she said, turning towards him, 'Coleman House is home to twenty-one children aged between twelve and sixteen, all of whom come from disadvantaged backgrounds and all of whom have behavioural problems of varying degrees of seriousness. They are placed here by the council, and we try to do our best for them but the law is not on our side. If they want to go out at night, they go out. If I or any of my staff lay a hand on them to try to stop them leaving, they can have assault charges laid against us just like that, and believe me they'd do it. Put bluntly, these kids do what they like because they know they can do what they like. Half of them can't write their names, but they all know their rights inside out. And often, I'm afraid, they simply decide they've had enough of us and walk out the door. Sometimes they come back; sometimes they don't.'

'Don't you try to look for them?' Malik persisted.

She looked at him in the way a teacher looks at a particularly foolish pupil. 'We're extremely understaffed. It's hard enough keeping control of the ones who want to be here without worrying about the ones who don't. And where would we look for her? She could be anywhere.'

'Did you report her missing?' I asked.

'I informed Camden Social Services and they will have informed the police, but I didn't report it myself. I didn't see much point.'

'How old is Molly Hagger?'

'Thirteen.'

I shook my head. 'It's a young age to be out on the streets.' It was. Far too young.

She turned to me now. 'Mr . . . ?'

'Milne.'

'Mr Milne, I can understand if you think I'm not taking Molly's leaving seriously enough, I can understand both of your concerns, but try to look at it from my point of view. I've been a careworker for a long time now, and I've tried to help a lot of kids make a better life for themselves. But the older I get, the harder it becomes. You see, a lot of the time these kids don't want to be helped. They get plenty of offers, I can promise you, but most of them just want to live fast, take drugs, drink. They're independent, but independent in all the wrong ways. They can't stand any form of authority but often they aren't capable of looking after themselves. They're not all like that of course, some do actually want to listen and learn, and they're the ones I find myself gravitating to. If I've tried to help someone, and they keep turning their noses up at that help, then eventually I have to stop.'

'And was Molly Hagger like that? Was she one of the ones who turned her nose up?'

'Molly came from a very difficult background. She was sexually abused from the age of four by both her mother and her mother's boyfriend. She was taken into care at the age of eight and she's been in it ever since.'

I thought of the girl in the photograph and felt mildly sick. 'Jesus . . .'

'It's far more common than most people think. You should know that, Mr Milne.'

'It doesn't make it any easier.'

'No, you're right, it doesn't. But, to answer your question, Molly wasn't one of our more difficult girls. She didn't resent her carers in the way some clients do, but she had a very different outlook on life that was a direct result of the experiences she'd suffered.'

'What do you mean?'

'Well, she had a very casual and very adult view of sex. She had male and female sexual partners from a very young age, and from the age of ten she was charging for her services to certain individuals.'

'Has she run away before?'

'She's walked out on a number of occasions and not been seen for some time. The last time of any significance was about a year ago when she took up with an older man. She ended up living with him for several months before he got tired of her and threw her out. That's when she came back here.'

'So you think that might have happened this time?'

'I would think, knowing Molly, that that's a very likely scenario.'

I nodded, more optimistic now that she was still alive. 'We're going to need to speak to all your other, er, clients, and the rest of the staff to see if anyone else knew Miriam Fox and might be able to give us any relevant information.'

'The majority of the clients aren't here at the moment. Most of them attend local schools, or are supposed to anyway. Those who are in the building now are the ones who have special learning needs, and require one-to-one tuition. They might not be too helpful.'

They weren't. There were seven of them altogether and we interviewed them one at a time in Carla Graham's office, with her present. Two refused to answer any questions at all with anything more than yes or no, and of the rest only one claimed to have heard of Miriam Fox, and that was Anne Taylor, the youthful legal expert I'd met earlier. She said that she'd known Molly 'a bit' and that Molly and Miriam had been friends, even though Miriam was older. Anne had seen Molly with Miriam a couple of times while out in the evenings (she denied knowing that either of them had been prostitutes), but claimed she'd never really spoken to Miriam beyond the usual pleasantries. 'She seemed a bit stuck up,' she told us. 'She thought she was better than anyone else.'

And that was it. Carla made some effort to get her charges to speak, but it was a losing battle. They weren't going to tell the police anything, not if they could help it.

After that we interviewed the other members of staff present, four of them altogether. Two of them recognized the photo of Miriam and identified her as a friend of Molly's, but once again, neither had had any meaningful contact with her so couldn't, or wouldn't, add any further information.

'I don't know how much help that was,' said Carla when we were finished.

'It's difficult to tell,' I said. 'That's the thing with murder inquiries. It can often be a long, slow process and it always involves talking to a lot of people. Most of the time you don't hear anything significant, but just occasionally you do, even if you don't notice it at the time.'

'Well, I hope you're successful. It's worrying thinking that there's some maniac out there who could easily kill again.'

'We'll catch the perpetrator. I'm sure of that.' I stood up, and Malik followed suit. 'Anyway, thanks for your assistance this morning. It's appreciated.'

'I'll show you out,' she said, getting to her feet and leading us out of the office.

At the double doors, I shook hands with her while Malik nodded briefly and walked out. 'We'll need to come back and speak to the other clients at some point,' I told her.

'Of course. It would help if you could phone ahead, though. I'd like to be here when you come.'

She had nice eyes. They were a deep brown colour, with laughter lines round their edges. I would make sure she was there when I came back. 'I'll do that. It'll probably be sooner rather than later. It's important to close every avenue of inquiry.'

There was a sound of hysterical yelling and shouting from one of the rooms down the hall. It sounded like one of the female clients was experiencing a lack of customer satisfaction. In reply, we could just about make out the calm, measured tones of one of the social workers. It was greeted with another blast of abuse. Talk about a hiding to nothing.

Carla Graham sighed resignedly. 'I'd better go and see what all that's about.'

'You certainly have a difficult job to do here,' I told her.

'We've all got difficult jobs to do,' she answered, a rueful smile playing about her lips, and turned to go.

'I think you had a bit of a thing for her,' Malik said, when I joined him outside.

I grinned. 'She's an attractive woman.'

'A little bit old.'

'For you maybe. Not for me.'

'A social worker, though, Sarge? It would hardly be a match made in heaven, not with your views.'

'Yeah. Somehow I don't think it's a goer.' But in an odd way I wished it could be. I needed some romance in my life.

It was getting on for one o'clock, so we grabbed some lunch at a nearby McDonald's. Malik plumped for Chicken McNuggets while I took the traditional route of Big Mac, fries, and a hot apple pie for pudding, washed down with a regular Coke. Not exactly the ideal start to my new diet.

'I didn't like her,' Malik said as he slowly chewed on a McNugget.

'I know you didn't.'

He swallowed. 'She was too cynical, you know? Like nothing would faze her.'

'It's no different to the way it is in our game. You build up a shell so that things don't affect you. You have to. I mean, let's face it, how would you like to work with those little fuckers?'

'No discipline. That's the problem.' He picked up another McNugget with his fork. 'Do you think any of them knew anything?'

'Anything of interest? I doubt it. I think we'd have known if any of them were lying through their teeth. They're not that good actors.'

'So it was a bit of a waste of time going down there, really.'

I smiled. 'Well, in some ways maybe.'

He ignored my comment, and changed the subject. 'I was surprised this morning by the preliminary findings.'

'That there was no sign of sexual assault?' He nodded. 'So was I. It sort of begs the question, what was she killed for?'

Malik hunted down and pinned his last McNugget. 'That's why we need to talk to the pimp.'

But talking to the pimp had not proved any easier for our colleagues than it had for us the previous day. When we got back to the station we heard that he hadn't been at home when DS Capper and three others had called there several hours earlier. Apparently, he had a girlfriend who lived in Highbury, and he was supposed to spend quite a lot of his time with her, but he hadn't been at her place either. Nor was she in residence. Both properties were now under surveillance and all patrols had been advised to bring him in for questioning should they come across him. So far no-one had.

When I left that afternoon at 4.20, citing a non-existent doctor's appointment as the reason for my departure (Malik made me feel guilty by looking concerned and asking if it was anything serious), the inquiry was heading towards thirty-six hours old with few substantial leads and a suspect against whom there was pretty much no evidence and who, so far, hadn't even got a viable motive.

There was, of course, still a lot of the race left to be run, as a sports commentator might say, but whichever way you looked at it the start hadn't been particularly inspiring.

9

After picking up the suitcase at King's Cross, I took it home, counted the contents (it was all there), and stuffed a jiffy bag with Danny's cut. I sealed the bag and placed the rest of the money, bar a couple of hundred spending, in a safe in my bed-room. It wouldn't stay there for long. I have a personal deposit box at a hotel in Bayswater where I stash my ill-gotten gains. One day I'm going to have a hefty lump sum. It doesn't pay interest, but it keeps growing.

I've known Danny for about eight years now. He was the brother of a girl I used to go out with. Her name was Jean Ashcroft and she was the only non-Force girl I've ever had a relationship with since joining up. We were together about a year, and for a while it looked like it was going to get serious. We'd even started looking at places to rent together, which is the closest I've ever been to any sort of real commitment, and I think it's probably fair to say that I loved her, as much as I've loved anybody in the sexual sense. But then Danny fouled things up. Not intentionally, mind, but a foul-up all the same. You see, in those days he was a bit of a rascal. Although he was intelligent and came from a respectable family, he didn't have a job, nor did he want one. He preferred dope dealing. It was easier, and it was more profitable. Somehow he managed to keep his illicit activities hidden from the rest of his family, including his sister, and so it turned out to be a terrible shock for them when one of his pathetically small-time deals went pear-shaped, and he ended up on the wrong end of a savage beating.

It was a typical piece of middle-class naivety, really. He was holding half a pound of speed he was meant to be selling to a contact of his, but the contact, deciding it was easier to steal the goods rather than buy them, set him up. On his way over to the contact's flat, three of the guy's mates ambushed him in the stairwell. However, since Danny hadn't yet paid for the stuff, he was loath to give it up. A very one-sided battle ensued and Danny ended up with a fractured jaw, smashed cheekbone, severe concussion, and God knows how many busted ribs. And he still lost the speed, which, by all accounts, had to be prised from between his broken fingers.

He was in hospital three weeks altogether, which, when you consider it was on the NHS, gives you some idea of the extent of his injuries. It really threw the cat among the pigeons as well. His dad seemed to think that, because it had happened on our patch, I should have known something about his activities and put a stop to them, or at least told him about them. So he turned against me. Danny's mum followed suit, being one of those people who are incapable of their own opinion. The thing was, I could have lived with that, no problem. I'd never liked either of them much anyway. The problem was Danny. Once he got out of hospital he wanted revenge on the man who'd set him up. He was also worried because the guy he'd bought the stuff from now wanted paying as well. In fact, he wanted a lot of favours and the only person he knew who was in a position to grant him any was me. I'd always got on well with Danny, even though he'd never been able to hide his dope dealing activities from me. In fact, I genuinely liked him.

So when he came to me begging for help, I said I'd do what I could. The guy who'd sold him the speed was a pretty low-level player, so a quick threat of prosecution and the possibility of worse got him out of the picture. It was the revenge thing that represented a problem. Danny wanted me to help him take the guy out, though help wasn't exactly the operative word since it looked like I would be the one doing most of the work. Danny was only five feet six and of proportionate build, so he wasn't what you'd call a useful ally. He wanted to ambush the guy in the same way he'd been ambushed, and return the kicking, but I talked him out of that one. I don't even know why I agreed to get involved at all. I could have just told him to cut his losses and be thankful that he no longer owed the other guy money, but

I didn't. Maybe it was a pride thing. Maybe I wanted him to look up to me. I don't know.

Anyway, I devised a compromise. A couple of months earlier I'd uncovered about fifty ecstasy pills in an unrelated search of a suspect's premises. Because we already had the suspect bang to rights on about a dozen other charges, I'd put the pills in my pocket, thinking they might come in useful at a later date, not so much as a commodity – even in those days there was a lot of controversy over the effects of E, and I didn't want anyone dropping dead of anything I sold them – but of course they had another use, and that was helping put away criminals who were proving particularly hard to pin down for their crimes. I'd never planted anything on anyone before, but I'd heard about enough cases to know that it usually worked. If it was carried out properly.

Which was the difficult part. The guy, whose name was Darren Frennick, didn't tend to leave his flat very much, apart from to do the odd deal, and we needed uninterrupted access. We thought about it for weeks, racking our brains for a way to get in there, before we came up with a simple yet foolproof solution. Frennick was an ugly bastard but, like all young men, he had a healthy sex drive. I knew a girl at the time who was a professional escort and who could be trusted with difficult jobs. So what we did was this. Having paid her a substantial amount, funded by Danny, and given her the tablets, we sent her round to the flat. She knocked on the door, and when Frennick answered she told him she was his escort for the evening. He started to claim ignorance, but she was a good-looking girl and he didn't want to look a gifthorse in the mouth, so he invited her in and kicked out the couple of mates he'd had round there at the time.

As we'd guessed, he didn't want to escort her anywhere, preferring instead to get straight down to business. But within seconds of his amorous advances she was claiming she wasn't that sort of girl and an escort meant just that. He asked her what the hell she was on about and continued with his pawing, which was when she showed him some of her kjung fu moves. One series of ferocious blows and kicks later and he was out cold on the floor. Quick as a flash, she used a pair of tweezers to remove the packet of pills from her handbag. Shebrushed them briefly against his fingers, then threw them under his bed. He was coming round by that time so she ran out of there, shouting and screaming, and immediately phoned the police on her mobile phone, saying that this man had tried to give her some pills and rape her. She gave the address and his first name, and the cops, knowing who he was, were round there like a shot. By which time, of course, she'd made herself scarce.

Five minutes later she called the police again, saying that she was sorry, she didn't want to get involved in pressing charges against the guy, but she had seen him put the pills back under his bed. Dispatch passed this information on to the officers on the scene, who'd entered the flat through the open door. A dazed and bloodied Darren Frennick was arrested and remanded in custody. He ended up serving nine months for supplying Class A drugs, which Danny didn't feel was revenge enough, but which I assured him was the best he was going to get.

And that should have been that. Except that it wasn't. I don't think Jean ever found out the full story, but somehow she got wind of the fact that I'd used an escort girl to set Frennick up, and worked out that this was a side of me she'd never seen before and one that she didn't particularly like. Things became strained after that, Jean repeatedly asking me if I'd ever slept with prostitutes, and not believing me every time I said no. First, the living-together lark went on hold; a couple of months later, the relationship followed suit.

By rights, I should never have forgiven Danny for fucking up what will in all probability turn out to be my one chance of getting hitched, but he was so grateful for what I'd done, and felt so guilty for the problems he'd caused, that I found it difficult to hold it against him. Jean and I never really saw each other again after that. She met this chartered surveyor from up north and moved to Leeds with him, but Danny and I continued to keep in touch. Occasionally we did business together. One time I sold him a couple of kilos of dope I'd liberated from its wrongful owner. He tried to move it on but ended up selling it to under-cover Drugs Squad officers and getting nicked instead. They leaned on him hard, trying to get him to name his source, but his experience with Darren Frennick had hardened him. He feared prison – who doesn't? – but he kept quiet, even though they told him that co-operation would surely mean a lighter sentence. He ended up doing eighteen months.

Danny was not the luckiest man in the world; nor was he, in criminal terms, one of the best at his profession, but I trusted him absolutely, and there are very few people I can say that about. That's why I took him with me when I went off to kill three men. Because I knew he'd keep his mouth shut.

He rented a basement flat up in Highgate, not too far from the cemetery, and it was twenty to six when I finally rang his door-bell. He opened the door slowly, keeping the chain on the latch, and poked his head round. His face was pale and there were bags under his eyes. He looked like a man with a lot on his mind.

'You're late, Dennis.'

'It's the pressures of policework. It makes punctuality close to impossible. Blame the government. They're the ones letting all the criminals out.'

He released the chain and let me in. I followed him into the kitchen, noticing that his feet were bare, and his shirt was hanging out the back of his trousers. A very slovenly state. It looked like he hadn't set foot outside the flat all day.

'D'you want a cup of tea, or something?' he asked, putting the kettle on.

'Yeah, thanks, a tea'd be nice.' I put the bag containing his share on one of the worktops and leaned back against the cooker. 'I've got your money here.'

He nodded, getting a couple of cups down from one of the shelves. 'Cheers.'

'Do you mind if I smoke?'

'You don't usually ask.'

'Well, I can see you're in a sensitive mood, so I thought I'd be polite.'

He turned to me, his face registering a vague disgust. 'This whole thing doesn't faze you at all, does it?'

I lit the cigarette. 'Of course it does. But it's been done now. We'll know to be more careful next time, but regrets don't change a thing.'

'It's not about regrets. This was a huge fuck-up, Dennis, and the cops aren't going to let go of it. Not until they've caught someone. And that means us.'

I took a drag on the cigarette, feeling tired of all the verbal sparring in my life. I'd once had the chance to become an apprentice plumber, which would have paid a lot more money for a lot less hassle. At this moment, I wished I'd gone that route.

'Danny, there's one thing about policework you ought to know. It's all about trails. If you leave a trail when you commit your crime, which most people do, then the police will follow it until they find you.'

'Don't patronize me, Dennis. I don't fucking need it.'

'But if you don't leave a trail then there's nothing to follow. The police just run into a brick wall.'

He sighed, then turned to pour the teas. I watched him as he beat the teabags with his spoon. He was agitated, badly so, I felt I might have overestimated his nerve. I took another long, thoughtful drag on the cigarette. Most cigarettes I smoke I don't enjoy. I think that's the case with the majority of smokers. You only put one in your mouth because you know that if you don't, you'll only be thinking about smoking and wondering when you're going to have your next one until you do. But this cigarette was different. It tasted really good.

'You know, looking at you with that makes me wish I'd started
smoking.'

'Do you want one?'

'You'd give me one as well, wouldn't you? Christ, Dennis, the things you get me involved in. And you a fucking copper . . .'

He passed me my cup of tea. It didn't taste very nice. Underbrewed and too much milk.

'I'm sorry about the job, Danny, I really am. I didn't know it was going to turn out to be customs men. If I had, I'd never have touched the thing with a bargepole.'

'So what were you told? Originally.'

'I was told it was three drug dealers. According to my contact, they were trying to muscle in on some friends of his.'

'And who was your contact?'

Danny had never met Raymond nor, as far as I knew, had he ever heard of him. I liked to make Raymond Keen, and my association with him, as quiet as possible. For obvious reasons. 'You don't want to know,' I told him. 'Seriously. There's no point.'

He thought about that for a couple of seconds, then let it go. 'So how did you know they were going to be there? At the Traveller's Rest?'

'Those blokes? Apparently my contact had set it up so that they were going there for a clear the air meeting with his associates. All I had to do was pick them off when they arrived.'

He shook his head and sighed. 'You know, I've been thinking about this shit all day. Ever since it happened. And if they were customs . . . Think about it. If they were customs, then how the fuck did your associate know they were going to be there?'

'He says they were corrupt. It was a blackmail job, that's all I know. They were crooked, they were obviously involved in something they shouldn't have been.'

'So, if that's the case, how do we know the police can't find a trail?'

'They can't find a trail through us.'

'But what if they can find a trail that leads to your contact? If those blokes were corrupt, then the cops are going to find out, aren't they? And if they were involved with the man who hired you in some way, then they'll be able to follow the trail back to him.'

'They won't. Everything was very carefully planned.'

'But that's not the worst of it,' he continued, ignoring my comment.

I looked at him. 'Really?'

'What if they weren't corrupt, Dennis?'

I was beginning to get tired of this. 'Look, Danny. My contact's a middle-aged businessman who's made a fair bit of money over the years. What I'm trying to tell you is that he's an intelligent man. He's not going to do anything that's going to get him in a load of shit.' I finished the cigarette and tea at the same time and threw the one in the other.

Danny signed. 'So what I've been thinking all day is this: Maybe there's more to this whole thing than meets the eye. This thing could be a lot bigger than we think. If those customs officers weren't corrupt then they were involved in something so sensitive that they had to die for it.' He emphasized the last words like a paperback detective making a speech to his assembled suspects. 'And if that's the case, then not only is your contact heavily involved, he's also got some fucking good contacts of his own to set this sort of thing up.'

'Well, if that's the case, then you shouldn't be worried. Because there's not much chance of us getting caught, is there?'

'Maybe not, but, well . . . you've got to think . . .'

'What? What have you got to think?'

He sighed again, choosing his words carefully. It took a long time to get what he wanted to say out. 'That what's the point in keeping us alive? We're loose ends, Dennis. Loose ends involved in something very, very major. And now we've done what we were meant to do, then, you know . . .' He let the sentence trail off into the distance.

'Jesus, Danny, you've got to get yourself into some gainful employment. You've been watching far too much TV. This isn't a fucking mafia film. If we keep our mouths shut and go about our daily business as if nothing's happened, then we'll be all right. I told you that on the night. Nothing that's happened since changes anything.'

'I hope you're right,' he said, but he didn't sound convinced.

I felt paternal towards him then. 'I am. Don't worry.' I stepped forward and patted him on the shoulder, not in a patronizing way, more of a man-to-man way. 'Just try not to think about it, and remember, in a few days' time it'll all have blown over.'

'Yeah, I know, I know. It's difficult, though. Sitting here all day.'

'Do you want to come to a pub quiz?'

'Eh?'

'A pub quiz. There's one I go to on Tuesday nights when I've got the time. It's teams of four. There's a couple of blokes I normally play with, but we're often short of a fourth.'

Danny looked at me aghast, his usually thin blue eyes bugging out like they were on mini springs. 'Are you serious? Fuck me, Dennis, I don't know how you can live with yourself.'

'What? Going to pub quizzes?'

'You know what I mean.'

'Like I said, we've just got to carry on as normal. And what's more normal than a pub quiz?'

'And to think my sister was going to marry you.'

'Lucky you came along and fucked it all up really, wasn't it?'

He shot me a guilty look then, which I knew he would. It was cruel really, making him pay again for something that happened all that time ago.

I grinned at him to show I was only joking, and clapped him on the shoulder again. Still very much man-to-man. 'Come on, it'll be a laugh. Shit, it's got to be better than sitting here biting your nails and gawking at the TV, waiting for your mugshot to appear.'

'I can't go back inside again, Dennis. Not after last time.'

'You won't have to,' I told him. 'I promise.' We looked at each other for a long moment. 'So, are you coming then?'

'Where is it?'

'Pub called the Chinaman. Just off City Road.'

Danny thought about it for a moment. It looked as though he was trying to work out whether he could afford to do something so frivolous when, by rights, he ought to be putting all his concentration into shitting himself. In the end it seemed he could afford to let his concentration slip for a few hours.

'Fuck it. Why not?' He picked up the jiffy bag. 'At least I won't be short of cash for a drink.'

10

'He was an accountant.' Malik chewed on his sandwich as he spoke.

'You spoke to your mate, then?'

He nodded, finishing his mouthful. 'Yeah, last night. He's been working round the clock.'

'I can imagine.'

It was twenty past two the following afternoon, and we were in the station canteen. A fairly unproductive morning had been spent helping to collate all the statements we and the other officers had taken so far in an effort to make some sort of sense of them. So far nothing was leaping out at us, and the one possible suspect, the pimp, had still not been found. Nor was anyone sure where else to look for him.

'How are they coming along with everything?'

'You know what it's like, Sarge. It was difficult for him to say too much but it seems they're working on a lot of leads. From what I can gather, they're concentrating on the accountant and trying to establish what he was doing with those customs officers.'

'Two customs officers and an accountant. It sounds like the name of a bad film.'

'It's an interesting combination, I'll give you that.'

I finished picking at the Caesar salad I'd ordered and pushed the plate away, thinking about the inevitable cigarette. 'What does your mate make of it all?'

'He said they'd already dug up a lot of info on the accountant and there was nothing to suggest he wasn't a sound guy. He didn't have a record or anything.'

I remembered the accountant's face, the shock on it as he looked down the barrel of my gun. I lit the cigarette. 'So what was he doing with them?'

'That's the million-dollar question. My friend says there was an official reason why they were together. He wouldn't say exactly what it was, but from what I can gather the accountant had information on something that was very useful to the customs men.'

'So they're pretty sure the customs men were part of some sort of investigation?'

Malik nodded slowly. 'That's my impression. He didn't say for sure, but I think that's the angle they're looking at it from.'

'So the only way the murderer would know they were there at that time—'

'Was if it was an inside job. It's a worrying thought. You don't like to think of the forces of law and order as being corrupt.'

'You think someone tipped the killer off?'

He shrugged. 'That's what it looks like. What else could it be?'

I hoped Malik's information was wrong – which, of course, it could have been. A lot of the time on big cases involving a lot of detectives, contradictory stories get thrown up. From my point of view, it would be a lot easier to believe that the three victims were the pondscum Raymond had labelled them. Not only did it make what I'd done a lot more palatable – at least to me – I also felt it would make it much more difficult for the investigating officers to come up with a result. If it was an inside job, then the list of people who would have been in a position to know where those men were going to be and when they were going to be there would be pretty short.

But at the moment, it was still conjecture. I knew I was going to have to find out more information from Raymond, but at the same time I was going to have to be careful about how I did it. I'd never looked at him as a threat before, but suddenly I didn't want to give him a reason for wanting me out of the way as well. Maybe there'd been more truth in Danny's words than I'd initially given him credit for.

'You look very thoughtful, Sarge. Everything was all right at the doctor's yesterday, wasn't it?'

'Oh, yeah, yeah. No problem. Nothing serious anyway. I'm just not looking forward to chasing around questioning the rest of those kids at the childrens home. It just seems like a hiding to nothing.'

We still had close to two thirds of the kids to take statements from, and, although I quite fancied the idea of seeing the alluring Carla Graham again, I didn't want to waste any more time talking to snotty little bastards who wouldn't help you if their lives depended on it. I'd already told Knox I didn't think we'd get anything helpful out of it, but he'd insisted. He wanted to make sure he covered every angle of the case, if for no other reason than to cover his arse from any future kicking by superiors frustrated by a perceived lack of results.

'Wasn't it you who told me when I started out that only five per cent of policework gets you anywhere, and it's always spread right across the one hundred per cent you have to do?'

I grinned. 'Did I really say that? Shit, that must have been a long time ago.'

'Two years. That's all.'

'I must have been lying.'

'So, what is the answer then? The secret of policework?'

I was about to tell him that it was not to give a fuck about it and make sure you earned an alternative income, when DC Hunsdon walked in. He looked pleased. There were only about a dozen of us scattered about the canteen and most were uniform. Since CID always like to stick together, he made his way over to us.

He stopped when he got to the table and leaned forward, smiling, hands on the top.

'I can see you're dying to tell us something,' I told him.

'We've got the pimp.' He spoke these words in the manner of someone saying, 'We've solved the case.' Somewhat optimistic, I thought.

'Oh yeah? Where was he?'

Hunsdon sat down and lit a cigarette. 'He came in here. Walked in with his brief about ten minutes ago.'

'Who's going to question him?' Malik asked.

'Knox is going to do it with Capper. They're going to lean on him hard.'

He didn't look at Malik as he spoke. Like a lot of the younger detectives, Hunsdon didn't like Malik. This was partly to do with the fact that he was a graduate, but also because he was Asian. There was a feeling that he got special treatment because of his ethnic background, a situation not helped by the way senior management tended to treat him as some sort of teacher's pet. The resentment was unjustified and stupid, but it was difficult to squash. It was a testimony to Malik that he never once acknowledged it.

'Do you think he did it?' I asked him.

Hunsdon shrugged. 'What else have we got?'

'Hardly a reason for pinning it on him,' I said.

'Yeah, but it's not just that, is it? The victim wasn't sexually assaulted but she was attacked in a way that was meant to make it look like a sexual assault, so it's probably not going to be a pervert. Plus, he was seen round the victim's flat just after the murder and attacked you when you tried to question him. And, if that isn't enough, he's got a history of violence, and he'd attacked the victim before. Put her in hospital a couple of months back with cracked ribs and concussion.'

'Yeah, but that's not the same as cutting her throat from ear to ear and hacking great holes in her genitals.'

'He fits, Sarge. Whatever way you look at it, he fits.' He said these last words firmly, and in a way that suggested there was no point continuing to argue with him.

Which there wasn't. Right or wrong, at least it meant that there was less work for the rest of us.

'How are you getting on with the mobile phone records? Did Miriam have one registered in her name?'

He nodded. 'Yeah, she did. And I tell you something, it took a fuck of a lot of phoning round to find out. The company's going to send us a list of calls she made and received over the past month.'

'Maybe it'll throw up something.'

'You never know,' he said, but he didn't sound that interested. In his mind, we'd already got our man.

11

As predicted, we ended up spending several fruitless hours at the children's home that afternoon trying to track down the various 'clients' we hadn't yet spoken to. We managed to pin down a few but no-one who could help us much. To be honest, it did prove to be a bit of a waste of time. Carla wasn't there either, which disappointed me. She had a meeting out in Essex and hadn't returned by five o'clock, which was the time we'd decided that we'd had enough. I phoned through to Welland and told him that he might as well send uniforms down for the rest of the statements because it simply wasn't worth using us for it, and he agreed without much resistance.

That evening it was Malik's turn to take off early. He had to pick his kids up from his mother-in-law's as his missus, who was some high-flying accountant, was off on a seminar in Monte Carlo or some other such exotic destination. It made me think. The last seminar I'd attended had been in Swindon. 'The Role of the Police Force in 21st-Century Britain' it had been called – about as interesting and informative as watching a car rust. I was definitely in the wrong job.

We left together and I took the tube down to King's Cross. I thought about heading back to the station and seeing what needed doing but decided a drink might be better instead. Welland had told me they were still questioning the pimp, and so far there was nothing of note to report, which didn't surprise me. You only turn up with your lawyer in tow if you don't want to say too much.

I found a pub on the Marylebone Road near the station which didn't look too shitty and took a seat at the bar. The barman was a young Australian guy with a ponytail and a silver ring through his eyebrow. There were only a few people in the place so we had a bit of a chat about this and that. He was a friendly sort, which is often the way with Aussies. I think it must be something to do with the fact that they're brought up in a nice sunny climate. I asked him what the crime situation was like over there. He told me it was pretty bad.

'It's getting worse too, y'know,' he said. 'A lot of guns around the place, and people more willing to use them.' I told him that that was the case everywhere. 'Don't I know it,' he said. 'Especially here. I always thought London was supposed to be a safe place.'

'I think you're about fifty years too late,' I told him, and we left it at that.

When I left the pub, shortly after seven o'clock, I decided to walk home and take in some of the sights of the red light district where Miriam Fox and her young friend, Molly Hagger, had plied their trade.

King's Cross isn't a lot like people expect a red light district to be. On the main drag there are the two railway stations on one side of the road, almost next to each other – King's Cross and St Pancras – while a few dodgy-looking fast-food outlets and amusement arcades cluster together on the other. A couple of ageing sex shops with their trademark blackened windows and garish lighting are the only sign that people come to the area with sex in mind, but even they look lonely and a little out of place. King's Cross is no Amsterdam or Hamburg. There's no obvious prostitution activity on the main roads, even after dark. The prostitutes might be there, but you wouldn't particularly notice them. The area tends to be fairly busy as the Marylebone Road links the west and east of the city, and there are always plenty of people about, which deprives the punters of their one great desire: anonymity.

But step away from the bright lights and into the dark, dimly lit backstreets and a new world awaits. Drifting in and out of view like ghosts are the whores and the crack dealers. Sometimes you don't even see them. Their disembodied voices reach out from the doorways and alleys and the questions they ask are always the same: 'Need any gear?' 'Looking for a good time?' Sometimes you can feel their eyes boring into you, trying to work you out, looking for your weaknesses, maybe deciding whether or not you're worth robbing. Cars ease idly by, sizing up the scene. If you look at them, you'll see that most of the time the occupant is a single, middle-aged man and they never return the look. They always turn away. These are the business-men searching for their illicit thrill. Some of them are just frustrated, and need a quick fuck to bring them fleeting satis-faction. Others are perverts, people who want to do things to a woman their wives and girlfriends would never countenance. People who want things done to them that you and I couldn't countenance. And somewhere among them are the psychopaths, rapists and killers sweeping the area in their constant hunt for prey. This other world exists fifty yards from King's Cross station, but unless you look for it you'll never see it, and unless you see it you'll never understand the sickness that keeps it going.

It was a mild night with a strong wind. In my raincoat pocket I clutched a small cosh I occasionally carry about with me, purely for emergencies. It's less than a foot long and easily concealable on a winter's day. I've never used it in anger before and I'd never think about wielding it while on duty – it's more than my job's worth – but I was glad I had it now.

Two ageing prostitutes, their faces cracked and wrinkled like old leather, stepped out of the darkness and into my path. They wore ridiculously short skirts and pantomime make-up. 'How about some, love?' said one, forcing a leering smile. 'With a real woman.'

'I'm a police officer,' I said, pushing past her as politely as possible.

'So? Even coppers need a bit of fun,' she shouted after me. But her enthusiasm had faltered.

I didn't say anything. What was there to say to that?

I felt sorry for her. I felt sorry for them both. According to some of the other guys on the case these older girls were bitter about the competition provided by their more youthful counterparts like Miriam Fox and her friends, which was no great surprise. It's difficult enough to compete with newer, better, different models, and even worse when they undercut you. This rivalry had resulted in a number of incidents where older prostitutes had attacked the young ones, and several where they'd actually called the police to tell them about underage activity in an effort to get the girls off the street. Now the two competing groups tended to keep apart, but it was youth that had the most success.

It was quiet tonight, a result no doubt of the investigation, but business would soon return to normal. In the end, nothing gets in the way of capitalism. That's what's always annoyed me about the British attitude to paying for sex. It's all well and good having a big moral stance against prostitution, but that doesn't stop it happening. It doesn't even curtail it. Far better just to regulate the trade so that the girls are clean, pimp-free and safe, and the red light districts become tourist attractions, not drug-infested no-go areas like the one I was walking through now. Girls like Miriam Fox would almost certainly still be alive if they'd worked in Amsterdam or Barcelona, or wherever they were sensible enough not to attempt to change the laws of nature.

The scream came from somewhere behind me.

I didn't even register it the first time. You expect a scream on a street like this. Then it came again, louder and more desperate. It sounded like a young girl – a teenager – but whoever it was was pleading for help, the voice growing increasingly hysterical, and I knew straight away that something was badly wrong.

I swung round fast. A car was in the middle of the road about thirty yards away with its lights on and engine running. The driver, who I couldn't see very well, was leaning out of the passenger side and holding onto a girl who was struggling violently with him. There didn't seem to be anyone else around.

A part of me didn't want to get involved. Ahead of me were the bright lights and security of the Gray's Inn Road. I might have been a copper but I was off duty, in my own time, and I could be taking a big risk coming between those two. If it was a domestic she wouldn't thank me, they never do. I could end up with a knife in my gut or a gun in my ribs, all for being charitable.

But that part of me's still in a minority, thank God. I pulled the cosh from my pocket, ran into the road, and sprinted towards the car. The girl was now half in and the screaming was getting louder and louder as she realized how close she was to being abducted. Her thin, bare legs flapped wildly as inch by inch they disappeared inside the vehicle, which was now slowly moving forward.

I don't know if he heard me coming or not. I didn't make any noise – there's never any point advertising your presence if you don't have to – but my footfalls on the concrete were loud enough. As I got there, the car shot forward, but not before I'd grabbed the girl round the legs and pulled. For a moment the driver held on and I had this terrible fear that he was going to drag me along the tarmac. I stumbled and half fell but held on for dear life, somehow managing to keep my feet. That was it for him. The game was over, he wasn't going to get his prey, so he let go and she flew out the door, landing in a heap on the road. The momentum knocked me over too and all I could do was watch while he made his rapid getaway with a screech of tyres, turning a corner before I could even focus on his number-plate.

I got to my feet, putting the cosh away, then helped her up. 'Are you all right?'

She looked at me for the first time and I recognized her instantly as Anne Taylor, the girl who'd been outside Coleman House when we'd arrived there the previous day. She looked a lot less full of herself now, though. Her eyes were tear stained and her make-up was running. The shock on her face was clear.

She nodded slowly, checking her skirt and top for any damage. 'I think so . . . Yeah, yeah, I'm all right.'

I took her by the arm and moved her onto the pavement. 'Did you know him?' I asked.

'Probably just some pervert,' she answered, without looking up. 'I've never seen him before.'

'What did he look like?'

This time she did look up. 'Look, I'm not interested in pressing charges or nothing like that.' She shook herself free of my arm.

'You know, a thanks might not go amiss. I mean, I have just

helped you out of a difficult situation. Anything could have happened to you then.'

'I know how to look after myself.'

'Yeah, sure.' I took out my cigarettes and offered her one. She took it and I lit it for her, lighting one for myself at the same time.

'Look, thanks. It was good of you.' It was given grudgingly, but I suppose it was better than nothing. What is it with kids these days? The little bastards have never got any manners.

'Do you want to grab a quick coffee somewhere? Calm yourself down a bit?'

'No, I'm all right. I'm fine.'

'Come on. I'm buying.'

I could tell she was thinking that a sit-down and a hot drink might be quite nice. The problem was the company. 'I don't want to sit there with you going on at me about this and that, and questioning me. I ain't got time for that.'

'Look, just a coffee and a cigarette. I could do with one myself. I'm not used to that sort of exercise.'

She gave me a dismissive look. 'Yeah, I can tell.'

We found a café on the Gray's Inn Road not peopled entirely with lowlifes. I bought two coffees and we found a booth at the back.

'I'm surprised you're out on the streets so soon after what's happened.'

'I thought you weren't going to go on at me. If you're going to fucking lecture me, I ain't interested. I could be out earning money, you know.'

'Or you could be in the back of that bloke's car, bound and gagged—'

'Look, I don't need this fucking shit . . .' She started to get up from her seat.

'All right, all right, I won't lecture you. I'm just worried about your safety, that's all.' She sat down again. 'You had a narrow escape out there tonight. Remember that.'

'Don't worry about me. I can look after myself.'

'Yeah, you said that. I expect Miriam Fox thought the same thing.'

'There's perverts out there all the time. It's one of the risks, isn't it?'

'I suppose if you put it like that, yes it is. When we spoke yesterday, you said you didn't know Miriam Fox was a prostitute. That wasn't true, was it? You knew.'

'You coppers are all the fucking same, aren't you? You never stop asking questions.'

I laughed. 'Look, this is purely off-the-record talk. Anything you say here can never be repeated in a court of law. You ought to know that. All I'm trying to do is find the person who murdered Miriam and take him off the streets. So he can't do it again.' I pulled out two more cigarettes, again lighting hers. 'It's in your interests, probably more than mine, to make sure that happens.'

She thought about it for a moment, her self-interest clearly wrestling with her innate distrust of the forces of law and order. I took a drag on my cigarette and waited for her. I was in no hurry.

'Yeah, I knew she was on the game,' she said eventually. 'Course I did, but I didn't have much to do with her. She was a real bitch.'

'In what way?'

'Well, she just rated herself, you know? She looked down on the rest of us like we was some sort of fucking scum. And she was a scheming cow too. Always talking behind people's backs, turning them against each other. I never liked her, so I kept out of her way.'

'She was with Mark Wells, wasn't she?'

Anne nodded. 'Yeah, and I don't have nothing to do with him.'

'Why not?'

'He's a nutter. You get on the wrong side of him and he tears you a-fucking-part.'

'Do you think he might have had something to do with what happened to Miriam?'

'I thought it was a pervert that did it.'

'It might have been, but we don't know at this stage. It might have been someone else. Someone who knew her. Someone like Mark Wells.'

She shrugged. 'I don't know.'

'Do you think he'd be capable of it?'

'Look, you shouldn't be asking me that. I don't want to start answering those sorts of questions.'

'Anne, whatever you say to me here won't go any further than this table, and your name'll never be mentioned. I'm just trying to build up a picture, that's all.'

'If Mark Wells ever heard I'd mentioned his name to you, he'd fucking kill me.'

I thought about telling her he was already in custody, but held back. I didn't want to prejudice her answers, no more than I had done already, anyway. 'He won't hear it. I promise. No-one will.'

'He's a vicious bloke. I've heard some nasty stories about him kicking the shit out of people if they piss him off, and I heard he knifed this geezer once because he owed him some money for something. But what would he want to kill Miriam for? She was earning him cash.'

Which was a good point, and one that was going to need answering.

'Anyway,' she continued, 'he's already short of girls.'

'What do you mean?'

'Well, Molly was one of his girls and she's gone now.'

I thought about my dream again. 'Where do you reckon Molly's got to? I'd like to find her and ask her a few questions about Miriam. They were good mates, weren't they?'

She nodded. 'Yeah, they were. Fuck knows why. She was about the only one who liked Miriam.'

'Can you think where she's gone to?'

She looked down at the table top, dragging constantly at the dying remnants of the fag. We'd had quite an adult discussion, and it was fair to say that in some ways she was older than her years, but at that moment, she looked her age. A kid trapped in an adult's world.

She sat like that for what felt like a long time, not saying anything. I sat back in my seat, thinking that maybe I'd annoyed her in some way. It was difficult to tell. When she spoke, it was without looking up, and her words were quiet.

'I don't think she's gone anywhere.'

I wasn't sure I'd heard her right. 'What? What was that?'

This time Anne looked me right in the eyes, and I thought I saw the beginnings of tears in them. 'I said, I don't think she's gone anywhere.'

12

'What do you think's happened to her, then?' I asked quietly.

'I don't know,' she said, looking away.

'Well, you must have a reason for thinking that way.'

'Look, stop hassling me with all these fucking questions.'

I paused for a long moment, thinking that I was glad I didn't work with kids. Especially teenagers.

'I just don't reckon she's gone anywhere, that's all. In fact, I'm fucking positive.' This time I didn't say a word, but I was intrigued. 'She wouldn't have left Mark. I know that.'

'Mark Wells?'

'Yeah. She loved him, you know? She'd have done anything for him, even though he didn't give a fuck about her. He's already got a couple of girls so he didn't need Molly. I mean, he fucked her, but that was it. She was just an earner to him.'

I thought of the smiling face in the photo-me images. She was too young for those sorts of complications. 'You don't reckon she may have just got pissed off with Wells and decided to sling her hook? From what we've heard, she's walked out and disappeared before.'

'No, I don't reckon that. The last time she left it was with her old boyfriend, but she hasn't been with him for ages. She wouldn't have gone away on her own. Not without Mark. She was well into him. Talked about him all the time.'

'Were you and her close?' I'd asked Anne this yesterday and got a negative response, but this time I thought she might tell me the truth.

'Sort of. She talked to me a fair bit. You know, about this and that. But mainly Mark. She was always talking about Mark.'

'What did Miriam think about Mark? Do you know?'

She shrugged. 'She used to fuck him, but that was it. She weren't in love with him. Not like Molly.'

'And when you saw Molly last . . . when was that? About three weeks ago?'

She shrugged again. 'Something like that, yeah.'

'Was that about the time she disappeared?'

'I saw her one day in the home and then she went out that night and no-one ever saw her again.'

'How did she seem when you saw her? Was she in good spirits or was she pissed off about things?'

'She was normal, you know. Just like she always is.'

'She didn't say anything about leaving, or anything?'

'No. Nothing.'

So where did that leave us? I wasn't even investigating Molly Hagger's disappearance and yet here was a girl who knew her, and who knew Miriam Fox, telling me that there was something very suspicious about the whole thing. Once again, I was reminded of my dream. It was as vivid now as it had been when I'd woken up in the darkness, sweating and fearful, but it had lost its power as a premonition. Was there something in what Anne was saying, or was it the imagination of a teenager at work? Molly could easily have taken off somewhere without telling Anne, who admitted she wasn't that close to her. It was also quite feasible that Molly hadn't been as obsessed with Mark Wells as Anne was making out. After all, she was only thirteen years old, and even I knew that thirteen-year-old girls are pretty fickle when it comes to love.

'You don't believe me, do you?'

'Yeah, I believe you, but if she hasn't gone anywhere, then where is she?'

'I don't know.' She shrugged her shoulders and looked at me with eyes that didn't belong to a kid. 'Maybe she's dead.'

'Do you think that? That she's dead?'

She nodded slowly and with worrying confidence. 'Yeah. I think so.'

I cleared my throat, not liking the feeling I was getting. 'Do you think the person who killed Miriam might have killed her too?'

'Could be.'

'The man who attacked you tonight . . . what happened?'

'I was standing in my normal spot when he pulls up in this car. I should have been with Charlene, but she didn't turn up tonight so I was on my own. He just beckons me over like a lot of them do, then when I get over there, I take a look and I don't like the look of him.'

'What was wrong with him?'

'He just didn't look right, you know? He had this horrible smile and there was something about him. He gave me the creeps.'

'Go on.'

'Well, he opens the passenger door and pats the seat, and he's sort of leering at me like some sort of fucking perv, and telling me to get in. But I reckon he's kinky; he looks the type. The type who'll take you out somewhere quiet and really give you a going over, so I say no thanks and start to go. But he just grabs me and starts pulling me in, telling me it'll be all right, that he's not going to hurt me, but he's fucking rough and he's pulling me by the hair as hard as he can, the bastard . . .' She paused. 'And then you turned up.'

'What did he look like?'

'Biggish guy. Fat. Bald. Fat face.'

'What sort of age?'

'I don't know. About fifty or something.' Which probably meant thirty.

'And you've never seen him before?'

She shook her head. 'There was just something about him, you know? I don't normally feel that way about punters. I mean, they're all fucking old and ugly, most of them anyway. But this one was different. I just knew he was dodgy.'

I tried to remember the make of car he was driving. It was a

Mercedes saloon, not particularly new, and I think the colour was light brown or beige. Not dark-coloured like the one that had picked up Miriam. Other than that I had nothing.

'It'd be good if you could make a statement.'

'Why? I've just told you what he looked like. Do you think he could have been the one who killed Miriam?' It looked as if the thought had only just occurred to her.

'I don't know. I really don't. Maybe.'

She shuddered. 'Fucking hell.'

'You'd do a lot better not working the streets, Anne.'

'I need the money.'

I thought about sitting there trying to persuade her as to the error of her ways, but I'm almost certain it wouldn't have done any good. Change comes from within. You've got to believe that what you do is wrong and needs to stop, and I was pretty sure Anne didn't feel like that.

'Come on, let's take you back to Coleman House.'

She snorted. 'Fuck that. I'd only been out there ten minutes when you came. I haven't earned any money yet.'

'Call it a night off.'

'My man don't believe in nights off.'

'And who's your man?'

'Come on, you're a copper. I ain't telling you that.'

'Well, I hope he's an improvement on Mark Wells.' As if.

'Yeah, course he is.'

'Then he'll understand, won't he?'

She laughed, much too cynically for a thirteen-year-old. 'He won't be happy if I don't earn him some cash.'

What a gentleman. 'All right, let me do you a deal. I'll give you forty quid if you go back to the home tonight.' It was a stupid gesture. The money would end up in the hands of her pimp or the local crack dealer, who were probably one and the same. And if Anne chose to put herself in danger, it was hardly my concern. Especially as whatever happened tonight, she'd be back on the streets tomorrow anyway. But I didn't want to be responsible for leaving her out there tonight.

'Forty quid. And what do you want for that?'

'Nothing from you. All you have to do is go back home for the night and stay there.'

'That ain't a lot. Forty quid's fuck all. I could earn ten times that.'

'It's all you're going to get. And you don't have to do anything for it.'

She thought about it for a moment. 'Make it fifty, and I'll do it.'

'You're in the wrong job. You ought to be a trained negotiator.'

I insisted on going back to Coleman House with her as I didn't trust her to go alone. We got a black cab and the driver gave me a dirty look when he saw her in tow. In the end, I felt dutybound to show him my warrant card so he'd know I wasn't some perverted punter who'd forgotten his transport for the night.

We didn't say much in the cab, and when we arrived she jumped out without a word along with her fifty quid, and disappeared inside. I could have just gone back home, but while I was there I thought I'd check to see if Carla Graham was around. Malik was right, she wasn't my type, but there was not exactly a wealth of good-looking women in my life, so I liked to make the best of any opportunities I got in that department. Even if it was just talking.

I had to ring the buzzer to get in. A woman's voice came over the intercom. She couldn't say her 'r's, and I recognized her as one of the staff members we'd interviewed yesterday. I think she'd called herself Katia, or something equally bizarre beginning with a K. A youngish girl with a revolutionary's stare who'd come across as the sort who thinks all coppers are Nazi stormtroopers just itching to truncheon a few minorities. I told her who I was and asked if it was possible to speak with Ms Graham.

'I think she's with Dr Woberts,' she told me. 'I'll just see if she can be made available.'

'Tell her I'll come back first thing tomorrow morning if it's more convenient,' I said, thinking that that would probably be less preferable to seeing me now.

About thirty seconds passed, then the door opened. 'Katia' stood there, looking overweight and tired. 'She's in her office,' she said, glaring at me as if I'd just pinched one of her nipples.

I nodded and walked past her. The place was quiet, making me wonder where everyone was. Up to no good probably. Anne would surely be out again in ten minutes making my cash gift to her an even bigger waste of time than I'd already thought.

I knocked on the door of her office but walked in without waiting for an answer. Carla Graham was standing by her desk talking to a short middle-aged man in a three-piece suit. She was wearing a light grey trouser suit with a white blouse. A simple string of pearls adorned her neck.

She smiled at me, but I thought there was a hint of effort in it which I've learned to get used to – you have to when you're a copper – but which still disappointed me, coming from her. 'Sergeant Milne. You must be working overtime tonight.'

I smiled back, stepping up to the desk. 'Unfortunately in our job it's difficult to keep to office hours. Thanks for taking the time to see me.'

'You only just caught me. This is one of my colleagues, Dr Roberts. He's a child psychologist.'

We shook hands.

'I'm not actually based here,' he said in a pleasant, almost feminine, sing-song voice. 'I do work at sites all over the borough.'

'I expect you're kept fairly busy, then.'

'We have a lot of children with special needs, but it's very satisfying work.'

'I'm sure it is,' I said, not meaning it at all.

'I understand you're investigating a murder,' he said, looking at me with undisguised interest. He had quite a jolly face, which struck me as unusual for his line of business. Most psychologists spend their whole lives with their heads up their arses. For a profession with such a huge and constant failure rate, they take what they do remarkably seriously.

'That's right,' I said. 'A girl not much older than some of the people you deal with. Her name was Miriam Fox. She was a runaway.'

He shook his head. 'It's a tragedy, Sergeant. I always feel if we can influence them while they're young, we can help prevent them taking the path that leads to this sort of thing.'

I felt like telling him that he and his colleagues had always had ample opportunity to do just that, but had clearly failed. But I didn't. The doctor looked a sensitive sort and I didn't want to upset him. For some reason, I actually thought he seemed quite a nice bloke. He reminded me of an eccentric music teacher I'd had in school who used to wear brightly coloured bowties and who was truly enthusiastic about what he did. I'd never liked music at school, it was one of those subjects that seemed to glory in its irrelevance, but I'd always liked classes with him.

'It must be a frustrating task,' I said.

'And how is the investigation going?'

'These things take time, but we're confident of a result.'

'I understand there's been an arrest.'

I eyed him curiously. 'That's right. How did you know?'

He smiled. 'I'm addicted to the news, I'm afraid, and now I have the internet on my laptop, I'm always checking what's happening. The local news said a man surrendered himself to the police today.'

'That's correct, but I can't comment any further on it, as you can appreciate.'

'Of course, of course, I understand. Forgive my inquisitiveness, Sergeant, I just always like to know what's going on.'

'Don't we all?' I told him.

A pregnant pause followed as Roberts presumably tried to think of something else to ask, but I guess he must have realized that he wasn't going to get much information out of me because he called it a day. 'Well, I mustn't hold you up. Good luck with the case.' He put out his hand and I shook it.

He said his goodbyes, excused himself, and I turned to Carla. She was looking even better than she had done yesterday and I had no choice but to try and picture her naked.

'I was just about to finish for the night, Mr Milne. It's been a very long day.'

'And I appreciate you seeing me, Ms Graham. Look, is there a pub near here? Maybe we can talk in less formal surroundings, if that would make things easier?' Christ, that came out easily.

She raised one of her eyebrows and gave me a funny look. Maybe I'd overstepped the mark, but you don't win prizes without buying tickets. 'Are you suggesting we go out for a drink?' There was enough of a hint of playfulness in her voice to tell me she wasn't offended.

I smiled. 'Well, technically, I suppose. But please don't feel it's your civic duty. We can talk here if you'd prefer.'

She sighed. 'There's a pub round the corner that's not too bad.

We can talk there if you want, but I can't stay too long. I'm exhausted, and I've got another long day tomorrow.'

The pub was a two-hundred-yard walk from Coleman House, far enough away to avoid seeing any of the home's clients. It was a huge place, built on two storeys, and was clearly popular with the student crowd. Although busy, it was spacious enough to accommodate everyone amply and there were still a few tables spare.

As we walked to the bar, Carla said hello to two people she knew – both men, both younger than me – and I found myself feeling mildly jealous. I ordered a vodka orange in a superficial attempt to appear sophisticated, and a vodka tonic for her.

'I thought police officers weren't meant to drink on duty,' she said when we'd found a corner table a respectful distance from anyone else.

'Well, I'm not officially on duty.'

She raised both her eyebrows this time. 'Oh. I was under the impression you wanted to see me regarding the investigation.'

'I do. That's the reason I'm here, but what I want to talk to you about is off the record. I'm here in an unofficial capacity.'

She looked interested, and now I had a bit of a problem. If I was honest with myself, the only reason I was there was to see her; everything else was somewhat peripheral. I was concerned about what Anne had told me but I wasn't quite sure how I was going to explain that.

'Go on.'

She was watching me closely, and I found myself watching her back. She had beautiful brown eyes that seemed to swallow you up. Not for the first time, I found myself wondering what the fuck she was doing managing a children's home.

'I ran into one of your clients this evening. Anne. She was in the middle of being abducted by one of her prospective customers.'

She looked genuinely concerned. 'Is she all right?'

'Yeah, she's all right. But she was lucky, Ms Graham. If I hadn't been there, I don't know what would have happened. Somehow I don't think it would have been a happy ending.'

'These girls . . .' She shook her head slowly. 'There's no telling them. It's as if they've got a death wish.'

'Well, it could be a wish that ends up being fulfilled.'

'I know, I know. What's so tragic about the whole thing is that Anne's got so much intelligence. She could really do something with her life if only she'd listen to people. Where is she now?'

'I took her back to your place. That's when I came in to see you.'

'You should have told me.'

'Don't worry. She's okay. She took it remarkably well. We talked for a while afterwards and she seemed concerned, particularly about Molly Hagger's disappearance. She seemed to think that Molly didn't just walk out—'

'What did she think had happened to her?'

'She wouldn't say for sure, but I think she felt something untoward had happened.' I briefly explained the reasons Anne had given me, without mentioning Mark Wells by name. When I'd finished I had to admit to myself that they sounded pretty flimsy.

Carla took a packet of Silk Cut out of her handbag and put one in her mouth, before realizing that she hadn't offered me one, and hastily pointing the pack in my direction.

I declined. 'My throat demands something stronger,' I said, taking a pack of Benson & Hedges out of my shirt pocket.

She lit my cigarette for me and I got a vague but pleasant smell of her perfume as I leaned forward.

'I thought you said you'd arrested someone for the girl's murder.'

'We have, and we're questioning him very closely, but we have to keep our options open. It might be that he's also responsible for murdering Molly Hagger. It might be that he's not responsible for anything.'

She took an elegant draw on her cigarette. 'Do you think she's dead?' she asked.

'I don't know. Anne was adamant that Molly Hagger would never have gone away of her own accord, but she could well be wrong.' I paused, then decided to jump in at the deep end. 'You can't think of any other girls who've left the home in the last few months who, perhaps, you didn't expect to lose?'

Carla gave me a reproachful look. 'Mr Milne, I understand your concerns, and I sympathize with them. If anything's happening to young girls it's essential it gets uncovered, but, with due respect, not every female client at Coleman House is a teenage prostitute. Some get involved in that sort of thing, I won't deny that, but they're in a minority, and we certainly don't keep the streets of King's Cross stocked up with underage girls. There are dozens of care homes in a three-mile radius of here who have exactly the same problems as we do. Do you really think it's likely that our clients are being picked off one by one by some unknown murderer?'

'No, no, of course not. I'm sorry if it came across like that. I'm just trying to look at every avenue.' I took a sip of my drink, noting that hers was getting dangerously near to the bottom of the glass. I didn't want her to go – not yet – but I wasn't doing too well at charming her into staying. 'Will you do me a favour, though? Just to indulge me.'

'What?'

'Will you just let me know if any of your clients absconds, or goes missing under suspicious circumstances? Please. Anything you say will be treated with the utmost confidentiality.'

She nodded. 'All right, but we get that happening a lot of the time, as I said to you and your colleague yesterday. Most of the time, it's just that. Them absconding. Looking for greener pastures. It's the same for all the homes, especially in a city the size of this one.'

'Yeah, I know. That's the problem. If you were, say, a killer, and you didn't want to get caught, they're just the type of girls you'd go for. Ones who can disappear without a trace and no-one's too worried.'

'But I do worry – we all worry – for our clients because we know the pitfalls that await them round every corner. But without resources, and without authority . . .'

'Yeah, I know. What can you do?'

'Exactly. But if any of the girls goes missing, I will let you know.'

'Thanks. I appreciate it.' I took a drag on my cigarette, knowing I had to do something to keep the conversation alive if I was going to keep her here. 'It seems ridiculous that these kids can just do exactly what they want when they're so, you know, unequipped for life.'

'It's a debate we have constantly within the profession,' she said. 'It goes against the grain for many of us to take authoritarian measures, but sometimes I genuinely feel there's no alternative. These children are vulnerable, they just don't know it.'

'It's funny,' I said, not wanting to lose the moment, 'but when I was a kid, my mum used to tell me what a cruel world we lived in. She always said enjoy everything while you're young, but be prepared, because when you get older you'll see that there are a lot of bad people out there. And you know what? I never believed her.'

'But you do now?'

'Yeah, I do now. If anything, she was more right than she could have known.'

'You're beginning to strike me as the sensitive type, Mr Milne.'

'I'm not quite sure whether I should take that as a compliment or not.'

She thought about that for a moment, looking at me over her glass. 'Take it as a compliment. It's how it was intended.'

'We're not all fascist bullyboys, you know. Some of us are actually quite nice people – especially when we're not at work.'

'I don't doubt it. And just because I'm in the profession I'm in, it doesn't mean I'd automatically think you were all fascist bullyboys.'

'But some of your colleagues do.'

'Some of the younger ones do, yes. When I first joined social services, I was probably a lot more black and white in my view of the forces of law and order too. But that was a long time ago.'

'Not that long, I'm sure,' I said with mock chivalry.

She smiled. 'Now that I will definitely take as a compliment.'

'It's how it was intended.'

She looked at her watch, then back at me. 'I really ought to be going, Mr Milne. Time's getting on, and I'm driving.'

'Well, have one last drink with me. It's a rule I've got that I always have to have a minimum of two drinks in every pub I go into. One drink means you're in too much of a hurry.'

'It's an interesting theory. All right, then, I'll have one more. But let me buy.' She stood up. 'Same again?'

'Please.'

I watched her as she walked across to the bar. She was wearing black high-heeled boots and she carried herself extremely well, moving with a grace I would normally associate with a model. Or maybe it was just me. I was already fully aware that I had the hots for her. I expect she knew it too, but it was only watching her then that I realized quite how much I wanted to rip her clothes off and make love to her on the spot. It had been close to six months since I'd last had sex so it wasn't going to take a lot to get me going, and the last time had been no great success either. On that occasion it had been a woman DC from the station who'd been as drunk as me, so it was never going to be a match made in heaven. She'd been engaged to a lawyer from the CPS and I'd got so worn out that I'd had to fake an orgasm. Twice. Although I must have done something right because she'd wanted to see me again afterwards.

This time, there was more than just a desire to have sex, although this came high on the list. I was attracted to Carla in a way I'm not used to. The last time I'd had a feeling like this was when I'd started going out with Danny's sister, and that had been a long time back.

She stayed for about another twenty minutes. I was desperate to go to the toilet for most of the conversation but held back, not wanting to give her an excuse to realize that she ought to be on her way home. We chatted about this and that, mainly to do with our respective jobs, and I found her an interesting and intelligent talker. She was single as well, which helped. Divorced with no kids, she said that most of the time she was married to her work. I told her I knew the feeling.

I kept looking for an opportune moment to ask her out but one never came, or maybe it's more accurate to say that my nerve let me down. I mean, she was a serious career woman with an air of authority about her more suited to a politician than to social services, and I was like a schoolboy in love for the first time with feelings that were more seventeen than thirty-seven.

When she'd finished her drink, she stood up and offered me a hand to shake. 'I really must be going, Mr Milne. It's been very pleasant. It's just a pity that the reason we've been brought together is so tragic.'

I stood up and shook, squeezing her hand tightly. 'Unfortunately, that's the way it goes sometimes. Well, it was nice to talk to you, Ms Graham.'

'You may as well call me Carla.'

'Well then, I insist you call me Dennis.' It sounded a really shite name when I said it like that. Really unsophisticated. Like Wayne, or Eric. For a moment I wondered why I'd never changed it to something better. Even Zeke would have been an improvement.

She smiled. 'Well, Dennis, I hope the investigation goes well.'

That was my opportune moment, but I bottled it. 'I'm sure it will. I'll be in touch if there's anything else we need. And obviously, as I said earlier–'

'I'll definitely let you know if any of the girls goes missing, but, as I told you, it does happen a lot, and there's usually an innocent explanation, if I can use a word like that.'

'Sure, I understand.' I finished my drink. 'Let me walk you to your car.'

'There's no need. It's only parked round the corner. I'd offer you a lift but I've got a very early start.'

'No problem, I understand.' At least my bladder would thank me.

I sat back down and she turned to go, then turned back again. 'Oh, one last thing. Tell me, how did you get Anne to go back to the hostel?'

'I bribed her.'

'With what?'

I felt a bit sheepish admitting what I'd done, but did it anyway. 'I paid her to go back. I gave her some money in lieu of any earnings she would have got by staying out there.'

I wasn't sure if this would please her or not. Probably not. But, surprisingly, she looked at me with what I thought was a measure of respect. 'You *are* a sensitive soul, Dennis.' She smiled. 'I'm almost certain it was a futile gesture. Girls like Anne aren't going to be redeemed suddenly, but I appreciate your concern.'

'Thanks,' I said, and watched her as she disappeared out of the door.

It was ten past nine and I was tired, a long way from home, and desperate for a piss. The evening's events had at least given me some insight into the type of world these girls inhabited, and the type of people out there preying on them. But whether it helped move the case on or not, I wasn't sure.

13

'We're going to charge the pimp,' Malik said excitedly as I walked into the incident room at a quarter to nine the next morning.

The place was buzzing, as is always the case when you've had a result, and most of the detectives who'd been involved were sitting about looking pretty pleased with themselves, although I couldn't see Welland anywhere, and Knox wasn't in his office. Charging Mark Wells and convicting him were two different things, of course, but it sounded like there was definitely room for a lot of optimism. Clearly there'd been some sort of significant breakthrough in the past few hours.

'You missed all the action, Dennis,' DS Capper said loudly. 'Where were you?' Capper was at his desk along with two of his

DC cronies, one of whom was my last sexual conquest – if you can count two faked orgasms as a conquest.

I stopped in front of them. 'What happened, then? Did he confess?'

'He will do. Now that we've got the shirt he was wearing when he killed her. Covered in her blood.'

Capper looked far too self-satisfied for my liking. It was hard enough speaking to him when he was having a bad day, well nigh impossible when he was having a good one. I said to the room in general that it was a piece of very good news, smiled as if I'd just been told I had a really big cock, and sat down at my desk. Malik followed me and seated himself on the other side.

I looked at him with surprise. 'Shit, that all happened fast. When did you hear about it?'

'I saw it on Teletext first thing this morning and came straight in. That was a couple of hours ago.'

'Who found the shirt, then?'

'We got a tip-off. Apparently one of Wells's girls called in last night and said that Wells had admitted to her that he'd killed Miriam Fox and dumped the clothes nearby. They did another search of the area and found the shirt. It went off to forensics in the early hours of this morning. The preliminary tests show an exact match between the blood on the shirt and Miriam Fox's blood.'

'That was quick.'

'Time's of the essence, isn't it? By lunchtime we'll have already had him for twenty-four hours.'

'So it's not a done thing yet?'

'No, but it looks like it's going to go that way. It's definitely the murderer's shirt and we've got a good link between it and Wells.'

'Who was the caller? Did she give a name?'

Malik shook his head. 'No, but you can't blame her, can you? She's not going to want any publicity.'

I nodded slowly and lit a cigarette. It was a fair point.

'What's up, Sarge? You don't look totally convinced.'

I yawned. 'Nah, I'm just tired. I didn't sleep too well last night.' I had a bit of a hangover as well. I'd left the pub shortly after Carla had gone but had stopped off at the Chinaman on the way home for a quick one. Unfortunately it had turned into a slow three. 'You wouldn't do an old man a favour, would you?'

'That old man being you?'

'That's right.'

'What is it you want?'

'A bacon sandwich and a nice cup of tea.' He gave me a dirty look. 'Please, Asif, I wouldn't ask if it wasn't an emergency.'

'You've got to change your diet, Sarge. You eat nothing but crap.'

'Well, get me an apple as well.' I fished into the pocket of my suit and brought out two pound coins. 'Please. Call it a personal favour. I won't ask again, I promise.'

He took the money reluctantly, checking that no-one was watching, and got up. 'This is a one-off, Sarge. Remember that. It's only because you look so bloody rough that I'm agreeing.'

'Your pity will be rewarded,' I told him piously.

When he'd gone, I started to think about this new development. I hadn't slept well because I'd been thinking about my conversation with Anne and the possibility that there was some sort of serial killer on the loose targeting underage prostitutes. It was a flight-of-fancy theory, really. Though they make ideal fictional villains and endless fodder for real-life documentaries, in reality serial killers are as rare as dinosaur turds. If there were more than two operating in this whole country of close to sixty million people at any one time, I'd be extremely surprised. But I suppose these things do occasionally happen, and if such a man was at work he'd picked the right sort of place and the right sort of victims to keep himself concealed. The only thing was, if Molly Hagger and any other girls had fallen victim to this man, where were the bodies? And why was Miriam Fox's left in such an obvious location?

These were the questions that had prevented me getting anywhere near the seven hours' slumber I need to function at what passes for optimum efficiency. I'd even managed to incorporate Carla Graham into the various theories and trains of thought I'd tossed about my brain. In the better ones, I'd solve the case, find the killer (even going so far as catching him as he prepared to despatch his latest victim), get a promotion, and end up fucking Carla's brains out.

Fat chance. But at least a man can dream.

The bacon sandwich tasted good anyway, and I was so hungry I even ate the apple down to the core.

At 9.15, Knox came into the incident room with a very tired-looking Welland. Welland sat down immediately and it looked like he needed to. Knox, meanwhile, addressed the rest of us. 'We've just told Mark Wells about the latest developments and once again he categorically denies any involvement, but, to use the old phrase, he would say that, wouldn't he? He certainly looks far more worried than he has been. As we all know, he's a cocky bastard, and he's lost a lot of that now. We should get the rest of the results on the shirt later this morning and they'll tell us whether it belongs to Wells or not, although from the way he's behaving, I feel fairly certain it's his.'

'So we're going to be knocking out the champers later, then?' This was Capper.

Knox smiled. 'It's far too early even to think about a celebration drink yet. We've done well, very well, and it's been a team effort, but until you hear otherwise, it's still business as usual.'

He strode into his office, leaving Welland where he'd sat down. One of the women DCs asked Welland if he was all right. 'Yeah, yeah, I'm fine,' he replied. 'Just a bit under the weather.' Someone suggested that he go home for the day, but he said he'd stick around and wait for Wells to be charged. 'I want to see that bastard squirm,' he said, with more vigour than I'd have thought his body would allow.

'He looks terrible,' said Malik quietly, turning to me.

'Yeah, I know. He should take a few days off. He needs it. And the taxpayer owes him a break. He's done a good job on behalf of society.'

Not that anyone had ever thanked him for it; or any of us, for that matter. It may be that it's not accurate to describe all coppers as unsung heroes, but neither is it fair to view them as the constant villains of the piece, which is usually the way we're portrayed whenever we get a mention on the box. And Welland, more than most, was one of the good guys. He'd put his all into policework, so now he might as well take something back.

'If I was him, I'd go for early retirement,' said Malik.

'If I was him, I'd have gone for it ten years ago.'

He gave me a disbelieving smile. 'No you wouldn't. You enjoy the whole thing too much.'

'Bullshit I do.'

My phone rang and I had a sudden rush of adrenalin, hoping it was Carla. But if she was the person I most wanted to speak to, then the person on the other end of the line had to be one of those whose voice I least wanted to hear.

'It's a Jean Ashcroft for you, Mr Milne,' said the civilian receptionist.

Christ, what the hell did she want? 'Thanks, can you put her through?' There was a pause as she came on the line. 'Hello, Jean. Long time no speak.'

'Hello, Dennis. Look, I'm sorry to bother you . . .' Her tone was strained, formal.

'It's no problem. No problem at all. What can I do?'

'It's Danny,' she said. 'I think he might be in trouble.'

'What makes you say that?'

'Well he phoned me last night and, you know, he never normally phones me, so I knew something wasn't right. He didn't sound himself, Dennis. It was all very strange. I think he'd been drinking, or smoking something, and he was rambling, going on about changing his life, doing something different, saying that it was definitely time to make the break and go . . . and he said something about having saved up some money, a lot of money.'

'Maybe he has.'

'He doesn't have a job, Dennis. He would never have been able to raise a lot of money,' she stopped for a quick sniff, 'unless he's involved in something. You know, something criminal. That's what I'm worried about. You know what he's like. It would break my mum's heart if anything happened to him again, especially after all that stuff before. And now with Dad gone.'

'Look, I understand you're worried about him. It's only natural. And I know he's had his brushes with the law, but he hasn't been in trouble for a long time now.' Malik was looking at me quizzically now, but I waved him away, intimating that it wasn't business. Not police business, anyway. He stood up and walked off. 'I don't think you should let one drunken phone call get you too concerned. Seriously, Jean.'

'You still see him sometimes, don't you?'

'Yeah, occasionally, but not as often as I'd like.'

'You know, whenever we speak, which I know isn't that often, but whenever we do, he always talks about you. I think he looks up to you. Would you do me a favour? Please. I understand what you're saying about not getting too worried, but would you go round and see him, just to check things out? See that he's OK.'

This was all I needed. 'I really think you're worrying unduly. Danny's no fool. He's done his time. He won't make the same mistake again.'

'Please, Dennis. I'm sure you're busy, but it would mean a lot if you could just check up on him.'

'OK, I'll see what I can do, but I'm sure it's nothing.'

'Thanks. I really appreciate it.' And it sounded like she did.

I took her number in Leeds and said I'd get back to her one way or another in the next few days. We talked for a few moments longer, but the conversation was stilted and uncomfortable. Far too much water had passed under the bridge, and I was happy to hang up. Jean Ashcroft had been a good-looking girl once upon a time, and good company too, but now she was nothing more than a half-forgotten part of my past. Danny had really fucked up by talking to her. He'd seemed fine the other night at the pub quiz. We'd had a few drinks, a few laughs, and had even come a close second to the winners, and when I'd left him he'd been OK. Not exactly full of the joys of spring, but OK nevertheless. It was clear, however, that being cooped up at home for much of the time, with just himself for company, was making him seriously paranoid, and that was dangerous. Fuck knows what he'd do if they ever really got close. I was going to have to give him a good talking to. Knock some sense into him. Get him to calm down.

What was it that American president once said? The only thing we have to fear is fear. Well, Danny feared fear, and it was beginning to make him a liability.

14

At 11.55 that morning the results from the lab came back con-
firming that hair samples found on the shirt belonged to Mark
Wells, and that it could safely be surmised that the shirt belonged
to him.

At 12.10, the questioning of Mark Wells by DCI Knox and DI
Welland recommenced. The suspect still denied any involvement
in the crime and became hysterical when told of the new evidence
against him, at one point attempting to assault both the officers
present. He had to be physically restrained before questioning
could continue. His solicitor then requested some time alone with
his client to discuss these new developments, and this was
granted.

At 12.35, the questioning once again resumed, Wells's solicitor
sticking to the position that his client had had nothing to do with
the murder of Miriam Fox. However, neither he nor Wells could
offer any realistic explanation as to why the shirt had been found
so close to the murder scene covered in the victim's blood. Wells
suggested that it must have been stolen.

At 1.05, twenty-seven-year-old Mark Jason Wells was formally charged with the murder of eighteen-year-old Miriam Ann Fox. For the second time that day, he had to be physically restrained from attacking his interrogators. During the ensuing altercation, his solicitor was accidentally struck in the face by Wells and required medical treatment for a bloody nose. In a rare moment of wit, DS Capper later claimed this to be a double result for the Metropolitan Police.

At 2.25, still a little sleepy from my canteen lunch of lasagne and garden vegetables, I was called into Knox's office.

Knox was sitting behind his spotless desk looking serious, which surprised me a little under the circumstances. 'Hello, Dennis. Thanks for coming in. Sit down.' He waved to a seat. 'You've heard the news, then?'

'About charging Wells? Yes, sir, DI Welland told me.'

'DI Welland's had to go home, I'm afraid.'

'He didn't look too good, sir, I have to admit.'

'He isn't, I'm afraid. In fact, he hasn't been his best for some time.' I didn't say anything, so he continued. 'He went for some tests a couple of weeks ago and he received the results this morning.' I felt a mild sense of dread. Knox sighed loudly. 'He only told me after we'd charged Wells. I'm afraid DI Welland has prostate cancer. There's going to be an official announcement this afternoon.'

'Jesus.' What a day. 'I knew something was wrong but I didn't think it would be anything like that. How bad is it?'

'Well, it's cancer, so it's bad. As to whether it's terminal or not, I don't know. Neither do the doctors. A lot depends on how he responds to treatment and his overall attitude.'

'There won't be anything wrong with that. The DI's a fighter.'

I suddenly felt like crying, which is something I haven't done in a long, long time. It was the injustice of it all. Here was a man who for thirty years had been trying to do the right thing and he was repaid with a life-threatening illness, while there were criminals and politicians out there who'd spent just as much time trying to line their own pockets and were as healthy as a new heart. The moment passed, and I asked Knox if he minded if I smoked.

'No-one should really be smoking in here, especially under the circumstances, but go on then.' He watched me light it and told me that I ought to give up. 'It won't do you any good, you know,' he told me sternly, which was a statement of the obvious if ever I'd heard one. That's the problem with health fascists. They never understand that you know as much about the facts as they do.

'A man's got to have some pleasures,' I said, which is my standard defence in these sorts of matters.

'Perhaps. But anyway, I digress. I didn't bring you in here to discuss any bad habits you might have. I wanted to speak to you because, at the very minimum, DI Welland's going to be on sick leave for three months, and I suspect it will be considerably longer. It might even be the case that he never comes back. So we have a temporary vacancy.'

I felt as though I ought to say something at this juncture but, because I couldn't think what, I kept my mouth shut. I was beginning to get the first stirrings of interest, though. The DI's position. I could handle that, even if it was only temporary.

'Obviously we want to promote from within the CID at this station, as that'll give us the continuity we need, and it'll give DI Welland the chance to slot back in, when and if he's able to return to duty.'

'I understand.'

'And it's for that reason we've decided to go with DS Capper as the acting DI.'

And to think I'd been getting optimistic. I fought hard not to show my disappointment at being passed over in favour of an idiot like Capper, but it was difficult.

'I wanted to tell you first before we announced it so that I could explain our reasons.'

'Which are?'

He gave me the usual management waffle about how Capper had more experience at plainclothes level (there was about two months in it); was better qualified (he'd been on more training and awareness courses than I had, most of which were about as useful as suntan lotion in a snowstorm); and had a more positive attitude towards certain aspects of the job (such as kissing arse).

What can you say to that?

'That's not to say that you're in any way a bad copper, Dennis. Because you're not. You're an extremely valued member of the team. I want you to understand that.'

'I understand, sir,' I said, hoping that we could bring this bout of making me feel better to a swift end.

'You've done a great job over the years.'

'Thanks.'

'I know you're disappointed.'

'I'm all right, sir.'

'That's understandable, but try to take some positives from it.'

'I will, sir.'

'Now, to wrap this Miriam Fox case up we have a task that requires experience and tact.'

'I'm all ears.'

'I want you to go down to see her mother and father and talk them through the progress we've made on the case. It'll be good public relations and it'll give them an opportunity to bring themselves up to date with what's been happening. They've been told by local police that charges have been laid against the man in custody, but that's all.'

'What else do they need to know?'

'It's felt both by the Chief Super and myself that they'd benefit from a personal visit by one of our more senior officers. I'd like you to go down there tomorrow morning and take DC Malik with you.' I think I must have made a face because Knox fixed me with a stern look. 'Look, Dennis, the Metropolitan Police has one hell of a lot of critics, as you know. Miriam Fox's father is an influential man and a local Labour councillor. We need to get people like him on our side.'

There was no point arguing. The decision had been made, so nothing was going to change it. I nodded to show that I understood. 'Is that all, sir?'

'Yes, that's it. Thanks for your understanding., Dennis. I knew you wouldn't let us down.'

I stood up. 'I'm sorry about the DI. I'd like to visit him, if it's possible. When does he begin his treatment?'

'Monday. I'll let you have the hospital details when I get them.'

'Yeah, that would be good. Thanks.' I took a last drag on the cigarette and looked about for an ashtray. There wasn't one, so Knox passed me a three-quarters-empty coffee cup with the legend World's Best Dad scrawled on the side. Better parent than man manager, then. I chucked the butt in and he put the cup back on his desk. 'It's good news about Wells, anyway.'

Knox nodded. 'Yes it is. It's always good to get a result this quickly.'

'Did we locate the car he was driving when he picked her up?'

'Forensics are doing tests on his car at the moment.'

'And is it a dark-coloured saloon?'

'It's a maroon BMW, so I think that counts. It would look dark-coloured at night on a dimly lit street. Why? Do you think there's a problem?'

I shrugged. 'Not necessarily. It's just that when Malik and I ran into him at Miriam Fox's flat he looked totally shocked to see us, and it was instinctive shock too, not put on. If he'd killed her he'd expect to see coppers at her place. Also, what would he be doing going back there?'

'Maybe there was some incriminating evidence he wanted to recover.'

'There wasn't. We checked the place thoroughly, remember.'

Knox sighed. 'Dennis, just what do you want us to do? We've got a violent pimp with plenty of convictions for assaults against women who's known to have attacked the victim within the last few weeks and whose shirt was found covered in her blood less than a hundred yards from where she was killed, and who's so far failed to provide us with any sort of alibi. We can hardly let him go, can we?'

'But it doesn't necessarily mean he's the one, does it? You only found the shirt because of a tip-off. And that's the only thing that really connects him to the murder, isn't it?'

'Well, it's a pretty big thing, don't you agree? It's definitely his shirt, it's got his hair fibres all over it, for Christ's sake.' He was beginning to get annoyed now. Knox was a man who liked to feel he was in control, he didn't like it when people started knocking holes in his theories.

I nodded slowly. 'True, but it's still the only connection. And there's still the little problem of motive. I mean, why did he kill her?'

'Dennis, what's your fucking problem? Have you got some alternative theory you'd like to share with us all? Because if not, stop trying to undermine all the work we've done.'

I thought about telling him about Molly Hagger's disappearance and the possibility that there was something more to all this than a simple dispute between a pimp and his whore, but

I held back. In a way I was too embarrassed to say something. I had nothing concrete at all, just a few flimsy ideas and that old classic: the instinctive feeling that something wasn't quite right.

'No, I don't have anything else, I'm just concerned we get the right man. The last thing we need is an acquittal and allegations of a frame-up.'

'I'm glad you're concerned. It shows you care. But believe me, Mark Wells is our man. If I wasn't damned sure, I wouldn't be charging him. OK?'

'OK.'

'And, Dennis, bear this in mind.'

'What, sir?'

'There hasn't been a single killing of a prostitute in the whole of the south-east with an MO like Miriam Fox's, so it's almost certain it was a one-off. Do you see what I'm saying?'

'Yes, sir.'

'Don't complicate matters, because a lot of the time they don't need complicating. Now, can you do me a favour and send DS Capper in?'

And that was that. I left the room without saying another word, wondering just how much worse things could get.

I found Capper over at the photocopier talking to Hunsdon. I told him Knox wanted to see him, and he went off with a sly smile. When he'd gone, I turned to Hunsdon.

'Have you got those phone records yet?' I asked him.

'Yeah, they faxed them through this morning. I've got them here somewhere.' He picked up a pile of papers from the in-tray and went through them quickly.

'Were they any use?' I asked him as he searched.

'Not really,' he said, handing me two sheets of A4 paper.

I took them off him and glanced down the first page, which detailed outgoing calls. There was a total of ninety-seven listed, all made in the twenty-eight days up until the date of the murder. The left-hand column gave the date and time of each one, the right-hand column identified the numbers called. The second sheet detailed the incoming ones, of which there were fifty-six.

'These numbers have got no names with them,' I said, looking up at him.

'That's right. That's why they're not much use.'

'Can't they identify the person each number's registered to?'

'Yeah, but apparently that takes a lot longer because it involves more than one company. There's a lot of cross-checking databases, that sort of thing, but they're on the case at the moment. I should be getting a list any time now.'

I put the sheets in the copier and ran a copy, giving the originals back to him. 'Look, can you give me the names of the people you're dealing with? I don't mind chasing it.'

He looked at me uncertainly. 'What's the point? They're not going to tell us anything. So she made calls to Wells and he made calls to her. That stands to reason.'

'Humour me.'

'The bloke I've been dealing with is called John Claire. I've got his number back at my desk.'

'Well, let's go back and get it, then.'

Reluctantly he returned to his desk with me in tow and dug out the number. I got the feeling he hadn't exactly been pushing himself to get the information on Miriam's records, but that was Hunsdon for you. He wasn't a bad copper in many ways, but he was a lazy bastard, and not the best at performing routine tasks, especially when he thought the tasks themselves were a bit pointless.

I wrote the number down and he asked me again what the point of chasing it up was.

It was, I suppose, a good question. I think at that precise

moment my interest stemmed from a real desire to put one over on Knox and Capper and wipe the smiles off their faces. Maybe Wells was the man responsible for Miriam's murder, but it just didn't seem to me to be as cut and dried as they all thought. For the sake of a couple of phone calls, I was more than happy to be the one who proved them wrong.

15

There were seven numbers which came up more than three times among the phone calls to and from Miriam Fox's mobile, and I decided to concentrate on finding out who they belonged to, as well as all the numbers she'd either called or received calls from during the last three days of her life. It was quite possible that they wouldn't tell me anything; even if they did, it was still going to be extremely difficult to get Knox to authorize any further investigation, particularly now that he'd charged Wells. But I still felt it was worth a try.

I called John Claire from my desk, but his line was busy. I lit and smoked a cigarette down to the butt and called him again, but it was still engaged. He was obviously a hard-working boy. I was going to give it five minutes and try him again but I never got the chance. A knifepoint robbery had occurred at a back-street newsagent's less than half a mile from the station and I was ordered to attend with Malik to take statements from the proprietor and any witnesses. We were there for about an hour, trying to calm down the proprietor's wife, who'd had a knife held against her throat by a kid of no more than thirteen while his five laughing mates had ransacked the place. The husband, who'd been out at the wholesaler's, was distraught. He harangued us and society in general for turning out kids who thought so little of using violence. We didn't try to argue with him. He was right. I told them we'd do what we could to apprehend the perpetrators and thanked them for their help. We then got a squad car to take the wife to hospital for a check-up and returned to the station to file our report.

At ten past five, I tried John Claire's number again. This time he answered immediately. I explained who I was and why I was phoning.

'Yeah, I was dealing with one of your colleagues, DC . . .?'

'Hunsdon.'

'That's right. I was trying to get together some information for him. Telephone records.'

'Yeah, I know. How far are you down the line? It's just I need them pretty quickly.'

'I've already sent them,' he said, sounding surprised. 'I emailed them to him this morning.'

'No, we've got the actual numbers, it's the people they belong to we need to know. Who the phones are registered to.'

'Yeah, I know. That's what I sent him. I sent him a list with the numbers on it yesterday. I had to chase down the names of the people and it took a bit of time. I said as soon as I got the information I'd get it across to him. And I did. This morning.'

Clearly, Hunsdon hadn't been checking his mail. I lit a cigarette. 'Maybe the network's down here today or something. Can you send it again?'

'Yeah, no problem.'

'I'll give you two places to send it to, just to make sure it goes through.' I reeled off my work and home addresses, and waited while he wrote them down. 'And can you do it immediately, please?'

'Yeah, of course,' he said, sounding a little nervous. 'No problem, officer.'

I thanked him, and hung up.

The mail hadn't arrived when, ten minutes later, Capper phoned through and asked to see me in Welland's office for a quick chat. He was sitting behind Welland's desk looking far too comfortable when I went in.

'I understand you've been told the news,' he said, making only a cursory attempt to contain his pleasure.

'That's right. Congratulations.'

He swung round slowly in Welland's mock leather seat. 'Thank you. Now, I want us to work together, Dennis. I know we haven't always seen eye to eye in the past, had our ups and downs, but it's important we all pull in the same direction.'

'I agree,' I said, avoiding calling him sir.

'How did it go this afternoon at the newsagent's? Do we know who did it?'

'I can't say for sure, but I think the one with the knife's Jamie Delly.'

Delly was the fourth and youngest boy in a family of petty criminals, all of whom possessed a nasty streak. He'd first been nicked at the age of eight for trying to set his school on fire; ten years earlier his mum had assaulted me with a frozen leg of New Zealand lamb when I'd tried to arrest her for shoplifting.

'That little toe-rag. Bit out of his league, isn't it?'

'Well, he's growing up now. Time to move on from nicking kids' dinner money and shoplifting.'

'Didn't his mother—?'

'Yeah, yeah. Leg of lamb . . .'

'You're lucky you didn't get the chop.' Capper grinned at his wit, showing an unruly set of stained teeth. I would have grinned too if I hadn't heard the joke at least a hundred times before.

'Can we get him for this?' he asked, becoming serious again.

'I should think so, if the proprietor's missus can pick him out in an ID.'

'Get one organized, will you?' he said in a tone that almost begged him to round off the sentence with a 'there's a good lad'. I nodded, and said that I would, keen not to rise to the bait, although wondering how long I was going to be able to put up with this man as my boss. 'Another thing, Dennis, before you go. I understand you were trying to take over Hunsdon's end of the Fox inquiry, telling him you'd chase up the information on the phone records. Is that right?'

'I thought there might be something in there somewhere that could be of use.'

'And you didn't think DC Hunsdon was capable of finding it?' He eyed me closely.

'I was just interested in seeing what I could find. Hunsdon had to make a couple of phone calls, I offered to make them for him.'

'We've charged someone, Dennis, all right? That's it, end of story. I can't have officers of mine going over old ground. We haven't got time. And if for some reason you're not busy enough, I can always assign you some more cases. Because we've got plenty of them.'

'OK, point taken.'

'Have you chased up these records?'

Instinctively I decided not to tell him. 'No. No, I haven't.'

'Good. Don't bother. Concentrate on the stuff that's assigned to you, OK? And if there's anything I can do to help, let me know. Like I say, I want us to work together.'

I asked him if that was all. He said it was.

'I'll get back to work, then,' I said, but I didn't. I got my coat, told

Malik I'd see him in the morning, and headed out of there.

16

I stopped at the Roving Wolf for a quick pint, then caught the bus home through the rush-hour traffic. It was half past six when I walked in the door, and I rang Danny's home number as soon as I'd shut it behind me.

He answered after three rings. 'Right,' I said, without preamble. 'Do as I say. Go to the nearest phone box, get its number, then phone me with it. Stay where you are and I'll phone you back.' He started to ask what it was all about, but I cut him off.

Five minutes later he called back and gave me the number. I wrote it down, then called it using Raymond's mobile.

'Christ, what the hell's this all about?' he asked, picking up the phone. 'What's all this cloak-and-dagger stuff?'

'I wanted to be able to speak freely,' I said. 'I got a call this morning, Danny. From your sister.'

'Oh, shit.'

'Yeah, that's what I thought. Now, tell me something. What the fuck are you phoning her for? I told you to just keep calm and let everything blow over.'

'I know, I know. It's just that it's fucking difficult, Dennis.

You know, I can't stop thinking about what happened. I'm even dreaming about it. I was in the pub last night and there was even talk that it had something to do with the Adamses. Do you know anything about that?'

The Adamses, for those who've not heard of them, are the shadowy North London crime family few people tend to know anything about, but whose name is usually linked to any so-called gangland crime where there are no immediate suspects. I'd have bet my life that Raymond had never even met one of the Adams family, let alone agreed to commit murder for them.

'Don't be fucking daft, Danny,' I told him. 'Do you really think I'd get involved with people like that? And do you genuinely believe that people like the Adamses sub out this sort of thing to blokes they don't even know. They've got plenty of resources of their own. So, who was saying all this shit, then?'

'There was a bloke called Steve Fairley in there. He was saying it. I wouldn't have taken much notice if it had been anyone else, but he's a bit of a player. Knows about these things. That's what worried me.'

I knew Steve Fairley. Tomboy had told me about him. If he was a player, then he was very much Vauxhall Conference. 'And you reckon the Adamses decided to tell him all about it, do you? You know, make sure as many people know about it as possible?'

'Look, I know it sounds stupid—'

'You're right. It does.'

He sighed. 'It's just getting to me, that's all.'

'But telling your sister, Danny, of all people. I mean, what the hell's she going to do to help you out of your predicament? Give you a character reference? Now she's been on to me saying she thinks you're in trouble, and can I go and visit you and find out what's wrong, and then get back to her. I don't need this, Danny.'

'I'm sorry, I really am. It won't happen again.'

'It better not.' I almost told him it was that sort of talk that could get us all killed, but held back. There was no point making him even more jittery than he already was.

'I didn't tell her anything important, I promise.'

'You told her you'd saved up some money, that got her suspicions going straight away.'

'Yeah, but there's no way she can link that to anything that's happened.'

'No, that's right, but if you start pouring out your heart every time you've had a few drinks then sooner or later something might slip out, something that could incriminate you and me, and that'd be a truly fucking stupid way to get caught. Now, let me tell you something. Every day that passes means they're less likely to catch us. The trail gets that little bit colder. Like I've said all along, all you need to do is keep calm and everything'll be fine. If it's any consolation, the only person who's got any idea of your involvement is me, and I'm not going to say a word to anyone. So you're OK, understand?'

'Yeah, yeah, I understand. I'll make sure I keep shtum. It was just one of those things.'

'Look, now you've got some money, why don't you take a little holiday? Get away for a few weeks. It's got to be better than sitting around trying to think of all the things that could possibly go wrong.'

'Yeah, maybe you're right.'

'When was the last time you had a holiday?'

'Shit, I don't know. Ages ago.'

'Well, fuck it. Treat yourself. It's dogshit weather. You're not going to be missing much. And by the time you come back all this will have died down and everyone'll be talking about some other heinous crime.'

'You've got a point. Maybe I will.' There was a long pause. Eventually he spoke again. 'I'm sorry, Dennis. I really am. I won't fuck up like that again.'

'I know you won't,' I told him. 'I know you're not that fucking stupid.'

'What are you going to tell Jean?'

I thought about it for a minute. 'I'll tell her I talked to you and that you've turned over a new leaf. Rather than aid and abet criminals in their criminal ways, you now try to put them behind bars where they belong. I'll tell her you're a police informant and that's how you've made some money, but that it's all very hush hush and she can't talk about it to anyone for fear of blowing your cover. Hopefully that way she'll leave you alone. What do you think?'

'I think you're a cunning bastard, Dennis.'

'Take that holiday, Danny. OK?'

'Yeah. Yeah, I think I will.'

'I'll talk to you soon.'

I hung up and walked into the lounge, sitting down on the sofa with my cigarette. Had I managed to calm him down enough to cross him off my list of worries? It was a good question. What I'd said was eminently sensible, if not altogether true. I wasn't the only person who knew of his involvement in the killings. I'd been forced to give some details about him to Raymond before he'd allowed me to take him on the Traveller's Rest job. Armed with those details, if Raymond really wanted to find Danny, he'd probably be able to. There was no point telling Danny that, though. Hopefully, he would take my advice and leave the country for a while. It would certainly make my life easier. If the truth be told, he was rapidly becoming a thorn in my side. For the first time I thought maybe it would be better for everyone involved if I simply took him out, and quietened his fears for ever. Not that I seriously thought I could ever pull the trigger on Danny. I'd known the little bastard too long. But if I'd been a more ruthless man maybe I'd have done more than let the thought rumble through my mind. That was a measure of how concerned I was.

I finished the cigarette and stubbed it out in the overflowing ashtray, remembering the mail John Claire was meant to have sent me. I got up, went through to the bedroom, and switched the PC on. While it booted up I went and got myself a beer from the fridge, feeling pleased that I was home for the night and cocooned for a few hours at least from the problems of the world.

Claire's email had arrived at 5.31, so at least he'd been true to his word. I opened up the attachment and saw that what he'd sent was a copy of the original document but with a third column tagged on containing the names of those to whom each individual number was registered.

I didn't recognize the first name on the list. It was a man, most likely a punter. The second name was a man's as well, again one I didn't recognise. The next number wasn't registered to a particular individual, which probably meant it was a pay-as-you-go mobile. Maybe it belonged to Molly Hagger. I thought maybe it would be a good idea to phone it and find out. The third name was Coleman House, which stood to reason.

I didn't read the fourth name. Or the fifth.

I was too busy looking at the sixth.

And wondering why Carla Graham had lied to me when she said she hadn't known Miriam.

17

I really didn't know what to expect as I turned the car into the short gravel driveway that led up to the Fox residence. The house itself was an attractive and spacious two-storey building constructed in an L-shape with a thatched roof and lattice windows, set in enclosed gardens. It was on the edge of a small village a few miles west of Oxford towards the Gloucestershire border, so a fair drive for Malik and me. It had taken us about two and a quarter hours through the usual heavy traffic, and it was now just after eleven.

'Just in time for a nice cup of tea,' I said, pulling up in front of the house.

Malik looked a little nervous. I guess he too didn't know what to expect from this sort of visit. It was never going to be easy. These people had found out only four days ago that their daughter had been murdered. They may not have seen her for close on three years, but they were still going to be in a state of shock. It would take years for their lives to return to normal, if they ever did.

To be honest, my mind was elsewhere. I wanted to know why

Miriam Fox had phoned Carla Graham three times during the last fortnight of her life, twice to Carla's mobile, and why Carla herself had made two calls to Miriam's number, the last of them just four days before she was murdered. That many calls was no accident. Those two had known each other, and the only conceivable reason why Carla hadn't said anything to us about their relationship was that she had something to hide, although what that something could be I had no idea. I'd phoned Coleman House straight away, ostensibly to let her know that we'd charged Mark Wells, but also to arrange another meeting so I could ask her about it, but she'd left for the night. I'd tried her again before we'd left this morning but she was in a meeting. I hadn't bothered to leave a message. There was no point alerting her to the fact that I was trying to track her down. For the moment it could wait.

I straightened my tie and banged on the huge brass doorknocker.

The door was opened almost immediately by a largish middle-aged lady in a sweater and long skirt. Although she looked tired, with large bags under her eyes, she appeared to be bearing up reasonably well. She had a light covering of make-up on and she even managed a smile of greeting. 'Detective Milne?'

'Mrs Fox.' We shook hands. 'This is my colleague, Detective Constable Malik.'

They shook hands as well, and then she stood aside for us. 'Please, come in.'

We followed her through the hallway and into a large, very dark sitting room. A fire blazed in the grate, and sitting in one of the seats facing it was a shortish bearded man with glasses. He stood up slowly on seeing us and introduced himself as Martin Fox. If Mrs Fox appeared to be bearing up well, then Mr Fox was the exact opposite. His whole body appeared slumped as if the guts had been knocked out of him, and even his speech was slow and forced.

The gloom seemed to spread from him like an infectious cloud. I got depressed just being within five feet of the bloke.

We sat down on the sofa and Mrs Fox asked us if we'd like anything to drink. We both opted for tea, and she went off to make a pot.

While she was gone, Malik told Fox that he was very sorry about his loss. He sounded like he truly meant it as well.

Fox sat back with his head against the seat, not looking at us. 'Did she suffer?' he asked, speaking slowly as if carefully choosing his words. 'When she died, did she suffer? Please be honest with me.'

Malik looked at me for a bit of help on this one.

'She would have died very quickly, Mr Fox,' I said. 'She didn't suffer. I can assure you of that.'

'The newspapers said only that she was stabbed.'

'That's the only details we released to the media,' I said. 'They don't need to know anything more than that.'

'Was she stabbed many times?' he asked.

'She died from a single wound,' I said, not mentioning anything about the mutilation.

'Why?' The question hung in the air for what seemed like a long time. 'Do they know, these people who commit these terrible crimes? Do they know the hurt they cause? To the ones who are left behind?'

I ached for a cigarette but knew without asking that this would be a non-smoking household. 'I think,' I said, 'that most really don't have a clue of the suffering they inflict. If they did, I'm sure a lot of them would think twice before doing what they do.'

'And do you think that this man . . . the one who killed my Miriam . . . do you think he knew what he was doing?'

I thought suddenly about the families of the customs officers and the accountant. I knew what I'd been doing. Had always known. 'I'm not sure, Mr Fox. It could well have been a spur-of-the-moment thing.'

'It doesn't matter. People like that should be put down. Like dogs.' Maybe he had a point. 'I never believed in the death penalty. I thought it was barbaric for a society to put to death its citizens, whatever their crimes. But now . . . now . . .' His face, still only visible in profile, was contorted with a terrible frustration. 'I'd pull the trigger myself. I really would.'

Before I could give him my standard police spiel that these feelings were understandable but ultimately counter-productive, Mrs Fox thankfully returned with the tea. Fox slipped into a sullen silence. Doubtless he'd been venting his spleen to her in similar vein all week. She sat down at the opposite end of the room to her husband so that we were between them, and poured the tea from a china teapot.

'The reason we're here,' I said, thinking that I really didn't have a clue what it was, 'is to update you on what's happening with the inquiry, and let you know what'll happen now that we've arrested someone.'

'Who is the man who's been charged?' asked Mrs Fox.

I told her who he was and what his relationship was to their daughter, careful not to give away too many details. Pre-trial, police officers have got to watch what they say in case they blurt out anything that might prejudice a fair hearing for the suspect.

'You think he's the one, then?' she said, when I'd finished.

'Bastard,' Fox added, with a violent snarl. Mrs Fox gave him a reproachful look, though she must have felt the same.

It was a good question. I was 50 per cent certain at best. Malik, from the conversation we'd had on the way down, was closer to 80 per cent. Like Knox, he couldn't see any viable alternative, which made drawing conclusions easier for him.

It was Malik who answered. 'We're very sure it's him, Mrs

Fox. As sure as we can be. There's substantial physical evidence linking him to the scene of the crime.'

'Good. I don't think I could stand an acquittal. Not on top of everything else.'

'We can't predict the future, Mrs Fox,' I said, 'or juries. We can only do our best. But I think the case is very strong.'

'Bastard,' said Fox again, still not looking at us. I think he meant Wells, but it was difficult to tell.

'Mark Wells will spend a considerable part of the rest of his life in prison if he's found guilty, Mr Fox,' Malik told him. 'And we're going to do everything in our power to make sure that happens.'

'It's not enough. No prison sentence is good enough for him. Not after what he's done.'

It was, I thought, amazing how socially liberal people like Labour councillors soon changed their tune on crime when it actually had an effect on them. At that moment, Fox looked to be only a couple of steps away from becoming a Charles-Bronson-type vigilante, although without the guns or the menace. Or, it seemed, the energy.

Mrs Fox looked across at her husband and gave him a brave smile. 'Come on, Martin. We've got to stop trying to be so bitter. It doesn't help.'

Fox didn't say anything. I took a sip of my tea and decided to try to finish this interview as swiftly as possible. But before I could continue my spiel about how there was going to be a long wait for the trial and how we would keep in touch regularly in the meantime, Mrs Fox suddenly burst into tears.

Malik and I sat there respectfully. Fox continued to sit in exactly the same position he had been in for the previous ten minutes, staring at an ill-defined point somewhere in the middle distance. I thought he was being ignorant. I know he'd had an immense trauma, but sometimes you've just got to be strong.

'I'm sorry,' she said, dabbing her eyes with a handkerchief. 'It's just . . .'

I put on a stoic smile. 'We understand. You've had a terrible loss. You've got to let it out.'

'I know. That's what the counsellors have been saying.'

'Don't worry about us,' said Malik.

'You know,' she said, looking at both of us with an expression of disbelief, 'it's such an awful, awful waste. That's the hardest part. When you think what she could have been. What she could have achieved if only she'd stayed here with us . . . people who loved her. Instead she ended up dying such a lonely and degrading death. Why?' This was the second time that question had been asked this morning. 'Why did she have to run away and leave us like she did?'

'Leave it, Diane!' snapped Fox, swinging round in his seat and fixing her with a rage-filled stare. Malik and I looked at him, surprised at the violence of his outburst, and his features relaxed a little. 'Just leave it. There's no point going over this again.'

But Mrs Fox clearly had matters to get off her chest. 'Do you know, in the three years she's been gone she never once tried to make contact with us? Not once. Not even a call to let us know she was all right. Nothing. Do you have any idea how that made me feel?'

'We have evidence to suggest that Miriam was taking quite a lot of hard drugs,' I said. 'Sometimes that can take over a person's life to such an extent that they lose track of what their priorities should be. Maybe that's what it was like for her. It doesn't mean she didn't care. It's just that the lure of the drugs may have been stronger.'

'She could have called, Mr Milne. Just once. If not for our sake then for her sister's. Chloe was only twelve years old when Miriam left. She could have contacted her.'

'Leave it, Diane. Please.'

'No, Martin. I've suffered as much as you. I should be allowed to say my piece.' She turned to us again. 'I miss Miriam terribly. I have done since the day she walked out of this door. I loved her more than anything I can describe, but that doesn't detract from the fact that what she did was unforgivable. To put us all, the whole family, through three years of living hell. That was . . . it was so selfish. I loved Miriam, I really did. But she was not a nice person. I'm sorry to have to say it, I really am, but it's true. It is, Martin. It's true. She was not a nice person.'

'Shut up! Just shut up!' His voice reverberated around the room, the slack, hollow face now fiery red with emotion.

'Calm down, Mr Fox,' I said firmly. 'Your wife's just trying to speak.'

'She doesn't need to say that. She doesn't know what she's saying. It's our daughter you're talking about, you know . . .' He faltered, slapped his head in his hands, and began sobbing loudly.

Mrs Fox stared at him for some time, her bottom lip quivering as she fought for control over her emotions. For a moment, I thought I saw a hint of contempt in her eyes, but I couldn't be sure. The atmosphere was thick with tension and I could see that Malik had sweat forming on his brow. It had been a difficult few minutes, but this was what the job was all about. This was what we were paid less than double-glazing salesmen for.

I broke the silence by briefly explaining the process for the next few months: the magistrates appearance today, the pre-trial preparations, the possibility of adjournment, et cetera, but I didn't think either of them was really listening. They looked lost; beaten by the whole thing. Fox had taken his head out of his hands, but once again he declined to look in our direction.

Finally, I put my empty teacup on the table and asked them if they had any further questions.

There was a long pause.

'I don't think so, Detective Milne,' Mrs Fox said finally. 'Thank you both for coming.'

We all stood up, including Fox, who looked as though he might fall back down at any time.

'Is there anything else you need?' I asked them both.

'No, we're receiving plenty of support from family and friends, and we've had some counselling.'

'Good. It's important you talk to people about your feelings.' I looked at Fox when I said this, but he looked away. 'It helps.' This was bollocks, of course. It didn't. Recovery comes from within, not from people who don't know you.

They both nodded, and we all shook hands again. Mrs Fox turned towards the door, then suddenly turned back towards us.

'One thing,' she said. 'You never mentioned the reason why this man ... why he killed Miriam.'

Malik got the answer in first, which was probably for the best. 'As DS Milne mentioned, the suspect hasn't admitted his guilt yet, so we're not entirely sure. However, since there were no signs of sexual assault, we believe it was the result of an argument between the two of them. Probably about money or drugs.'

She shook her head. 'It seems such a petty reason to end some-one's life; to destroy every dream they've ever had.'

'There are no good reasons for murder,' said Malik. 'They all leave the same amount of pain.'

She managed a weak smile. 'I think you're probably right.' She led us out to the front door and stopped in front of it. 'Thank you both for coming. It's very much appreciated, I promise you. Even if it's not that obvious. And I do apologize for getting so emotional. It's very difficult ...'

We both told her once again that we understood entirely. With that, the door opened and we were out of there.

There was a pub a few miles down the road and we stopped for a drink and an early lunch. It was empty. We ordered our drinks from the bored-looking landlord and took a table in the corner.

'What did you think of it in there?' Malik asked, sipping his orange juice.

I knew what he was getting at. 'I detected a bit of an atmosphere and I got the feeling that maybe Mr Fox felt a little guilty about something.'

'Yeah, that crossed my mind. Do you think, you know, anything ever went on between him and Miriam?'

'It happens. It happens in a lot of families, rich and poor. And I suppose it would explain a lot: like why she went away in the first place, why she put up with a life as an underage prostitute, why she never made contact with them. But we might be completely wrong. I get the impression she was a difficult kid anyway. Anne Taylor called her a real bitch when she was talking about her, and not even to phone your mum or your sister through all that time . . .'

'It makes me think that maybe now we've got a motive for Wells. If she had that sort of difficult personality, and it looks like she did, then she could easily have had a major falling-out with him.'

'It's possible.'

'Maybe he thought he was being clever by making it look like a sex crime.'

'It's certainly a viable theory.'

'But you're still not convinced?'

I sighed. 'Not entirely, no.'

'There's a lot of evidence building up, Sarge.'

'Yeah, there is, but there are unanswered questions too. Stuff that puzzles me. Like why Wells came back to the flat.'

'Maybe he's just thick. Plenty of criminals are.'

I told him about the phone records. 'It looks like she and Carla had at least five conversations in the last weeks of Miriam's life. What I can't understand for the life of me is why Carla would pretend not to know her, when it's clear she did. Not unless she had something to hide.'

'And you think it might have something to do with the murder?'

I shrugged. 'I don't know. All I know is that I don't like unanswered questions, and I don't think there's an innocent explanation for it.'

'I told you there was something dodgy about her. I could see it right from the first minute. So, what do you intend to do about it? There's no way Knox is going to want any extension of the inquiry. Not now he's got Wells.'

'I'm going to go and see her, Asif. Make some excuse why we need to talk, then spring it on her.'

'Are you sure that's the reason why you want to see her?'

I gave him a withering look. 'It's definitely the most important reason.'

'Well, let me know what you find out. Although, I still think it was Wells who did it.'

Our food arrived. A tired-looking ploughman's lunch for me, a chilli con carne that bore more than a passing resemblance to dog food for Malik. The landlord gruffly ordered us to enjoy our meals, although I didn't think there was much danger of that.

'Don't say anything about this thing with Carla Graham to anyone else,' I told him, taking a bite of stale bread. 'Capper got wind that I was getting the phone records off Hunsdon and he told me to leave it alone. I don't want to give him any more ammo to fire at me. Not now he's the boss.'

'Don't worry, I won't say anything.' He spooned down a few dollops of chilli, then looked at me seriously. 'You know, I thought it was bad them making him acting DI instead of you. You could do that job one hell of a lot better.'

'It's all politics, Asif. If you play the game, you go places.'

'Then why don't you play the game, Sarge? Forgive me if I'm speaking out of turn, but you're wasted at DS level. You should be running murder investigations, not just being a little cog in them.'

I forced down a fatty lump of ham, then pushed the plate away. I wouldn't have enjoyed that meal if I hadn't eaten for a week. 'I play it,' I said, lighting a cigarette, 'I just don't play it with the same enthusiasm any more, now that the rules are always changing.'

'You can't live in the past, Sarge. The world changes. Even the Met changes. The secret's to adapt. Change with it. Learn the rules. You could still go places.'

'They made you DS, didn't they? Put you in Capper's role.'

He looked surprised. 'How did you know? Knox only phoned me last night. He said he wasn't going to announce it until this afternoon.'

'He hasn't said a word. Not to me, anyway. I guessed. There was something on your mind this morning when we drove down here. You were quieter than usual. Also, you were the obvious choice.'

'You think so?'

'Yeah, I do. You're a fuck sight more talented than any of the other DCs we've got. You'll make a good DS. When's it effective from?'

'Monday, if it all gets sorted out.' I took a drag on my

cigarette but didn't say anything. 'You're not pissed off are you, Sarge?'

I turned to him and smiled. 'No. I'm glad it's you and not anyone else. Congratulations. You deserve it. Unlike Capper.'

'You know, I don't want to sound clichéd or anything, but I've learned a lot working with you. It's been a real education.'

'Don't overdo it. It's me you're talking to, not the DCI.' But I was secretly pleased. I'm just like anyone else. I like compliments, even if they're not entirely truthful.

'Well, I mean it, anyway.'

He went back to eating and I went back to smoking, blowing my cancerous fumes up at the olde worlde beamed ceilings.

'Thanks,' I said. 'It's appreciated.'

Ten minutes later we were back in the car, heading home.

18

We weren't back in Islington until close to five o'clock. An accident on the M40 had caused massive tailbacks, and since neither of us had any idea of alternative routes, we were forced to crawl along at ludicrously slow speeds for hours along with thousands of other irate drivers.

I got Malik to drop me off near home. Somehow I couldn't face going back to the station where the talk would doubtless be of promotions and terminal illnesses, and where I suddenly felt as much an outsider as I ever had. Welland had been an ally, a man who'd often stood up for me in the past. Now he was gone. As a replacement, Capper had to be what a media commentator would call 'the nightmare scenario'.

When I got in I checked my messages. There were none on my home phone, but Raymond had left one on his mobile. He wanted to see me as soon as possible and gave me a number to call back on. He signed off by saying it was urgent, but nothing to worry about too much, whatever that was meant to mean. It was unlike Raymond to leave messages for me, unless it was important. I phoned the number he'd left but it too was on answerphone service, so I left a message for him saying I'd meet him at our usual spot at two the following afternoon unless I heard otherwise. I wanted to see him anyway. There was, it was fair to say, a lot to discuss.

After that, I tried Carla Graham, but she'd left Coleman House for the day and I didn't want to risk calling her on her mobile. She might wonder where I'd got the number from. I told the woman on the other end of the phone that it was the police and asked when Carla was expected back. I was told she was on weekend day shifts and would be in the following morning. I said I'd call her then.

Outside it was raining, but I fancied a walk, and maybe a drink somewhere, so I strolled round the corner to the Hind's Head, a quiet little place I frequent occasionally.

There was no-one in there and I didn't recognize the lone bar- man. He was reading the paper when I came in. I took a seat at the bar and ordered a pint of Fosters, lighting a cigarette and removing my damp coat.

There was a slightly crumpled copy of the *Standard* next to me on the bar. Since the barman didn't look too chatty and there was no-one else to talk to, I leaned over and picked it up.

The shock hit me right between the eyes like an express train.

The headline was in huge block capitals covering half the page: E-fit of Customs Killer. Facing it on the opposite side of the page was a detailed photofit picture of a thin-faced man, thirty-five to forty, with short dark hair and eyes that were just slightly too close together.

If I'd asked an artist to paint a quick picture of my face, he couldn't have done a better job. The likeness was uncanny.

The whole world seemed to cave in on me as the full implications of what I was looking at flooded into my brain like water surging through a burst dam.

Now I knew that more than at any other time in my entire life, I was in real danger. Not just from the cops but from people whose faces I didn't even know.

But who knew me. And who now realized that I was a lot better off to them dead than alive.

Raymond was right. I should have fucking shot her.

Part Three

UNRAVELLING

19

At exactly 12.55 p.m. the next day, I arrived at R.M. Keen's Funeral Home for the Recently Bereaved, a mouthful if ever there was one. Set slightly back from the road in the attractive, leafy setting of Muswell Hill, it was definitely the sort of place you'd like your corpse to be stored before it went up in smoke. The building itself, hidden from the road by a gentle canopy of beech trees, was a converted nineteenth-century chapel with old-fashioned lattice windows which looked to have kept much of its original character. Fresh flowers sprouted from stone vases on either side of the oak door. I half expected to be greeted by the vicar's wife. There was a gravel car park out front containing a couple of hearses, a sprinkling of other cars, and Raymond's royal blue Bentley. So at least I knew he was there.

The door was locked. A sign on it asked prospective customers to use the intercom and kindly wait for assistance, so I did just that. A few seconds later a grave, middle-aged voice, sounding not unlike Vincent Price, bade me good afternoon and asked how he could be of assistance. I'm all for creating the right atmosphere, but I think this bloke was taking it a bit far.

'I'm here to see Mr Raymond Keen,' I said as gravely as I could.

'Is Mr Keen expecting you?'

'Yes, he is.'

'And your name is?'

'Mr Milne. Mr Dennis Milne.'

'I'll just see if Mr Keen is available.'

Raymond, of course, wasn't expecting to see me for another hour, and in a completely different location, but I was no longer taking any chances. The e-fit had spooked me sufficiently to start distrusting everyone. Raymond was not going to want me falling into the hands of the police, and if he had to I knew he'd have no qualms about guaranteeing that I didn't. The only thing going in my favour was the fact that he didn't know I'd been stopped at a roadblock that night, and had given the police my true identity. At least I hoped he didn't know. At this point it wouldn't have surprised me that much if it turned out he had someone on the inside of the police investigation as well.

Vincent Price came back over the intercom. 'Mr Keen will see you now. Please come in.'

I opened the door and walked into the foyer, which was done out in oak panelling. Vincent was sitting behind a large, very tidy desk, although in the flesh he looked more Vince Hill than Price.

He gave me the standard gloomy look. 'If you go down the hall, Mr Keen's office is the last door on the right.' He pointed to a poorly lit corridor leading to the back of the building, and I followed it down, not bothering to knock when I reached the last door on the right.

Raymond was smoking a fat cigar and poring through a number of open files spread out in front of him. God knows what they contained. It could have been anything. VAT receipts, profit and loss accounts, information so valuable people had to die for it . . .

He looked up and smiled broadly as I came in. 'Dennis, this is a rare honour, and most unexpected too. Please, take a seat.'

I sat down in a comfortable, high-backed leather chair that probably cost what I got paid in a month. 'Yeah, sorry about the intrusion, Raymond. I thought it might be easier if we met here.'

He continued smiling. 'Really? And why's that?'

I met his stare and held it. 'Suffice it to say I'm a little bit nervous at the moment.'

'Yes, I'm sure you must be. That photofit of you was a remarkable likeness. Frighteningly so. The question is, what do we do about it?'

'There's nothing we can do. We'll just have to sit tight. It's highly unlikely anyone who knows me'll think I did it.'

'I should hope not. If they did, it wouldn't say much about you, would it?'

I lit a cigarette, thinking that Raymond almost certainly didn't know about the police questioning me near the scene.

'Well, you asked to meet me, Raymond. So what can I do for you?'

'Too many people know about what happened. Your mate, the one who drove you, he's one of them . . .'

'He's all right. He won't say anything.'

'How can you be sure of that?'

It was a very good question. Hopefully, because he'd left the country. I hadn't heard from Danny the previous night after my e-fit had appeared, so I assumed, or hoped at least, that he'd taken my advice.

'The reason I took him was because I knew I could trust him not to start panicking.'

'Have you spoken to him since?'

'Yeah, when I gave him his share. He was pissed off he'd been lied to about the targets, but then so was I . . . but it wasn't a major problem for him. He'll be all right.'

'You've not spoken to him since the photofit came out, then?'

'No, but he told me the other day he was off down the Caribbean for a couple of weeks. To spend a bit of his money.'

'A wise move,' he said, shuffling some of his paperwork around the desk. 'And you're sure that's where he's gone?'

'Well, as far as I'm aware, yeah. What are you getting at exactly?'

'Just making sure. I wouldn't want to think he's got all worried and gone to the police.'

'He wouldn't do that.'

Raymond eyed me closely. 'So you'll vouch for him, then?'

'He won't cause any problems. Like I said, that's why I took him.'

'Good, good.' He nodded his head slowly. 'I only wish I could say the same about the other guy.'

'Which other guy?'

'Our man. The one there on the night, out the front. Waiting for them to arrive. That's what I wanted to see you about.'

'What do you mean?' As if I didn't know.

'He's a nice lad, don't get me wrong, and it's a hard decision to have to make, especially as I know his mother so well, but . . .' He sighed, then looked at me as if inviting some sympathetic understanding. 'He's a liability too. I think we're going to have to deal with him.'

I'd never actually met Raymond's man, the one who'd radioed in the victims' arrival, but I remembered he'd sounded youngish, no more than twenty-five, and although he'd put on the tough-guy act when talking to me I knew he'd been shitting himself on the night. You can always tell. There's always something just that

little bit shaky in the voice of someone who's battling unsuccess-
fully to control fear. Not that he'd had much to worry about. All
he'd had to do was watch out for the Cherokee and inform me
when it turned up. I'd had the hard part. I assumed I was going
to have the hard part now.

'So, what are you telling me for?'

'You know exactly why. You're my most reliable man, Dennis.
A difficult job like this requires the touch of an expert touch, not
some rank amateur.'

I dragged hard on what was left of my cigarette and shook my
head. 'Jesus, Raymond. This is getting out of hand. We can't just
keep on fucking killing people.'

'He's the last one, Dennis. You can claim a bet on it.'

'You said that to me five days ago. Your exact words were: "It
won't happen again." That was Monday. Today's Saturday.
What are you going to want me to do next week? Assassinate the
fucking Pope?'

'Look, I wasn't to know that the little bitch who saw you'd
have a photographic memory, was I? I told you you should have
shot her. The fact is, this fucking photofit's got everybody
nervous. Very nervous.'

'And that's another thing, Raymond. Who exactly is this
everybody you're working with? I hear on the news that I've
killed an accountant who, as far as anyone knows, had an
unblemished record. So, tell me, who are your associates, and
what did they want this guy dead for?'

'The more you know, Dennis, the worse it'll be for you. You
know that. Think about it.'

I sighed. 'If I take out this other guy, then what's to stop me
being the next on the list?'

'Dennis. At the moment, you're all right. I know you can't go
to the police and make any sort of deal. Everybody knows that.

You're too heavily involved. There's so much blood on your hands, it's dripping onto the carpet.'

'Thanks.'

'I'm just trying to make you feel better, that's all.' He shot me a smile that I think was meant to show he knew how I felt, and pointed his cigar in my direction. 'And if you don't know anything about the reasons behind what happened then, again, you're no threat to anyone. No threat means there's no point in taking you out, so you stay alive. Which is what you want.'

'And Danny?'

'Your mate? Well, if you say he's all right, he's all right.'

I sighed. 'I just don't like the way things are going, that's all. It's getting out of hand, and in my experience that's when things start to go wrong.'

'Look, Dennis, I don't need it either, but it's what's got to happen. The bloke's name is Barry Finn. He's been walking round the last few days like someone's got a pair of shears wrapped round his bollocks. He's jittery, and it's noticeable. It's not a situation we can allow to continue.'

'And how much are you offering in payment?'

He raised his eyebrows. 'Dennis, this is all about making sure we all stay at liberty, not about making a quick profit. Be serious.'

'Fuck that, Raymond. This whole thing's about profit, and don't pretend otherwise. You want me to kill him, you're going to have to pay up. I'm taking a risk here.'

'You're taking a bigger risk by not doing it, I promise you.' There was the first hint of a threat in his voice.

I looked up at the nicotine-stained ceiling, focusing on a flimsy, dust-covered spider's web that hung forlornly there. I looked for the spider, but guessed he was long gone.

'When do you want him taken care of?' I asked wearily, knowing full well that I had no choice.

'As soon as. Preferably before the end of the weekend. Definitely by Monday.'

'It's not going to be easy. If he's as paranoid as you say he is, he's going to expect someone to take a pop at him.'

'Did he see you on the night?'

I shook my head. 'No. We just talked on the radio. I couldn't even tell you what he looked like.'

'That's another reason to use you. He's worked for me for a long time so he knows what most of my people look like.'

'And if I do it, I want it to be the end of it. Understand?'

Raymond nodded. 'Yeah, I understand. It will be.'

His mobile rang. He looked as though he was going to ignore it, then decided it might be important, and took the call.

I took the opportunity to light another cigarette. Raymond listened to whoever was talking on the other end for what seemed like quite a long time, told the caller to get over to the funeral home straight away so they could discuss whatever it was that needed discussing, and pocketed the mobile. It sounded like our meeting was over.

'You're going to need to give me all the details on this guy,' I told him. 'Photograph, address, any other relevant information.'

He smiled. 'No need.'

'What do you mean?'

He patted his jacket where he'd replaced the mobile. 'That was him. He's on his way over here now.'

20

'This is what I call a stroke of good fortune,' Raymond said, rubbing his hands together.

'Don't tell me you want it done here?'

'Why not? It's as good a place as any. In fact, better. Are you carrying?'

I was. A six-shot 2.2 I'd bought from Tomboy years back which I kept for emergencies only. I considered my current plight to be as close to an emergency as I was likely to get and I was fully prepared to use it to defend my liberty and maybe my life, although I didn't like the idea of turning it on someone who presented no direct threat.

'I am, but I don't want to get it dirty. I need it for protection, and if I have to fire it again down the line I don't want to have to worry about this thing getting back to me. '

'Don't worry about that. No-one's ever going to find the body.'

'How can you be sure?'

'Just take my word for it. It's not going to be found.' Have you got a silencer?'

'Of course not. I wasn't planning on carrying out any assassinations today, believe it or not.'

He shrugged. 'No matter. The walls are thick in this place. It was built when things were made to last. No-one'll hear anything.'

'Raymond, for fuck's sake. This sort of thing needs planning. I can't just take someone out off the cuff. Not with ten minutes' notice.'

He stood up and fixed me with a hard stare. 'Of course you can. Think positive, Dennis. The problem with you is you're too fucking negative about everything.' He looked at his watch quickly. It was a Cartier or Rolex. Flash bastard. 'Now we've got to get things sorted out. He doesn't live too far away so he'll be here soon.'

I started to say something but he shifted his bulk out of the chair and walked past me towards the door, leaving me no option but to follow. He strode purposefully down the hall and up to the front desk. Vincent was still there.

'I've got some business that needs sorting, Frank, so I'm going to have to shut up shop. We're not expecting any deliveries, are we?'

'No, not today, Mr Keen,' he answered in that funereal drawl of his.

'Well, do me a favour and make yourself scarce, there's a good man.'

He didn't need asking twice. He'd obviously had to piss off at short notice before. I didn't like the way he looked at Raymond either. There was fear in his expression. He knew things about Raymond he'd rather not know, that was my impression. He nodded, got his coat, and went out the door without another word.

'So, how are we going to do this?' Raymond said, looking

about him for pointers. One word described his overall attitude: excited. He seemed genuinely excited at the prospect of committing murder. 'Come on, Dennis. Help me out here.'

I thought about trying to reason with him but knew there was no point. I could have walked out and left him to it, but it wouldn't have done me any good. One way or another, Raymond's man was going to die, and at that moment I guessed that if I co-operated in his demise I might be helping myself at the same time.

'The best thing is to put me on reception. When he arrives, I'll let him in and tell him to go down to your office. He'll go down, you'll start talking, then I'll come down and knock on the door. You'll ask me to come in, so in I come. I'll have a couple of coffees ready. I'll put them down, you carry on talking to him, and when his back's turned to me, I'll shoot him.'

'I don't know, Dennis. I don't really want it done in my office. Can't you just do it in here?'

'How?'

'Well, either when he opens the door, or when you've directed him down the hall. Maybe you can just walk up behind him and pop him while he's en route.'

I shook my head. 'It wouldn't work.'

'Why not?'

'Too risky. If he's as nervous as you say he is, he'll probably suspect something like that. He'll be watching his back on the walk down to your office, and if I try anything, chances are it'll fuck up. Same with shooting him when he walks in the door. There's too much scope for failure. It's got to be done in an enclosed place where he can't escape.'

He nodded slowly, digesting my words. 'All right, fair enough. But we're going to have to do something about your clothes. You look far too casual to be working in a place of rest, even on a

Saturday.' He disappeared into one of the rooms off the hall and reappeared a few seconds later with a shirt and black tie. 'That should fit,' he said. 'There's nothing I can do about the jeans. Hopefully by the time Barry notices them he'll be half a second away from a fully ventilated head.'

I took the gun out of my leather jacket pocket, removed the jacket and the sweatshirt I was wearing underneath, and chucked them down behind the reception desk, out of sight. I then hurriedly pulled on the shirt and tie and stuffed the gun down the back of my waistband. The shirt was a bit small and I couldn't do the top button up – not without choking myself, anyway – but I didn't suppose Barry would be paying too much attention.

'You've got to sound very respectful when you speak as well. We're very customer-orientated in this business. Try to talk slowly, and sound like you're thinking about what you're saying.'

'I'll see what I can do.'

I sat down behind the desk and lit a cigarette.

'Blimey, Dennis, you can't just sit there with a fag in your mouth. It doesn't set the right fucking tone. Respectful, remember.'

'It's Saturday, and we're not expecting punters. Call it a perk for having to work odd hours.'

He shook his head in an annoyed fashion, but let it go. 'Right, let's get this straight. You send him down to my office, we start talking—'

'You offer him a cup of coffee because you're having one yourself. You phone through to me in reception, and I go and make it. Now, where's your coffeemaking equipment?'

'That door behind you goes into a kitchen. All the stuff you need's in there.'

'Fine. I'll bring it down, and we'll take it from there.'

I couldn't help thinking what a mistake I was making getting involved in such a hastily planned murder. Some time soon my luck was inevitably going to run out.

Raymond appeared to read my thoughts. 'All this'll be over soon, Dennis. Then we can get back to making money, pure and simple.'

I nodded, taking a drag on the cigarette. 'I'm thinking . . . after this I might do what my driver's doing – you know, take a long holiday somewhere. Maybe even permanent.'

'The crime figures'll go up without you, Dennis.'

I managed a humourless smile. 'Somehow, I don't think so.'

The sound of wheels on gravel outside stirred me from my thoughts.

'He's here,' Raymond said, looking out of one of the lattice windows. 'I'll get down to my office.'

I straightened my tie, feeling almost like a new guy on his first day in the office, and put out the cigarette.

A few seconds later the buzzer went and I leaned down to the intercom speaker and asked, in as grave a voice as I could muster, who was there. I'm not a bad mimic, and it came out pretty well.

A flustered voice asked for Raymond. 'We are closed at the moment, sir,' I told him.

'He's expecting me. My name's Barry Finn.'

I told him to hang on while I checked with Mr Keen, sat there for a few seconds, then came back on the line. 'Please come in.' I pushed the small red button on the intercom, which I assumed released the lock and was pleased to find out that it did. That could have fucked things up, if I couldn't even open the door.

Barry Finn was slightly older than I'd expected, about thirty, no more than five feet seven tall with a mop of dirty blond hair. He had the pinched, wary features of a small-time villain and his eyes were darting about in overdrive. Just like Len Runnion's always did. This was a man carrying a lot of weight on flimsy shoulders. Immediately I knew Raymond was right to want him out of the way, although it didn't say much about his judgement that he'd used him in the first place. Still, maybe you could have said the same about mine.

I gave him a stern, headmasterly look and pointed him in the direction of Mr Keen's office. He didn't say a word and took off down the hall. It felt strange knowing that he only had a few more minutes of life left in him, and a bit sad to think it was going to be spent worrying about something he could do nothing about.

Now it was time to wait. Raymond, however, was not hanging about. Within two minutes he phoned through, gruffly telling me to get him a coffee, not bothering to say please. I was glad then that I wasn't a full-time employee of his. He had the sort of brash attitude with his staff that gives capitalism a bad name.

I checked the gun for the second time since sitting down and took the safety off before replacing it in the waistband of my jeans. Then I went into the kitchen and put the kettle on. While I was waiting for it to boil, I gave the place the once-over. I've never been in an undertakers' kitchen before, and wasn't sure what to expect. Maybe a few jokey pictures of the employees posing with the corpses, or some coffin-shaped fridge magnets. But there was none of that. Everything looked depressingly normal. Clean and tidy as well. Scattered about the walls were postcards from various far-flung destinations. One was even from Dhaka in Bangladesh, which struck me as an odd destination to spend your holidays. The photograph was of a toothless, bare-footed rickshaw driver smiling at the camera. I took it off the wall and saw that it was from Raymond. He said that the weather was too hot and he was looking forward to getting back. If the photo on the front was the best the Bangladeshi tourist industry could do, I couldn't blame him.

The kettle boiled and I poured Raymond's coffee, substituting the two sugars he'd ordered for salt, just so he'd know I wasn't his skivvy. I found a battered Princess Diana memorial tea tray, put the cup on that, and headed off down the hall.

To keep up the ruse, I knocked on the door and waited until I was called in, which took all of about a second.

Raymond beamed at me as I stepped inside and Barry looked round quickly, just to check that everything was all right. 'Ah, thank you, Dennis. Just what the doctor ordered. Are you sure you don't want one, Barry?'

Barry shook his head, but didn't say anything.

I walked over and Raymond took the cup from the tray, managing a brief thanks. He turned back to Barry. 'So don't worry about it,' he told him. 'It's not going to be a problem.'

Still holding the Princess Diana commemorative tea tray, I reached down and pulled the gun from my waistband.

Barry must have sensed I was still in the room. As Raymond continued to gabble, he turned round at the exact moment I raised the gun. The wrong end of the barrel was only three feet from his head.

His eyes widened and his mouth opened. Before he could say anything, I pulled the trigger, wanting to get this over with as soon as possible.

But nothing happened. The trigger didn't move. I squeezed harder. Still nothing. The fucking thing was jammed.

'Don't kill me! For fuck's sake, don't kill me!'

The words were a frightened howl, and it struck me then that it was the first time anyone had ever had the chance to ask me for mercy. It hurt, because it made me feel doubt. Doubt that I had the strength to kill a man face to face in cold blood. He raised his arms in surrender, the mouth opening and shutting ever so slightly like a tropical fish, unintelligible pleas for mercy trembling out. I felt like I was frozen to the spot, like I was completely and utterly incapacitated. What did I do now? What could I do now?

'For the love of God, Dennis! Shoot the bastard!'

Reflexively I pulled the trigger. Again, nothing happened. I knew then that the weapon was useless. It was never going to unjam in the next five seconds.

'Come on!' yelled Raymond, his face red with frustration.

Barry half turned to his boss, still keeping one eye on the gun. 'Mr Keen ... Raymond ... what are you doing? I won't say nothing—'

'Finish it!'

'The gun's fucking jammed, Raymond!'

'Oh, for Christ's sake!'

In a surprisingly deft movement, he reached over, grabbed a medium-sized statuette of a golfer taking a swing from the side of his desk, and whacked Barry over the head with it. It broke immediately, the golfer's head and torso flying across the room. Barry yelped in pain, but that was about it. He was hardly incapacitated.

This seemed to galvanize Barry into action. Seeing that he was dealing with people who'd have difficulty killing a rumour, he jumped to his feet in an attempt to escape, whereupon I slammed the tea tray into his face, knocking him back down again. He lashed out with his legs, but I jumped aside and tried to hit him with the butt of the gun. It caught him on the arm as he raised it to protect himself, and with his other hand he punched me in the kidneys. This time it was my turn to yelp in pain. I staggered backwards, creating an opening between him and the door. He was off the seat like a greyhound out of a trap and heading towards salvation.

I suddenly had a vision of spending the rest of my days behind

bars, stuck in segregation along with the paedophiles and inform-
ants, and it was that which stopped me from letting Barry Finn
go. Raymond was yelling something, but I couldn't hear it. I
jumped on Barry as he reached the door and tried to pull him
backwards, dropping the gun in the process.

But Barry had a lot of incentive to get out of there and he
wasn't going to give up easily. Despite my best efforts, which
included trying to gouge his eyes, he managed to open the door
and stagger unsteadily down the hall with me on his back. He
managed about four paces before Raymond came running round
the front of him, his face a panting mask of adrenalin and
rage.

'All right, Barry boy, let's go quietly now.'

But Barry wasn't going to go quietly, not if he could avoid it.
He desperately tried to dodge round Raymond with all the agility
of a pantomime horse.

Raymond stood his ground, and punched him hard in the
stomach.

Barry gasped as the wind was taken out of him. He fell to his
knees and held that position for maybe a second, before toppling
over onto his side. I jumped off his back, thinking that Raymond
must have one hell of a punch on him. Which was when I saw
the bloodied knife in his right hand.

'Pick him up, hold him,' he demanded excitedly.

Barry was crawling along the floor on his stomach, blood oozing out from under his body. Raymond kicked him viciously in
the side, which I thought was a bit unnecessary, but he had the
look of the sadist about him that day. I've seen it plenty of times
before. Sometimes they just get carried away.

'Go on, pick him up, Dennis. Now.'

Barry coughed and tried to say something, but it just came out
like a splutter. I felt sick. This was different from a shooting. It

was so much more messy and, in a bizarre way, so much more personal.

I stood behind him and pulled him up by the arms. His body made a horrible squelching sound as it disengaged from the pool of blood forming below him, and I had to fight to stop myself from puking.

Raymond's face split open in a wild, maniacal grin and his eyes widened dramatically, as if they were trying to drink in as much of the scene as possible. Again Barry tried to get words out, but it was too late. The hand containing the knife darted out and there was a splitting sound as the blade peeled through soft flesh. Barry gasped. Raymond stabbed again. And again, his face beaming savagely, lost in the joy of murder, his right arm pumping like a demented piston. Barry tried to struggle but his movements were weak and drawn, and every thrust of the knife took just that little bit more out of him. The blood dripped heavily onto the floor and I struggled to hold him upright, slipping slightly in the mess below.

'Please,' I heard him whisper through clenched teeth, or maybe it was just air escaping, I don't know.

Either way it was over, and finally his resistance went altogether and he slumped in my arms. Raymond had stabbed him at least a dozen times.

Raymond stood back, panting with exertion, and admired his handiwork. His crisp white shirt was spattered with gobs of blood. 'All right, he's gone. You can put him down now.'

I laid him gently on the floor and stepped away. There was blood everywhere, although thankfully the dark hardwood flooring served to disguise the worst of it.

Raymond, still holding the knife, wiped sweat from his brow. 'It's a shame he had to go like that. I always quite liked old Barry. What the fuck happened with your gun?'

'It jammed,' I said. 'It happens sometimes.'

'This is a fucking mess, Dennis. By rights you ought to clean it up as it was your gun that caused it.'

'What are we going to do with him?' I asked, still partially numbed by what had just happened. I'd never seen so much blood in my life. It seemed every drop Barry had owned was now spread out between me and Raymond. Every now and again his body twitched malevolently. A faint but growing odour of shit drifted silently through the still air.

'Well, he's already beginning to go a bit ripe, so we'd better get him packaged up. We'll stick him in one of the coffins for now.'

He put the knife down next to the body and motioned for me to follow him. We walked back down the hall and he opened up a door a little bit further down on the opposite side from his office. A number of coffins were stacked up in lines on shelves against one wall. They all looked to be much of a muchness, although some were bigger than others.

Raymond took a quick look at them, then selected the one he wanted and pulled it down. It was a cream colour – almost white – with iron handles, and it looked quite cheap – which, I suppose, stood to reason, since he wasn't going to be making any money out of Barry's disposal. I got one end of it and we took it outside and put it down on one of the few dry spaces on the floor, before lifting Barry's bloodsoaked corpse up and chucking it in. Although I worked hard to avoid it, a few splashes of blood got on my jeans, which basically spelled the end for them. Raymond put the lid down, and after that we cleared up the rest of the mess as best we could, which took a good twenty minutes and involved me doing most of the mopping up while Raymond acted in something of a supervisory role.

When we'd finished, I went and got myself a glass of water

from the kitchen. I drank it down fast, then poured myself another and drank that down as well. I was still feeling nauseous so I took some slow, deep breaths and focused on one of the postcards. This one was from India, from somewhere called Mumbai, which I hadn't heard of. I wondered briefly who'd gone there for their holidays, but didn't bother to look.

When I felt a little bit better I walked back into the hallway.

'Are you all right?' Raymond asked. He was kneeling down beside the coffin hammering in nails while chewing on a cigar. He looked a bit knackered, but that was about it. You wouldn't have guessed he'd just stabbed an employee of his to death.

'I don't ever want to have to do that again,' I told him.

'You know how it is, Dennis. Sometimes you've just got to do these things.'

I snorted. 'There've got to be better ways to earn a living.'

'Too right, and after this I'm going back to concentrating on my core business. There's big money to be made in undertaking. And it's a steady market. You see this?' He banged the coffin with his hammer. 'One of these costs thirty-seven quid from the manufacturers. Thirty-seven quid. But you know what? The cheapest one I sell'll cost a punter four hundred. That's a one thousand per cent mark-up. And the beauty of it is that no-one argues. I mean, who the fuck's going to negotiate over the price of their nearest and dearest's funeral costs? Only a right heartless bastard'd think about doing that. And thankfully there aren't too many of them about.'

There wasn't a lot you could say to that. 'So what are you going to do with the body?'

'I'll put it in the back of one of the hearses and drive it up to some associates of mine.' I raised my eyebrows. 'They're professionals, Dennis. Don't worry. They know how to make people disappear.'

'Are you sure you can trust them? This is a body we're talking about here, not a caseload of porno videos.'

'Let's just say I've worked with them before and they've proved reliable.'

'And they can be trusted to get rid of him?'

He stood up and smiled at me. 'Dennis, you of all people should know that if you want to make someone disappear, and you know what you're doing, then, bang' – he clicked his fingers – 'they'll just vanish into thin air. Never to be seen again.'

I thought of Molly Hagger then and shuddered.

'Grab the other end, will you?' he said.

I did as I was told, and together we loaded the coffin into one of the hearses so that it could begin its final journey to an anonymous resting place.

21

It was twenty past three when I picked up the phone and called Coleman House. I was back at home, sitting on the sofa with a cup of coffee and a cigarette.

Someone whose voice I didn't recognize answered, and I asked to be put through to Ms Graham. I could hear my heart thumping. I wasn't sure whether it was because of the shock of what I'd been a part of earlier, or simply nerves at the prospect of speaking to a woman I fancied, and trying to get her to see me.

I pictured Barry Finn. I could hear the gruesome gasping noises he made as Raymond stabbed him, like an old man with emphysema.

'Hello, Mr Milne. Dennis.'

'Hi, Carla, sorry to bother you.' My heart was beating louder than ever. For a second I wanted to put the phone down and get the hell out of my flat. Go for a run or something. 'You heard about the charges being laid for the Miriam Fox murder?'

'Against the pimp? Yes, I saw it in the paper.'

'I tried to reach you to tell you yesterday but you were out, and I didn't really want to leave a message.'

'Thanks for letting me know. I suppose that means you won't have to come back here again.'

'That's right.' I paused for a moment, wondering how best to put this. 'There were a couple of things I wanted to run by you, though.'

Her tone didn't change. 'What sort of things?'

'Nothing to worry about, just some background information I need. I'd rather not discuss it over the phone. Is it possible we could meet somewhere?'

'Is it very urgent?'

I didn't want to alarm her. 'Not particularly, but it would be nice to get it out of the way.'

'I'm trying to think when I'm around . . .' She didn't sound unduly worried. 'I've got a lot on this afternoon.'

'This evening?' I ventured.

She thought about it. 'How about tomorrow evening? That'd be easier. Why don't you come round to my flat? It's up in Kentish Town.'

This was an invitation if ever I'd heard one. 'Yeah, of course. I could do that. What's the address?'

She told me, and I wrote it down in my notebook. 'I'll find it. What sort of time?'

'I normally eat at about seven. Come round after that. About eight?'

It sounded as though we were arranging a date, and I suppose in a way we were. 'Eight o'clock's fine. I'll see you then.'

We said our goodbyes and I hung up, not knowing whether to feel pleased with myself or not. I was glad that I was going to get the chance to see her again, even if what I had to say wasn't exactly going to endear her to me. I was interested too in what her answers were going to be. I didn't at that point think that she'd had anything to do with the murder, but something had definitely been up between her and Miriam Fox and I wanted to know what it was.

I sat there for a few seconds mulling over the possibilities, but I found it difficult to concentrate. The problem was, I couldn't help thinking about Barry Finn. Usually I can rid my mind of inconvenient thoughts – its something you've got to be able to do if part of your life involves ending the lives of fellow human beings – but this killing had hit me a lot harder than any of the others. It was the indignity of it. Right now, he was probably laid out on tarpaulin in someone's garage being slowly and carefully dismembered like a piece of rancid meat.

Knifing a man to death in cold blood while he struggled to understand what the hell was going on, then sentencing his relatives to years of torment by removing all traces of his existence; making him vanish into thin air, like Molly Hagger and who knows how many other lost souls. Whichever way you chose to look at it, it was a shameful way to make a living.

I picked up my coffee, went to take a drink, then decided I needed something stronger. A lot stronger. Outside, the day had become grey and cloudy, and it had begun to spit with rain. There was a half bottle of Remy in the cupboard so I poured myself a couple of fingers, and filled a pint glass with the contents of a can of Heineken from the fridge. There didn't seem any point doing things by half measures, and I had nowhere to go for the rest of the day.

I drank the brandy down in one, lit a cigarette, and took a good draw of the beer. I smoked the cigarette down to the butt, finishing it at about the same time I finished the beer. I poured myself some more brandy, drank it down, lit another cigarette. I didn't feel any better. I could still picture Barry Finn. I could hear the noises he made as he died: that horrible gasping as he fought for breath through punctured lungs. Futile. All futile. I thought of the pleasure Raymond had taken in the murder, like a kid playing his first ever Playstation game. I'd never really taken him for a sadist before, but I wouldn't underestimate his potential for cruelty again. Would he have worn that same smile had he been killing me? Somehow I felt sure the answer was yes. Maybe, he was even now planning my demise with his mysterious associates, men adept at making bodies disappear.

And how close were the coppers to me? Had the young cop at the roadblock talked to the investigating officers? Were they checking my background, viewing me now as a possible suspect? Had they gone further? Was I under surveillance even as I sat here getting drunker and drunker?

Paranoid thoughts were suddenly swarming through my brain like steamers on a tube train. There seemed no end to them, and no way to escape the strength-sapping fear they generated. I'd never had a panic attack before, but I could feel one coming on.

I filled the brandy glass again and found another can of Heineken in the fridge. I drank the one, then took a long gulp from the other. I tried to imagine what it felt like to take a knife in the gut. I'd read somewhere once that it was like being hit with a cricket bat, except twice as bad. I got the feeling it was plenty worse than that, especially when you were being held in a vice-like grip by someone you'd never met before and the one doing the knifing was your employer, someone you knew and trusted. Christ, I hated myself; for just a few seconds, I truly hated myself. I was no amoral bastard who didn't give a fuck about his actions. I felt guilty. I knew I'd done wrong, I really did, and that was what was getting to me.

At some point the drink hit me hard. Cricket bat hard. I came over very tired and knew I was going to have to lie down. In a way, it was a relief. I lay back on the sofa and let the weariness wash over me, finally ridding my mind of its demons.

I don't know for how long I slept. Maybe a couple of hours, something like that. I needed it anyway, however long it was.

I was woken by the sound of the phone ringing. It was pitch black in the room and I could hear the rain coming down outside. My mouth was desert-scrub dry and I had a headache, a result of the fact that I'm not used to drinking brandy during the day. I closed my eyes again and waited for the call to go to answerphone.

It was Malik. I picked up as he was starting to leave a message.

'You sound in a bad way, Sarge,' he told me in a manner that was far too cheery for my liking.

'I've been asleep. You woke me up.'

He started to apologize but I told him not to worry. 'I needed to wake up anyway.' I yawned. 'Where are you phoning from?'

'The station.'

'What are you doing down there? It's your day off.'

'Just doing a little bit of overtime.'

'Very conscientious.' And sensible too, now that he was on the verge of promotion. It was important to show enthusiasm while you could still manage it. 'So, what can I do for you on this shitty, wet evening?'

'We've found the murder weapon in the Mark Wells case.'

I was suddenly more interested. 'Oh yeah? Where was it?'

'In a park not far from Wells's flat. It was in some bushes. A kid looking for his football found it.'

'Prints?'

'No, but you can't have everything, can you? It's definitely the weapon that killed her. A butcher's knife with a ten-inch blade. It's got her blood all over it.'

'How do we know it belongs to him?'

'He threatened people with a very similar knife on two separate occasions in the weeks before the murder. It's his knife, Sarge. It's definitely his.'

'Shit. And, you know, I still wasn't convinced.'

'They're doing a load of other tests on it as well. Just in case he left any DNA traces.'

'I'm glad that bastard's going down. That'll teach him to hit me.'

'And that's not the only thing. Wells's brief came in today.'

'He's recovered from his injuries, has he?'

'No, it's a different one now. He sacked the other guy. Anyway, he comes in and says that Wells has been thinking about this business of the shirt and he reckons he did own a shirt like the one we found once, but that he gave it away a long time back.'

'He gave away his shirt? Who the hell does that?'

'Yeah, and get this. He reckons he gave it to one of his girls.'

'Which one?'

'Well, that's the thing. He said he gave it to Molly Hagger.'

22

We both agreed that this sort of story wasn't going to get Mark Wells very far in court, especially as, conveniently, the person he'd supposedly given it to had disappeared into thin air. I wasn't entirely sure whether this new information cemented the case against him or not. The fact that I'd only just woken up, having not long consumed nearly half a bottle of brandy mixed with beer, didn't make matters any easier.

'Have you seen Carla Graham yet?' he asked.

'No, not yet.' I resisted the urge to tell him I'd made an appointment with her. 'I don't suppose I'll bother now. It doesn't look like there's much doubt it's Wells, and there's no point raking up stuff that's got nothing to do with the murder.'

'It'd be interesting to see why she lied.'

'Yeah. Maybe I'll ask her if I ever run into her again.'

The conversation moved on to other things, all of them brutal. Malik told me that we had another possible murder inquiry on our hands. An eighty-one-year-old lady had held onto her handbag after a gang of young muggers had decided to relieve her of it, and had fallen on her head during the struggle. She was now in intensive care and the doctors were doubtful she'd pull through. Two people had been glassed the previous night in a pub fight, and one was going to lose his eye. One arrest: a nineteen-year-old who was already on bail for another assault. I recognized the name but couldn't picture his face. Three more suspects were still at large.

I asked Malik about the Traveller's Rest case. Had he spoken to his mate about it again? He said he hadn't, and laughingly told me that the e-fit and my face bore a startling resemblance.

'Do you think so?' I asked him.

'What? Don't you?' He said it in a manner that suggested he couldn't believe I couldn't see it.

I reluctantly agreed that there were similarities, but assured him I'd had nothing to do with it. 'But if you don't see me Monday, it means I've fled the country.'

'Somehow I think I'll be seeing you Monday, Sarge.'

I told him he didn't have to call me that any more, not now he was DS.

'Oh yeah, I suppose I don't. See you Monday then, Dennis.'

I think I preferred Sarge.

I said my goodbyes and rang off. It was almost six o'clock, and I had nothing to do. I don't really have many friends, as such. It doesn't usually bother me. I'm not the sort to get bored. I work fairly long hours and I don't mind my own company. But tonight I didn't feel right. I wished there was someone I could talk to about my predicament, though Christ knows what I'd say. That I was a part-time professional killer as well as a copper, that I'd murdered more people in the past week than some self-respecting serial killers manage in the whole of their wicked careers; and how things were now spiralling out of control and my life was in danger. I'm not sure I'd have got much in the way of sympathy. I certainly didn't deserve any.

I'd bought myself some more of that creamy prawn risotto, so I made that for my supper, and washed it down with a couple of glasses of sparkling mineral water. Then I had a long shower, cleaned my teeth, and put some fresh clothes on.

In the end, I didn't bother going anywhere. It was raining too hard, although on the weather forecast they said it wouldn't last. Apparently a cold spell from Siberia was on the way. Nice. *Die Hard 2* was on one of the Sky movie channels so I watched that for a while, glugging steadily on a bottle of red wine until I finally fell asleep at about the time the evil South American dictator murders his guards.

I'd seen it twice before, so I wasn't worried. I knew he'd get his comeuppance and Bruce Willis would see that justice was done, just like a true copper should, not by following a load of bureaucratic rules and resigning himself to remaining a shitty little cog in a large and inefficient machine, but by bypassing the courts, the probation service and the prisons – those eternal obstacles to true punishment – and just blowing the heads off the baddies instead.

Which, if you're honest with yourself, is much the best way.

23

Danny phoned just after midnight, as I was emptying the ashtray into the bin in the kitchen. I thought about letting it go to answerphone but, given the circumstances, anyone phoning was probably worth talking to, and I picked up after the third ring.

I was disappointed to hear his voice, and the obvious fear in it. 'Dennis?'

'Danny. What is it? I thought you'd taken my advice and taken off for a bit.'

'Look, I saw the picture—'

'Careful what you say, Danny,' I said firmly. 'If you want to talk, do what we did last time, OK.'

'I'm scared, Dennis. Really fucking scared. And this time I'm not exaggerating. I've booked a flight, right, like you said. I'm off to Montego Bay tomorrow on the eleven thirty flight out of Gatwick . . .' His words were tumbling out. I stepped in to interrupt him again, fearful he was going to say something stupid, but he was determined to speak. 'But I was out tonight, down the pub for a quick drink, and I was on the way home just now and this car pulls up outside my flat with these two blokes in it. They slow right down, and clock me, and then one of them reaches down to pick something up.'

'All right, all right. Where are you now?'

'I'm at home. As soon as I saw them I was down the steps like shit off a stick. I got the key in the lock just as one of the blokes appeared at the top of the steps. He had something in his hand. I think it was a gun or something. I just turned the key, ran inside and double-locked the door behind me.'

'Has he gone, this bloke?'

'Yeah, yeah. I think so.'

'And you're pretty sure it was a gun he was carrying?' I was conscious that someone could be listening into this call, but I knew I was never going to get him to a payphone now.

'It looked like it, yeah. He had a long coat on and he had one hand in his pocket. He was pulling something out of it. I thought it was a gun.'

'But you didn't see for sure?'

'No, but I'm not fucking around, Dennis. This bloke was after me. I'd bet my fucking life on it.'

'OK. Calm down. What did he look like?'

'I didn't get much of a look. It was dark and I was trying to get away. He was dark-skinned—'

'Asian?'

'No, more Mediterranean or Arab.'

'And you'd never seen him before?'

'No, never.'

'How old?'

'I don't know. Maybe thirty.'

I tried to collect my thoughts for a moment. 'All right. Stay put. Make sure all the locks are shut on the doors and windows.'

'They are. I've done all that.'

'Good. I doubt if they'll hang around, whoever they are. No point getting people's suspicions up. All you need to do is stay put tonight, and catch that plane tomorrow. Just keep your wits about you when you leave the flat.'

'Who do you think they were, Dennis? Anything to do—'

'I told you,' I snapped, 'careful what you say. To be honest with you, they could be anyone. There are enough fucking criminals about. I can vouch for that. They may just have been opportunistic robbers.'

'No. They were definitely after me.'

'Well whoever they are they didn't get you, so keep calm. And remember, tomorrow night you'll be sitting on a beach sipping cocktails, away from all this shit and knowing that everyone'll have forgotten about it by the time you get back.'

'Look, Dennis. Can you come over? Just to check things are all right. You know, I'd appreciate it. It's just that I'm on my fucking own here.'

I sighed. 'Danny, it's gone midnight and I've drunk enough to sink a fucking battleship. I doubt if I'd be in a position even to find your place—'

'I'll pay for a taxi, don't worry about that.'

'Come on, what is this? You'll be all right. They'll be gone now, I guarantee it. And if you hear anything later, anyone trying to break in, just dial nine-nine-nine. Seriously, it'll be OK.'

Now it was Danny's turn to sigh. 'OK. OK, I'll do that. I just wanted to run it by you, that's all. If I'm in danger, then you're going to be too. Maybe you ought to think about a holiday as well.'

'Maybe I will. Perhaps I'll join you on the beach at Montego Bay in a few days. Look, take care, eh? And call me when you get back.'

'No problem,' he said, which were the last words he ever uttered to me. For all I know, they could have been the last words he ever uttered, full stop.

I hung up and walked over to the window, looking out across the quiet, rain-swept street. Nothing and no-one moved down there. Part of me felt guilty that I hadn't gone over to see him, but what could I have done? The advice I'd given him was as good as he was going to get, and I genuinely didn't believe he was in any danger, not now that he was safely inside his flat.

At the same time, however, I think I already knew his experience had been more than a simple street robbery. It was just that I didn't want to admit it to myself. Because, as he pointed out, if they were after him then, for all Raymond's protestations to the contrary, it meant they were almost certainly coming for me next.

24

At half past ten the following morning, I phoned Danny and got his answerphone. I didn't leave a message. I tried him on his mobile but it was switched off. I tried both numbers again an hour later, and again got no answer. In the cold light of day, I decided that he'd got off all right and was now thirty thousand feet above the Atlantic heading for the sunny Caribbean.

At a quarter to twelve, I went out and got some breakfast at a café I know on Caledonian Road, trying hard to forget my many troubles.

Carla Graham lived on the top floor of an attractive white-brick Edwardian townhouse set in a narrow cul-de-sac that had too many cars parked along it. I paid the sullen-faced cab driver a twenty and wasn't offered any change so, rather than argue, I left it at that and walked up the steps to the front door.

It was five to eight, and the night was cold and clear with an icy wind that found its way right through to the bones. There was a flashy-looking video entry system and I rang the buzzer for number 24C. After a few seconds, Carla's voice came over the intercom.

'Hello, Dennis,' she said, sounding not too displeased that I'd made it.

I smiled up at the camera and said hello, and she told me to come straight up the stairs to the third floor. The imposing-looking front door clicked open and I stepped gratefully inside. It locked automatically behind me.

She was waiting for me at the top of the stairs with the door open behind her. Although only casually dressed in a black sweatshirt and trackpants, she still looked close to stunning. It was something in the way she carried herself. Hers was a natural beauty, the sort you can tell looks just as good at six a.m. as it does at six p.m. Her hair looked recently washed, and once again I noticed a light aroma of perfume as we shook hands. What she was doing in the grim and worthy world of social work remained as much a mystery as ever.

'Please come in,' she said with a smile, and led me inside, through the hallway and into the lounge. 'Take a seat.' She waved her arm, indicating that I could park myself anywhere.

It was a sumptuous room with high ceilings and big bay windows that gave it an airy feel, even on a cold winter's night like this one. The floor was polished wood and partially covered with thick Persian rugs. All the furnishings were obviously expensive yet tasteful, and the walls were painted in a light, pastelly green that shouldn't have suited it but somehow did. Normally I wouldn't have noticed any of this, or very little of it anyway, but this was the type of room that demanded attention.

'This is very nice,' I said. 'Maybe you should have been an interior designer.'

'It's one of my hobbies,' she said. 'It's a lot of work, and it costs a bit of money, but it's worth it. Now, what do you want to drink?'

There was a half-full glass of red wine on the coffee table next to an expensive-looking bottle. A cigarette burned in the ashtray.

'Well, if it's not imposing, I wouldn't say no to a drop of that wine.'

'I'll get you a glass,' she said, and stepped out of the room.

I removed my coat and sat down on a comfortable chair, feeling more than a little awkward. It was an odd situation. On the one hand, I was intensely attracted to Carla Graham, while on the other, I saw her as someone who at the very least was withholding information in a murder inquiry and who, at worst, was a suspect. In the end, I found it difficult to decide whether I'd rather fuck her or nick her. I knew I wanted to do one of the two.

She came back and poured the wine before handing me the glass. Once again I caught the smell of her perfume. I realized, with some horror, that it was giving me the beginnings of a hard-on.

She sat down on the sofa opposite me, picked up her cigarette out of the ashtray, and looked earnestly in my direction, as if she had no idea why I might be there.

'So, what can I do for you, Dennis? You said there were some things that needed clearing up.'

I cleared my throat. 'Yeah, there are. Mark Wells, the pimp we've charged, suggested that he once gave one of his shirts – a dark green one with medium-size collars – to Molly Hagger. This would have been a few months ago, and it would have been far too big for her. Did you ever see a shirt like that in Molly's possession?'

She furrowed her brow, thinking about it for a couple of seconds. 'No, I don't recall anything like that. Why would he have given her a shirt?'

'I don't know. He just said he gave it to her. I expect he was lying.'

'Why's it relevant to the case?'

'It probably isn't. Just something I wanted to check.' She gave me a puzzled look. 'What might be more relevant, though,' I continued, lighting a cigarette, 'is why you told me at our first meeting that you didn't know Miriam Fox when I know you do.'

If my statement had shocked her, she didn't show it. She just looked put out that I'd effectively accused her of lying, especially as I was sitting in her comfortable chair enjoying a glass of her good wine. And it was good, too.

'I don't know what you're talking about, Detective Milne.' No Dennis now. 'I never knew Miriam Fox.'

I locked eyes with her, trying to stare her down, but she held my gaze. 'Look, Carla . . . Miss Graham. There's no point denying it. I've seen Miriam Fox's phone records. There are five calls logged. Three were made by her, two by you.'

Carla shook her head, her face a picture of innocence. 'There must be some mistake.'

'There's no mistake. I checked. And I double-checked. You had five conversations with Miriam in the last few weeks of her life, and God knows how many before that. Now, I want to know what those conversations were about, and why you wanted them kept hidden.'

'Look, I don't have to answer questions like this. I want my lawyer present if you're going to carry on.'

'Do you? Are you sure about that?'

'Yes, I'm very sure. Here you are, near enough accusing me of murder in my home—'

'I'm not accusing you of anything. I'm just trying to tie up any loose ends. At the moment, we're simply two people having a conversation. None of what you say's admissible in a court of law.'

'So why the hell should I talk about it?'

'Because if you don't, I'm going to have to go back to my superior and tell him about the phone records. At the moment, I'm the only person who knows anything about them. If your explanation satisfies me that you know nothing about the murder, I'm prepared to keep it that way; if it doesn't, I'm going to tell him anyway. At least this way you get your chance to tell me your side of the story without anyone else being involved.'

'So you're here unofficially? Like the last time we met?'

'I'm here in a semi-official capacity. It could go either way. Now, what were those conversations with Miriam Fox about?'

She sighed, as if bowing to the inevitable. 'I suppose I half thought this was what you were coming round about.'

She finished her cigarette and immediately lit another one, taking a deep drag. I sat watching her impassively, wondering what I was going to hear, and what I was going to do when I'd heard it.

'Miriam Fox was blackmailing me.'

'What about?'

'About an area of my private life.'

'Go on.'

'She knew something about me that I would rather have kept secret and she was trying to exploit the situation to her advantage. She was like that.'

'So I keep hearing. And this area of your private life ... what is it exactly?'

She looked me firmly in the eye. 'I'm what's colloquially called a lady of the night, Detective Milne. I escort middle-aged, usually middle-class, men for money. Sometimes I fuck them.' There was a defiant expression on her face as she spoke, as if she was daring me to criticize her.

I didn't bother rising to the bait. I've heard plenty of worse revelations than that in my time, although I have to say it did catch me off guard. 'Well, I suppose it stands to reason. You don't get these sorts of furnishings on civil servant's wages.'

'You're not shocked that a person in my position is involved in something like that?'

I smiled and took a decent-sized sip from my wine, thinking that this was something of a surreal moment. 'People in positions a lot higher than yours are involved in that type of thing, though usually as customers rather than suppliers, so, no, I'm not shocked. Is this a regular thing, this escort work?'

She nodded. 'Yes, I suppose it is. I tend to do a couple of nights a week, sometimes more.'

'Is that what you were doing last night?'

'None of your business.'

'So how did some low-level street girl like Miriam Fox find out about your extra-curricular activities? I presume you weren't . . . moving in the same circles.'

'Let's just say she found out.'

'How did she know who you were?'

'Two or three years ago, when she first ran away, she was arrested for soliciting and ended up at Coleman House. She didn't stop long, a couple of weeks at most. She was a very difficult girl to handle and she seemed to have a hatred of authority. I think there might have been problems at home that had helped to shape her personality, but she never talked about them. In fact, about the only time she did talk was to throw abuse. There were quite a few confrontations with staff, including myself, and then one day she decided she'd had enough and walked out. Like a lot of the girls do.'

'Wasn't it a bit dangerous to suggest to us when we first interviewed you that you didn't know her?'

She shifted in her seat and put one leg up on the sofa. It was a vaguely provocative pose, although she didn't seem to notice it.

'Not really. None of the current staff were there, when she was there, and originally she gave a false name when we took her in. It would have been difficult to check up on it, and why would you have bothered?'

Which was fair enough, I suppose. 'And when was the next time you saw her?'

'But you said she was blackmailing you.'

'She was. Look, I'd really rather not go into details, Mr Milne.'

'I'm sure you wouldn't. But it's important I know.'

'So you can calculate whether I'm telling the truth or not?'

I nodded. 'Basically, yes.'

She picked up her wine and took a large drink, as if fortifying herself. 'Look, I'll be honest with you. I don't actually know how she found out. I can guess, but that's about it.' I waited in silence for her to continue. 'Let me start with how it works. My clients tend to be businessmen, men with plenty of spare money. The usual procedure is for us to go somewhere for dinner, then back to a hotel, or their place, for the rest. That way, I keep control of the proceedings, and don't get myself into any situation where I'm unnecessarily vulnerable.'

'That stands to reason.'

'A few weeks ago, though, one of my regular clients – a high-powered lawyer, and someone I've been seeing for several years – was caught kerbcrawling in King's Cross. You might have heard about it.'

I nodded, remembering the case vaguely, though not the name of the punter concerned. Kerbcrawling wasn't big news these days, even when it involved such a richly deserving case as a wealthy lawyer.

'Apparently, it was the second time it had happened to him. He'd been caught doing the same thing a few years ago in

Paddington.' She shook her head, as if annoyed with herself for getting involved with someone so unreliable. 'I was worried, I didn't need that sort of hassle, not the sort that could easily compromise me. Afterwards, I went round to his place and confronted him. I asked how often he did it and he swore that both times had been one-offs. He was obviously ashamed about it. He was also obviously lying. No-one's that unlucky. So I asked some of the girls in the home if they knew anything about him, whether he'd ever propositioned any of them, more as a matter of conversation than anything else. It was easy enough to do. The case had made some headlines in the local paper, so people seemed quite happy to talk about it.'

'And?'

'And several of the older ones had had some involvement with him. One had even got to go back to his apartment in Hampstead Heath, the same place I'd visited on many occasions. Apparently, he also liked to do it without a condom, which might have been one of the attractions of using street girls. They don't tend to be so fussy. So I ended our arrangement with him straight away. I'm not interested in dealing with people who lie to me and who have such a dubious attitude to the sexual health of both themselves and others.'

'Then two, maybe three days after I'd confronted him, I got a telephone call at Coleman House. It was Miriam Fox. She told me she knew that I'd been seeing the lawyer, and that I'd been getting paid for my time.' She sighed. 'As I said, I couldn't honestly say exactly how she found out. I think he must have used her services a number of times, so she'd almost certainly been at his apartment at one time or another. Maybe she found some evidence that I'd been there.'

'Like what?'

'I told you, I don't know. Maybe she was leaving one night

when I was arriving; maybe she was watching the place and saw me there. You know what some of these street girls are like: they go to a place, then tell their pimp how many valuables the punter's got, then they plan to rob it. She could have been surveying the apartment for her pimp, and saw me.' She shrugged her shoulders hopelessly. 'The point is, she knew. That's all I can tell you."

'What did she want from you?' I asked.

'The same as most blackmailers. Money. She told me that if I didn't pay her five thousand pounds, she'd expose me to the local authority and the newspapers.'

'That must have given you a bit of a shock.'

'It did. I couldn't believe what I was hearing. It just seemed so ... unfortunate.'

'What did you say to her?'

'There were other people in the room with me at the time so I couldn't really say a lot. I got a number off her and told her I'd phone her back. When I did call her back, she repeated her demand for the money. I told her I didn't have that sort of cash and we had a bit of an argument. Eventually she said she'd settle for two thousand. For the time being. Those were her words. For the time being. I repeated that it was going to take a while. She gave me a week.'

'Did you ever give her any money?'

'I never actually met up with her at all. A week later she phoned me on my mobile – I'd given her the number – and I stalled her again. I said I'd managed to get some of it, but not enough. I told her she'd have to give me another week. To be honest, I didn't know what to do. I knew it wouldn't stop with just one payment, that she'd come back to me for more and would keep coming back until she'd bled me dry. I mean, she was a drug addict and she wasn't going to beat her addiction suddenly. And she was the sort of girl who would have told the authorities anyway, just to spite me.'

'What happened after the other week was up?'

'I phoned her on her mobile and left a message. I told her I was no longer interested in giving her any money and she could go fuck herself as far as I was concerned."

'That was a bit of a brave move.'

She shrugged again. 'It was a calculated risk. I'd given it a lot of thought. I knew she'd probably report me, but I was hoping that neither the authorities nor the papers would take the word of some crack-addicted runaway. And even if they did investigate, I thought I'd probably be able to cover my tracks well enough so that they wouldn't discover anything. Anyway, she called back the next day and tried to persuade me that I was making a mistake. She was pissed off that I was calling her bluff, and she sounded pretty desperate as well. Perhaps she owed someone some money – her pimp, or somebody like that. In the end, I was almost feeling sorry for her.' She managed a slight smile when she said this, and took a sip of her wine, more confident, it seemed, now that she'd got this off her chest. 'We talked for a couple of minutes, she got quite hysterical, called me a bitch, said I'd regret messing her around, and then I just hung up.

'And that really was the end of it. It was the last time I spoke to her. A few days later she was dead.' She lit another cigarette, and I noticed her hands were shaking a little. 'That doesn't sound good, does it? Someone blackmailing me, and then they end up murdered?' Again, I didn't say anything, just sat there and let her speak. 'That's the reason, or one of the reasons anyway, I didn't say anything to you. So, now you know. What are you going to do about it? Are you going to tell your superior?"

'Well, it would be difficult to avoid the fact that you've got a motive for wanting her out of the way . . . but then so have a few other people. She was clearly the sort of girl who attracts enemies. Did you kill her?"

She looked me in the eye. 'No, I didn't. I had nothing to do with it. I might have had a motive, but not a strong enough one. Even if someone had believed her, I wouldn't really have been losing that much. I'm getting tired of the job at Coleman House anyway. It never seems to be doing anything to improve the lot of the people I'm meant to be helping, and I doubt if it accounts for more than a third of my earnings these days. I certainly wouldn't kill anyone over it.' She finished her wine and poured the last drops from the bottle in equal measures into her glass and mine. I doubt if there was more than a mouthful each. 'Do you believe me, Mr Milne?'

It was a good question. On balance, yes, I did. Her story sounded plausible. Coincidental, but still plausible. More so than any alternatives I might have thought up, and I was almost certain she hadn't delivered the fatal blow. She was tall and lithe, but it had been a man, and a strong one at that, who had killed Miriam Fox. That meant that for Carla to be guilty she would have needed to have got someone else involved in the plot, which, as far as I could see, would have defeated the object of it in the first place. And she was right too. All to defend a job managing a care home for delinquent kids? Somehow I didn't think so.

I sighed. 'I'm not going to take it any further, put it like that.'

'But you don't believe me?'

'I don't really know what to believe. It's a pretty strange story, you've got to admit that. One minute you're a high-powered social worker managing a kid's home, the next you're an escort girl with a nice line in kinky customers.'

'You certainly know how to make it sound degrading.'

I gulped my mouthful of wine. 'Well, isn't it? Getting fucked for money by middle-aged men who'll dip their wick with anyone who'll take the cash off them? It's hardly what you'd call satisfying and useful work.'

'I'm not going to apologize for what I do. I provide a service, nobody gets hurt, and sometimes, you know ... sometimes it is quite satisfying. And if I get paid for it too ... it's all the better, isn't it?'

'I don't know. Is it?'

'Have you ever paid for sex, Mr Milne? Dennis?'

I smiled. 'Why? Are you offering?'

She smiled back. 'I'm very choosy about who I sleep with.'

'Well, I guess that's me out then. A nosey, cynical copper's hardly a prime catch.'

She didn't say anything and we sat in silence for a few moments, both, I think, pondering our positions in the world and what we'd actually achieved. It struck me then that the two of us weren't really all that dissimilar. Both leading murky double lives we'd far rather keep deeply buried. The difference was, I'd kill to preserve the secrecy of mine. At least I hoped it was the difference.

'Do you want another drink?' she asked me eventually.

I looked at her, not sure whether she actually wanted me to stay or not. She gave a weary smile back, which I took to mean yes. 'Are you having one?'

She nodded. 'Why not?'

I watched her as she turned round in her seat and removed a bottle of brandy from a cupboard behind the sofa. Her bottom looked remarkably pert.

'Will this do?'

'Perfect,' I said as she put two fresh glasses down on the table and poured a hefty slug into each.

I offered her a cigarette from my pack, but she opted for a Silk

Cut. I lit mine and sat back in my seat, thinking that there was something about her story that turned me on. The prim, well-spoken manager who turns into the whore by night. I know it's the fantasy of a lot of men, and in that respect I was just like everyone else.

'So how did a respectable lady like yourself get into . . . escort work?'

She took a drink of the brandy and pulled the sort of face you pull when you're quaffing neat spirits. 'It's a long story.'

'That's just the way I like them.'

'I was married for a long time to a man I really cared about. He was a social worker, like me. We met at university, fell in love, and that was it really. Neither of us really believed in marriage, but I think we wanted a way of showing how committed we were to each other. We both totally believed in what we were doing; I suppose people do when they're young. We didn't have a lot of money, but it didn't really seem to matter. We rented a nice little two-bedroom flat in Camden, and things were good. You know what it's like when you're in love. You're happy with your lot.'

I nodded to show I understood, but I wasn't sure if I did.

'Then, one day, he told me he'd met someone else. A girl in the department. He didn't even seem that sorry about it. He talked about it as if it was one of those things; something that couldn't be helped. All our time together, eight years of marriage, the whole relationship . . . it ended just like that.' She gave me a look that demanded understanding, if not sympathy, her face a combination of sadness and anger. 'He moved out the next day and applied for a transfer to York, which was where she came from. Apparently she was pregnant and wanted to be closer to home. Sometimes I think that's why he went for her. Because she wanted kids, and I wanted to wait for a while.'

'It must have been very hard on you,' I said, stating the fucking obvious.

'It was. I was suddenly on my own for the first time in a long time, and what made it worse was that without Steve I couldn't pay the rent on the flat, so I had to move out of there too, and that part really hurt. I'd worked so hard to make it a home, spent hours and hours getting it just right, and in the end it was all for nothing.

'So, there I was, broke, single, and depressed. Even the job didn't seem to be going right. I was moving up the ladder, but not as fast as I'd have liked, and the work was providing a lot of frustrations. Kids who you put so much time into, who you really thought were going to make it, ended up overdosing on smack and barbiturates, or turning their back on you, and all that bureaucratic interfering. It was a real low point in my life, probably the lowest. At one time it even crossed my mind to, you know . . .' She trailed off.

'But eventually I pulled myself together and life went on. But I was a changed person, Dennis. I lost a lot of my idealism, I was harder, more focused. Then, one day, I read an article about a housewife who worked in the days as a part-time call girl. She didn't do it for the money. I think she was more interested in the adventure, and maybe the sex, but she seemed happy with the way it worked out and at the time money for me was still very, very tight, so I thought, I could do that. I'm attractive, I'm quite good company. And I'm certainly lonely enough to appreciate the attention, even if it was from people I wouldn't normally have associated with. So I decided to give it a go.'

'You've been doing it for a while, then?'

'I suppose I have. I've never really thought about it. It's a part of my life now.'

'I still can't believe it,' I said, taking a sip of the brandy. 'When

I first met you I'd never have guessed that, you know, you were involved in this sort of thing. I'm not condemning it. It's just a bit of a shock.'

Carla shrugged.

'And do you enjoy it?'

She appeared to think about it for a moment. 'Sometimes. Not all the time. Maybe not even much of the time. But sometimes. So, how about you? Did you always want to be a copper, or did you just fall into it?'

I took a long drag on my cigarette. 'I think I always wanted to be one. You know, when I was growing up, I had this real sense of justice. I hated bullies, and I hated it when people did something bad and got away with it. I thought it would be really good to do a job where you could stop that sort of thing from happening, and when it had already happened you could punish the perpetrators. I also thought it would be a bit of an adventure.'

'And has it been?'

I took a couple of seconds to answer. 'Well, I suppose it's had its moments, but, to be honest with you, they've been pretty few and far between. A lot of the time it's just endless paperwork and dealing with people who live shitty lives and do all these shitty things to each other for the most mundane reasons. And, you know, you can never seem to stop them.'

'That's human nature, Dennis. It's what a lot of people are like. They grow up without values, alienated from the society they live in. You can't just turn them into model citizens at the drop of a hat.'

'But everyone's taught right from wrong. Whether it's in the media, at school . . . It's just a lot of them aren't interested. They have no fear of doing wrong; that's the problem. I guess it's because they have no respect for us, the people who are meant to be stopping them. You should hear the shit we put up with every day.'

She smiled. 'It's probably exactly the same as the shit we put up with every day.'

'Why do we do it, eh?'

'Because we care,' she said, and I suppose that was as good a reason as any. Although the problem I had was that I'd stopped caring a long time ago, and perhaps, in a way, so had she.

I finished my brandy and she refilled the glasses. When they were full, she picked hers up and raised it for a toast.

'To the carers,' she said.

'To the carers,' I intoned.

We clinked glasses, and once again I got a smell of that wonderful perfume. I was feeling relaxed now, at ease with the world; the drink and the company removing the heavy loads of worry from my shoulders.

We talked for a long time. An hour . . . two hours . . . maybe more, I can't honestly remember. Pretty much a bottle of brandy's worth. Not really about anything in particular. Just things.

At some point I began stroking her smooth bare feet while we chatted, my head spinning with booze and lust and confidence as my words tumbled out. Her toes were painted a beautiful plum colour and I bent down to kiss them one by one, taking them into my mouth, revelling in the intimacy of the contact. She moaned faintly, and I knew then that I'd conquered her. That this was it. That I was going to make love to the woman I'd fantasized about these past few nights, who I'd thought was far too good for me, but who had now shown her true, vulnerable colours, and who I wanted with a desperation that even now I find impossible to describe.

25

When I woke up I had that feeling you sometimes get where you don't know where the hell you are. Well, where I was was in a beautiful king-sized bed in a darkened room. To my right, I could see the dull half-light of a winter morning peeping round the edges of long, crimson curtains. I was on my own in the bed, but there was a faint smell of perfume in the air and the noise of someone moving about coming from somewhere outside the door.

It took maybe three seconds to work everything out and remember the events of the night before. The sex had been surprisingly ferocious; either she was a very good actor (which I suppose a lot of women in her situation must be) or she'd really been enjoying herself. I preferred to think it was the latter, and was pleased with my own performance, which had been solid if very much second fiddle to that of the opposition. I guess she'd had a lot more practice than me.

I sat up in bed and looked at my watch. It was twenty past seven and my head hurt. Monday morning, the start of a new week. I wasn't looking forward to going back to the station, and once again thoughts of jacking it all in drifted into my mind. I had the money to make a move. It was just a question of whether I had the guts.

The door opened and Carla appeared, dressed in a thin black kimono-style dressing gown, carrying two cups of coffee. She was looking six a.m. good.

'Oh, you're awake, then?' she said, handing me one of the cups. 'I thought I was going to have to pour a bucket of water over you.'

'I'm usually a pretty heavy sleeper,' I said, 'and I had enough exercise yesterday to put me out until this afternoon.'

She smiled but didn't say anything as she put her cup down on top of a chest of drawers and switched on the main light. She slipped off the dressing gown to reveal a naked body that seemed to have aged perfectly. I watched her hungrily as she slowly dressed, starting with expensive-looking black underwear.

'It's a pity you've got an early meeting,' I told her.

'Don't I know it,' she said, without looking round. 'I've got a hangover from hell. Drinking at home always seems to do that to me.'

I bit the bullet. 'Are we going to see each other again?'

She pulled on a pair of tights. 'Look, Dennis, I don't want to hurry anything, you know. Last night was, well, a one-off.'

'Is that what you want it to be?'

She came over to the bed and sat down on it, facing me. 'Remember what you came over here for: to question me about a murder in which I was a suspect. You still haven't told me straight that I'm not one. Things happened, but that's because we were both pretty inebriated. It's not exactly the ideal way to start a relationship, is it?'

'I'm not proposing marriage, Carla. It'd just be nice to see you again, that's all.'

'Do you know what you're getting involved in, Dennis? I see other men. It's not something I'm going to stop overnight, and I don't know how easy you'll find it to deal with that.'

'I'm quite a liberal guy.'

'You're a copper.'

'I'm a liberal copper and I had a good time last night. I got the impression you did too. It's an experience I want to repeat, that's all. Shit, I'd even pay for it.' She shot me a bit of a dirty look. 'I'm joking,' I told her.

'Look, I'm not trying to give you the brush-off, Dennis, but my life's complicated. The last time I had a boyfriend, he tried to get me to change the way I live, and I'm not the sort of person who likes to be told what to do. I value my independence. And I know it sounds shallow, but after what I went through after the divorce, I value the money as well.'

I leaned over and patted her on the knee, letting my hand linger there for a moment. She didn't, it has to be said, seem desperately interested.

'I understand, but I'd appreciate it if we could at least pop out for a drink one night.'

She stood up and pecked me on the forehead. 'Yes. We can do that. Give me a call some time.'

Realizing that I wasn't going to tempt her back into bed, I got up and started putting on my crumpled clothes – clothes I was now going to have to turn up for work in.

By the time I'd located everything and put it on, Carla was at the dressing table applying the finishing touches to her face. I stopped beside her and bent down to kiss her on the head. She patted me on the hip in a way that reminded me of the way you pat a dog.

She must have seen the creases of disappointment on my face because she managed a weak smile. 'I'm sorry, Dennis. I'm not the best person in the mornings. I take a while to get going,. It's normally lunchtime before I can get enthusiastic about anything.'

'No problem. I understand. I'll call you, then.'

'Yes.'

'Have a nice day.' That one just slipped out, for want of something better.

I winked at her as I shut the bedroom door behind me and headed out, wondering if I'd done something wrong. Probably, although whatever it was I couldn't for the life of me work out. But that's women for you. Complicated and unpredictable.

Just like my days were becoming.

26

Work that day was mundane. There was a meeting first thing about the mugging of the old lady. Apparently she'd survived the weekend but had yet to regain consciousness, and Knox was pissed off. Things were not going well in our division crime-wise, and the clear-up rate on offences of violence was now hovering below the 20 per cent mark, which, as he told us, was utterly unacceptable and wouldn't look too clever in the performance league tables.

To remedy this, however, there was going to be a series of raids the following morning at the homes of a number of mugging suspects, aged between twelve and sixteen, one or more of whom could well have been involved in the attack on the old lady. There were nine homes in all to search, so it was going to involve all of us. 'It's time to take the battle to them,' he concluded loudly, but for me the message was muted. I remembered him saying exactly the same thing a few months back about crack dealers in the area. We'd simultaneously raided a total of fourteen premises in an operation Knox had cunningly codenamed 'Street Shock', had recovered drugs with a street value of more than twenty-five grand, and made a total of nine arrests. Five were later released without charge; one absconded while on bail and hadn't been seen since; one pleaded guilty and received a fine and suspended sentence; one was acquitted by a jury who believed his story that he hadn't known the stuff was in the house; and one was now in custody awaiting trial, having previously been released on bail and re-arrested twice in the space of three weeks for dealing. The only shock was the one the tax-payers would get if they ever discovered what a pathetically negligible effect such an expensive and time-consuming operation had had on both the criminals and the local crime figures. It was hardly a wonder our clear-up rate was so bad. Most of the time, it just wasn't worth the bother.

I had a brief chat with Malik after the meeting had concluded, but neither of us had time to cover much ground. He was now heavily involved in the mugging case and was keen to make a good impression.

After that, Knox had me writing up reports on all my current cases, which took all morning and a good part of the afternoon. He told me Capper wanted to take a look at what I was working on to see if there was any mileage in giving me additional resources; in other words, to see if there were any mistakes I was making. Apparently, the two of them were particularly keen for movement on the armed robbery case, which appeared to have ground to a complete halt. Which was true. It had. But I wasn't quite sure what more I or any of my colleagues could do to kick-start it. If no-one gives you information and the perpetrators haven't left any obvious clues, a detective's room for manoeuvre is somewhat limited. But it transpired that the Chief Superintendent had had a meeting with representatives of the Kurdish community (both the stabbing victims – the shop's proprietor and the customer – were Kurds) who'd told him they wouldn't rest until the culprits were caught. They had also raised that possibility, so dreaded of all senior Met officers, that racism might be playing a part in holding things up. Obviously, the Chief Super was keen to show his community bridge-building skills, and since much of the work on the case had been done by me, I was going to have to indulge in some serious arse-covering. Knox also suggested that at a later date I too might have to prostrate myself in front of these so-called representatives of the community so that they could have a go at me as well – another good reason to resign, if ever I needed one.

It was difficult to concentrate on the report writing. I kept thinking of the sex with Carla, and wishing that I could repeat the experience. I had to make a conscious effort not to call her number. I knew she wouldn't appreciate it. Not today. She was, as she said, a woman who liked her independence. Fair enough. I'm a man who likes mine – most of the time anyway – but I still harboured hopes that I could get something going with her.

Some time around lunchtime, Jean Ashcroft phoned again. She asked me if I'd been round to see Danny. I told her I hadn't but that I'd phoned him, and everything seemed all right. She said she'd tried to get hold of him but he wasn't answering his phones, and I mentioned that he'd gone away on holiday for a couple of weeks.

'Did you find out where he was getting his money from?' she asked. 'It's just not like him to have any, you know.'

I told her that I wasn't sure (I'd given up on the police informant story, thinking it might prompt her into further investigation), but said that I didn't think it was anything to be overly concerned about. 'Maybe he's got less money than you think,' I added. 'You can get these last-minute deals for hardly anything now, so I expect he just picked up something cheap. I checked with some colleagues up his way and they say he's not in the frame for anything they've got on the go.'

'But he didn't say anything about what was worrying him?'

'No. But I wouldn't read too much into it. He didn't sound like he had anything serious on his mind, and I can usually tell. It's my job.'

'Did you say it was yesterday he went on holiday?'

'That's what he told me he was doing when I called him.'

'Well, I've tried his mobile this morning and he's still not answering.'

I said that this was probably because he couldn't get a signal where he was, and I think I managed to convince her not to panic about it. 'He'll call back soon, I'm sure,' I said, but for the first time I began to get a bad feeling about it all. I made a mental note to call Raymond when I got the chance, just to confirm that neither he nor his jittery associates had tried to track Danny down. Finally, I said my goodbyes to Jean and got back to my report writing.

I left the station at five thirty that night, having got the feeling that under Capper I was going to be pushed to one side of things, and that my time at the station really was coming to an end. I fancied a drink, if only to get rid of the dry, sour taste in my mouth and the worries constantly surfacing in my head, but decided instead to go and visit DI Welland in hospital. It was duty, really. I don't like going to hospitals (who does?), but Welland needed some moral support. When I'd been put in one three years ago, having received an enthusiastic tap on the head with an iron bar when an arrest went wrong, he'd visited me three times in the six days I'd been in there. The least I could do now was return the favour.

He was being treated at St Thomas's, and it was five past six when I got there, armed with a jumbo box of wine gums, which were always his favourite, and a couple of American true crime magazines.

Hospitals always smell so uninviting and, in England at least, they usually look it too. Being a copper, I've had to spend more than my fair share of time in them. Aside from the many visits I'd made to interview victims and sometimes the perpetrators of crime, I'd ended up being on the receiving end of treatment on three separate occasions, all work-related. There'd been the iron bar incident; the time during my probationary period when a mob of rampaging Chelsea fans had used me for kicking practice; and an incident early on in the Poll Tax riot when a huge crop-headed dyke had whacked me over the back of the head with a four by four while I'd been trying to resuscitate some old granny who'd just fainted. In that case my assailant had been arrested on the spot and, ironically enough, had turned out to be a nurse.

Welland was in a ward at the back of the hospital and they'd got him a private room. He was sitting up in bed in his pyjamas reading the *Evening Standard* when I knocked and went in. He was much paler than usual, as if he was a bit seasick, but he didn't appear to have lost any weight, and all in all he didn't look quite as rough as I'd expected.

He looked up and managed a smile when he saw me. 'Hello, Dennis.'

'How are you, boss?'

'I'm sure I've been worse, but I can't honestly remember when.'

'Well, you look all right for it. Have they started the treatment yet?'

'No, it's been postponed until tomorrow. Lack of specialist staff, something like that.'

'That's the NHS for you. They make the Met look over-manned. Here, I brought you these.' I put the wine gums and magazines down by the side of the bed. He thanked me, and with a quick gesture offered me a seat.

I sat down in a threadbare chair next to him and said something else to the effect that he looked remarkably healthy given the circumstances, which is the sort of inane bullshit you have to come out with at times like this, even though no-one ever believes it. I once remember telling a girl whose face had been partially melted by acid thrown at her by an ex-boyfriend that she'd be all right in time. Of course she wouldn't and neither would Welland.

'It's good of you to come, Dennis. Thanks.' He sat back further into the pillows, looking tired, and I noticed that he sounded short of breath when he spoke.

'Well I wouldn't say it was a pleasure, sir, because visiting a hospital never is, but I wanted you to know we hadn't forgotten about you or anything.'

'How is work? I miss it, you know. Never really thought I would, but I do.'

'It's the same as ever,' I told him. 'Too many criminals, not enough coppers. Plenty to keep us busy.'

He shook his head. 'It's a hiding to nothing sometimes, isn't it?'

'It sure is that,' I agreed, wondering where this conversation was going.

'You know something, Dennis. I've always thought you were a good copper. You know the job, you know what it's all about.'

He turned his head and looked at me just a little bit too closely for my liking. I had the feeling this was going to turn into one of those deep conversations about life and policework I could really do without.

'I've always done my best, sir.'

'We've known each other a long time, haven't we?'

'Yeah, we have. Eight years you've been my boss now.'

'Eight years . . . Christ, is it that long? Time just goes, doesn't it? One minute you're a young copper with it all in front of you, and before you know it . . . before you know it, you're this . . . Sat in a hospital bed waiting to begin the treatment that could save your life.' He was no longer looking at me, but was staring up at the ceiling, seemingly lost in his thoughts. 'Funny how things go, isn't it?'

'Yeah, it is.' It was. 'Eight years.' I shook my head. 'Shit.'

'You know, these days they've got so many new faces. All these graduates who've come in with their new ideas. A lot of them are good blokes, don't get me wrong, and women . . . but they don't really understand the fundamentals of policework. Not like you and me. We're old school, Dennis. That's what we are. Old school.'

'I think we're a dying breed, sir. In a few years' time we'll be gone altogether.'

'And you know what? They'll miss us. They don't like us, they think we're dinosaurs, but when we're gone they'll miss us.'

'People never get appreciated until they're gone,' I said.

'That's exactly it. These new people – these men and women with their degrees – they just don't understand policework. Not like you and me, Dennis. They don't know that sometimes you've got to bend the rules to get on.'

I felt a sudden sense of shock. I'd always been very careful not to involve Welland in any of my murkier dealings, and as far as I was aware he knew nothing about any wrongdoing I'd ever committed.

'I've always tried to play it fair, sir. Sometimes I've had to lean hard on people, but it's always been by the book.'

'Sometimes you've got to do these things,' he said, continuing as if I hadn't spoken, still staring up towards the ceiling. 'People don't realize the sort of job we have to do, the sort of scum we have to deal with the whole time. They just take the whole thing for granted. Do you remember when the Home Secretary visited that time?'

I remembered all right. Two years ago it had been. He'd marched in all smiles, pumping hands left, right and centre. Telling us how he was going to increase recruitment and how he and the government were going to introduce legislation to make it easier for the police to gain convictions and harder for the criminals to avoid the long arm of the law, which, needless to say, had never happened. Come to think of it, he'd used the phrase 'taking the war to the criminals' as well. Maybe that's where Knox had got it from.

'Who could forget?' I said.

'He talked about how he really empathized with us, how he knew how hard the job we had to do was. But he didn't. None of them do. If they did, they'd untie our hands and pay us more. Make it worthwhile upholding the law.' He sighed. 'Sometimes you've got to bend the rules a bit, make a few pennies here and there to supplement things. If a piece of evidence goes missing, who's going to notice? In the end, it's only going to get burned anyway. Why not make something out of it?'

Still he wouldn't look at me. I felt increasingly uncomfortable sitting there in that shitty little room listening to things I really didn't want to hear. In a way, he sounded as though he was rambling, but I knew he wasn't.

'What are you trying to say, sir?'

'You know what I'm trying to say, Dennis. I know you've bent the rules in the past—'

'I've always tried to play it fair,' I said, repeating the phrase

I'd used earlier, but it sounded lame now, and I knew it. 'I don't think I've—'

This time he turned and faced me. 'Dennis, I know you've done things in the past you shouldn't have. I know it. No question. Stuff's gone missing, sometimes bad stuff like dope, and you're the only person who could have taken it.' I tried to say something, but he put up a hand to stop me. He wanted to say his piece, and nothing was going to stop him. 'You're a good copper. You always have been. But I'm not blind. And I'm not stupid. I'm not saying you're bent, not by any means, but I know you've cut corners and made a bit of illicit cash here and there; done a few dodgy deals. Fair enough, I say. You've worked hard over the years. You've put away a lot of very nasty people, people who'd probably still be free if it wasn't for your efforts. I know that in a couple of cases you've had to use – how shall I put it? – unconventional means to put people down. And I understand that, I really do. The law's a straitjacket sometimes. I know it and you know it, because we're old school. These new people, they don't have a clue how it works . . .' He turned away again, presumably signifying that he'd got what he wanted off his chest.

For a moment I just sat there, not sure what to say. What could I say? He had me bang to rights, and the thing was, I'd never seen it coming. Maybe I'd just been far too cocky for my own good. I exhaled slowly and wished I could have a cigarette.

'You know what I like about you, sir? You never mince your words.'

'No point. Not when you're in my position.'

'What have the doctors said about the . . . the er . . . ?'

'The cancer? You can say the word, you know.'

'Do they think they've got it early?'

'It doesn't look too good, Dennis. It might be all right, but the odds aren't in my favour. I'm not sure how much they're in yours either.'

I felt an immediate spasm of fear. 'What do you mean, sir?'

He sighed, and there was a short silence before he continued. 'I want you to be careful, Dennis. I've always liked you, you know. A lot more than sometimes I've let on. I liked the way you never backed down. You've got guts, and that's something in very short supply these days.'

'What are you trying to say, sir?'

He turned to face me again. 'I'm saying, watch your back.'

'And what's making you say that?' I asked, my voice steady. 'What have you heard that I ought to know about?'

'I had visitors earlier.' There was a pause. I didn't say anything. He sighed. 'Two men from CIB.'

So they were on to me. In a way it had always been coming, ever since they'd issued the e-fit, but I still had difficulty containing my shock. 'What did they say?'

'They asked a lot of questions.'

'What kind of questions?'

'About your background, your attitude ... all sorts. They wanted to know whether you had more money than might be expected of a serving copper, whether there'd ever been any suggestion of ... corruption.' He emphasized the last word, taking his time to pronounce it.

'What did you tell them?'

'I told them you were a good copper, that I couldn't think of a bad word to say about you except that maybe sometimes you were too eager to get a conviction.'

'Thanks, sir.'

'Whatever it is you've done, Dennis, be careful. Because they're on to you.'

I sat there for a couple of seconds as the full magnitude of his words sank in. In a strange way, I felt relieved that Welland hadn't linked me with the e-fit. I don't think I could have handled receiving the odium of someone I respected. Not after everything else.

'Don't worry, sir. It's nothing serious. I promise.'

'Sure. I understand.'

Again there was a silence, this time broken by me suggesting it was time to leave. 'I need to think about things,' I told him.

'You've got to get yourself back on track,' he told me. 'Be a good boy for a while.'

'Yeah, I know.'

'You're a good copper, Dennis.'

'Maybe.'

'And it was nice of you to come and see me. I appreciate it. I really do.'

I stood up and patted him gently on the arm. 'It was no more than you deserve. Thanks for saying good things about me.'

He gave a nod of acknowledgement, and I turned to go.

'One thing that was funny,' he said as I reached the door.

I stopped and turned back. 'What was that, sir?'

'Just that for some reason they seemed really interested in your firearms training.'

I shrugged, not giving a thing away. 'You know how it is. They've got to ask these things. Maybe they want to fit me up for a few murders as well.'

He managed a weak smile. 'You never know with the lot they've got up at CIB.'

I turned away from his gaze, hoping I'd imagined the knowing look.

27

Unravelling. It was all unravelling, so fast that I couldn't keep up with it. With each passing hour, my room for manoeuvre was becoming more limited. The gates to freedom were closing, and unless I made the right decision, and made it quickly, my life was effectively finished and I could look forward to the rest of my days behind bars, segregated from the bulk of the prison population for my own protection. As for how long would that be? Thirty years? At least. Triple murder. Maybe even quadruple murder. Thirty years without a single taste of freedom.

Sitting alone that night at a corner table in the Chinaman, the drink doing little to calm my nerves, I tried to consider my options. They clearly had me down as a suspect, I could no longer doubt that. The copper at the roadblock had seen the e-fit and had put two and two together. Doubtless, by now they'd have got hold of a recent photo of me to show their main witness, the girl at the hotel, and presumably she'd picked me out as the killer. The question now was whether this, on its own, was enough evidence to secure a conviction. At the moment they clearly felt there was no point snatching me off the streets and charging me. There could have been several reasons for this, the most obvious being that they wanted me to lead them to who-ever it was who had ordered the killing. Another would be that they wanted to gather further evidence against me without my knowing it, then spring their trap. Obviously, given my integral role in the saga, they would know there was no point offering up the carrot of a more lenient sentence for co-operating. I had no incentive whatsoever to tell them anything, however hard they leaned on me, and they'd know that.

It was a potentially embarrassing situation too. A serving police officer in a reasonably high position within the Force, and a background that included seventeen years' pretty much unblemished service, being arrested on suspicion of three counts of murder. No-one in authority wanted that scenario, not until they were truly convinced that I was the man they were looking for. This at least gave me a slight chance of escaping the fate that was otherwise in store. But the fact remained that I was almost certainly now under close surveillance. Even more embarrassing than having me arrested was not having me arrested with news leaking out that I'd been in the frame but had slipped through the net.

I finished the scotch and water I was drinking and casually surveyed the pub, looking for anyone who didn't belong. Police surveillance teams can be good, especially if they're using the best people they've got, but if you're aware that you're under their gaze it makes their job one hell of a lot more difficult. I clocked a middle-aged guy at the far end of the bar in a cheap-looking black suit with his tie askew and the top buttons of his shirt undone. He was talking animatedly to Joan, the landlady, and it looked like he was telling her a joke. I watched him for a couple of seconds, then scanned the rest of the bar. A few stools down from him were a couple of businessmen types I recognized, and down from them were a group of younger blokes, only just out of their teens, clustered around the jukebox. Two couples were at separate tables just in front of the bar, one of them I recognized, the other I'd never seen before. The second couple were sitting there looking bored and not really saying much to each other, so they were probably married. The woman looked up and caught my eye, but there was no momentary sense of concern there at being rumbled. She wasn't police. In fact, she actually appeared quite pleased I'd been looking at her and shot me the briefest of smiles. Her husband, or whoever he was, didn't seem to notice, so I smiled back before turning away.

There were maybe a dozen other people in the place all told, sprinkled across the tables, all seemingly involved in their own private conversations. I didn't concentrate my attention on any-one for very long. The last thing I needed was for the surveillance team – if, of course, there was one – to realize I was on to them. The moment that happened, I'd be straight into custody, and maybe they might even be able to trace my awareness of their operation back to Welland, and I didn't want that to happen. The DI had done me a favour by covering my arse and letting me know what was happening, particularly when you took into consideration the fact that they'd been asking about my firearms experience. A lot of people would have forgotten their loyalties at this point and blurted out everything they knew. But not Welland. He knew the score. Or thought he did, anyway. Thinking back, I was sure that I'd imagined the look of suspicion on his face. There was no doubt that had he realized the full extent of my crimes it would have been a different story. One of the things going in my favour was that few people were ever going to think me capable of mass murder, which probably wasn't something to brag about, but was at least useful.

I lit a cigarette, thinking there was nothing to hold me back from running. This whole thing wasn't just going to go away. Not now. The investigating officers were going to keep sniffing around until they had the information they wanted. Then, one way or another, they were going to pull me in. And if Jean Ashcroft heard about any of this, she was likely to tell the cops about Danny, and then the shit really would hit the fan.

Danny. I'd tried his mobile again when I'd left the hospital, hoping he'd pick it up and tell me he was sitting on the beach sipping a pina colada, but it had still been switched off. I tried it again now, dragging on my cigarette as I waited vainly for a response. The longer he didn't respond to calls, the more I was forced to conclude that something bad had happened, and this left another problem. Raymond and his associates didn't need to keep me alive either. If they too got wind of what was going on they would definitely come for me – if they weren't coming already. Either way, my future looked grim so long as I stayed put.

But running away from everything – my career, my life: it was a big step. And then there was Carla Graham. Maybe she didn't want anything serious, but it was just possible that I could change that. Amid all this, she was the only positive thing keeping me going.

I picked up my mobile and thought about calling her. I was aware I might piss her off, but events were moving too rapidly for me to sit back and be patient. If she rejected me now it wasn't actually going to make a great deal of difference. I stared at the phone for maybe ten seconds, then put it down. I'd wait until tomorrow.

I finished my cigarette, then went up to the bar to get another drink. Joan was still chatting to the middle-aged man, and they were laughing like old friends, though you could tell from the way she excused herself from the conversation that they didn't actually know each other.

'What can I get you, Dennis?' she asked, before turning back to the guy. 'You see this bloke here?' she said, meaning me. 'Changes his drink all the time. You can never tell what he's going to have. Isn't that right, Dennis?'

'A man should never be too predictable,' I told her, and ordered a bottle of Pils, as if to prove the point.

As she turned away to get it, I gave the guy a brief smile. He smiled back awkwardly, then looked away. I noticed he was drinking Coke. Suspicious in a place like this, but not unheard of.

Another youngish couple came in and I found myself eyeing them closely. She sat down at a table near the bar and removed her hat and scarf, appearing not to notice me. Her boyfriend/colleague approached the bar and I turned away and paid for my drink, careful not to draw attention to myself. Jean asked me if I was dealing with the case of the old lady who was mugged. She told me that the victim was the mother of one of her former regulars. I told her I wasn't, but that I thought there might be arrests soon. 'It was kids who did it, and kids always end up giving themselves away. They can never keep their mouths shut.'

'Little bastards,' she said. 'They should bloody hang 'em.'

Which were probably the sentiments of 80 per cent of the population, not that it would ever make any difference. Usually, at this point, I'd have put on my police hat and tried to convince both myself and my audience that the perpetrators would end up receiving their just punishments, but this time I didn't bother. They wouldn't.

'Don't ever rely on the courts for justice, Joan,' I told her. 'They're afraid of it.' I turned to Coke Drinker. 'Isn't that right?'

'I never talk politics,' he answered, without looking me in the eye. 'It's too easy to make enemies.'

'Well, someone should do something about it,' Joan grumbled, and went off to serve the guy who'd just come to the bar.

I didn't bother returning to my seat but drank my beer quickly and in silence. When I'd finished I looked for Joan but she'd disappeared out the back. I nodded to Coke Drinker, who nodded vaguely back in my direction, and walked out.

The cold spell from Siberia had well and truly arrived, and an icy wind ripped through the narrow street. I pulled my coat tight around me and started walking, occasionally looking back. The parked cars lining both sides were empty and no-one came out of the Chinaman behind me.

After about fifty yards I turned into a side street and waited in the shadows, shivering against the cold, telling myself I was a fool because if they were following me it would only confirm what I already suspected, and would make no difference to my predicament.

But still I stood there. Five minutes passed. Then ten. A car came by slowly with two men in it, but I couldn't make them out properly. It carried on and accelerated away at the end of the street.

An icy rain began to fall and I broke cover, heading for home, but keeping to the shadows, not knowing who was going to be waiting for me when I got there.

28

When I got near my flat, I surveyed the street carefully, looking for anyone or anything that might be out of place, but it seemed the cold had driven everyone indoors. Only when I was satisfied that the silence was genuine did I walk hurriedly up to my front door and ram the key in the lock, still half expecting some hidden assassin to emerge from the darkness, or a shouting posse of armed police to charge me, screaming staccato orders.

Nothing happened, and there was relief when the door closed behind me for the last time that night.

The first thing I did when I got upstairs was phone in sick. I didn't know how much they knew at the station about the investigation into me but I found it hard to imagine that Knox wouldn't have been informed of it by now. Next I rang Raymond's mobile, but he wasn't answering, and neither was Luke, his bodyguard, so I left a message asking for him to call me and telling him I wasn't going to be at home for the next couple of days. Just in case he was thinking about sending anyone round. Then I made a cup of coffee and told myself not to panic. Foresight, if not right, remained on my side.

I went to bed about ten o'clock and fell asleep surprisingly easily. I remained out like a light the whole night, and for once I actually felt partially refreshed when I awoke the following morning at just after eight.

It was now time to plan my next move. Each day I remained here the chances of my being arrested grew higher, which meant that I was going to have to take the plunge fast. I needed to shake off my surveillance, grab the money from the Bayswater deposit box, and go to ground for a bit. As soon as I started running and they realized that I was on to them, that was it; there'd be no turning back. I was going to have to keep running for the rest of my life.

I went round the corner to get a paper, acting as casually as possible and not spotting anything or anyone untoward, then returned to read it over a light breakfast of toast and coffee. There was no obvious mention of the Traveller's Rest investigation within its pages and nothing on the Miriam Fox case. Now that an arrest had been made and charges laid, there'd be no further mention of her murder until the trial, and probably not much coverage then. Instead, there were the usual tales of woe from Britain and abroad: a farming crisis; renewed famine in Africa; a couple of food scares; and a liberal sprinkling of murder, mayhem and fashion tips.

When I was on my sixth cigarette of the day, I decided I had nothing to lose by calling Carla Graham. I phoned her office from Raymond's mobile, concerned about the possibility that my own phones had been bugged. She picked up on the fourth ring and I was relieved to hear no meeting-type noises in the background.

'Hello, Carla.'

'Dennis?'

'Yeah, it's me. How are you?'

She sighed. 'Busy. Very busy.'

'Well, I won't keep you long.'

'I was going to call you today anyway,' she said.

'Oh yeah?'

'Look, I don't want you to take this too seriously, but you said to let you know if anyone else went missing.' An ominous sensation crept up my back as partially buried thoughts suddenly unearthed themselves like zombies in a graveyard. 'And someone has.'

'Who?'

'Anne Taylor.'

Anne. The girl I'd shared coffee with less than a week ago. The girl I'd saved from abduction.

'Jesus, Carla. When did this happen?'

'She was last seen on Sunday afternoon.' She seemed to sense my unease. 'She's done this before on several occasions so I don't think there's any real cause for alarm. And obviously, there is a man in custody for the murder.'

'I know, but it isn't as cut and dried as that. There are a lot of unanswered questions, and everyone's innocent until proven guilty. You of all people should know that.'

'I still don't think you should read too much into it. Anne is that type of girl.'

'And so was Molly Hagger, but you can't help getting concerned. When did Anne last go missing like this?'

'About a month ago.'

'How long was she gone for then?'

'A couple of nights. A similar length of time to this. That's why we haven't been too worried. The last time she went AWOL it was because she was off on a binge with an older woman. She got stoned, fell asleep, and when she woke up twenty-four hours later she came back here.'

'And before that? When did she last go missing before that?'

'I can't remember. A few months ago. Look, Dennis, no-one here thinks anything untoward's happened.'

'So why were you going to phone and tell me?'

'Because you asked me too. Personally, I think Anne's doing her usual thing, which is going out, taking drugs, and doing exactly what she fancies, regardless of what anyone tells her, because that's what she's like. But I felt I ought to tell you because you were worried and I suppose I'd never forgive myself if Anne did end up like Miriam Fox, dead in some back alley with her throat cut, and I hadn't bothered reporting it. Although I still think the chances of that happening are fairly remote.'

'OK, OK, I get your point. I don't like it, though.' And I didn't. Anne's disappearance had sown more doubts in my mind. Maybe somehow, defying all the odds, Mark Wells wasn't our man. Not that it should have mattered; I had far bigger fish to fry now. I sighed. 'Look, do me a favour and inform the police. Tell them what's happened.'

'Dennis, you *are* the police.'

'Not any more I'm not.'

'What are you talking about?'

'I resigned. Yesterday.' Not quite true, but it might as well have been.

'Are you playing games, Dennis? Because if you are, I'm not interested.'

'No, I'm not. Honestly. I handed my notice in. It's been a long time coming.'

'But what are you going to do? I mean, are you trained for anything else?'

Killing people, I thought.

'Not really, but I've got a bit of cash put aside. I thought I'd maybe head abroad for a while. Do some travelling. I've always wanted to do something like that.'

'Well . . . Good luck with it. I hope it works out for you. When are you hoping to go?'

'As soon as I can. Probably before the end of the week.'

'You know, I think I'm jealous.'

'You could always come with me.'

She laughed. 'I don't think so. Perhaps one day I'll come out and visit you.'

'You should do. What's keeping you here?'

'I can't believe I'm actually being encouraged to be more of a rebel by a policeman. I don't know, Dennis. At the moment I'm happy the way things are.'

'Are you? Really?'

There was a short silence on the other end of the line before she spoke again. 'It just wouldn't work. I don't know you well enough. I think we should leave it at that.'

'OK, but it'd be good to see you one last time before I go.' As soon as I said this, I knew that this was a risk I should not be taking, but I didn't seem able to help myself.

'Yes,' she said, 'it would, but I don't know when we're going to get the chance.'

'Look, I remember you saying the other night that you liked poetry. They're doing a reading by some contemporary poets tonight at a place called the Gallan Club, not far from me. Why don't we meet there for a drink? It's a nice spot.'

Carla ummed and aahed for a few minutes, but finally agreed to come over for an hour or so. I began to tell her where the club was but it turned out she knew the place vaguely anyway. 'And don't forget to tell the police about Anne,' I added. 'Report it formally. You never know what might have happened and it's better to be safe than sorry.' Again she told me that she thought there was nothing to worry about, but I insisted and she ended up agreeing to do it.

After I'd hung up, I made another cup of coffee and lit cigarette number seven. Anne Taylor was not my concern. Even if I'd stayed a copper and remained connected to the Miriam Fox murder case, she would still not have been my concern. Mark Wells was almost certainly Miriam's murderer. But I couldn't help wondering what had happened to Molly Hagger and where Anne had got to. I would certainly have expected really to have surfaced by now. Her best friend had been killed, and it was difficult to believe that she wouldn't have at least shown her face to find out what was going on, or contact the authorities if she believed Wells was responsible. And now Anne had disappeared only a few weeks after Molly. There might, as Carla clearly thought, be a perfectly logical explanation for it, but for me it was all too coincidental, particularly on top of the attempted assault the previous week. I couldn't help but feel that I was missing something, something neither I nor any of my erstwhile colleagues were aware of, but try as I might I couldn't put my finger on what it was. And, with everything else, it felt like it wasn't worth trying.

But sometimes, you know, it's difficult to let go. So I picked up my home phone, this time not caring who was listening in, and made a call to Malik's mobile.

It rang ten times before he answered, and when he heard my voice I couldn't tell whether he was happy that it was me or not. I wondered briefly if he knew that his superiors were on to me.

He asked me how I was feeling, having presumably heard that I'd phoned in sick, and I told him I was OK just a little under the weather.

'I haven't been sleeping too well. I think I need a holiday.'

'Why don't you take a couple of weeks? You're bound to be due it.'

'I am. Maybe I will.'

'Anyway, what can I do for you, Dennis?'

Dennis. I was never going to get used to that from him. 'How did the raids go this morning? Have we laid any charges yet?'

'We pulled in everyone we were meant to, but no charges yet. You know what it's like with these kids. It's like treading on egg shells. You're not even allowed to raise your voices with them in case they get upset.'

'I'm sure one or more of them did the old lady.'

'I think everyone's sure of that. It's proving it that's the problem, not that I have to tell you that.'

'How is she?'

'The old lady? Touch and go. What I think personally is that one way or another she's going to die as a result of what happened. It might take a few weeks – it might even take a few months- – but either way, those kids were responsible.'

I agreed with him. 'Look, the reason I'm calling is the Miriam Fox case.'

'Oh yeah?' He spoke the words without much enthusiasm. I told him what Carla had told me about Anne's disappearance while he listened at the other end. When I'd finished, he asked me what I was doing talking to Carla. 'I thought you weren't going to bother contacting her.'

'She contacted me. I told her to if anyone else went missing. And this one seems like one coincidence too many. Two young girls, both no more than fourteen, disappear within a month of each other from the same children's home. At the same time, a girl both of them have had some association with, and who was best friends with one of them, is murdered. All three were prostitutes working the same area of King's Cross. I know people disappear, and I know we've got Mark Wells in custody, and that the evidence against him's good, but something about this just isn't right.'

'Like you said, people disappear . . .'

'Yeah, I know. I know. People disappear all the time, especially teenage crackheads, but with this frequency? And we know one met a violent end, and one of the others was assaulted during an attempted abduction just a matter of days ago, something I was witness to. And now we've got this thing where the evidence against the suspect in the murder – the shirt – is linked to one of the missing girls.'

'I wouldn't read too much into that, Dennis. Giving the shirt away to someone who's not around to deny it is just an easy excuse for Wells to use.'

'Has anyone been trying to find her?'

'Who? Molly Hagger? Not that I'm aware of. But if you're concerned, you should be talking to Knox, not me. Why don't you see what he has to say about it?'

'Because I know what he'll say, Asif. That we've got a man in custody, that there's no evidence for extending the inquiry further . . .'

'And he'd have a point, wouldn't he? You're right, it all seems a bit coincidental, but what can we do about it? On Hagger and the other girl, there's no evidence that anything untoward's happened, and, as you say, they're not the sort of girls whose disappearance is going to cause anyone any surprises.'

'I just wanted to run it by you. See what you thought.'

'And I appreciate you thinking of me. What I'd say is this. It's strange, but strange is all. Maybe you ought to keep your ear to the ground and see how things pan out, maybe have a few words with some of the street girls, but I wouldn't worry about it too much yet. There's plenty of other things to concern yourself with, and you shouldn't be thinking about them anyway. You ought to be in bed resting and getting yourself well so you can come back here and help us out.'

But I'd never be going back to help them out. I'd miss Malik, even if he had started calling me Dennis and dispensing advice just a little bit too readily. He was a good copper, though, and the thought that perhaps I had played a small part in getting him that way felt good. I told him he'd be doing me a favour if he could keep his ears open for any relevant developments among the King's Cross whores, and he told me he would. I thanked him, said that I'd see him shortly, promised him t I'd get to bed straight away and take it easy, then rang off.

But I didn't go to bed. Instead, I spent the rest of the day mulling over my plans and making preparations; occasionally phoning Danny's mobile, always without success; sometimes stopping to look out of the window at the iron-grey sky and pondering the fates of Molly Hagger and Anne Taylor; wondering what secrets Miriam Fox had taken to her grave.

And all the time something was bothering me, and I couldn't put my finger on what it was. Something I'd missed; something that flickered and danced round the recesses of my memory like the shadows of a flame, irritating me because it was important in some ill-defined way but I was unable to coax it out, however hard I tried.

And as darkness fell on my last night as a serving police officer, and the rain the forecasters had warned us about finally swept in from the west, I realized I was still just as ignorant of what had happened in the Miriam Fox murder case as I had been on the morning I'd first stared down at her bloodstained body.

29

I phoned a minicab to take me down to the Gallan Club, and it got me there at about a quarter to eight. It was raining steadily and, though not as cold as the previous night, there was still a bite in the air.

I'd never been to the Gallan before, even though it was only about half a mile from where I lived. I'd walked past it plenty of times though, most notably the previous day when they'd had a blackboard outside saying that tonight was contemporary poets night. It wasn't really my cup of tea, but I suppose it made a change from sitting around in the pub. It was quiz night at the Chinaman as well, and it would be the first time I'd missed it for non-work reasons for as long as I could remember.

The interior of the Gallan was small and dimly lit. The stage, empty when I walked in, was at the end furthest from the door, while the rest of the floor space was taken up by evenly clustered round tables. A bar on the left-hand side ran the length of the room. All of the tables were occupied, and a small crowd milled about the bar. Most of those present were the type of people you'd expect at a poetry evening where the headline act was someone called Maiden Faith Ararngard: fresh-faced students in long coats, sipping delicately at their beers; a group of eco-warriors with an overabundance of piercings and pantomime clothes; and a few older intellectual types who looked as though they spent every waking hour in the hunt for hidden meanings to pointless questions.

I'd half expected this type of line-up and had dressed down as far as my wardrobe would allow so that I didn't look too much out of place. It hadn't worked. Faded jeans and a sweatshirt with a hole in the elbow were never going to blend me in with this crowd, although at least I was pretty much guaranteed there'd be no undercover coppers in here. Like me, they'd have stuck out a mile.

Carla hadn't arrived, so I went to the bar and ordered a pint of Pride from a guy with a bolt through his nose and a beard that was close to a foot long. He gave me a bit of a funny look like I'd come dressed as a Doctor Who villain, but he was efficient, and that's always the most important trait for any bar-man. I paid for my drink and stood close to the door so that I could see Carla when she made her entrance.

I didn't feel particularly comfortable in there, and in a way that said something about her and me. She knew we were never going to be an item; it was me who found it difficult to accept. But accept it I was going to have to do. From tomorrow I was on the run. I had a false passport in my possession which I'd got from one of Len Runnion's contacts a few months back. It had been an insurance policy after a CIB investigation into a couple of ex-colleagues at the station had given me a case of cold feet. It was a good one, too. I'd grown a ten-day beard and put on some glasses for the photograph and it looked very unlike me. But I wasn't going to be able to use it yet. There'd be an all-ports alert out for me as soon as I broke cover, which would mean me having to lie low for a couple of weeks until the fuss had died down. Maybe I'd drive down to Cornwall or up to Scotland, somewhere a bit isolated. Not for the first time that day, I experienced a strangely exhilarating feeling of apprehension.

I was vaguely amused to see that the first act up was Norman 'Zeke' Drayer, a.k.a., apparently, the 'Bard of Somerstown'. Norman was dressed in a lincoln green jacket with tassles that looked as though it was made of felt, a pair of cricket whites, and knee-length black boots. Thankfully, he didn't have a hat with a feather in it on his head, or he'd have been a dead ringer for Robin Hood.

He danced onto the stage to polite applause and immediately opened up with a bawdy ballad about a buxom country girl called Annie McSilk and the difficulties she had fending off the advances of amorous farmers. It was actually quite good, and I had a few laughs in spite of myself, even if it did go on a bit too long. Unfortunately, it was also the high point of his act. The next three poems in his stint veered off into the boring half-Wworld of social justice and had me looking at the door every twenty seconds for any sign of Carla. By the time he danced off the stage, with theatrical bows all round, the applause had been all but drowned out by the buzz of individual conversations.

I was jealous of the people in there, jealous because they had nothing to fear. I watched them as they talked among themselves, discussing their issues as if they were of real importance, safe in their cocooned little worlds.

I felt a tap on the shoulder and turned round to see Carla

standing there. Her face was more heavily made up than usual, but the effect seemed to add to rather than detract from her beauty. She was dressed in a long black coat, underneath which was a simple white blouse and a pair of tight-fitting jeans. She greeted me with a brief peck on the cheek and I told her she looked good.

'Why, thank you, kind sir,' she replied with a faint half smile.

'What do you want to drink?'

'I could murder a vodka and orange.'

I got the attention of a barmaid, who came over and took the order.

'So, you're really going then, Dennis?' she said, when the barmaid had gone. 'You know, I really didn't think you'd have the bottle.'

'Appearances can be deceptive,' I told her. 'Any news on Anne?'

'Nothing yet, but one of the other girls said that she'd been seeing a new man, and apparently she'd talked about going off with him.'

'Really? Well, let's hope it's that then. Did you report it to the police?'

She nodded. 'I did. They didn't seem that interested.'

'Did you tell them about Molly?' She nodded again. 'And they still weren't interested?'

'They're street girls, Dennis. They do this sort of thing. You know, I don't know how you're going to handle not being a copper. You're just too interested in whatever's happening around you.'

'It'll do me good to get out of this place. Perhaps when I'm away from it, I won't worry about everything so much.'

She smiled. 'We'll see. You'll probably be back inside a month.'

'Somehow I don't think so.'

'Well, keep in touch, won't you? Send me postcards from your various destinations.'

'Of course I will.' I eyed her closely. 'You know, I don't want to sound too sickly about this, but I'm going to miss you. I think we could have done OK together.'

'Do you?' She returned my look. 'Maybe, but like I said, Dennis, now's just not a good time.'

I nodded. 'Fair enough. I'd better make the best use of tonight, then.'

'Make sure you do,' she said with a smile. 'My time doesn't come cheap.'

There wasn't a lot you could say to that.

A table came free on the other side of the room from the bar and we took it as the next act, a plain-looking girl with spindly legs called Jeanie O'Brien, came on. She was carrying a stool, which she sat on to face the audience.

'I know her,' Carla said. 'I've seen her perform before. She's good.'

She was too, but I wasn't really listening. Unfortunately, Carla was, which meant that the conversation was strained and pretty one-sided, with me doing most of the talking. I finished my beer quickly, wondering why on earth I'd risked everything by sticking around for one more night.

'Do you want another drink?' I asked her eventually.

She looked at her watch. 'One more. Then I've got to go.'

I was coming back towards our table with the drinks when I ran into the Bard of Somerstown himself. Drayer acknowledged me straight away and immediately looked nervous.

'Er, hello officer. How are you?'

I stopped in front of him. 'Not bad, Norman. A most distinguished performance out there earlier.'

'Oh, you saw it, did you? I' afraid it wasn't one of my best. What are you doing here anyway? Not that I mind, of course, but it just doesn't seem to be your sort of gig.'

'It isn't. Not really. But the lady I'm with—'

'Oh yeah. I saw you with her earlier.'

'Well, she's into poetry.'

He nodded vaguely. 'Oh yeah, nice.'

I looked over at our table. Carla was elegantly puffing on a Silk Cut, staring into space. At that moment she really did look like a high-class escort girl, aloof from the world around her. And I wondered then whether she felt anything for me at all, or whether she'd just bedded me because I'd been there at the time.

'I heard you arrested someone for Miriam's murder.'

'That's right.'

'Do you think it's him?'

How many times had I been asked that? As if I was going to say no. 'The evidence points that way,' I replied, but I wasn't really thinking about what I was saying. I was looking over his shoulder at Carla, and I was thinking. Turning stuff over and over in my mind.

'Because, you know, I was thinking, when I saw you earlier, that it was odd.'

I looked back at him. 'Odd?'

'Well, when I saw the woman you're with, I thought she looked familiar. And I tried to remember where I'd seen her before.'

'And? When have you seen her before?'

'Well, that's the funny thing. I wouldn't have remembered if I hadn't seen her with you just then.'

'Where did you see her, Norman?'

'In the hall outside my pad.'

I tried to keep the desperation out of my voice. 'When? When was that?'

'A couple of weeks back.'

'Before Miriam's murder?'

'Yeah, yeah. It would have been.'

'Why didn't you tell us this when we came round to visit you last week?'

He sensed my displeasure. 'Because, you know, well, you only seemed interested in what male visitors she'd had, and I couldn't even have told you if she'd been at Miriam's place or not. I just saw her and I thought she looked nice. And then I sort of forgot about it until tonight, when I saw her with you. There's no problem, is there?'

I shook my head, focusing my mind elsewhere. Putting together the final pieces. It was a while before I spoke. 'No. There's no problem.'

'Is there anything wrong, man? Are you OK?'

I nodded slowly, and looked away from him. 'Yeah, I'm fine. Just a bit tired, that's all.'

So Carla had been lying again. I should have known her story was bullshit, but maybe I'd been concentrating on too many other things to have seen the holes in it. I looked at her once again, and this time she looked back. I think she must have seen something in my face that told her I knew, because her eyes widened. Drayer turned round to follow my gaze and started to say something, but I wasn't taking any notice. Then Carla's eyes widened even further – she must have recognized him too.

I pushed past Drayer and strode up to the table, slamming the drinks down on it.

Carla stood up, the concern etched across her face. 'Look, I can explain. I didn't want you to know that I'd paid her—'

I grabbed her tightly by the arm and pulled her towards me. 'Dennis. You're hurting me.'

'You're fucking right I am. You've played me for a fool, Carla.'

'Let go of me,' she hissed, eyes narrowing. 'I admit it, I lied. I did meet her, but—'

'You didn't just meet her, did you? You killed her. Either that or you know exactly who did.'

'What on earth are you talking about?' Her expression was one of utter astonishment, but I wasn't falling for that one again.

'When we were talking this morning, you said to me you didn't want Anne Taylor to end up like Miriam Fox. Dead in a back alley with her throat cut. Those were your exact words. Remember?'

She tried to shake her arm free. 'I told you to let go—'

'But the only people who could possibly know that Miriam Fox had her throat cut were us – the police – and the murderer.'

'No, no, no.' She shook her head wildly. 'I don't know what you're talking about. You . . . you're accusing me of killing that girl. You bastard!' She yelled out these last two words, and people started turning round to look at us. Then, with her free hand, she reached down, picked up her drink, and chucked the contents of it in my face.

The alcohol stung, and I blinked rapidly, momentarily releasing my grip on her arm. Before I could recover, she pushed me back into one of the chairs, turned and stormed out.

But I wasn't letting her go that easily, not until I'd found out what had really happened. I stood back up, rubbing the stinging alcohol out of my eyes, and started after her, but I'd made only five paces when a big guy with thick dreadlocks stepped in front of me and blocked my path.

'All right, mate, leave her alone.'

'Out of my way. I'm a police officer!' I snapped, realizing as soon as the words were out that this was not the sort of venue to be declaring your links with the oppressive capitalist system.

'Well, fuck you, then,' he said evenly, and punched me on the side of the head.

I stumbled back while his rake-thin girlfriend grabbed hold of him and told him not to get himself into any trouble. He started telling her to leave him be, but he never finished the sentence because I came forward with my trusty little truncheon in hand and smacked him round the face with it. He went down hard, hitting the floor with a satisfying thud, and his girlfriend screamed. I kept walking, keeping my head down, making for the door, once again caught completely unawares by the speed and direction of events.

30

It was raining even harder when I got outside. I looked up and down the street but could see no sign of Carla. It was quiet out there tonight. The traffic was running smoothly and there didn't seem to be many people about. About fifty yards away I could make out a black cab waiting to turn right into a side street, and I wondered if she was inside it. I didn't bother trying to find out, knowing it would be gone long before I got there, and instead lit another cigarette and stood where I was, trying to take in what I'd just heard. She'd stitched me up perfectly. I'd genuinely thought there'd been a shared attraction when all the time her sole purpose had been to throw me off track. And it had worked, too. Far too easily.

There was a bus shelter across the road and I jogged over to it, fiddling around in my pocket for the mobile. When I reached the shelter I dialled Malik's home number. His wife answered after a couple of rings. I'd met her once or twice in the past, and when I came on the line she asked me how I was. I told her I was fine, but that it was urgent I talked to him. 'It's about a case we were working on.'

'I don't like him getting too many calls at home, Dennis. He works hard enough as it is.'

'I know, I know. I wouldn't ask if it wasn't important.'

Reluctantly, she went off to get Malik and he came on the phone a few seconds later.

I didn't beat about the bush. 'Carla Graham. You were right about her. She's a conniving, cynical bitch and she was involved in the Miriam Fox murder. I don't know how or why, but she's definitely involved. I think it might be something to do with blackmail. Drayer, that poet guy we met when we went round to Miriam's flats, he remembers seeing her—'

'Whoa, Dennis, slow down. What is this? When did you see Drayer?'

Out of the corner of my eye I saw two figures walking towards the bus shelter. They both had their heads down, which I thought was strange. They were ten yards away and walking purposefully.

'Just now. Two minutes ago.'

Eight yards. Seven yards. They both had their hands in the pockets of their long coats. Malik was talking into my ear. Suddenly I wasn't listening any more.

Six yards. One of them raised his head, and our eyes met. I knew straight away that he was here to kill me.

There was no time even to freeze with the fear that shot through me.

Keeping as casual a face as possible, and still clutching the phone to my ear, I turned slowly on my heels and then, without warning, broke into a manic sprint, the adrenalin coursing through me. I dropped the phone in my pocket as I ran, sneaking a rapid peek over my shoulder. My movement had caught them by surprise, but only for a second. One pulled a sawn-off shotgun, the other a revolver. They lifted them in my direction, still walking purposefully, not even breaking stride. And still only a matter of yards away.

I didn't think. I just didn't have time. Reflexively, I veered sharply right and began running across the road. A car was forced to brake suddenly, its tyres skidding on the slick tarmac. I heard the driver shouting something angry but unintelligible.

An explosion shattered the night air and something whistled past my head. I kept running, keeping low, trying to move in a zig-zag pattern to make it more difficult for them to hit me. More shots, this time from the revolver. Close. Far too close. Any second now and I was going to get a bullet between the shoulder blades.

I could hear them right behind me, charging after me across the street. I hit the pavement on the other side and ran, crouching, using parked cars for cover. The shotgun blasted its load again and a shower of glass from a rear windscreen sprayed the ground. There was no way I was going to outrun these boys. They knew it. I knew it. All I could do was to keep going. With my head down and my body straining forward, I continued down the pavement as fast as my legs would carry me, knowing that all this effort was probably going to be in vain but too desperate to care.

From somewhere in the direction of the Gallan club I heard a woman scream in terror as she saw what was happening. For a split second I imagined her standing horrified above my bullet-riddled corpse. At that moment I was so frightened I could have pissed my pants.

Then, without warning, I caught a glimse of a man in a suit running across the street in an effort to get between me and my pursuers. He was holding something up in his right hand. A warrant card. He must have been a member of my surveillance team.

'Police, police! Drop your weapons!'

He'd got onto the pavement behind me and was standing in front of the gunmen. Ahead of me, on the other side of the street, I could see his partner – a shorter, fatter guy who looked a few years older. I recognized him straight away as the guy at the bar in the Chinaman the previous night. The Coke drinker who never liked to talk politics. He was waiting to cross the road to apprehend me, but a car speeding down the street was holding him up.

'Police! Drop your weapons now!'

It was the tall one again, but his voice betrayed his desperation as he suddenly realized he'd almost certainly bitten off more than he could chew. I kept running, but briefly turned round. He was ten yards behind me and the gunmen had stopped in front of him. One was looking round him at me, and I could sense his urgent desire not to let his quarry disappear.

There was a second's silence. instinctively I slowed down as the drama played itself out. On the street cars were stopping to get a look at what was happening, allowing the other copper to cross. He ran towards me, but he too was watching his colleague. It looked like the whole street was.

The shotgun barked again, and the man who'd tried to prevent my execution flew backwards through the air. He seemed to hover above the ground for an indeterminate but memorable period of time before hurtling downwards with a crash, as if an invisible hand had tipped him out of its palm. He lay there, not moving.

His colleague froze. Still in the middle of the road. And then he put a hand to his mouth as the shock of what he'd just seen hit him. He tried to shout something, something that could give him some control over a chaotic situation, but nothing came out.

And before he'd even moved, my pursuers came after me again, the shotgun guy reloading and running at the same time. His friend with the handgun was ferociously quick. He came at me in huge bounds, reminding me bizarrely of one of the two-legged hunting dinosaurs in *Jurassic Park*, and there was a fixed, maniacal smile on his face. For a moment I felt like I was in some sort of slow-motion nightmare, that whatever I did, however fast I moved, he was going to catch me. But I kept running, knowing there was no choice, not daring to look back as the shots cracked around me. And as I ran, my lungs and throat filled up with phlegm and I couldn't breathe. I knew I was just seconds away from the end.

There was a yelp and the sound of someone slipping, and I looked over my shoulder to see handgun man falling onto the wet ground, holding the gun up in the air. Relief didn't even cross my mind. The one with the shotgun was right behind him, and by now he'd reloaded. He jumped over his colleague, then stopped, lifted the weapon to his shoulder, and prepared to fire. Eight yards separated us. Even though I was still running, he couldn't miss.

Coming up on my left was a Chinese takeaway. It was my only chance. I flung myself forward onto the pavement at just the moment he pulled the trigger, taking it at a roll. The shot flew shrieking over my head and into the distance, and I was immediately back on my feet and charging at the takeaway door like a runaway bull. He fired again, but I'd already hit the door at a dive. It flew open and I fell inside, hitting the tiled floor elbow first, ignoring the pain that shot right up my arm.

I wanted to lie where I was for a couple of seconds and get my breath back, and it took a huge effort of willpower to force myself to my feet. I heard footsteps on the pavement outside and I knew that they were only seconds behind me. The lone customer in the place – a middle-aged man with a checked shirt and an expression of sheer dismay – stood watching me silently. Behind the counter, the young Chinese server, who couldn't have been a day over eighteen, looked just as confused by the whole situation.

I turned round as shotgun man appeared at the door. He levelled the weapon, the customer swore and fell back onto one of the chairs, and I charged the counter. The Chinese guy shrieked and dived out the way as I rolled over it like it was an assault course obstacle, crashing down the other side. The shotgun barked again and the glass covering the menu board above my head exploded into a hundred pieces that fell about me like jagged snowflakes as I wriggled maggot-like across the floor.

The door marked 'Private – Staff Only' was my only means of escape. I headbutted it open, crawling on my hands and knees, and desperately pushed my body through. I was in a small corridor leading through to the kitchens. Back in the shop, I could hear shouting and the sound of someone else coming over the worktop. I ran forward into the kitchens where half a dozen Chinese in chef's whites were busy at work. They all turned round as I charged in, and one jumped in front of me.

'No, no. Not allowed. No customers!'

I looked round desperately for an exit door, knowing I had seconds.

The chef, who just about came up to my chest, grabbed me by the lapels of my jacket. 'No customers! You must leave!'

He began pushing me backwards, and another younger chef armed with a wicked-looking meat cleaver started coming round the main worktop. I spotted the back door behind them in the corner. It was held slightly ajar by a piece of cardboard. I felt a surge of relief and panic in roughly equal measure.

Hearing the rapid footfalls in the corridor behind me, I screamed something incoherent and pushed the chef aside. He fell into a load of pots and pans and cried out. The other chef, the one with the cleaver, went to raise it above his head, and I thought momentarily that this would be a very stupid way to die, cut down by an irate kitchen worker while fleeing a professional assassination team.

I ripped the warrant card from my pocket, the last time I would ever use it. 'Police! I only want to get out! Get out of my way!' I charged past him, and he actually did get out of the way. There was a load of panicked shouting from all around me, and I knew that my pursuers were in the room.

I kicked the door open without pausing and ran out into the litter-strewn back yard as it slammed shut, rattling, behind me. A few yards ahead was a wall piled up with rubbish, facing on to the backs of terraced houses. I could have run for it but I didn't think I'd make it over before they put a hole in me. It was a time for hard decisions.

Resisting the temptation to bend over and throw up, I side-stepped and positioned myself by the door on the opposite side to the direction it would open, knowing that if I fucked this up then they would have me. No question. But there was little time for fear. Within a second, there was a commotion from inside the kitchens, more shouting – most of it foreign and unintelligible – and then the door flew open again and shotgun man came charging into view, automatically looking towards the wall ahead.

With a speed I didn't think I was capable of, I threw myself into him, grabbing the gun in the process. I shoved it upwards, pushing all my weight against his body, the power and surprise of my attack forcing him back so he blocked the doorway. At the same time, instinctively, reflexively, whatever you want to call it, he pulled the trigger, not having had the time to realize that the barrel had just been thrust into position right beneath his chin.

The noise was louder than anything I think I've ever heard in my life. It ripped through my ears and shook my whole body right down to the toes. A huge splash of blood soaked my face like warm, vile treacle as the top of his head was ripped away, its contents scattered high up the door and across the windows. He fell backwards, and I tugged the weapon from his grasp.

His partner was right behind him and he was forced to get out of the way as the corpse hit the floor. He looked down at the bloody head, then back at me, his face a mask of rage.

'Bastard!'

He raised the gun and I threw myself backwards as he fired, landing on my back on the paving slabs. He fired again, missing my head by inches, the bullet ricocheting up off the concrete. But I'd swung the shotgun round now so it was facing him, and finally it was my turn to pull the trigger.

I tried to balance it and take aim, but time was too short. The weapon kicked in my hand and a huge meaty chunk of his left leg just above the knee disappeared. The leg collapsed uselessly, and he collapsed with it, dropping the gun as all his efforts were put into howling in agony. He was still sitting upright when I got his head in my sights and pulled the trigger again.

But the weapon was empty.

The Chinese had gathered around the door and were looking down at the carnage with a mixture of fear, shock and morbid excitement on their faces. I was panting heavily, I was exhausted, but this wasn't over yet. In the distance, above the ringing in my ears, I could hear the sound of sirens converging on the scene from all directions, but it sounded as though they were still some way distant.

I got to my feet and waved the weapon at my audience. They all scuttled out of the way and I stepped forward, grabbed the wounded would-be assassin by his hair and dragged him outside, before picking up his gun and putting it in my pocket. I shut the door and turned to face him. His howls had now subsided into heavy, desperate breathing interspersed with little shrieks of pain through clenched teeth. He was holding onto the huge wound with both hands in a vain attempt to stem the copious flow of blood.

I leaned down. 'Who sent you?' I hissed, between pants. 'Who sent you?'

He looked Mediterranean, Turkish perhaps, and I put him in his early thirties. He could easily have been the guy who'd spooked Danny. Probably was. He could even be the man who'd killed him. Because, by now, I was sure he was dead.

He didn't answer. He didn't even look at me. In the distance, the sirens were getting louder and more numerous. Time was running short. I hit his hands with the butt of the shotgun, forcing him to release his grip on the wound. As he did so, I thrust my hand into the torn flesh and scraped my fingernails along it. His scream would have deafened me under normal circumstances, but I was partially deaf anyway.

'Who sent you?'

'No speak English,' he whimpered, shaking his head. 'No speak English.'

This time I slammed the butt into the wound, and when he put his hands on it instinctively, I slammed it into them too. He was screaming, so now I cracked him in the face to shut him up, cutting his lips. Blood spewed down his chin.

'Who the fuck sent you? Tell me! Now! Who?' I grabbed him

by the hair again and snapped his head back so he was looking me right in the eye.

I think he saw the ruthlessness in my expression and realized there was no point delaying any further, even though the sirens were coming in from all sides. 'Mehmet Illan,' he whispered.

'Who?'

'Mehmet Illan.'

'Who the fuck is he?'

Before he could answer, there was the sound of footsteps from inside the kitchen and I heard someone running through. I took a step back and raised the butt so that it was level with my head. This time, as the door opened, Coke Drinker emerged, panting into the darkness and right into my line of fire. I heard one of the Chinese staff shout 'Look out!' in a high-pitched, dramatic voice, but it was way too late for that. I hit him full on in the face with the butt, demolishing his nose like soft fudge and scattering flecks of blood across both cheeks. He went down on both knees, hands covering his injured face, and I knew he was no longer any problem. There were other voices coming from the street, shouting, giving orders. Coppers' voices, doing what they do best: bringing situations under control.

Still packed with adrenalin, I dropped the shotgun, turned, and ran for the wall, vaulting up onto it in one less-than-graceful movement before manoeuvring myself over. I slid down the other side and landed in more sacks of rubbish. I was now in someone's ill-kept back garden. There was an alley running down the side of the adjoining house, so I clambered over the rickety wooden fence separating the two gardens and followed it, emerging on the next street. I crossed it straight away, then began jogging in the opposite direction to the Gallan, trying to wipe the blood from my face.

I heard a police car approaching behind me so I

darted into another sidestreet and kept running. The car continued on, missing me, and I kept going, trying to put as much distance between myself and the carnage as possible.

But exhaustion was taking hold. I had a stitch in my right side and I was having difficulty breathing. My legs felt as though they were going to go under me at any moment, and the only thing keeping me going was the fear of getting caught.

And the desire for revenge. One way or another the people who were trying to fuck me up and put me out of existence were going to pay for their crimes. I wasn't going to die that fucking easily.

Another hundred yards, another hundred and fifty, and then I could run no more. I half jogged, half staggered into a dingy-looking back alley by the side of a school and found a spot out of sight of the road. I sat down against the wall and panted my breath back to normal – a task that seemed to take for ever. Above my head, the clouds unloaded their rain on the city. Slowly, the sirens faded away.

The desire for revenge. It was the only thing I had left in the world.

Part Four

THE BUSINESS OF DYING

31

I could have walked away from the whole thing. Gone underground, waited a few months, then left the country. That was
basically what I'd intended to do, but, in the end, I felt that I
couldn't leave things as they were. Questions needed answering,
and scores needed settling. It was as simple as that. Everyone had
fucked me up: my bosses at work, Raymond Keen, and now even
Carla Graham.

Carla Graham. That she was somehow involved in the murder
of Miriam Fox was no longer in doubt. It was almost certainly
not her who'd pulled the knife across her throat, not given the
size and depth of the wound. But she definitely knew who'd done
it. And why. It was her motive for being involved that intrigued
me the most because for the life of me I couldn't understand
what it could be. She was right about the blackmail plot – it just
didn't seem enough to kill someone for. And what about the
evidence against Mark Wells? Were he and Carla in it together?
It was difficult to conclude otherwise, given the evidence against
him, and yet it made no sense. Neither could I understand why
he'd gone round to Miriam's flat after the murder and been

genuinely shocked to discover police officers there. If he'd been the killer, surely he'd have expected that and avoided the place?

I was still in the dark, and I didn't like it. I should have cut my losses, but I guess I'd simply hit the point where everything had gone so far downhill that I no longer cared what happened, as long as I got the chance to get even with the people who'd been pulling the wool over my eyes through all this.

That night, after getting my breath back and wiping the worst of the blood off my face, I hurried home through the back streets and threw on a single set of new clothes, before hailing a cab on City Road and getting it to take me to Liverpool Street station. From there, I got on the Underground and took the Central Line right back across town to Lancaster Gate, before making my way to Bayswater using a combination of walking and the bus.

It was five to eleven by the time I arrived at the hotel where I kept the safety deposit box. I knew the owner vaguely from my previous visits, and he was at the desk in the cramped foyer when I walked in, smoking a foul-smelling cigarette and watching football on a portable TV. He nodded as I approached, and I told him I wanted a room. Without taking his eyes off the TV he leaned over, removed a key from one of the numbered hooks on the wall behind him, and put it down on the desk.

'Twenty pounds per night,' he said, in a thick foreign accent. 'Plus twenty deposit.'

I told him I wanted to book for three nights and counted out four twenties. He took the money, again without taking his eyes from the TV. 'Up the stairs to the third floor. It's on the right.' One of the teams scored and the commentator shouted excitedly in Arabic or Turkish, or something like that, but the owner didn't bat an eyelid. I assumed he supported the other side.

The room was small and horrifically done out in 1970s style orange and purple, but it looked clean, and that was good enough for me. It was private, too. I wouldn't draw attention to myself staying here, where the remainder of the occupants were almost certainly going to be newly arrived illegal immigrants and asylum seekers, and where the owner probably wouldn't go voluntarily to the police about anything.

I threw off my clothes and lay down on the bed, lighting a cigarette and taking a deep breath. The chase was on now, but the police were still in a difficult position. They couldn't just print my photo in the next day's papers. It might have been pretty obvious that I had been involved in the Traveller's Rest killings, but they still couldn't be absolutely sure that I didn't have an alibi for the night in question. For all anyone knew, I could have had a mistress up in Clavering I'd been seeing on the sly; I could have been with her on the night in question. And maybe it was simply coincidence that the killer looked so much like me. For the first, and probably the last, time in my life I actually gave thanks to those who had drafted the laws of our great country for making them so obviously in favour of the criminal. They needed hard evidence against me, and maybe at the moment they just didn't have enough. They'd be pulling out all the stops to find me, but they'd still be doing it with one hand tied behind their backs. For that reason, and that reason alone, I still felt there was hope of evading capture.

I finished the cigarette and lay there for a long time, staring at the ceiling and wondering where I was going to be in a year's time. Or even a week's. Out in the hallway a door slammed and I heard a lot of shouting in a foreign language. A man and a woman were arguing. It lasted about two minutes, then there was the sound of someone running down the stairs. I picked up the mobile and wondered whether it was worth trying Danny again. I decided against it. Somehow I knew he wouldn't answer.

I sighed. Somewhere out there, Raymond Keen was relaxing,

enjoying the fruits of his success. Some time soon he'd find out that the attempt on my life had failed, which was going to be more than a little inconvenient.

And some time after that he'd find out that he'd made a big mistake trying to silence me.

32

I left the hotel at just after eight o'clock the following morning, dressed in the clothes I'd changed into the previous night, and took a walk in the direction of Hyde Park. It was a brisk morning and a watery sun was fighting to push its way through the thin cloud cover. I stopped for breakfast and coffee at a cafe on the Bayswater Road and took the opportunity to take a look at the papers.

The shooting incident at the Gallan was front-page news, as I'd expected. However, at the time of going to press, details were still fairly limited. They'd named the dead police officer as Detective Constable David Carrick, aged twenty-nine, but the man I'd despatched remained anonymous. I wondered if they'd ever find out who he was. The report confirmed that a third man had suffered gunshot wounds at the scene and was now under police guard in hospital, where his condition was described as serious but not life-threatening. For the most part, the story revolved around the drama of the shoot-out, with the inevitable witness reports, but it was clear its authors didn't have any real idea what it had been all about. There was a quote from one of the Met's assistant chief constables saying that gun crime, though on the rise, was under control in London, although I don't suppose many of the readers believed him. The paper's leader column assumed that drugs had been the motive behind the shooting and claimed that the government was going to have to do something radical to quell demand among the nation's youth. Which was a sensible enough viewpoint, even if it remained to be seen whether drugs had actually been the motive in this case. Whatever Raymond and his associate, Mehmet Illan, were involved in was still a mystery. The only thing I could say for sure was that it was both illegal and highly profitable, drugs, I suppose, was as good a guess as any.

When I'd finished eating and reading, I carried on down the Bayswater Road in the direction of Marble Arch and stopped when I found a phone box just off the main thoroughfare. I wasn't sure how Malik would react to my call – badly, probably – but he was in a better position than me to do something about the Miriam Fox case.

He answered his mobile after one ring. 'DS Malik.'

'Asif, it's me. Can you talk?'

There was a short silence.

'About my call last night—'

'Look, what the hell's going on, Sarge? The word is you're involved in a lot of very bad stuff, that you had something to do with the shooting last night. A police officer got killed—'

'I won't piss you about, Asif. I've had some problems. I've got into bed with a few of the wrong people—'

'Oh shit, Sarge. You of all people. Why the fuck did it have to be you?' He sounded genuinely hurt.

'It's not what you think.'

'Isn't it? They told us this morning that you're a strong suspect in the Traveller's Rest killings. Is that why you were so interested in how the investigation was going?'

'Oh, for Christ's sake, Asif. It's me you're talking to. The man you've worked with for four years. Do you really believe I'm a triple murderer?' I was conscious that there were probably people listening in to this call and they would be trying to trace its source urgently.

'So what were you doing up there that night? They said you were stopped at a roadblock near the scene.'

'I was stopped, but I was on the way back from Clavering. I've got a woman up there, someone I see occasionally.'

'You've never told me about her.'

'She's married. You wouldn't have approved. But that's not what I'm phoning about. Believe what you want to believe, there's nothing I can do about that. But I want you to investigate Carla Graham. She's definitely involved in the Miriam Fox killing and maybe those other disappearances I was telling you about as well.'

'How do you know?' He was trying to keep me talking, there was no doubt about that.

'I just do. She knew things only someone involved could know, and that's definite. All I'm asking is that you put some tabs on her, check her background. Maybe even lean on Wells some more.'

'We can't. He's been charged.'

I exhaled loudly. 'Just look into her background. That's all I'm asking.'

'All right, I'll see what I can do.' There was a short pause. 'What were those men after you for last night?'

'Because I made a mistake. I got involved in something I shouldn't have, and now they want to make me pay the price.'

'I never took you to be corrupt, Sarge ... Dennis. What the hell made you think you could get away with it?'

I ignored the question. 'I'm sorry. I truly am.' I wanted to say something else, but I didn't know what, and I didn't have the time anyway. He started to repeat the question but I hung up, sad that now even he was against me. But not really that surprised.

I jogged across the road and into Hyde Park, feeling like a pariah. I didn't think they'd had time to get a trace on me, but there was no point hanging around to get proved wrong, so I made my way slowly back to Bayswater, figuring that my next move was to buy some clothes and a toothbrush.

33

As the day wore on, I couldn't help thinking that Carla Graham was going to get away with her role in the murder of Miriam Fox. Malik hadn't seemed overly interested in what I had to say: even if he did believe me, there was no way Knox or Capper or anyone else was going to act on it. In the end, what was there to act on? Just the word of a disgraced police officer who was now on the run.

It bothered me that justice wouldn't be done. I suppose you could say that justice is rarely done in this world and that the vast majority of people don't get the fate they deserve, but that would be missing the point. I knew Carla Graham had done wrong and I wanted her to be called to account for it. I also wanted to find out whether she could shed any light on what had happened to Molly Hagger and Anne Taylor. I was pretty certain by now that Molly was dead and it was important to me to find out why and how. And who it was who'd killed her. It would, I thought, be a chance to atone for my many sins. Even if no-one ever realized that I'd solved the case and punished the perpetrators, at least I would have the satisfaction of having redeemed myself in my own eyes. Which was a lot better than nothing.

It wasn't going to be easy to get Carla to talk voluntarily. I knew that. Knowing her, she'd already have some story concocted as to how she'd found out about the manner of Miriam Fox's death – she was obviously pretty creative in that department – and would be fully aware that one verbal slip-up on her part to a man who'd just resigned from the police force was not exactly going to do a great deal to build a criminal case against her. But get her to talk I would. Carla Graham was a tough cookie who'd be able to withstand some pretty rigorous questioning, but this time it wouldn't do her any good. I would be visiting her in a very unofficial capacity. And with nothing to lose.

By four o'clock that afternoon, I'd decided on my strategy. At ten past, I found a callbox in Kensington, phoned the *North London Echo*, asking to speak to Roy Shelley. I went on hold to the sound of Marvin Gaye's 'Heard it Through the Grapevine', and it was about a minute before he finally came on the line.

'Dennis Milne. Fuck me, I haven't heard from you in a while. What do you want? Renew your subscription?'

'No, I might have something for you. Something that'll sell a lot of papers.'

'Oh yeah?'

'But I need something from you first.'

'You're not pissing me about are, you, Dennis? No disrespect, but I don't want to waste my time here. There's talk of redundancies at this place at the moment and I don't want to be first in the queue.'

'You'll be last in the queue if you run this story, Roy. It's big stuff, I promise you. The sort of stuff the nationals love.'

I could almost hear his interest cranking up at the other end. I'd known Roy Shelley a long time. He was what you'd call an old-school reporter. A pisshead who could sniff out information faster than any copper I knew.

'Can you give us a little snifter?' he asked. 'Just so I've got some sort of idea what to expect.'

'Not yet, but I promise you it'll be one hell of a lot better than you can imagine. It might even turn out to be the story of your career. But, like I said, I need something from you first.'

'What?' His tone was suspicious.

'Does the name Mehmet Illan mean anything to you?'

He thought about it for a moment. 'No. Should it?'

'I don't know. But can you do me a favour and find out anything you can about him. He's Turkish, I think.'

'Well, he would be with a name like that.'

'I would imagine he's based somewhere in North London, and he's definitely involved in a lot of dodgy dealing.'

'What kind of dodgy dealing?'

'I'm not a hundred per cent sure, but I think, if you ask around enough, you'll find people who know him. But try to be discreet.'

'And is this guy part of the story you've got?'

'He's a part of it, yes. But just a part. There's a lot more besides. How soon can you get me the info on him?'

'It could take a day or two.'

'Too long, Roy. I need it fast. The sooner I get it, the sooner you get your story.'

'Dennis, I don't even know who the bloke is.'

'Yeah, but you can find out. That's why I called you. I'm uncontactable at the moment, but I'll call you back at ten a.m.

tomorrow. If you can get me the gen by then, I'd appreciate it.'

'This'd better be a good story, Dennis.'

'It is. I promise you. And something else too.'

'What?'

'Whatever you do, don't tell anyone I called. And don't make any attempt to get hold of me either. I can't explain why at the moment, but all will be revealed very shortly.'

'Christ Almighty, you're sounding like a fucking Robert Ludlum book. At least give me a sniff of what's going on.'

'Roy, if I could, I would. But I can't. Not for a day or two anyway. Just be patient. It'll be worth it.'

He started to ask another question, but I said my goodbyes and hung up.

After that, I made another phone call, but the person I was after wasn't in. No matter. It could wait.

I stepped out of the phone box and hailed a passing black cab. I got him to drop me off halfway up Upper Street, paid him his money, and went to pick up my car, which was parked on an adjoining street a couple of hundred yards up from my flat. I knew they'd be looking out for me on the off chance that I was stupid enough to return home, but they'd only have a couple of people watching the place, and my car was parked far enough away to avoid getting spotted. I was relieved to see that it was exactly where I'd left it more than a week earlier, which for London isn't too bad. It started first time, too. Maybe my luck was changing.

My first port of call was Camden Town. After hunting around for what seemed like a long time, I found a free meter on a residential street and then made my way over to Camden High Street to get my bearings before heading in the direction of Coleman House. I passed the pub where I'd first had a drink with Carla only a week earlier and, after hesitating for a moment, went inside. At this time in the afternoon it was still quite quiet, with only a sprinkling of students, old codgers, and the un-employable dotted about the place. That would all change in half an hour when the after-work crowd started to pour in.

I ordered a pint of Pride from the bar and asked the barman where the payphone was. He told me it was in the corridor lead-ing to the toilets. There was no-one around when I walked in, so I dialled Coleman House reception.

'Carla Graham, please,' I asked in as official a voice as I could muster.

'She's not here at the moment,' said the voice at the other end, a woman whose tones I didn't recognize. 'Can I ask who's call-ing, please?'

'Frank Black. Black's Office Supplies. I'm actually returning her call. She was interested in some prices.'

'Can I put you through to her assistant, Sara?'

'Well, it's actually Miss Graham I need to speak to. Do you know when she's back?'

'I'm afraid she won't be in until tomorrow now. She's at a seminar this afternoon.'

I said I'd phone back, and hung up. After that, I tried Len Runnion's number again, but there was still no answer.

I went back into the bar, took a stool facing the wall near the door, and drank my drink. A mirror stretched right around the wall at head height, and my reflection stared back at me mournfully. I looked a mess, mainly because I hadn't shaved that day, which was deliberate. I was growing a beard now, in keep-ing with my passport photo. I was also going to have to fatten up a bit. I'd been at least half a stone heavier in the photo, and to be on the safe side I wanted to add another half stone on top of that. I'd had a McDonald's for lunch, which had been a good start, but I was going to have to have a similarly fatty supper for it to have any effect. From now on I was on a diet of greasy, bad food in large quantities until further notice. And I'd probably be one of the first people in the world to actually benefit from it.

I felt like I needed Dutch courage for what I was about to do, so I ordered another pint and drank that with a couple of cigarettes and a bag of cheese and onion crisps I didn't want but felt sure I ought to have. By the time I'd finished it, the predicted after-work crowd had materialized and the bar was three deep with loud, suited individuals and young secretaries out for a good time. The clock above the bar told me it was twenty past five.

Outside, darkness had long since fallen and the streets were crowded with commuters and early Christmas shoppers. The day after tomorrow would be the first of December. The year had gone fast, as they always seem to do. This time, however, I'd be glad when it had been and gone. Memorable it might turn out to be, but for all the wrong reasons.

By the time I got back to the car it had started raining. I jumped in and fought my way through the crawling rush-hour traffic, hoping that I got to Carla's flat before she did. My plan was to wait outside until she arrived, then apprehend her at the door. I'd try to get inside through charm alone – I didn't want to cause a scene – but if she didn't want to play ball, I'd pull the gun I'd taken ownership of the previous night. I didn't think she'd argue with that. After that, I'd play it by ear.

But the traffic was a lot worse than I'd expected and I wasn't totally sure of my bearings, so it was well gone six when I pulled into Carla's cul-de-sac. I managed to squeeze into a parking space about twenty yards down from her building and cut the engine. I could make out her flat through the outstretched skeletal branches of a beech tree. There were several lights on. So she was home.

I cursed silently. I should have got there earlier rather than dawdled over my pints. Now it was going to be difficult to get inside. I lit a cigarette and weighed up my options. I didn't think she'd let me in if I rang on her buzzer. We'd hardly left on the best of terms, and she had no reason to talk to me. What was I going to say? That I wanted to come up and accuse her of murder for a second time? Breaking in was another option, but I remembered the building's security system being fairly elaborate. The door had been new and the lock was a five-bar. I didn't think my housebreaking skills stretched to that, not without equipment.

Which meant waiting for an opportunity to present itself. I finished the cigarette, took a swig from a bottle of Coke I'd brought with me, and lit another cigarette, wondering what I was going to do when and if she admitted her part in the whole thing. I could hardly make a citizen's arrest, not in my position, and I didn't think I had the stomach to kill her in cold blood. Which kind of cut down my options. Yet somehow I still felt that I was doing the right thing by coming here. I had to get to the bottom of this before I could continue with my life.

I think I'd been there about ten minutes, maybe a bit less, when a car drove into the cul-de-sac looking for a parking space. I slid down in my seat, not wanting to draw attention to myself, and the car continued past. When it got to the end it made a torturously slow U-turn in the limited space available and drove back out again. About a minute later, I saw the driver, a middle-aged businessman, walk past on Carla's side of the road. He stopped when he came to Carla's building and fished about in his coat pocket for his keys.

I stepped out of the car and crossed the street as casually as possible, coming up behind him as he was mounting the steps. He heard my footfalls and whirled round, his face etched with the automatic fear city dwellers always experience when someone approaches them from behind at night. His expression eased a bit when he saw it was a man in a shirt and tie, but remained suspicious nevertheless.

'Yes. Can I help you?'

I pulled out my warrant card and showed it to him. 'I'm here to see Miss Carla Graham,' I said authoritatively, looking him right in the eye. 'I understand she lives on the top floor.'

He put his key in the door. 'That's right. Well, you'd better buzz her—'

'I'd rather she didn't know who it was, sir. You see, I'm not one hundred per cent sure she'll want to speak to us.'

He looked at me curiously but decided in the end that I was probably who I said I was, and turned the key in the lock. 'I assume you know where to go,' he said, as I followed him inside.

'Yes, I do. Thanks.'

'Sorry to seem suspicious, but you know what it's like.'

'Dead right. You can never be too careful these days.'

He moved off down the hall and I made my way up the stairs, remembering back to that night just three days ago when I'd walked up them the first time. A lot had changed since then.

When I got up to the third floor, I stopped outside her door and listened carefully. The television was on with the volume turned up high. It sounded as though it was switched to the news. I pressed my ear against the door and tried to pick out any other sounds, but couldn't hear anything.

I reached down and tried the handle, but it wouldn't give. The door was locked, so I leaned down and checked the lock itself. It was an easy one. Reaching into my pocket, I pulled a credit card from my wallet and manoeuvred it into the tiny gap between the door and skirting. The lock gave without resistance, and slowly I turned the handle.

I stepped into the hallway and gently eased the door closed

behind me, putting the chain across it to delay her if she tried to make a getaway. There were no lights on in the hallway itself but the sitting-room door on my left was open, providing some light. I stopped and listened again. Nothing. Not a sound.

Making as little noise as possible, I slowly put my head round the sitting-room door.

The room was empty. In the corner, the TV blared as a news reporter in some dusty war-torn location gave a dramatic run-down on whatever conflict it was he was covering. A half-drunk cup of coffee sat on the teak coffee table, and next to it was an ashtray with two butts in it. I waited a moment, then, still hearing no sound from anywhere in the flat, walked inside. I leaned over and dipped my finger in the coffee. It was cool, but not cold. Maybe half an hour old. No more than that.

I retreated back into the hallway. Immediately to my right was the kitchen. The door was half closed but the light was on inside. I pushed it open and had a quick look but, like the sitting room, it too was empty. That only left two rooms, one of which was the bathroom, right opposite me at the end of the hall. Its door was wide open. I crept up, paused for a moment, then reached round and pulled on the light.

Empty.

Which left the bedroom.

I assumed she must have gone out for something; either that or she'd taken a very early night. It didn't matter. I could wait for her easily enough. I didn't suppose she was having a romantic tryst in there, otherwise I'd have been able to hear her. Carla was not a woman who could enjoy a quiet fuck.

I stepped forward and listened briefly at the door. Again, just silence.

Slowly, ever so slowly, I turned the handle. The door creaked open.

It was pitch black. Even without looking, I could tell the curtains were closed. I stepped inside, waited a moment, then reached for the light switch, trying to remember which side of the door it was on. Again, no sound. No sound at all.

I picked the right side, found the switch, and flicked it on. It seemed very bright and I blinked rapidly as my eyes refocused.

It took me two, maybe three seconds to see the huge dark stain that spread high up the wall behind her kingsize bed. Beneath it, lying face forward on the heavily bloodstained sheets at a slightly skewed angle from the wall and with its arms and legs spread wide, lay the fully clothed corpse of Carla Graham. She was wearing a white blouse, whole swathes of which were now crimson, black trousers and socks. One of her bedside lamps had fallen off its perch and now lay on its side on the floor, the only obvious sign of a struggle, and her hands were gripping onto great clumps of the sheets. There was a vague, airless smell in the room but nothing like as pungent as the stench in the funeral home after Raymond had murdered Barry Finn.

I stepped forward, still finding it difficult to believe what I was seeing, and gingerly approached the body. I didn't want to touch it, not without gloves on, but I wanted to check that she was actually dead, although with that much blood it was difficult to believe she could be anything but.

Her eyes were open. Wide. Terrified. But still beautiful some- how, even in death. We could have been something. We really could have. At that moment, I felt a bitter regret that it had come to this.

The gaping wound in her throat was partly obscured by her hair, but I could see that it was very deep and very wide ... similar to the one that had ended Miriam Fox's life. Out of the corner of my eye, I watched a droplet of blood ease slowly down the wall. I looked back down at Carla's throat. The blood was still oozing out of the wound, though its flow was now down to a trickle.

She had died only a short while before. A very short while. Ten, fifteen minutes. No longer than that. The blood hadn't even coagulated yet. I'd been outside for about ten minutes, sitting in the car. No-one had left the building in that time. It had taken me five minutes to get up the stairs, give the flat the once-over, and come into the room where I stood now. That was fifteen minutes in total. In my estimation, she'd almost certainly been alive fifteen minutes ago.

Which meant only one thing.

I heard the movement behind me and whirled round at just the second the knife came flashing through the air in a great arc, still dripping with Carla's blood. I jumped backwards and banged into the bedside table. The blade swished past perilously close to my skin, almost touching it, only an inch separating me from certain evisceration.

My attacker was a big man, well over six feet with a build to match. He had a black baseball cap pulled low over his face, but I could make out the look of steely determination beneath it. There was no way he was going to let me live. Not now I'd seen him.

He stumbled slightly with the momentum of his swing and I jumped forward, grabbing him by both wrists and kicking him as hard as I could in the shins. He flinched with pain but maintained his balance, and pushed me back against the table, at the same time twisting his way out of my grip.

Now he had both hands free again, and he brought the knife up in a rapid thrust aimed at my belly, but I leaped aside, landing on my back on the bed, my head resting on Carla's still warm corpse. I could feel the blood-drenched sheets wet against my body. I tried to kick out as he lifted the huge knife above his head but his legs were pressed up tight against mine, making movement next to impossible.

He brought the knife down hard, but I wriggled violently and grabbed his arm with both hands, pushing it to one side and banging it against the wall with all the strength I could muster. He didn't release his grip. Instead, with his free hand he punched me hard in the face and I felt a terrible pain shoot through my cheek. He punched me again, a triumphant look in his eyes, and my vision began to blur.

Then, suddenly changing tactics, he stopped punching me and reached over to grab the knife from his other hand, which I had pinned against the wall. In doing so, he relaxed the pressure on my legs, and before he had a chance to stab at me again I kicked out wildly, cracking him in the knee with the heel of my new brogues. He jumped backwards out of range of my feet and his cap flew off, revealing a thick head of unkempt hair. The loss of it appeared to distract him momentarily, like Samson losing his locks, and I took the opportunity to roll across the bed, forcing myself over Carla's slick, greasy body.

I seemed to roll for ages before finally crashing down the other side. I could hear my attacker coming round the front of the bed, and I desperately hunted through the pockets of my coat for the gun I'd taken the previous night. I got a grip on the handle and tried to tug it out, but it snagged on the material. He was coming into full view, replacing the black cap on his head, the knife held wickedly aloft. Only feet away. I felt the material around my pocket tear. I pulled again, desperately trying to get it out, panic threatening to fuck up everything.

Suddenly the handle came free and I whipped the gun out, pointing the barrel at my assailant. He saw it and stopped dead, then made a split-second decision turn and run for the door. I located the safety catch, flicked it round, then sat up and took aim. He was almost through the door but I managed to get off a shot. It went wide and high, hitting the upper door frame. He kept going, disappearing from view, and I jumped to my feet and started out after him.

When I came out into the hallway he was at the front door, fiddling with the chain. He turned, saw me, gave me one last defiant look, and pulled it open. I fired again as he started down the stairs, but again the bullet went wide and high. It was no wonder the Turk hadn't been able to hit me the previous night. The sights on this gun were so out of kilter I'd have had to aim at the ceiling to get any chance of actually putting a hole in my target.

I could hear his heavy footfalls on the stairs, taking them two at a time. There was no way I was going to catch him now. I stopped where I was, panting with exhaustion and shock. That had been close. Far too close for comfort. That made two attempts on my life in twenty-four hours, neither of which had been that far from success. So far I'd emerged unscathed, but it was only a matter of time before my luck ran out.

And now I was never going to get any answers from Carla Graham.

But her killer would know them. And luckily for me I knew him. Or knew his name, anyway.

There's a true story that goes like this. A thirty-two-year-old man once kidnapped and repeatedly raped a ten-year-old girl. He took her back to his dingy flat, tied her to a bed and subjected her to a prolonged and sickening sexual assault. He might have killed her too, apparently he'd boasted in the past of wanting to murder young girls for a thrill, but a neighbour heard the girl's screams and called the cops. They turned up, kicked the door down, and nicked him. Unfortunately, he later got off on a technicality and the girl's father ended up behind bars, and later under the ground, for trying to extract his own justice. I remembered the case because an ex-colleague of mine had worked on it. It had been two years ago now.

The rapist's name was Alan Kover, and he was the man who'd just tried to put a knife in me.

There were more footsteps on the stairs, this time coming up. I placed the gun back in my pocket and walked over to the front door. As I was shutting it behind me, the guy who'd let me in emerged from round the corner. He was carrying a heavy-looking torch that I think was his best effort at a weapon, and wearing a very concerned expression.

'What's going on?' he asked. 'I've just seen a man with a knife come charging down the stairs.'

I started down towards him. 'Call the police,' I said.

'But I thought *you* were the police.'

'Not any more I'm not.'

'Then who the hell are you?'

I pushed past him without stopping. 'Someone who hopes good luck comes in threes.'

34

'Mehmet Illan. Forty-five years old. Turkish national, he's been resident in this country for the last sixteen years. He's supposedly just a businessman, but apparently he's got previous convictions in Turkey and Germany for drugs offences, though no record here. He's got a number of companies on the go doing all sorts: import/export – mainly foodstuffs and carpets; a chain of pizza parlours; a PC wholesalers; a textile factory. You name it, he's got an interest in it somewhere down the line. But the word is that a lot of his companies are just fronts for money laundering, and that his real profits come from elsewhere.'

'Oh yeah? Where?'

'Apparently he used to import a lot of heroin overland from Turkey and Afghanistan, although no-one's got any hard evidence of that, but now he's in the people-smuggling business. You know, asylum seekers.'

'I hear there's big money to be made in that sort of thing.'

'Very big. These people come from all over the place and they'll sell everything they've got to get the money to pay the smugglers. The going rate can be as much as five grand per person, so one lorryload of twenty people can be worth a hundred K to the people doing the smuggling. If they only shift a hundred a week, they're still clearing half a million, and chances are they'll be shifting a lot more than that. It could be thousands.'

'And you think this guy Illan's involved in that?'

'That's what I'm hearing. My information says he's a major player, but he's done a good job of keeping himself as far away from the action as possible, so no-one's got anything concrete on him. What's your interest in him anyway?'

'I might have got something on him. You'll hear about it before the end of the week. You'll be the first to know.'

'Whatever it is, be careful, Dennis. This guy is not to be messed with. You know those three blokes shot dead the other week – the customs men and the accountant . . . ?'

'Yeah?'

'The accountant was something to do with one of his front companies, and the talk is that Illan was the guy behind the murders, although proving it's another matter. So, he doesn't

fuck about. You piss him off, you die. If he's prepared to commit triple murder, he's prepared to kill a copper.'

'Don't worry, I'm not going to do anything stupid.'

'So if you didn't know anything about this guy – and I assume
you didn't otherwise you wouldn't have been phoning me – what
is it exactly you've got on him?'

'Be patient, Roy.'

'Patience doesn't sell newspapers, you know that.'

I put some more money in the phone, knowing that I was
going to have to give him something.

'I think I can prove a link between him, some other criminals,
and the deaths of those three blokes.'

I could hear his breathing change at the other end. He was
excited, but nervous at the same time in case I was bullshitting.

'Are you serious?'

'Deadly.'

'So, why are you telling me? Why aren't you arresting these
people?'

'It's a long story, Roy, but basically you're going to have to
trust me.'

He sighed. 'I knew it was too good to be true.'

'I've resigned from the Force,' I told him. 'There were a couple
of minor irregularities. It was with immediate effect. That's why
I haven't arrested anyone yet.'

'Christ, Dennis. Really? What did you do?'

'Suffice to say I've had some involvement with people who
know Mehmet Illan. Not major involvement, but enough to get
me sacked. And enough for me to know a few things about
them.'

'Tell me more.'

'Not now. I need you to do something else for me. It shouldn't
take five minutes.'

'What is it?'

'Alan Kover. Remember him?'

'The name rings a bell.'

'He was that child rapist who got off on a technicality. The girl's father got arrested trying to burn his flat down and ended up committing suicide. It was about two years back, over in Hackney.'

'Yeah, yeah, I remember.'

'Kover's still walking the streets and I need to find him. Urgently.'

'Is he involved in this?'

I decided to lie. It was easier. 'He might be, I'm not sure. Can you get me his current address?'

'Dennis, you're asking me to do a lot here. This sort of stuff could get me in one fuck of a lot of trouble. What the hell are you going to do to him, anyway?'

Again, I lied. 'Nothing. I just need to speak to him. You do this for me, I promise no-one'll ever know it was you, and you'll get the exclusive on this story. After this, the whole of Fleet Street'll be beating a path to your door. I promise.'

'It might not be that easy. He might have changed his name.'

'He had previous convictions so it's unlikely he'll have been able to change his name. He should be on the Sex Offenders Register.'

Roy sighed. 'I'll see what I can do.'

'It's important, and I'm going to need the information quick.'

'Give me more of a snifter on this story. Something to really whet my appetite.'

'Get me Kover's current address by tonight and I'll tell you a bit more then.'

'This'd better be fucking good, Dennis.'

'I'll call you on this number at five tonight.'

'I've got a meeting. Make it six.'

'Six it is. And same thing applies. Don't tell anyone you've heard from me.'

The beeps went as he started to say something else, and I hung up without saying goodbye.

I stepped out of the phone box into the morning rush hour and made my way slowly back towards the hotel.

35

'With you in a minute,' came a voice from the back of the shop as I shut the door. I pushed the bolt across and switched the sign round from OPEN to CLOSED – not that I expected to be disturbed. Len Runnion's shop is hardly a mecca for retail activity. Still, always easier to err on the side of caution.

He appeared behind the counter wiping what looked like a Chinese ornamental vase with a cloth, presumably to get rid of fingerprints. When he saw me, he attempted a smile, but it wasn't a very good effort and his eyes started darting around alarmingly, always coming back to the vase in his hand.

'Oh, hello, Mr Milne,' he said as jovially as possible. He put the vase down under the counter. 'What can I do for you?'

'Guns,' I said, approaching him. 'I want some guns.'

His eyes seemed to go into overdrive, and he took a step back. I think there was a look on my face that scared him. 'I don't know where you'd get them sort of things from,' he said nervously. 'Sorry, I can't help on that one. I make it a point never to go near any sort of weapon.'

I stopped on the other side of the counter and eyed him carefully. 'I'm no longer a police officer,' I told him, 'so I'm not interested in nicking you for anything. Now, we can do this the easy way or the hard way.'

'Look, Mr Milne, I don't know what the fuck you're talking about so I think you'd better leave if that's the sort of thing you've come for.' He was more confident now that I'd told him I was no longer with the Force.

However, the confidence was shortlived. I pulled out the gun I'd taken from Illan's man and pointed it directly at his chest. 'I'm not fucking about, Leonard. I need at least two firearms other than the one I'm pointing at you, preferably ones that are magazine loading. Plus a reasonable quantiity of ammunition.'

'What the fuck is going on here, Mr Milne?' he asked unsteadily, his eyes for once very much focused as they stared at the gun. 'Is that thing real?'

'Very much so. Now, I know you deal in illegal firearms, everyone knows that.'

'I don't know what you're talking about—'

'Yes you do. You know exactly what I'm talking about. You're going to supply me the two weapons I've just asked for now – today – or I'm going to kill you. It's as simple as that.'

'I've got no guns. I promise.'

'You know something, Runnion, I've always disliked you. And I'll bet you shifted those tax discs from that Holloway robbery as well.'

'No, I didn't. I'm serious—'

'But you know what? That's nothing to do with me any more so I'm not even going to pursue it. I'll leave that to other people. But what I will tell you is this: if you don't get me these two guns this afternoon, you are a dead man. It's as simple as that.'

I moved the gun upwards so it was pointed directly between

his eyes. A bead of sweat rolled down his forehead and onto his nose. He blinked rapidly, but remained stock still. I think I'd convinced him I was serious.

'Please stop pointing that thing at me.'

'Are you going to get me what I want?'

'It's going to take some time.'

'Have you got the ones I want in stock?'

'I don't carry stock. Not of that—'

'Stop lying. I repeat: have you got the ones I want in stock?'

'I can get you two guns like that, yes.'

'Where are they?'

'I've got some gear over in a lock-up in Shoreditch. Guns. I should have what you're looking for. Now, please stop pointing that thing at me. It might go off.'

I doubted I'd have hit him if it had, but I wasn't going to tell him that. I lowered the gun and smiled. 'Let's go over there now. Have you got transport, or shall we go in my car?'

'I can't go now, Mr Milne. I've got things I've got to do.'

I laughed, but there was no humour in it. 'We're going now,' I told him. 'My car or yours?'

He sighed, then looked at me as if he still couldn't quite believe I was doing this. I looked back at him in a way that convinced him I was.

'We'll take mine, then,' he said. 'It's out the back.'

He went and locked up the front of the shop properly, then the two of us exited the rear door, fighting our way through the boxes of crap, unsafe electrical goods, and stolen property that made up the vast bulk of his inventory. The back door emerged into a tiny potholed car park containing two cars that looked like they were just about ready for the knacker's yard. We got into the slightly more respectable of the two – a rusty red Nissan which had probably looked quite flash and sporty back in the mid-1980's – and drove slowly out into the street.

The mid-afternoon traffic was heavier than usual due to an accident on Commercial Road backing things up and it took three quarters of an hour to make a journey that wasn't much the wrong side of a mile. We didn't speak a lot on the way. Runnion did ask a few probing questions about who it was who'd provoked my ire and whether I was going to kill or simply wound them, but I told him to keep his mouth shut and his eyes on the road, and after a while he got the message. I felt strangely detached from the whole thing. I was doing everything instinctively without any real thought as to the possible consequences. Nothing really seemed to matter. I had a plan, and if it succeeded I would be pleased, but if it failed, then so be it. I might even end up dead, yet, sitting there in the choking traffic, even that thought held no fear. And the funny thing was, it wasn't such a bad feeling to have. It felt almost liberating to know that this world, so often wrought with pressures and tensions, was no longer of real importance. Life for me had come down to a set of tasks that I would either complete or not complete. It was as simple as that.

The lock-up was one of a row on a narrow back road off Great Eastern Street. Runnion parked up on the pavement directly outside, and we got out together. There weren't many people about- a few City types taking shortcuts, the odd courier – and you wouldn't have thought you were only a couple of hundred yards from one of the largest financial districts in the world.

I stayed close to Runnion, keeping my hand in my coat pocket with the gun. 'Don't get any ideas about running,' I told him as he opened it up. He didn't say anything, and stepped inside. I followed him in, trying not to look too conspicuous, and pulled the shutter down behind me as he switched on the light.

Unlike his shop, the lock-up was remarkably tidy. There were boxes piled up on both sides but there was space to move about in the middle. At the far end, under a pile of tarpaulin, was a wooden strongbox which Runnion had to unlock. From inside it, he removed a large holdall which he put on the floor.

'Pick it up,' I told him. 'We're going back to your house.'

'What?' He looked at me, aghast. 'What for?'

'Because I want to take my time choosing and this isn't the place to do that.'

He started to argue, but I pulled the shutter back up and waited for him to walk out. He put the holdall in the back seat, secured the lock-up, and we were on our way again.

Runnion lived in a row of reasonably well-kept terraced houses in Holloway. I'd raided it once with Malik and a couple of uniforms looking for stolen property, which, predictably, we hadn't found, but I remembered it being quite a homely place. That had been about a year ago now and he'd been married at the time to a surprisingly pleasant wife who'd even offered us a cup of tea as we rummaged through their possessions, which is something of a rarity. She'd left him now and I kept enough tabs on him to know that he lived on his own.

Because we were moving away from Commercial Road, it took a lot less time to get to his house, even though the traffic was still heavy. We went inside in silence and sat down in his sitting room. There were a couple of dirty plates on the floor and various other bits and pieces of rubbish. Nothing like as tidy or as homely as I remembered it.

I motioned for him to sit down. He thanked me sarcastically, putting the holdall down on the floor between us. He was a lot cockier now than he had been, a result no doubt of the fact that he was getting used to the situation.

'Do you mind if I smoke?' I said, lighting a cigarette without offering him one. He shook his head and mumbled something, lighting one for himself. I sat back in my seat and took the gun out of my pocket. 'OK, show me what you've got in there.' He unzipped the bag and gingerly took out a shabby-looking .22 pistol. 'That's no use to me,' I told him. 'Keep going.' He put the .22 on the carpet and reached back into the bag like a miserable Santa, emerging this time with a sawn-off pump-action shotgun. I shook my head, and he carried on. Next up was more in tune with what I wanted: a newish-looking MAC 10 sub machine pistol. There was no magazine in it, but after a quick rummage around Runnion came up with two taped together. 'I'll have that one,' I told him, and he put it to one side.

He pulled out a further three weapons – all handguns – and told me that was all he'd got.

I smiled. 'Well, it's not bad for a man who likes to keep away from weapons.' Still holding onto my own gun, I gave each of them a brief inspection and settled for a short-barrelled Browning. 'Have you got ammo for this?' I asked him.

'Should have,' he said, and once again began a search of the bag, bringing out a couple of mint-condition boxes of 9mm bullets which he put with the MAC 10 and the revolver.

I took a long drag on my cigarette and watched him carefully as he put everything else back in the holdall. When he'd finished, I stood up and picked up my newly acquired weapons. I put the MAC 10 in the pocket of my raincoat, along with the magazines, and stubbed my cigarette out in an overflowing ashtray. I picked up the Browning and inspected it again, removing the magazine, checking the bullets.

'You haven't got a silencer for this, have you?' I asked.

'No, I fucking haven't,' he said, remaining seated.

'Well, I hope when it comes down to it, it works.'

'I'm sure it will.'

I released the safety and pulled the trigger.

It did.

36

'I've been hearing some funny rumours today, Dennis.'

'Oh yeah?' I leaned back against the phone-box glass and took a drink from the can of Coke I was holding. All part of the new diet. 'What sort of rumours?'

'That you're involved in a lot of serious shit. That the police are looking for you with a view to questioning you about some very nasty crimes indeed. Possibly even murder.'

I whistled through my teeth. 'Serious allegations. Where did you hear them from?'

'Are they true?'

'Behave. You've known me for close to ten years. Do you really think I'd be involved in murder?'

'And I've been in journalism for close to thirty years and one thing I've learned is that people are never what they seem. Everyone's got skeletons in their closets, even the vicar's wife. And some of them are pretty fucking grim.'

'I've got skeletons, Roy, but they don't include murder. Now, have you got the information we were talking about?'

'I'm concerned, Dennis. I don't want any of this coming back to me.'

'It won't. Don't worry.'

'That's easy for you to say.'

'What do you mean, easy? I'm the one who's on the run. Look,

I promise all you'll get out of it is a fucking decent story.'

'When? You keep telling me this, but so far I haven't got a thing to go on and I've put my neck on the line for you.'

I sighed and thought about it for a moment. 'It's Thursday now. You'll have your story by tomorrow.'

'I'd better do.'

'You will. So what's the address then?'

'What are you going to do to him?'

'I need to ask him some questions. That's all. He can solve a puzzle for me.'

'44b Kenford Terrace. It's in Hackney. That's all I know. And don't ever fucking tell anyone you heard it from me.'

37

I sat for a long time in the cold darkness waiting for Alan Kover.

His flat, not the one in which he'd committed the infamous rape, was stark in its minimalism. There was only one chair in the cramped little sitting room. It faced a cheap portable TV which had a small cactus plant on it, the only decoration of any kind in the whole room. I sat with my back to the door, watching the blank screen. Watching and waiting and thinking. Kover was the last key in the mystery surrounding Coleman House and its inhabitants. From the wound on Carla's throat, and the way she'd been attacked from behind, I felt sure that he had also been the man who'd murdered Miriam Fox. But such a scenario still threw up far more questions than answers. Presumably, Kover and Carla had been involved together in Miriam's killing. There was no other way she could have known the details of it. But how the hell had two such disparate personalities come together, and what on earth did they kill Miriam for? And what, if anything, did her death have to do with the disappearances? Kover and me, it seemed, had a lot to talk about.

I wanted to smoke. Badly. But I couldn't risk doing it in his flat so I opened my third can of Coke of the day and took a sip. What depressed me about this place was that there was nothing remotely homely, or even human, about it. It was like a bad attempt at a show home created by some very lazy people. I'd checked it over thoroughly, just to see if there were any clues as to what had been going on, but had found nothing. Nothing at all. Just kitchen cupboards with pots and pans in them, a wardrobe with some clothes, a bathroom with a toothbrush and soap. Not a thing that could tell you anything about his personality. For a few minutes I'd even thought I'd got the wrong address, but then I'd felt about under the bed and had pulled out a load of crumpled, dried-out tissues, and I knew then that this was where Kover resided. They'd said he had an unusually high sex drive, but he was sensible enough, having been on the receiving end of police attention, not to leave anything about that could get him into trouble. There were some unlabelled tapes piled up on the video recorder beneath the telly but I doubted if they contained anything incriminating.

I looked at my watch for the hundredth time since breaking in: 8.20 p.m. This time eleven days ago I'd been sitting outside the Traveller's Rest in the pouring rain with a man who was almost certainly now dead. I'd tried Danny's mobile three more times since the attempt on my life, and he still hadn't answered. The message kept saying that the phone I was trying to call was probably switched off and that I should try again later, but I knew there was no point. He would have answered by now. Even in Jamaica.

Behind me, I heard a key turn in the lock. Slipping out of the chair, I moved through the darkness until I was standing behind it as it slowly opened. A large figure emerged carrying a shopping bag and, though I couldn't make him out properly, I could tell it was Kover. The cosh came silently out of my pocket and, as he shut the door and turned to switch on the light, I cracked him hard over the back of the head.

He went down on his knees without a sound and stayed in that position for a second, so I hit him again. This time he toppled over on his side, and I knew he was out cold.

I worked fast. Grabbing him under the arms, I pulled him over to the chair I'd been sitting in, and flung him in it. He was already moaning and turning his head so I knew he wouldn't be under for long. I picked up the length of chain I'd brought with me and wrapped it three times round his upper body, securing it tightly to the back of the chair before padlocking it and chucking the key into my pocket. Next I produced some masking tape from my coat and used it to secure his legs and gag him.

By this time his eyes were fluttering and he was coming round. I lit a cigarette, savouring the first taste, and went round switching on all the lights before filling up the kettle and switching it on to boil. There was a four-pack of cheap lager among his shopping so I pulled off one of the cans and opened it, putting the rest in his sparsely populated fridge. I took a long drink – my first alcohol of the day – and stood watching him.

It took him a minute or two to realize where he was. He saw me, and his eyes widened. I smiled at him. He attempted to move, realizing then that he was helpless. I put my fingers to my lips to indicate that he should be quiet, then removed the tape from his mouth.

'What's going on?' he demanded. His voice was surprisingly high-pitched for a big guy and, though it sounded confident on the surface, there was a hint of nervousness which, under the circumstances, was no great surprise. 'I'm not saying nothing without my lawyer here.'

This was an interesting statement. It meant he knew exactly who I was. Maybe Carla had told him. I laughed and took a drag on the cigarette, stepping backwards. I had a perverse feeling that I was going to enjoy finding out.

'You tried to kill me last night,' I said.

'I don't know what you're talking about.' He struggled against his bonds. 'Now let me out of all this stuff. I could sue you for this.'

I pulled the tape back over his mouth and stubbed the cigarette out on his carpet. 'You know who I am, don't you?' I said. 'You know I'm a copper.' I paced slowly round the chair. 'Unfortunately, what you don't know is that I've left the Force. And what you also don't know is that I'm a killer, and that I've killed people who've deserved it a lot less than a piece of shit paedophile like you. So what I'm saying is this: I'm not like anyone who's ever questioned you before. I'm not here to put you behind bars. I'm not here to try to find out why you do the things you do. I'm here to find out some answers and if you don't give me those answers I'm going to blow your fucking brains all over this shitty wall, and that's after I've kneecapped you.' I stopped in front of him and pulled the Browning from my pocket, placing the barrel hard against his forehead. His eyes widened. 'OK? First question: why did you kill Carla Graham?' Once again, I removed the tape from his mouth.

'I don't know what you're talking about,' he blustered, looking down at his hands. 'Honestly.'

I pushed the tape back, then turned and walked into the kitchen, picking up the freshly boiled kettle.

He knew what was coming when he saw me emerge with it, but

there was nothing he could do. Desperately, he struggled in the seat as I stopped in front of him, stood there for a moment, then ever so gently tilted it until the boiling water dribbled slowly out and onto his upper left thigh. I increased the flow a little, moving to his other leg, watching as his face stretched tight and red with pain and his eyes bugged out of his head. I stopped, paused for maybe three seconds, then repeated the procedure, this time chucking a little on his groin for good measure. His wriggling became hysterical and a surprisingly loud moan came from behind the tape as he tried to cry out. His face was now beginning to go purple.

I stood back and watched him for a little while, a serene smile on my face. I felt that I was performing a worthwhile task, probably the most worthwhile task I'd performed in my whole career.

Without warning, I chucked a load more over his groin, waited while the pain racked through him in great agonized bursts, then put the kettle down and took a drink from the beer.

'Right. I hope we understand each other now. There's no limit to the pain I'll inflict on you if you don't answer my questions truthfully, so it's in your interests to just get it over with. And in case you think about crying out.' I reached down beside the chair to where the small jerry-can of petrol sat and poured its contents all over his body and head. 'If you thought hot water was painful, then nothing will prepare you for this.'

I put the can down and removed the tape. This time I crumpled it up and chucked it on the floor. I was confident I wouldn't need it again. He'd answer my questions now all right. Kover gritted his teeth, still fighting against the effects of the scalding, and turned uncomfortably in his seat.

'Now, let's start again. Carla Graham was involved in the murder of Miriam Fox. I know that for a fact. And I suspect you were too. What I'm missing is the reason. Whatever it was, you and her fell out about it, and you responded by butchering her on her own bed. Now, let me tell you something. There's no point in you not telling me the whole truth or protecting anyone else who may be involved or whatever, because if I get one word of a contradiction in your answers, then you'll burn. It's as simple as that. And I know you know that I'm serious.'

'Look, I didn't even know her! She was just—'

I pulled a lighter from my pocket and stepped forward, igniting the flame so it was only inches from his petrol-soaked face. Instinctively, he turned his head, but I followed it with the lighter and the flame remained right in his field of vision. He let out a fearful moan.

'You know, Kover, you're a very slow learner. I know you knew her. There's no way you got through the security door into her building without being let in, and there was no forced entry to her flat because I was there just after you, remember? You knew her and, for whatever reason, I think she was expecting you. So, I'm going to ask again: why did you and Carla murder Miriam Fox, and why did you then kill Carla?'

There was a long pause. The moment of truth. It was like opening a door, although even in my darkest nightmares I could never have been prepared for what I heard that night.

'I killed her. The one last night. But I didn't know her, I swear it.'

'Then what did you kill her for?'

He sighed, his face still reflecting the pain he must have been in. 'Because I was told to.'

'By who?' He didn't say anything. 'By who, Kover? There's no point protecting anybody here, you know. Not in the position you're in.'

'This bloke who worked with her. He was the one who told me to do it.'

'What's his name?'

'Dr Roberts.'

'Dr Roberts, the child psychologist? The guy from Coleman House?'

'Yeah, him. That's how I got in the flat. He had keys. I think he took duplicates.'

I was confused. 'What did he want her dead for?'

'She was on to him for something.'

'And what was that?'

'Look, it's all a bit complicated.'

'I don't care how complicated it is. Start talking.' I flicked on the lighter again, just to remind him that I wasn't fucking about. It had the desired effect.

'She knew he'd had something to do with the murder of the whore. The one you lot found last week down by the canal.'

'Miriam Fox?'

He nodded.

'You killed her, didn't you? Miriam Fox.'

'Yeah, I killed her,' he said eventually.

'So, Carla Graham had nothing to do with the murder?'

'No.'

I felt an overwhelming gloom then. Guilt sank slowly down onto my shoulders. Guilt that I had seen only the worst in her. That I'd misjudged her and that her anger at my false accusation had been genuine. And that, in the end, I'd done nothing to save her.

'How did Carla find out about Roberts's involvement?'

'I don't know for sure, but I think he told her something only the killer could have known, and for some reason she picked him up on it yesterday.'

So that was how she'd known the manner of Mirian's death. Roberts must have let it slip while talking to her. I felt another terrible pang as it became clear that, by confronting her in the Gallan, I'd effectively colluded in signing her death warrant.

'And so he called you to sort it out?'

He nodded again, not looking at me. 'Yeah, that's right.'

'So how did a respectable child psychologist know a convicted lowlife paedophile like you? How did he know you so intimately that he could call upon your help to commit murder? Twice.'

'He just knew me, all right?'

'No, it's not fucking all right. I'd tell me if I were you. And while you're about it, I'd also tell me why the two of you murdered Miriam Fox.'

'She was blackmailing Dr Roberts,' he said eventually.

'What about?'

'He was interested in little kids.' Was. That was interesting. I'd pick him up on that later. 'She found out about it.'

'How? I'd have thought she was a little bit old for a child molester.'

'She was. But he was diddling one of her mates from the home. Her mate must have told her about it and she started putting the squeeze on. Told Dr Roberts he'd have to pay her to keep quiet.'

'So she had to die?'

He nodded, looking away. I took a drink from my beer and watched him closely.

Roberts's number must have appeared on Miriam's phone record too, but in my shock at seeing Carla's name there I'd overlooked it. Perhaps if I'd been concentrating harder I could have wrapped this whole thing up a lot sooner. And Carla would still have been alive.

'And that's it, then?'

He looked up at me, his face asking to be believed. 'That's it. That's how it was. You know, I didn't mean to get involved. I wish I hadn't. I really do. I just want to be left alone now; you know, to get on with my life.'

I sighed. 'Two people dead just because some crack-addicted street girl threatens to make accusations.'

'That's how it was,' he said, an irritatingly earnest look on his face. 'I honestly wish I'd never got involved.'

'I bet you do.' I lit another cigarette. 'That Miriam Fox must have been some blackmailer.'

'She was. She really knew how to turn the screws.'

I sighed, then walked over to Kover. I leaned down close to his face and lit the flame on the lighter. He cowered back in the seat again. 'You're lying,' I told him. 'It was more than just a case of a doctor abusing his patient, wasn't it? Tell me the truth. What was going on between you and Roberts, and why did Miriam have to die?'

I kept the flame inches from his petrol-soaked face, determined that I would get the whole truth out of him. It wasn't that his story wasn't plausible, although it still didn't explain his relationship with Roberts; it was more that he was too keen to get me to swallow it. I've seen that sort of behaviour before from criminals. They want you to believe a certain series of events, even if it incriminates them. The reason's simple: they're usually hiding something worse.

'I'm telling you the truth,' he spluttered desperately. 'I swear it.'

I took a punt. 'What about those girls who went missing from Coleman House, Kover? What about them?'

'Look, I don't know—'

'You've got ten seconds to start talking. Otherwise you burn.'

'Look, please—'

'Ten, nine, eight, sev—'

'All right, all right, I'll tell you!'

I flicked off the lighter and stood up. 'It had better be the truth this time. Because otherwise I start the counting again at seven. Maybe even five. I'm tired of being fucked around.'

'All right, all right.' He paused for a moment to compose himself, then opened his mouth to say something. Then stopped. I think I knew then that it was going to be very bad. 'Me and Dr Roberts . . . we had a little business going.'

'What kind of business?'

'Girls. Young girls.'

I dragged hard on my cigarette, feeling full of dread. 'Tell me how this business worked.'

There was another pause while he thought about answering. In the end, though, he knew, like I knew, that he had no choice. 'I had a client, a bloke who wanted young girls. Except, the thing was . . . he wanted them permanently.'

'What do you mean?'

'He wanted girls who weren't going to be missed.'

'What was he doing with them?'

'Well, you know . . .'

'No, I don't know. Tell me.'

'I think he was killing them.'

'Why? For kicks?'

'I think so, yeah.'

In my time as a copper, I'd come across cases where paedophiles had murdered their victims. Sometimes to make sure they couldn't tell anyone what had happened, but more often than not because the act of murder served to heighten the pleasure of the sexual act. Killing while coming. There are some people in this world for whom that's the ultimate thrill.

'Jesus.' I shook my head, trying to take it all in. 'So how did it work?'

'Dr Roberts would pick the girls, the ones he thought could

disappear without it getting noticed, ones he was treating. He'd give me the rundown on their movements, tell me the best time and place to snatch them, then I'd do the rest.'

I stared at him, feeling sick. 'And how many times did you do this? How many girls disappeared?'

'We didn't do it much.'

'How many?'

'Four altogether.'

I dragged hard on the cigarette. 'Over how long a period?'

He thought about it for a moment. 'I don't know, about eighteen months. Something like that. The girl – the whore – she got a sniff of what was going on. Dr Roberts chose one of her mates for taking, and somehow she rumbled it. That's when she started blackmailing him, saying she'd expose him to the cops unless he paid her.'

'Did you know the name of Fox's friend? The girl Roberts . . . picked?' I found the last word difficult to say.

He shook his head. 'No, no. I never knew their names.'

'It was Molly Hagger.' He looked back at me blankly. 'Her name was Molly Hagger, and she was thirteen.' He looked down at his hands again, not saying anything. 'And Miriam Fox had to go because she was threatening to go to the cops?'

'Yeah. I picked her up pretending to be a punter. Then I did her.'

'I know. I saw the body.'

I stood there for a long moment, trying to digest what I'd heard, wanting at the same time to throw my guts up until there was nothing left. I have never felt so sick and depressed, so weary of it all, as I did standing there in that cramped little room with this fucking monster.

'And who was the last one you took? Was it a girl with black hair about the same age?'

'No. That girl, Fox's mate . . .'

'Molly. Her name was Molly.'

'She was the last one. The client didn't like us doing it too often. Otherwise it raised suspicions.'

Which left another mystery. What had happened to Anne Taylor? Although that one at least would have to wait for another day.

'And this client of yours, what's his name?'

Kover looked me right in the eye.

'Keen,' he said. 'Raymond Keen.'

38

I tried hard to hold in the shock that smacked me right between the eyes. Raymond Keen, a man I'd known for seven years, a man I'd killed for, involved in something so terrible that just the birefest thought of it made my skin crawl.

'I know Raymond Keen,' I told him. 'It doesn't seem his style to kill kids in some sort of sex game.'

'Why would I lie?' he answered, which at this juncture was a fair point. 'He's the client. I don't know if he's getting the girls on behalf of someone else.'

I thought about it for a moment. Raymond, after all, was a businessman. It was difficult to believe that he could be involved in a business quite so base and sick as the planned murder of children, but in the end no more difficult to believe than the involvement of Roberts, whose job it was to look after the mental welfare of children, and I had no doubt that Kover was telling

the truth about his part in all this. There was, I suppose, a ruthless logic in it all. Somewhere out there there were people –
hopefully few, but who could tell – who got their sexual thrills
from killing kids. Perhaps Kover was right, and Raymond was
simply tapping into this vile market, using kids whose disappearance wasn't going to attract much attention. And like all his
ventures he was keeping as far away from the action as possible.
It was easy to see why and how he'd recruited someone like
Kover, who was never going to have any sort of moral problem
in sending kids to their deaths. But Roberts? That was far more
difficult to swallow.

'So, where's Roberts now?'

'I had to tell Mr Keen about what happened with the other
woman, that I'd had to kill her. He was worried about Dr
Roberts letting stuff slip and giving the game away, so he got me
to do Roberts as well. Just to stay on the safe side.'

'How did you kill him?'

'I asked to meet him last night to discuss things. I picked him
up outside his flat. When he got in the car, I just leaned over and
stuck a knife in his guts, then locked the doors. Then I drove up
to Mr Keen's place. He said he'd take it from there.'

'You have been busy these past few days. So, Mark Wells—'

'Who?'

'The man who's been charged with the murder you committed.
Or one of them, anyway.'

'Oh yeah, the pimp.'

'Was he involved in any way?'

Kover shook his head. 'No. He had nothing to do with it.'

'So how did you manage to set him up?'

'Dr Roberts did it. At first he wasn't going to bother, but he
got cold feet when you lot came knocking. He said you came to
Coleman House asking questions. I think it spooked him a bit.'

'How did he get hold of Wells's shirt?'

'It was in the girl . . . Molly's possessions. She told him once that the shirt reminded her of him. I think she was in love with the bloke or something. The possessions were still at the home, so Dr Roberts just took it out and planted it. He was cunning like that. Then he phoned, put on a woman's accent, and tipped off you lot.'

I remembered his pleasant sing-song voice. If anyone could have impersonated a female, it would have been him. Bastard.

'What about the knife?'

'He'd heard from girls at the home that this Wells liked to threaten people with a big butcher's knife, so that's what I . . . that's what I killed her with. I kept the weapon, and just to, you know, fix him up perfect, Dr Roberts planted it near his place.'

'And that was that.'

'That's how it happened.'

'Raymond supplies you with a mobile, right?'

He nodded. 'Yeah.'

'Where is it?'

'Why? What do you want it for?'

'Don't fuck me about, Kover. You're the one who's tied up and drenched with petrol. Where is it?'

'In my pocket.' He just about managed to pat the outer pocket of his coat.

I stepped over and removed it, switching it on. 'I'm going to dial Raymond's private number now. When he picks it up, you're going to tell him you want a meeting with him as soon as possible. Preferably tonight. I expect he'll be reluctant. Don't worry. Be aggressive. Insist. Get a time. Make sure you definitely get a time. And don't give a fucking thing away. Understand? You fuck this up and you'll burn like a piece of charcoal.'

'Look, please. Just let me go. I've told you what you wanted to know.'

I punched in the numbers and put the phone to his ear. Just to show I meant business, I flicked the lighter on again and waved it gently in front of his face.

A minute passed. It didn't look promising. Then Kover was talking.

'Raymond, it's Alan. I need a meet. It's urgent.' There was a pause, and I could just about make out Raymond's booming tones at the other end, although I couldn't hear what he was saying. 'Something's come up. Something I can't talk about over the phone.' I leaned forward so that my ear was close to the phone. I could smell Kover's dry, sour breath. Raymond said something about being unavailable for a while. Kover kept trying, saying that he desperately needed to talk. I think Raymond asked him why again, and he tried to explain that it was confidential, that it was something that had to be discussed face to face. He carried on in this vein for maybe another minute, then he began to listen. Then he said OK a couple of times and the line went dead.

I stood back up and lit yet another cigarette. 'Well?'

'He says he doesn't want to meet anyone, but if it's an emergency, then I should get up to his house tonight. Before midnight. He says it's at—'

'Yeah, I know where it is.' Raymond's main residence was a mansion on the Hertfordshire/Essex border. I'd never been there before, but I was aware of its location. I dragged on the cigarette. 'Did he say he was going anywhere? After midnight?'

'No, he didn't say anything.'

'One more question. How the hell did you and Roberts ever get involved with Keen?'

'Dr Roberts knew him from somewhere. And I knew Dr Roberts.'

I didn't bother asking how Kover and Roberts knew each other. Doubtless it was down to their shared interest.

Sighing, I turned and walked over to the window. The view was of a gloomy monolithic towerblock which was so close that it would have blocked out the sunlight, had there been any. Outside it was raining hard, and fog was obscuring the glow of the bright orange street lights. A man, his coat pulled up so it was almost completely covering his face, hurried past on the street below. He was half running, as if simply being outside was enough to put him in mortal danger.

As I stood there looking out, I remembered back to when I'd been a kid of thirteen. We'd had a field out the back of our house with a huge oak tree in it. We used to climb it during the summer. My dad used to come back from work every night at half past six, rarely earlier and never later, and me and him and my sister would go out into the field and play football. We did it every night, unless it was raining, and it was best in summer when the sun went down behind the tree and the neighbours' kids came out and joined in. They'd been good days, probably even the best days of my life. Life's good when you're a kid; it should be, anyway. I pictured Molly Hagger, the little blonde girl with the curly hair. Thirteen years old. Her last hours must have been a confused, terrifying hell. Abducted from the grey, bleak streets of a wet, cold city – a city that had put her on to drugs and stolen any last scrap of innocence she had – and taken away to be used, beaten, destroyed, for the pleasure of men who dripped with the sickness of absolute corruption. Men who would steal a life just to create a better, more satisfying orgasm. She should have been playing football and having fun with parents who cared. Instead, her remains lay anonymous and forgotten, some-where they'd never be found. Forgotten by everyone, even by her best friend, who'd tried to use the situation for her own selfish advantage.

Forgotten by everyone except me.

'Look, can you let me out of here? I need a doctor for these fucking burns. I'm in a lot of pain.'

I continued to stare out of the window, puffing thoughtfully on my cigarette. I thought of Carla Graham and wondered if, had she lived, we'd have got anywhere together.

'You know, Kover,' I said, speaking without looking at him, 'I've done a lot of bad things in my life.'

'Look, I've answered your quest—'

'Some of them really bad.'

'Don't do anything stupid, please!.'

'This, however, is not one of them.'

I swung round, and before he could react the cigarette had left my hand. The funeral pyre began to burn, the roar of the flames drowned by his screams.

39

Raymond Keen. The instigator of it all. Like a fat, malevolent spider, he'd watched over this bloody web of murder, greed and corruption, unworried by who got caught up in it and how they met their ends. Only he could supply the final answers to my questions. And only by ending his life could I finally redeem myself in my own eyes, and the eyes of those who would sit and judge me.

I drove across the rain-soaked city, my mind a wasteland of torn images. Somewhere inside I felt fear, a fear that I might die in my pursuit of justice and revenge, that my time on this earth might be only hours from completion. But hatred conquered it.

It was a hatred that seemed to rise right up from the unmarked graves of not only the children Raymond had murdered, but from every victim of every injustice in the world. In the end, this consuming hatred would only subside when my revenge was complete.

I stopped at a phone box on a lonely back road in Enfield and put a call through to the number of a restaurant in Tottenham that Roy Shelley had given me. A foreign-sounding man answered and I asked to speak to Mehmet Illan. The man claimed not to know anyone of that name, which I'd half expected.

'Look, this is urgent. Very urgent. Tell him it's Dennis Milne and I must speak to him.'

'I told you, I don't know no Mehmet Illan.'

I reeled out the number I was calling from. 'He will want to speak to me, I promise you. Do you understand?' I repeated the number, and I got the impression that he was writing it down.

'I told you—'

'I'm only going to be on this number for the next fifteen minutes. It's a payphone. After fifteen minutes I'm gone, and he'll regret the fact that he missed me.'

I hung up, and lit a cigarette. Outside, the rain continued to tip down and the street was empty. There were lights on in the houses opposite and I watched them vaguely, looking for signs of life. But there was nothing. It was as if the whole world was asleep. Or dead.

The phone rang. It was barely a minute since my call to the restaurant. I picked up on the second ring.

'Dennis Milne.'

'What is it you want?' The voice was slow and confident, and the accent cultured. He sounded like he was from one of the higher social classes in his native land.

'I want you to do something for me. And in return I'll do something for you.'

'Is your line secure?'

'It's a payphone. I've never used it before.'

'What do you want me to do?'

'I want you, or some of your representatives, to get rid of Raymond Keen. Permanently.'

There was a deep but not unpleasant chuckle at the other end. 'I think you're making some sort of mistake. I don't even know a Raymond Keen.'

'Raymond Keen's going down. I've got evidence that's going to convict him of some pretty horrendous crimes.'

'I don't see what that's got to do with me.'

'If he goes down, he'll talk, and my understanding is you've got an interesting business relationship with him. One you'd rather keep secret.'

'What evidence, exactly, do you have on this Raymond Keen you're talking about?'

I took out the portable tape player on which I'd recorded the interrogation of Kover. 'This,' I said, pressing the play button and putting the machine next to the mouthpiece. I'd wound it forward to the most incriminating part and was pleased at how good the sound quality was. Kover detailed Raymond's role in the murder not only of Miriam Fox but of as many as four young girls as well. I switched it off before I got to the bit where I incinerated him.

'It sounds like a lot of that so-called confession was given under extreme duress. Surely, then, it would not be admissible in a court of law?'

'Maybe not, but if it fell into the hands of the police, I'm certain they would have to act on it. And I think you'd find they'd leave no stone unturned to put him away, and if they did that . . . well . . . I imagine they'd turn up a lot of stuff that would affect other people. And those people might get tarred with the same brush. And who wants to be closely associated with a child killer? Because I can assure you that's exactly what Raymond Keen is.' There was silence on the other end of the line. 'Raymond's at home at the moment. I think he's getting a little nervous about things. In fact, I think he might be preparing to fly the nest even as we speak, so you're going to have to be quick about things. If he's still alive in twenty-four hours the police are going to get that tape I've just played you plus all the other evidence I've unearthed on Raymond's nasty little sideline.'

'And after that? If Raymond Keen disappears, what guarantees are there that there will be no further repercussions?'

'I'll have got what I wanted. The tape'll be destroyed because, as you say, it incriminates me as well, and I'll disappear off the face of the earth.'

'You could be recording this conversation, What's to stop it being used against Mehmet Illan at a later date?'

'You're just going to have to trust me on that. Whatever happens, if Raymond's still alive tomorrow night, I'm going to the police. If he isn't, I won't. And to be honest, I'd prefer not to.'

'It would be useful if you disappeared sooner rather than later.'

'The moment Keen's gone, so am I.'

'OK. Well, thank you very much for your call.'

'One last question. My driver for the hit at the Traveller's Rest. Do you know what's happened to him?'

'I'm afraid I can't help you there.'

I didn't say anything. Maybe he was telling the truth, maybe he wasn't. He hung up without further preamble, and I slowly replaced the receiver in its cradle. Would he take the bait? I thought he had enough incentive, but I couldn't be sure, and I wasn't a hundred per cent certain he had the necessary fire-power to carry out an assault on Raymond's place. After all, the two men he'd sent against me had hardly been armed to the teeth. One had had a sawn-off, the other a revolver with a badly sighted barrel. And they hadn't exactly been accomplished assassins either. But he was going to want Raymond out of the way, and badly, which counted in my favour.

I got back in the car and thought about driving back to Bayswater, but decided against it. I hoped that I had just sentenced Raymond Keen to death, but maybe Illan would call my bluff and do nothing. I decided I had to go to Raymond's house, to check that he was there and what the level of his security was. I was armed, so if he was on his own I'd finish him off myself, but only after I'd found out who else, if anyone, was involved in the killing of the kids.

It was a quarter to ten and still raining when I pulled up just down the street from Raymond's residence. It was a big, modern house set behind high walls in two or three acres of land, part of a very plush new estate built on what was once farmland, a mile or so out of the nearest village. Only he and Luke lived there now. Raymond's wife had died ten years ago, supposedly the result of natural causes, but in the light of what I'd heard about Raymond these past few hours, even that diagnosis had to be taken with a pinch of salt. He had three kids, all girls, ironically enough, and all grown up and moved away, so it would just be him and whatever security cover he had.

I got out of the car, took my raincoat containing the MAC 10 and the Browning out of the back seat, and put it on. The street was empty, with not a single car parked on it, and the houses were far enough apart to give the area a real sense of privacy. I assumed the sort of people who lived here were City bankers and lawyers, high fliers who liked to think that they'd achieved something in life because their houses had eight bedrooms and walk-in wardrobes. They were going to get one hell of a shock when they found out what one of their neighbours had been up to, but, you never know, perhaps they'd enjoy the controversy. At least it would give them something to talk about.

The wall bordering Raymond's property was ten feet high and topped with short, vertical spikes to deter intruders. I walked up in the direction of the front gate, keeping an eye out just in case this place too was under surveillance. Not surprisingly, the imposing wooden gates were locked and access was via an intercom system. I walked back to the car and drove it slowly down until it was parallel to the wall. I then brought it up onto the kerb and as close to the wall as I could. Hoping that no-one was going to pay too much attention to my vehicle and its strange parking position, I listened for a moment and, hearing nothing, clambered up onto the roof. My head was now just below the top of the wall.

I took a deep breath and jumped up, grabbing hold of two of the railings, scrambling upwards until my feet were at the top of the wall and I was bent over almost double, my toes touching the railings only inches from my fingers. It was a painful position to hold. Below me I could see a thick, wiry hedge that looked as if it would provide an extremely painful landing. Gingerly I stepped over the railings and tried to turn myself round so that I was facing out on to the road, but started to lose my footing. As I slipped, I jumped at the same time, just managing to clear the hedge. I landed awkwardly on the grass, a sharp pain shooting up both legs, and rolled over in the wet, hoping I hadn't broken anything. I lay where I'd fallen for a few seconds, letting the pain in my ankles fade away, and then slowly got to my feet. I took the MAC 10 from my pocket and loaded the magazine into it, flicking off the safety at the same time.

The house was about fifty yards in front of me, a large

three-storey rectangular structure that looked like an attempt to recreate, with some success, one of those country houses of old. There was a drive that went right down to it before widening to encompass the whole façade of the building. Raymond's blue Bentley was parked outside, along with a Range Rover that I think belonged to Luke. What immediately caught my attention was the fact that Raymond's boot was open, as was the front door to the house. There were a lot of lights on inside and I got the feeling that something was going on.

The lawn leading up to the house was peppered with apple trees, giving enough cover for me to make a cautious approach. When I got to the edge of the driveway, about ten yards from the front door, I crouched behind one of them, shivering against the wet, pondering my next move. I didn't want a confrontation, not if I could help it. Far better to let Illan do the dirty work.

The sound of voices came from inside, and Raymond emerged with Luke in tow. Both were carrying suitcases. Raymond was complaining loudly about the inclement weather, though quite what he expected of England at the end of November was beyond me.

'I'll be glad to fucking get away,' he told his bodyguard as they placed the cases in the back of the Bentley. 'I'm not fucking bull-shitting you, I've had enough. It's no wonder our ancestors conquered the fucking world. Anything to have got out of this shithole.'

They turned to go back inside, Raymond still moaning, Luke still grunting in a weak effort to sound interested in what his boss was saying. So, my guess had been right. He was fleeing the coop. An intelligent move. The only problem from Raymond's point of view was that it wasn't going to happen.

I moved out from behind the tree and crept over the gravelled driveway until I was up at the house. Then, slowly, I made my way round towards the front door. Because of the way the porch jutted out a few feet from the rest of the house, I had good cover. So much so that neither Raymond nor Luke spotted me when, a few moments later, they came striding out to the Bentley with two more suitcases.

Without warning, I stepped out of the shadows, raised the MAC 10 and walked towards them, my feet crunching on the gravel. They both turned round at exactly the same time. Raymond looked momentarily shocked, but quickly regained his composure. Luke just glared and reached into the pocket of his leather jacket.

'Get your hands where I can see them. Now!' I pointed the weapon directly at him.

He continued to glare, but slowly raised his hands. Raymond did the same.

'What's the problem, Dennis?' he asked. 'What's all this?' His voice sounded genuinely surprised, but then Raymond had always been a good actor. At one time he'd even convinced me that he was nothing more than a loveable rogue.

'I think you know what the problem is, Raymond. Firstly, I'm not best pleased that you've tried to have me murdered—'

'Dennis, please. I don't know what—'

'Shut the fuck up, and stop playing me for an idiot. And secondly, and more importantly, I've unearthed some disturbing information about you which I want to discuss in more detail before I fill you with holes.'

His expression didn't change. It was all still hurt and shock, as if he truly couldn't understand why he was being held at gunpoint by someone he'd always trusted. 'Look, Dennis, I've always tried to—'

'Alan Kover.' This time a flicker of concern crossed his face. 'I've just finished having a chat with him. He filled me in on some interesting details regarding the work he did for you.'

'I've never heard of an Alan Kover,' he said loudly, but with a marked lack of conviction.

'Details about kidnapping young kids—'

I heard movement on the gravel behind me. Immediately I knew I'd made a mistake by addressing Raymond and Luke with my back to the front door. I started to turn round, but before I could fully react my head seemed to explode with pain as something hard struck it with a lot of force. I felt my legs buckle beneath me and I sank to my knees as I was hit again. I tried to hold onto the MAC 10, knowing that it was probably my only chance of survival, but it seemed to slip effortlessly from my grasp. My head spun and the whole world felt like it was floating away from me. All the time I cursed myself for being so stupid.

I fell forwards onto the gravel but managed to roll onto my side. Above me stood Luke's younger brother, Matthew, an iron bar in his hand and a less than Christian look on his face.

Raymond came into view and gave me a nasty little kick in the ribs. 'Fucking hell, Dennis, you're beginning to really annoy me now. You keep popping up like a fucking unwanted jack-in-the-box. Why can't you just get out of my face?' I wanted to tell him that I would have done if only he'd left me alone, but the act of speaking seemed one effort too far, and it would have been futile anyway. 'Get him inside, Matthew. Out of the fucking way.'

'What do you want me to do with him, Mr Keen?'

'Lock him in the cellar. I'll phone Illan. His boys can come and deal with him. It's their fucking fault he's still here in the first place. And make sure they don't do anything to him here. I don't want any mess in my house.'

'No problem, Mr Keen.' He leaned down and pulled me up roughly by the shoulders. Although conscious, I wasn't in much of a position to resist.

Raymond put his face up close to mine. 'Goodbye, Dennis. I'd say it's been a pleasure knowing you, but it hasn't been. Not at all. You were always a miserable cunt. You strike me as the sort of bloke who'd be a lot happier dead, so maybe I'm doing you a favour.' He gave me a patronizing slap on the cheek, enjoying my helplessness. 'Ta ta.'

He stood up and turned away. 'Have we got everything then, Luke?'

'Seems so, Mr Keen,' Luke mumbled in reply, slamming the boot shut.

'Then let's get out of here. I can't stand another fucking day of this rain.'

They both clambered into the car while Matthew picked up the MAC 10 and, with his free hand, dragged me backwards along the gravel and into the house. He hauled me through the porch and set me down in the large inner hallway by the rather grand-looking staircase that led up like some Hollywood film set to the main balcony. For some reason, I couldn't help thinking what a sumptuous place it was that Raymond owned.

He turned and went to open the door under the stairs, but it was locked. He fiddled in his pocket for a key and ended up producing a whole bunch of them. As he searched for the one he wanted, still holding both the gun and the iron bar, I felt my strength slowly coming back.

'Don't you fucking try anything, son,' said Matthew, seeing a flicker of movement in my legs.

'I wouldn't do this if I were you,' I told him in a strained voice. 'Getting involved in the murder of a police officer. You could go down for twenty years for this.'

'Shut up and don't fucking speak!' he snarled, but I could hear the nervousness in his voice.

'And what's your boss doing while you're organizing my murder? Running away, like he always does—'

'I told you to shut up!' he snapped, and turned back to his task, this time leaning the MAC 10 against the wall in front of him so that he could hunt through the keys more easily.

I remembered the gun in my other pocket. It struck me that in his hurry to get away, Raymond had been very slipshod, and Matthew was obviously no pro. Slowly, I started to reach down into the pocket. At the same time, Matthew found the key he wanted and placed it in the door. He turned round quickly to check what I was doing, and I think he saw that my hand had moved. He started to say something, but suddenly the angry crackle of gunfire came from somewhere outside. Another burst followed, then several individual shots, then through the open front door came the sound of a car reversing rapidly. It seemed Illan had taken my advice. And quickly, too.

Matthew turned and ran towards the door, shouting at me to stay where I was in tones laced with panic. Inexplicably, he left the MAC 10 where it was but continued to clutch the iron bar for dear life, as if the one offered him more protection than the other. I heard him curse as he reached the front entrance. More shots followed, and there was the sound of glass shattering.

Slowly, I forced myself to my feet, shaking my head to try to rid it of the grogginess I felt. I stumbled slightly but kept my balance. The back of my head felt as though it was on fire, but at least I was alive. For now.

I took the gun from my pocket. I'd already released the safety and it was cocked and ready to fire. The car screeched to a halt right outside the front door, kicking up gravel, then there was the sound of another car stopping right behind it. I heard Raymond's voice, panic-stricken now, then Matthew disappeared from view, screaming his brother's name. Raymond yelled at him to get back inside and there was the sound of running feet. There were more shots, and from somewhere a scream of pain.

I stopped and took aim at the hall door. A split second later, Matthew came running through it, followed immediately by Raymond. Raymond's face was covered in tiny cuts. There was no sign of Luke. I didn't hesitate but opened fire in rapid succession. My first bullet hit Matthew in the face and he flailed backwards, temporarily blocking Raymond as a target. I hit him again in the stomach and upper body, and he and Raymond fell to the floor together.

Almost immediately, a hooded gunman came charging through the doorway, holding a pistol. He turned and swung it in my direction so I kept firing, not knowing what else to do. I hit him in the shoulder, and I think the chest. He whirled round in a ferocious pirouette before banging into the doorframe then momentarily disappearing from view.

The gun was empty. On the floor, neither Raymond nor Matthew moved. I took a step backwards and suddenly a second gunman burst in. Knowing where my shots had come from, he crouched down and unloaded a volley of fire in my direction. Dropping the gun, I dived for cover and rolled round the other side of the staircase and temporarily out of range. I heard him running towards me and with every last bit of strength I had left I wriggled over to the MAC 10, grabbed it, and rolled round.

He was coming round the side of the staircase, gun out-stretched in front of him. He fired as soon as he saw me, the first bullet ricocheting off the expensive cream carpet, not far from my head. Two more bullets flew past me, equally close, and I pulled the trigger of the MAC 10.

The whole world seemed to explode in noise. A hail of bullets ripped through my attacker, sending him dancing in a ferociously manic jig as his body seemed to burst open. Ornaments, furnishings, glass . . . everything seemed to shatter as the bullets tore apart their target and flew off in all directions, stitching an angry blood-splattered pattern right across the wall. A dozen small wounds blended together and became a gaping hole in his midriff, exposing pale lumps of fat and the first writhing coils of intestine.

The magazine emptied in the space of a couple of seconds, the spent shells forming a pile on the carpet. For a moment, the gunman kept his feet, stumbling awkwardly about like a blind man, both hands clasping his guts and trying to put them back where they belonged. But I think it must have dawned on him that it was a futile exercise, and he fell to the floor and lay there moaning weakly.

For a couple of seconds, I didn't move. My head was pounding and I felt an intense tiredness. But I knew it was nearly over. All I had to do now was make sure Raymond was beyond help and make my getaway. Then I would have done what I'd set out to do, and I could sleep for as long as I wanted.

I got to my feet and looked over at Raymond and Matthew. Both were lying motionless in a heap by the door, their faces red with blood. Out in the porch I could hear the sound of someone moaning, presumably the other gunman. At the same time, the other car – the one that had been carrying Illan's assassins – reversed and turned round in the drive, before pulling away.

I approached the door and gingerly put my head round it. The gunman was lying on his front and a pool of blood had spread out below him. He still had hold of the gun, but his grip looked weak. He was trying to crawl towards the front door but didn't seem to have the strength to make it. I stepped towards him, leaning down to pick up the gun.

And then, for the second time that night, I heard a noise behind me. I swung round, eager not to get caught out again, just as Raymond, bellowing like an angry bull, charged me. He threw a punch, but I managed to read his intentions and dodged it, although I was unable to get out of his way as he ran into me head on, and I toppled over backwards under his weight.

I landed heavily on the back of the gunman, who let out a weird high-pitched squeal as the air was forced out of him. The gun fell from his fingers with a clatter. Winded myself, I desperately tried to parry the blows Raymond rained down on me. I managed to catch him on the chin with a punch of my own, but it wasn't enough to cause any real damage. He hit me back in the the spot where Kover had caught me the previous night, my already tender right cheek, and I felt something break.

Sensing that I was fading, he reached across me and went for the gun. And that was when I thought of Molly Hagger and the anonymous, gruesome death she must have suffered. Only thirteen years old. Still a fucking kid. And I knew I couldn't die without making Raymond Keen pay for his crimes. With a strength born of pure rage, I shot upwards, knocking him off balance, and headbutted him bang on the bridge of the nose. I heard the bone snap with a hideous crack and he screamed in agony. Out of the corner of my eye, I saw him bring up the gun, but his grip had loosened with the shock of my blow and I ripped it out of his hand, smacking him on the side of the head with the butt at just the moment he punched me again, knocking me backwards.

But this time I kept hold of the gun, and swung it round so it was pointed straight at him. His eyes widened and he froze. I sat back up, and this time he made no effort to resist. With one hand, I grabbed him by his thick mane of hair; with the other, I pushed the barrel against his eye.

'Now, now, Raymond. Easy does it.'

I pushed him backwards and got to my feet, still holding the gun tight against him. When we were both standing up, I gave him a shove and walked back into the inner hallway with him retreating in front of me. Blood poured liberally out of his damaged nose.

'Look, Dennis, I've got money. Plenty of it. We can come to some arrangement.' This time there was no mistaking the fear in his voice.

I stopped in front of him, keeping the gun trained on his face. Five feet separated us. 'I know everything that's been happening with Kover and Roberts and those kids.'

Raymond shook his head, then looked at me. 'Shit, Dennis, I never meant to get involved in it all, I really didn't.'

'That's what Kover said. I didn't believe him, and I don't believe you. Now, while you're here, there are a few questions I need answering.'

'OK.' He was playing for time.

'Every time you give me a wrong answer, or one I don't believe, I'm going to shoot you in either a foot or a kneecap.'

'Easy, Dennis. Come on.'

'How the hell did you and Roberts ever get involved together?'

'I've known him for years.'

'How?'

'I met him at a charity function once.' I snorted at the irony, but didn't say anything. 'We got friendly. I found out he had something of a coke habit so I started supplying him with the stuff – for a nice low cost, of course, which he appreciated. I liked him, you know, even though it didn't take me too long to find out about his little perversions.'

'Go on.'

'He had money troubles. Big money troubles. And not a lot in the way of scruples. Like most of them kiddy fiddlers.' He sighed. 'You know how it is, Dennis. Sometimes you can just see the evil in people. I saw it in him.'

I wondered then if he'd ever seen it in me.

'And what happened to the kids? Where are they now?'

'Dead. All dead.'

'Why? What did you do with them?'

'If it's any consolation, Dennis, I didn't kill them. I had a client, a bloke who was very, very sick. He got off on torturing children. Liked to suffocate them while he was, you know, doing his thing.'

'Jesus.'

'I wouldn't have got involved, I really wouldn't have done, but he was – is – an important man. We needed him for the business. If there was any other way–'

'Raymond, there's always another way. And what the fuck did you get out of letting him do that sort of—' I couldn't say it. 'What did you get out of it anyway?'

'We filmed him. He used to do the deed in this house I rent up near Ipswich, and we put a hidden camera in there to record him at it. We kept the tapes to make sure he told us everything that was going on.'

'And who is this sick bastard?'

'His name's Nigel Grayley.'

'And what's his use?'

'He's third in command at Customs and Excise.'

In the far distance, through the sound of the rain, I could hear the first sirens. It felt like a long time had passed since the first shots had been fired, but in reality I doubted if it was much over three minutes.

'So that's how you found out about where they were taking the accountant?'

He nodded, and I thought I detected shame in his manner. His shoulders were stooped and it looked like a lot of the *joie de vivre* had disappeared, probably forever.

'What was the accountant going to expose about you and your associates?'

'We've got a big illegal immigrant racket going. Have done for years. It was going so fucking well too. We had the infrastructure, the inside contacts. Everything was going fine, no-one was getting hurt, and then that prick decided to blow the whistle.'

'Where are the tapes? The ones you made of this Grayley guy?'

Raymond exhaled slowly. 'You don't want to see them, Dennis. You really don't.'

'I know I don't. But I know people who will.'

'Fucking hell, Dennis, I really wish it hadn't all ended like this.'

'The tapes.'

'There's one in the boot of the Bentley. Down by the spare tyre.'

'What the hell's it doing there?'

'I was going to drop it in a safety deposit box on the way to the airport. I didn't like leaving them all here while I go away, just in case the house burned down.'

The sirens were getting nearer. Now it was my turn to sigh. 'You know, Raymond, this is one of the most horrendous fucking stories I've ever heard.'

'I know, Dennis, I know.' He looked down at his shoes.

I knew it was time to kill him, but even now, for some reason, it seemed difficult.

'And what about Danny? My driver? What happened to him?'

He came at me fast, almost too fast, his bulk moving at an unnerving speed, and he was almost on me by the time I pulled the trigger, the bullet snapping his head back. I fired again, hitting him in the throat, but his forward momentum drove his body into me and knocked me back into the doorframe. I pushed him out of the way and regained my footing, watching as he writhed on the carpet. He rolled round onto his back, making horrendous gurgling noises. He tried to say something, but the only thing that came out of his mouth was blood, huge torrents of it. His head was bleeding severely, and I knew the end was near for him.

I lifted the gun and went to deliver the killing shot, but decided against it. Why let him go quickly? Better that he died with time to consider the terrible wrongs he'd done.

And so, leaving him choking his last breaths, I walked out of the house to the Bentley, stepping over Luke's bullet-ridden corpse as I made my way round to the driver's seat. The keys were still in the ignition and the engine was still running. There wasn't a windscreen, but I felt that for the time being I could live with that.

I put the car into gear and pulled away.

40

The following afternoon, at a hotel in Somerset, I put the tape from Raymond's car into the video recorder in my room, and watched for thirty seconds. It was enough. I have seen many dreadful things in my time. I've been an inner-city copper for close to twenty years so there aren't that many sights that can shock me. But this did.

Molly Hagger was on the tape. She was sitting on a bed in a sparsely furnished room, her hands tied behind her back. She was naked but for a pair of black frilly knickers but she still looked thirteen, maybe even younger, and she was in great distress, sobbing fearfully. A naked man appeared in front of her, side-on to the camera. He was balding, middle-aged, and worryingly thin. I vaguely recognized his face. I think, perhaps, that I'd seen him before on the television. He had a hungry look in his eyes and an angry erection. As I watched he struck Molly round the face and called her a dirty little whore. There was an intense pleasure in his voice. He grabbed her by her curly hair and pulled her towards him, slapping her again. She cried out in pain as he forced her to her knees and thrust himself roughly into her mouth.

I switched off then. There was no point in watching any more. It was too distressing. And I knew, without a doubt, that he had ended up killing little Molly Hagger, and that Raymond had filmed it all in glorious technicolour. The hardest part was realizing that outwardly here was a respectable man who had probably shaken hands with royalty before now; the sort of person who appeared on television to give his weighty opinion on events in the world of Customs and Excise. The sort of man who underneath the façade is a foul, deceitful monster who can keep that fact hidden from almost everyone who knows him.

An hour later, I posted the tape along with a detailed report on what I believed had gone on to DS Asif Malik. As promised, I also posted a briefer version of the report, careful to take out any mention of Nigel Grayley so as not to prejudice any future trial, to Roy Shelley at the *North London Echo*. In neither report did I mention my own part in the affair, although I had little doubt that that would become common knowledge soon enough.

An hour after that, I paid my bill and continued my drive westwards in the rental car I'd hired in the name of Mr Marcus Baxter, a travelling salesman from Swindon.

Epilogue

I approach the Philippine Airlines desk with a smile, and get a smile in return from the Oriental girl. She's older than her colleagues, somewhere in her thirties, and I expect she's the one in charge. She greets me happily as if it really is genuinely good to see me, and asks me the usual questions about whether it was me who packed my suitcases or not, and all the rest of it. I answer everything correctly, and we have a quick banter about what the Philippines are like at this time of year. 'I've never been there, you know,' I say, and she tells me that I won't be disappointed. 'No,' I reply, thinking that it's been years since I sat on a palm-fringed beach, 'I know I won't.' She briefly checks my ticket, sees that it's all in order, and flashes me another smile as the cases begin their journey along the conveyor belt.

'Have an enjoyable trip, Señor Baxter.'

'Thanks very much. I will.'

I move away from the desk and head towards passport control and my new life. I'm not nervous. There's no need to be. Three months have passed since that night at Raymond Keen's house and, in a land of constantly changing images and an ever-shrinking attention span, I am already yesterday's man. I look different, too. I wear a full beard now and glasses, and my face looks fatter. I've put on weight elsewhere too, mainly round the waist, the result of country cooking and quitting the cigarettes. You wouldn't recognize me from the photos they showed in the papers. No-one would.

And I feel better too, like a new man; a man who's put the past behind him. There are regrets, of course. That Carla went to her death soon after I'd called her a liar is something that will stay with me for a long time. But, in the end, the past is the past, and I'm happy to say that. I have achieved more as an individual than I ever achieved as a police officer. Thanks to evidence found on Raymond's premises and my reports to Malik and Shelley, Mehmet Illan and at least half a dozen of his associates are behind bars awaiting trial for their involvement in one of the largest people-smuggling operations in British history. Nigel Grayley, a married father of four, will never go on trial for his crimes, however. Four days after his arrest he slashed his wrists with a smuggled razor blade and bled to death in his cell. An inquiry is now under way to ascertain how he got hold of the blade, but no-one's shedding any tears, and the tabloids celebrated the news, which was fair enough. The world is a better place without him.

The remains of Molly Hagger and the other girls have not been found. Most people accept that the secret of their whereabouts died with Raymond, but there are others, myself included, who think that maybe Illan could shed some light on the mystery. But he isn't talking, and neither is anyone else who might know. In the end, you can't really blame them. No-one wants to be associated with that particular crime. Predictably, Danny never did make it to Jamaica. A week after Raymond's death his body was discovered with gunshot wounds in the boot of a stolen car in the Heathrow Airport long-stay car park after a security guard had detected a particularly repulsive stench coming from it. I was sad but not surprised when I read about it in the papers.

One piece of good news that has come out of all this, though, is that Anne Taylor is alive and well. I'd mentioned in my report that she'd gone missing too, even though Kover had denied abducting her, but a few days later she turned up in one piece, having gone on a jaunt to Southend with another, older girl in search of a new market for their services. She's still heading down a rocky road, one that could yet put her in an early grave, but at least for the moment she continues to breathe the same air as you and I.

Mark Wells had the murder charges against him dropped and has begun legal proceedings against the Metropolitan Police for wrongful arrest, demanding an estimated two hundred thousand pounds in compensation. However, his case has not been helped by the fact that less than a month after his release he was re-arrested after being secretly filmed trying to sell crack cocaine and underage girls to an undercover police officer. He's been in custody ever since.

And so, through all this, there's only one participant who hasn't been brought to justice. One Dennis Milne, multiple murderer. I was specifically and publicly named as a suspect in the Traveller's Rest killings two days after the discovery of Raymond's corpse, and though there's been what police describe as a major manhunt, I've so far managed to evade capture. I suspect now that I'll evade it for ever. I've got enough money for now and I've got a friend in the Philippines for whom I can do some work when funds finally begin to run low. I know I'll always be able to rely on old Tomboy.

Do I deserve to escape? I've thought about that a lot these past months. I've done great wrong, there can be no doubt about that, and if I could be put in the same position again knowing even half of what I know now, there's no way I would have pulled the trigger on that cold, wet night and sent three innocent men to their graves. But you can't change the sins of the past, you can only work to limit those of the future, and try to carry out deeds that help to make the world a slightly better place. In that, I think I have been at least partially successful. Would the world be a better place without me in it? On balance, I think probably not. Bbut then I would say that, wouldn't I?

And to those who may one day sit in judgement? What would I say to them?

Just two words.

Forgive me.